Michael B Fletcher is a writer of adult and YA speculative fiction including fantasy, science fiction and horror. His first book *Kings of Under-Castle*, a collection of humorous adventures featuring two rogues living under a medieval castle, was published by *IFWG Publishing Australia* in 2013.

Book 1 of his *Masters of Scent* fantasy trilogy was released in 2022, with *Tumblers of Rolan* following a year later. The final book in the trilogy, *Shadow Scent* will be released in 2024.

Fletcher has also co-authored *Kat*, a YA science fiction, with Paula Boer, to be published by IFWG Publishing in 2024.

Fletcher has had over 100 short stories published, many with a 'dark' or fantasy bent, in magazines and anthologies in Australia, USA and the UK. An anthology 'A Taste of Honey', containing 43 of these stories was published by Double Dragon in 2021.

He lives in Tasmania, Australia with his wife, Kim.

T0118839

Other Michael B Fletcher Titles by IFWG Publishing

Kings of Under-Castle (humorous short fiction collection)
Masters of Scent (Book 1 of the Masters of Scent trilogy)

Masters of Scent Trilogy: Volume 2

Tumblers of Rolan

by
Michael B Fletcher

Tumblers of Rolan

All Rights Reserved

ISBN-13: 978-1-922856-47-0

Copyright ©2024 Michael B Fletcher

Printed in Garamond and Iskoola Pota font types.

IFWG Publishing International
Gold Coast

www.ifwgpublishing.com

For my three sons

Nicholas, Christopher and David

who have helped challenge my imagination and hone my story-telling skills through many years of interactive bedtime stories.

Chapter One

"**W**atch it! Hold it!"

Kyel flinched, one eye on the whirl of scents before him, the other on the man near him. He stifled an angry retort and concentrated.

He could see the major scents: darker soil odours, lighter granitic notes from the rocks of the hillside, and duller portions from the sparse vegetation mixing. They coalesced in a ball close to his head. Occasionally a portion sloughed off, breaking up and dissipating into the air. The ball grew smaller as it drifted away, making his control harder.

"Heavier, stronger scents, with body. Drag them from somewhere. Add them from your memory. Whatever. Just do it!"

Kyel pulled at the ball while trying to find a binding scent from his olfactory memories. He remembered the stink of the river with rotting reeds and chose it, forming the motes and thrusting it out into the ball of scents.

"Yes! Yes! Now bind it, tie it together."

The ball slowed and flattened, resisting the light breeze flowing down the hillside.

"Keep at it!"

He tried to hold it together, bring it back while the breeze did its best to frustrate him. He could see it clearly, like a translucent blanket hovering, its edges fraying despite his efforts.

Sweat dripped into his eyes. It didn't help that Targas was constantly interrupting, breaking his concentration. He tried to lower the ball, keeping its structure until he could lay it over a boulder, but the moment it touched the rock it disintegrated in a puff of scents, gone in an instant.

He slumped forward from his seat on a rock.

"What sort of wine-rotted effort was that, Kyel?" Targas leant towards the youth, his light eyes intense. "You'll never get to be a full scent master if you can't hold your concentration."

"I thought I did fairly well."

"Fairly well doesn't cut it, Kyel." Targas ran his hand through his dark hair. "You've got to be able to hold your concentration. You've the skill. You can see the scents well, manipulate them and bind them as I've taught you. But you have to practise. What if you're being attacked?"

"Attacked? Here? No likelihood of that," Kyel said, realising he was referring to the war between their people and the Sutanites years before.

Targas stood. "We paid dearly in that fight, if you recall."

Kyel shifted on his seat. "Of course I remember!"

"Fine! You know best!" Targas flung his hands into the air before bending over, a fist knuckling his temple. His arms dropped to his side and he looked unseeingly at the sandy-haired youth for a few moments before turning and striding away.

Kyel's mouth tightened watching Targas heading down the hillside to slip through the narrow gateway leading to the business part of the town of Lesslas.

The tavern, he thought bitterly, *always the answer for Targas, the famous hero of the revolution.*

He flung a chunk of granite, which rebounded from the boulders, creating puffs of grit imitating the spirals of light scent already filling the valley. Kyel's eyes followed the rock while his hand felt for another.

He sat on a large boulder, grateful to be alone, until he heard a rattle of gravel nearby. He looked for Tel, his lizard companion, but nothing moved on the sun-baked rocks.

Probably followed Targas to the tavern.

Kyel's vantage point showed the line of rugged hills leading south to the broad plain, beyond which the purple haze of the Sensory Mountains blocked his view. He knew another, much larger plain lay beyond the barrier formed by the Great Southern River, which broke through at the city of Regulus. The river flowed wide and mighty to Ean's capital city, Nebleth, before continuing to the sea at Port Saltus. His memories from that time were not good ones and he resented Targas for forcing him to remember.

He thought of his friend Luna. They had been chased through those hills by the ruthless trackers of the old Sutanite regime. Later they had teamed up with Targas, an uncertain, unpredictable companion who had since become a permanent fixture in his home, partnering with his older sister, Sadir. And having a baby with her.

"Bloods!" Kyel swore, cursing the day he had met Targas.

Luna's face, framed in blonde curls, broke into his thoughts. He remembered her laughter as they shared quieter moments, holding her hand, wiping away her tears as they sought comfort before their brutal interrogation at the hands of Septus, one of the Sutanite leaders.

But Septus is dead, he thought grimly. *Thank Ean for that. And Jakus, his leader, was long gone, injured and fleeing back to Sutan.*

A tear trickled down his cheek as he thought how Luna had stopped Septus from killing their friends at the battle of the Salt Ways, at the cost of her own life. She had died a heroine. "Why couldn't it have been me? What did I do to stop them?" He cried out as he swiped at the tears, angry that even her face was fading from his memory.

The war had finished. They had won and driven the Sutanites from Ean. He had returned to Lesslas with Sadir and Targas and attempted to resume a normal life. But how, with Targas always there, reminding him of what he'd lost? And then Anyar had been born. More responsibilities, because of Targas.

"I could've learnt a trade, like my father before he disappeared—so long ago now," he mumbled, shaking his head. "But I can't, I've gotta grow my scent talent. Why won't Targas and the others leave me alone? The war's over. There's no need!" He felt the fine fair bristles covering his cheeks. He thought back to another person, one who even now pulled at his heart, Nefaria. Her alluring form hovered in his mind, that smile lighting her dark eyes, the touch of her hand and her soft voice.

"Nefaria," he said quietly, "why wouldn't you let me come with you? I wasn't too young, I wasn't. Why did you leave with that old decrepit, Jakus? You couldn't have loved him, surely. He didn't love you. Maybe he's dead now. Yes, and you'll be free to come back for me. Yeah, maybe."

He slung another rock high into the sky, where it seemed to hang in the air. He pushed out with his mind, grabbed skeins of passing scent and sought to weave a blanket, solid and strong like Targas had been teaching him. He tried to prevent the rock from crashing to the ground, momentarily slowing it before it rebounded from the boulder-littered slopes.

"Blast!" he muttered. "Be easier if I had some of that magnesa again. It really helped." He still thought of its taste, how it left a smooth, mellow feeling, allowed him to direct his scent senses with far more ease. He recollected the red crystals Jakus, the leader of the Sutanites, had given him. *Yes, he wasn't all bad, especially when Nefaria was with him.*

Something skittered nearby and the grey, scaly head of a Conduvian scent lizard poked out from between two boulders, fixing him with a black-eyed stare.

"Tel, you're here." Kyel grinned, pivoting on the rock towards the arm-length lizard. Another, almost as long, also emerged. "And you've brought your friend, too."

The other lizard, slimmer but with a wider belly, stopped and stared at him before scurrying up to Tel and pushing into his flank. More scrambling signalled the arrival of three smaller scent lizards.

"Ah!" nodded Kyel, "So that's what you've been getting up to. Found someone you like better than me. Figures. No one cares about me. Except"—he ran fingers through his sandy hair as a wan smile lit his face—"maybe Nefaria?"

Tel scrabbled, claws clinging to the top of a nearby boulder, and aligned his body to get maximum sun exposure. His family soon followed and lay scattered over the rocks in the same east-west alignment.

"Well, at least you've got your priorities right." *If only life were that simple for him.*

He reached for another rock, wondering about Nefaria. Had she left Jakus? Would she come back? "She might even be in Ean looking for me. Pah!" He flicked the stone into the air as hope faded from his eyes.

The kick drove high into Targas's sinuses, the back of his throat numb, a fire burning its way to his stomach. The drink hit with a thump and lay smouldering.

"Getting there," he gasped, eyes streaming, tanned face contorted. "Needs some work, though."

"Lizards' teeth," croaked Jeth, "I'd lose all me customers, even with this amount of malas." He eyed the small cup in his hand. "Just as well we only used one of these women's cups. Not likely drinkers here would want such a small one. They reckon the bigger the better."

Targas looked across at the stained leather apron restraining the ample belly of his friend, then to the solid fingers clasping the little cup. He grinned, straightening his worn brown tunic over grey trousers as he shifted on his seat before reaching for the jug. "We're certainly looking the part of experimenters, Jeth." He took another sip.

"It's all very well getting the grapes and malt, but there's more to making a quality malas than that," Targas continued, thinking back to the difficulties of making the raw spirit base and the metal tubing, boiling the alcohol off rough grape wine, then selecting key ingredients for maturation in wooden barrels.

"Yes, it's a start," said Jeth. "Then I've gotta train me customers to like and pay for it. Reckon I'm getting a headache with all this testing, and I've gotta be opening soon. Let's hope it's not too busy." The big man rose with a sigh and then looked hopefully at Targas. "Like to help me set up?"

"Sure," responded Targas. "Better than going home at the moment."

Jeth raised his eyebrows as he walked away.

Targas shook his head as he thought on what he had said. Things were tense between Sadir and himself. They'd returned to Lesslas after the final battle of the rebellion at Nebleth and the near fatal fight with Septus, the Sutanite head of the seekers. He only wanted to recover and live a normal life.

Their love and commitment to each other had grown. At the rebel stronghold, Sanctus, they'd explored senses together. For Targas, it was an awakening, and had taken him to another level of scent experience. They'd felt as one, knowing what each other was thinking and feeling. Subtle scents were picked up and acted upon without conscious thought; they wanted to be together and expand each other's scent consciousness.

He knew her healing ability had vastly improved during the rebel campaign to rid Ean of the Sutanite oppression, and he gladly helped her in achieving her aptitude. Sadir wasn't a typical scent master but she had something else, a scent aura of mystery, an empathy that promised a difference—of what he was unsure—but watching a person he cared for unfold into another stage of being made it worthwhile. The arrival of Anyar brought a new element into their lives; she was now a quiet, solemn young girl with her mother's heart-shaped face and brown hair and his light eyes.

Targas felt proud of his family, even of Kyel, who was now a young man. Targas rubbed his chin, thinking how accommodating Kyel was of his partnering his sister. Targas hoped Kyel accepted him and his current role as trainer despite ongoing difficulties.

But I keep spoiling it. Dark thoughts come into my brain and I start a fight. Can't control it. Targas shook his head.

"Targas," called Jeth, "weren't you going to give me a hand?"

The sun had set by the time he left the tavern and headed up the hill. He had become familiar with the cobblestone road winding past the town hall and into the narrow street. Sadir's house was one of a row of co-joined cottages, small but adequate for the four of them. It became a squeeze when one of their friends from the war came to stay. Still, they didn't mind; the euphoria of surviving the hell that first Jakus, then Septus, had put them through deflected concerns about the minutiae of daily life.

He grimaced, remembering the first time he had gone down that road years before, fleeing the enemy's seeker collection team. He, Sadir, Kyel, and of course Luna, little knew what was in store for them. And Luna had paid the ultimate price. Targas shook his head as if the memory could leave his skull. *What I wouldn't give for some memory loss now*, he thought. The grisly face of Septus, now safely dead, rose in his mind: the staring eyes, torn cheek exposing blood-covered teeth. He shivered and lengthened his pace.

Chapter Two

Targas pushed open the door of the cottage and walked quietly into the main room, and was greeted by a waft of cooking. Sadir was tending a pot on the small stove in the far corner. He paused, drinking in the sight of her slender, gown-covered form, the curve of her thigh, her wavy brown hair. A rush of feeling erupted in his chest. *Blood's grace, but I love that woman. But there's something different around her, a different sense, something...* He couldn't quite put a finger to it.

"Targas!" exclaimed Sadir, turning around. "You're back." She put the spoon in the pot and came towards him, wiping her hands on her apron.

He smiled, relieved all was right. The uncertainties he'd felt in the tavern and the gruesome memories on his walk home fell away.

She clasped him around the waist and held tight, head pressed into his chest. "I missed you," she murmured.

"Par." Anyar's small arms encircled his leg, her head buried into his waist.

Targas absorbed the odours of the room underlying the smell of cooking. The dominant scent was *woman*, Sadir, the most satisfying of all. The smell of Anyar was fresh, like a bloom of fruit gushing into his nostrils. Kyel was another, older odour—he hadn't come home. A touch of scent he'd noticed as he entered brushed against him again, but even as he puzzled over it he got a distinctive aromatic waft. *Ah,* he thought, *I have smelt that before.*

"Sadir," he asked, "what's that smell? Not Rolan cordial, by any chance?"

Targas felt Sadir stiffen against him, then pull away.

"I've been by myself with Anyar all day," she spoke firmly, "and I enjoy the cordial now supplies are easier to get. Besides, you've been at the tavern most of the day; drinking an underdone malas, if I'm any guess."

A darkness rose in his mind at the implied criticism in Sadir's voice. He tried not to react, yet knew he would.

"What did you mean by that?"

"I merely said," Sadir said, backing off several steps, "that you haven't been home much to help with Anyar and Kyel. Whether you're with Jeth or somewhere else I wouldn't know, but malas does have a very distinctive smell."

Targas made a determined effort to hold back, his face reddening with the strain. He watched Sadir waiting, eyes wide, a tinge of fear in her scent aura. Anyar released her grip and moved away. He took a deep breath.

"You know I'm trying to recreate the malas I used to make when I was in Tenstria, my homeland. I doubt I'll ever go back there, so if I can work it out it'll be a good way to earn a living."

"Yes, but…"

"Further, I must keep working on my talent. There's always pressure from one or another of Lan's people dropping by to see when I can get involved in the governing of Ean, training or some such. I think the impact of my role in the war has worn off."

"I know, but I need you here, to help me and this family to live our life how it should be enjoyed. You're training Kyel to a high scent standard but he needs you much more than he's willing to say. He's becoming a man and you don't make the time."

"Enough, Sadir," Targas's voice rose. "I'm trying my best, aren't I? I'm always doing what others think I should, trying to please everyone. Well, what about me, what about what I want, eh? I'm getting sick of all this. Pity the tavern's so far away." Targas looked back at the door, then paused.

Kyel stood there, his face pale, eyes staring from under his mop of sandy hair. He pushed past Targas, heading for the door leading to the bedrooms.

"Where're you going?" asked Sadir. "We were starting to worry about you."

Kyel stopped, hand on the door latch. "Me? Worrying about me? Then why are you shouting at each other?"

"Listen, Kyel," said Targas, "your sister and I were merely discussing your training, how I needed to spend more time with you."

"Yeah, and not at the tavern?" Kyel snapped. "Then how come you're arguing? I can't remember the last time I came home when you weren't."

"Now…" Sadir moved over to him and placed a hand on her brother's shoulder.

"No, you're as bad as him!" Kyel pulled away and dashed through the door.

"Kyel." Sadir's hand went to her mouth. "Please…"

"That's it," said Targas. "I don't have to listen to this!" He headed for the front door.

"But Targas, there's dinner"—Sadir flung a hand towards the stove—"and I wanted some time with you." She leant against the wall holding a hand over her tear-filled eyes as the door slammed. Anyar began to cry in short, hiccupping coughs.

Kyel lay on the firm mattress, toes jammed against the wooden end of the narrow bed. He struggled to take a deep breath to slow his racing heart.

"Why did I come home?" he hissed. "For this? Another fight?"

His eyes searched the wooden beams above his head, the dim light making a vague swirl of scents too hard to see. "Wish I could just be a top scent master, make the scents take me away from here, be wanted, be part of something else rather than stuck in this hole of a town."

He let his breath out in a slow huff and wiped at watery eyes.

The scents were hard to break up. He tried to take and solidify their motes the way he knew Targas could. "Too dark. Too hard. Wish I had some of Jakus's magnesa, then I'd be able to. It made it so easy." He ran the tip of his tongue across his lip, longing for the tang of the crystal and the subsequent rush of warmth, the feeling of power. "Maybe I should find some, build up my talent, not have to do what they tell me. I could go away, do my own thing, be liked, cared about even. Not just someone who can't get it right." He spat at the ceiling.

"Yeah," he nodded in the dark. "That's what I could do. Get some magnesa. Nefaria would help me. She cares about me, too. Maybe even get Jakus to give me some more.

"Yeah, better than staying here getting yelled at."

The bedroom door creaked. Kyel lifted his head, ready to snap, but slumped back and beckoned with his hand.

The young girl hurried over and climbed across his chest, their noses almost touching as she looked into his eyes.

"Anyar, not too close or I won't be able to breathe," he gasped, pushing at the brown hair tickling his face.

She put her arms across his shoulders and snuggled along the length of his body.

"Aww, you're upset too, aren't you?" Kyel rubbed her on the back. "Probably can't understand why they're fighting. Why they can't get on. After all they have you, and you're the best thing about them.

"Find it hard to leave you," he added, giving her a hug.

"Leave, Uncle Ky?" she murmured in a small voice.

"Nothing," he murmured.

"Kyel," Sadir's voice sounded from the kitchen, "could you and Anyar come and eat before everything gets cold?"

He sat up slowly, lifting his niece and put his feet on the floor. "Gee, you weigh a bit now." He heaved Anyar into a more comfortable position before carrying her to the door.

"I suppose you want a hand?" he asked, slipping Anyar onto one of the chairs at the wooden table against the wall.

"Just some salt, if you think you need it." Sadir spooned liquid from a pot on the small black stove set in the corner of the main room.

"What's for dinner, anyway?" he asked, glancing at the set face of Anyar watching her mother's back.

"Doesn't matter," her voice came faintly. "Overcooked anyway: sodden tubers, greens and perac casserole that's almost mush."

"Can I get us a drink?"

"Tea for me. Anyar can have milk from the pantry."

Kyel went through the door. For a moment he leant back against the wall of the small room breathing in the familiar odours, the scents of home. A murmur from Anyar made him straighten and reach for the covered jar of milk on a shelf and a small container of salt. By the time he returned, Sadir was sitting and three pottery plates lay on the table. He poured Anyar a mug of milk, put the salt down, took two cups to the stove and poured dark tea from the kettle.

The meal went silently, each wrapped in their thoughts.

"Ky?"

He looked up.

Anyar waved a spoon.

"My Par's gone."

"Uh, yes. He's out, uh, working." Kyel looked over at Sadir, who shrugged.

"Working," she mouthed.

He watched Anyar turn her attention to her meal, then shook his head.

"This isn't as it should be, is it? Us being together. Him training me, yet we're trying to be a family, and always fighting."

"He went through a lot, you know, especially at the end of the war. It's not been easy to settle down again."

"Listen to you. You're defending him, yet he's always picking fights, if not with you, then me." His spoon clanked into his bowl.

"But"—Sadir glanced at her daughter, who concentrated on her food—"when he came back he couldn't get over all that had happened. Some...something has changed, inside him. He wasn't like that. Maybe he'll settle, and get back to the Targas we know?"

"Yeah," Kyel grumbled. "I don't know whether I want to wait around for that to happen. I had friends too, you know, during the fighting, good friends, especially...especially Luna," he gulped.

Sadir stretched out an arm and clasped his shoulder.

"And"—he shook her hand off—"even Nefaria. She was nice to me, really nice, for a supposed enemy."

"Oh, Kyel." Sadir slumped in her seat. "Things will get better, I know they will."

K yel ate his meal in silence, mind slipping back to those momentous events of the war. Luna would forever be in his thoughts. He remembered her tear-filled face looking into his, the fear of what was to come in the dungeons of Regulus castle and his attempts to be brave for her. But he had failed her and himself. He was still a failure.

He felt his sister's eyes on him, pitying him.

"I think I'll have an early night," he growled.

He closed the door behind him and stood in the darkness, thinking hard. *I've gotta go back. Prove myself. Nefaria will help.* His eyes lit at the thought. *She was my friend, my only true friend. So I'll find her and show them.*

He struck a fire starter, lit the lantern and then pulled his pack from a cupboard, laid it on his small table and unbuckled the flap. "Money. I need some." He took a small pouch from under his mattress. "Yes, I'll need it, especially if I've got to go all the way to Sutan for her.

"Anyar will be fine. She's got my sister and…Targas. There's nothing for me here now. Not got much to take." He piled his brown travelling cloak, a spare set of trousers, underclothing, two shirts, socks, a knife and soap in his pack. He tightened the straps and placed it at the foot of his bed. "I'll leave next day, when Sadir's taken Anyar to the old woman who looks after her, and gone to work. I'll be far on my way by then, closer to finding Nefaria. Be more of a family than I've got now." He climbed into his bed and waited for the night to be over.

Chapter Three

The short, thin figure in a long grey robe, hood lying behind his bald, sun-browned head, smiled as he saw the town of Lesslas.

He had reached a well-built stone bridge spanning a small river before continuing to a wooden palisade surrounding the town. The gates were open and unattended with all traces of the previous rulers' penchant for control of the population gone.

He heard a low bleat beside him and looked up into the dark eyes of his travelling companion, grinning as its large ears swivelled away from him. "Who are you talking to?" he murmured to the perac. "Some of your friends?"

The animal's attention was focussed on a herd of similar long-necked beasts with colours ranging from fawn and grey to black, grazing on the other side of a stone fence.

The grasslands spread a considerable distance on either side of the dusty road, culminating in low foothills behind Lesslas to his right. On his left the country, interspersed with islands of short trees and bushes, gradually descended through a vast valley that ended with the Great Southern River half a day's journey away.

No wonder Lesslas is known for its perac wool industry with these vast grazing tracts, he thought. *It is certainly a peaceful place now. Still, it is time to move along and see how Targas and his family are.*

His face lost its smile as he thought of Targas's contribution to the Sutanites defeat and the peace that now reigned in Ean. Before the war, Targas had been drawn into the land to aid the Resistance and been pursued by the tyrant Jakus, ruler of Ean and his offsider Septus, eager to capture his unusual scent talent. Throughout, Targas had been desperately trying to come to grips with his own scent abilities. That he had achieved so much with the Resistance and was influential in defeating the Sutanites said a lot for the man's character. But now he had settled down with Sadir, the sister of young Kyel.

"Sadir," he murmured, "turning out to be a fine young woman with latent scent talent."

Targas had been omitted from the setting-up of a stable government in Ean, and the establishment and training of the youth for future defence of the land. He had appeared content to stay in Lesslas with his partner, and not return to his home country of Tenstria. Now concern for him from some of his friends had filtered back to the Eanite leader.

"Yes," he said, focussing on the road before him, "it is time I caught up with Targas." He pulled on the perac's lead and started moving his sandalled feet down the road. The occasional passer-by nodded to the Eanite scent master as he passed.

He entered the gates, catching sight of the town hall at the highest point where it dominated the town. Its two levels were crowned by a tower, open on all sides to allow for the trapping and monitoring of scents by the Sutanite rulers. The locals had smashed in those openings once government had returned to the people. *Understandable,* he thought, *but somewhat hasty.* The Sutanites system of receiving and sending scent messages was reasonably efficient and a valuable tool. *Still, it is early days and they'll be made use of again, as is already happening in the cities.*

He picked up his pace along the cobbled road. He knew Sadir's house was not much further, but his route had the advantage of going past the tavern where it was possible that Sadir would be working. *Perhaps Targas will be there as well? Besides, the long journey from Sanctus does bring on a thirst.*

He eyed the stone building as he tied his animal to the railing where a number were already tethered. Lan waited while his perac settled and began to drink from the water trough in front of the railing before pushing open the battered, solid wood doors and entered the relative coolness of the tavern.

He assessed the wave of scents rushing at him, recognising the large innkeeper, Jeth. He was bending behind a scarred wooden bar and filling an earthenware mug from a barrel set under the counter. The room was dominated by the bar and low wooden beams criss-crossing the ceiling. A number of nooks against the walls were occupied by groups of people in the herdsman or trader clothing of non-descript loose tops and baggy trousers. The several women present added a splash of colour, primarily blues and yellows.

The hum of conversation barely slowed as he entered and walked towards Jeth, while sifting the scents for Sadir and Targas.

"Welcome, Lan." The broad face of the owner broke into a smile. "Good to see you again."

Lan smiled in return as he caught the welcome in the man's scent aura.

"I am pleased to be here," he responded.

"You'll be wanting a drink, no doubt?" Jeth plonked a mug redolent with malty scents onto the bar. "I'll get yours in a minute," he said to his previous customer. "This here's one of the heroes of the revolution. Can't keep him waiting."

Lan nodded pleasantly to the wide-eyed stare of the herder at the bar and then looked around the room while taking a sip of the beer. He caught sight of Sadir serving at a table just as the flavours of the drink began to hit.

"My thanks, Jeth." Lan put his mug down. "I will go and speak to Sadir, if I may?"

"Certainly." Jeth began pouring a beer. "And Targas is here too; in the cellar, if you want him."

"Sadir," said Lan gently, touching her on the shoulder as she finished serving. She swung around, saw Lan's smiling face and burst into tears.

Ignoring the startled looks of the couple at the table, Lan pulled Sadir into his shoulder and moved away.

Jeth jerked his head towards the back of the bar.

Lan nodded and took Sadir to a small table wedged in a corner behind the serving area. He pulled two stools together and sat comforting her while she sobbed.

"Come now." Lan lifted her dark brown head to look into her tear-filled eyes. She quickly wiped her nose with her serving cloth and sniffed.

"Sadir, even if I had no scent talent I would know something is wrong. Your worry is for Targas and your family?" Lan patted her hand.

She nodded and sniffed again.

"Take your time."

Bit by bit Sadir told Lan of her concerns with Targas becoming very moody, quick to lose his temper and, although contrite afterwards, hard to live with.

"Yes, I can see how it is affecting you. And the others too?"

"Kyel is having difficulty. I mean, we aren't helping, because he walks right into the middle of our arguments." Sadir paused and wiped her brown eyes. "It's getting so he doesn't respond to either of us. I don't even think he's doing the scent control lessons you and Targas left him. He's certainly unlikely to be going to training in Sanctus with the other young people. And he's hardly ever home unless he's looking after Anyar."

"Mmm, you working here with Targas is probably not conducive to good family relationships." Lan looked around the room. "Has Kyel developed any interests?"

"Other than his lizard, Tel, nothing. After all this time he's still fretting over what happened in the war. Occasionally talks about Luna, and also that Sutanite, Nefaria, but he doesn't mix with any of the townspeople. No friends of his own age."

"I am reluctant to ask, but what does Targas do with his spare time?"

"Malas," spat Sadir, her mouth tightened. "Wine-rotted malas. Ask him."

A large trapdoor had banged open next to him and a familiar dark head began to emerge.

"Lan!" cried Targas. "When did you arrive? And Sadir—Oh." Targas took in the tear-stained face of Sadir and the scents of concern around them.

"I think we need to talk, Targas," said Lan.

They paused at the top of the ridge above Lesslas, found a huddle of boulders and made themselves comfortable. Targas leant against a warm rock face, angled so he could catch the rays of the descending sun. Lan sat several steps away, where he was able to look down over the town and back northwards along the route he'd travelled several hours earlier.

"I remember coming this way some years ago now," murmured Targas. "It was my first view of Lesslas. I didn't know what to expect." He rubbed his hand through his dark hair. "It was the first time I could really rest after coming into Ean. Kyel was going on about the Sutanite seekers, his sister and safety, and I didn't know what to expect. Then Sadir—she was…" He put his elbows on his knees, rested his head in his hands and looked at the sun. "I think I've ruined it, Lan. I think I'm gradually destroying the special thing that we have and I don't know why. I don't know why!" Targas stared out into the distance.

The scent master leant forward and took Targas's hands, his dark eyes assessing. "Link with me; let yourself go."

Lan began to hum, a familiar vibration that caused Targas to join in. Scents grew stronger, a vanilla aroma grew thicker, filling the space around them until it seemed the air had become opaque. The odours infiltrated their minds, pushing into every cell, every fibre, breaking into their very scent structure.

"Let it go, Targas. Allow it." Lan sensed a blockage in Targas's scent, a strength that was more than just the man—a force resisting the gentleness of the ritual, not allowing the flow through the channels and pathways within their brains or full access to their scent memories.

"Ah!" yelped Lan suddenly as the linkage snapped.

Targas jerked back and banged his head into the rock. "Ow! Blood's teeth!"

"Ah," groaned Lan, "I must apologise for that. I did not realise."

"Realise what?" said Targas, rubbing at the back of his head. "Did you find out something? Anything? A reason?" His boot rapped the ground, a harsh sound in the quietness.

"Patience, and I will attempt to make sense of what I learned." Lan rubbed the beads of sweat off his brow and leant forward to look into Targas's light eyes.

"I do not know what I expected, but not what I found. You have developed as a scent master, truly you have since last we did this. I had enough time to sense that." Lan nodded to himself. "But what I did not suspect is the blockage in your mind. I do not remember you having such. And unfortunately it defies me. I attempted to push in but I was blocked, stopped if you will. You are strong, very strong."

"Hold on." Targas broke eye contact. "Are you saying there's something there but you don't know what? That I've got something in my mind blocking me and my scent pathways?"

"No, that is not what I mean. I still see your scent powers, but there is something else. Whether it's that that is influencing you, I do not know. Maybe time will help you overcome it? Maybe it is just a phase you are going through as you develop, mature?"

"So what you're saying is you don't know, that it may or may not be something, and if it is, you hope I can overcome it over time?"

"Please, Targas," said Lan, brow wrinkling as he patted Targas's knee, "I am not saying help cannot be given, but only after we see if you can overcome this on your own. The good thing is you are aware of the problem, both you and Sadir, and that is significant. If it continues, then…" Lan paused. "I think I know someone who is far better with the ways of the mind than me. Yes, she will help.

"But for the moment, we had better return. Sadir will be home by now and I have had a long and wearying journey."

The sun had set behind the western mountains by the time Lan and Targas reached Sadir's house. They noticed the door was ajar.

"That's unusual," said Targas. "Normally the door's closed."

"Mmm," murmured Lan.

As Targas reached forward for the door it was dragged from his grasp. Sadir's eyes were wide, her face white.

"Kyel! I can't find him anywhere. His clothes and bag are gone!"

Targas reached out but she pushed past. "It's your fault. Your fault! Look after your daughter!" Sadir yelled as she ran down the street.

"Come, Targas," said Lan as he ushered him through the door. "We need to mind Anyar and see if we can determine what has happened."

"But Sadir…"

"I surmise she'll be checking with friends and will return later. In the meantime, we should go inside." The click of the door closing seemed loud inside the empty cottage.

He was glad he had his own perac, that he was old enough to own an animal and not have to ask his sister or Targas when he wanted to take it out of the communal stables near the tavern. Kyel had a momentary pang of guilt at the protests of the beast as he alternatively rode it at pace, then jogged beside it. But he just needed to get away, away from well-meaning people, from Lesslas and from his frustrating life.

His mind turned from those he'd left behind to what lay ahead. He had made a decision, as a man. It was his decision, and he would follow it through. He fought hard to retain Nefaria's face and form in his vision, not thinking about what he would do if he couldn't find her. It was enough to be going on the journey, to have a reason, to make sure she still thought of him and would welcome him.

"First to Nebleth. That was where I lived and trained when the Sutanites had me. There I was respected and had Nefaria looking out for me. If she's not there I'll go further, even…even if I must catch a ship to Sutan." His voice grew husky as he moved along the track to the top of the hill.

He slowed, looking for a place to camp for the night as darkness descended.

Chapter Four

Jagged granite spires trimmed with hoar frost reached into the pale clouds; at their base lay the remains of millennia of erosion. Low bushes, grey like the rock, did little to soften the harshness of the surroundings.

The clearing, secluded and almost inaccessible, was full of life.

Alethea surveyed the group before her, eyes bright and assessing. She was rugged up in the greens of her people, thick wool jacket covering padded trousers to mid-thigh. She absently wiped the end of her nose with a gloved hand; mornings always brought a sniffle, no matter how much she was used to early rising.

"Telpher," she called softly, "mind the girth strap."

The broad-shouldered man lifted his head from the woollen side of the perac, fogged breath obscuring his face. "Will be done. Don't like to lose cargo, nor break even one tumbler."

Alethea's attention had already moved on. One of the animals was objecting to its load. She blew a soft drift of calming scent at its long-necked head and the perac steadied, looking at her with a quizzical expression out of large brown eyes. She smiled and continued to watch over the preparations of the trading team, even as Telpher's response prompted a memory.

The trade between Ean and her country had only resumed on a regular basis once the Sutanite rule ended. They had continued to get limited supplies to the native Eanites during the long years of occupation, but the journey was hazardous. The rebels' stronghold of Sanctus, high in the western mountains on Ean's border with Rolan, had been as far as they could safely go.

Alethea's duties usually prevented her from spending time away from Rolan. As Mlana of her country she held the wellbeing of her people in sacred trust. Understanding the movement and interplays of the sensory forces in the atmosphere had been a crucial skill held by generations of her kind; few had the ability, innate, not learned.

On very rare occasions a Knowing discerned in the complex patterns of scent flow over the lands had foretold major changes in the natural order. The consequences of that Knowing four decades past still weighed heavily on Alethea, sapping her energy at the remembering. Visits to Ean after that had been brief and few. Her latest Knowing was confusing, necessitating her return to Ean. At least two individuals figured, one a damaged hero who still had to play a significant part in the country's future, the other a younger male whose influence would not come until later. And then, there was a woman—maybe more than one… Youth and talent figured highly. Again, it was all lost in the mists of time, with danger figuring prominently. Not all would survive. She shivered. Such portents could not be ignored.

"Mlana Alethea?"

She jumped at Drathner's voice. "Forgive me. I was elsewhere."

"Would you care to have a last look over the group before the Sending?"

"Yes. Thank you." Alethea, her head level with Drathner's shoulder, strolled amongst the animals and their handlers, looking for disharmony in the scents and checking the stability of the crates containing the highly desired, cordial-filled Rolan tumblers. She nodded to each person and absorbed the odours of the animals, assessing their readiness for the journey. All was as it should be. People were moving from foot to foot to keep warm, and the laden perac becoming fractious.

Drathner clapped his hands. All heads turned to Alethea as she stepped onto a flat-topped rock. The tall figure of Boidea nodded in support as Alethea responded to the warmth of feeling from those before her.

With all attention focussed on her slight form she raised her arms, looked to the columns of granite cradling the clearing and began to hum. The resonance of the sound was picked up by her people and grew until the clearing resounded around them. The scudding scents of the air mingled with those of the rock, earth and vegetation. They visibly thickened and filled the space above them, swirling in ever-increasing circles. The sound magnified. Alethea was moving to a rhythm that flowed from the people into the animals, and soon the group was a single swaying mass. The darkening scent spiralled over the group. Small portions infiltrated the mouths and nostrils of the people and animals. Everything blurred and softened. The cold rolled back. A sense of belonging and of comfort filled the void. The hum slowly faded.

Alethea smiled as she took Drathner's hand to step from the rock. She walked with him to the head of the column and took the lead of a veteran perac. The animal lowered its head to nuzzle Alethea before she gently urged it after Drathner's animal, now entering a gap in the walls of granite. A rocky path worn by generations of traders began the difficult trek through the mountains.

"A long way ahead of us," Boidea's melodious voice came from behind. "I'm looking forward to the journey, though its potential dangers are a little unsettling."

Alethea half-turned to catch a glimpse of her companion, a highly skilled mystic in her own right. "Do not worry, Drathner has done this trip many times and has not lost anyone." She turned to look at the rump of the leader's animal swaying with irregular motion along the narrow rocky path. "A few have had frost cold and occasionally animals have been taken by avalanches and the odd attack by vorals."

"Vorals? Up here?"

"Yes, up here. I expect they're too high for any competition from the k'dorian lizards… They're attracted to the honey."

"It's all rock and snow." Boidea raised her hands towards the craggy peaks above. "Surely nothing could live up here, not the pria or their hives?"

"Boidea, we're blessed with big animals right across Rolan and Ean. I think that is partly because of where they live. Big means more power and usually, as is the case with pria and those dreadful hymetta the Sutanites used in Ean, they can travel long distances. At any rate it's not too long a flight from the thickets of flowering mountain trees to where they build their hives. The vorals will follow a strong inbuilt memory to seek out the honey. Their tough skin can take a lot of pria stings without harm, and their thick fur keeps out cold."

"I hope we don't see a voral," she muttered. "They mightn't be overly large, but they're mean."

"We better just be on the lookout for them, Boidea. And where you put your feet as well," she added as her companion stumbled on the uneven surface. "A wrenched ankle could have untold consequences on this journey."

The trek was mind-numbing and physically wearying. Alethea had to rely on the surefootedness of her perac as she put one foot in front of the other. She felt her heart labouring as they began to climb again after the early descent. *I'm getting too old for this. But the call was strong and must take me where it will.*

She had to force herself not to call to Drathner and ask him for rest. She knew they had to pace the caravan through the mountains, and suitable camping sites were few.

A scudding gust of ice particles dashed across her face, peppering her with pinpricks of pain. She cried out.

"Mlana, are you hurt?" called Drathner's concerned voice across the strengthening wind.

"No. No, I'm alright…although I am tiring a little," she replied, raising her voice to be heard.

"Our camp area is just ahead, not far. We can rest soon," said Drathner, his square face topped with peppery hair appearing over the side of Alethea's animal. "I am sorry the journey is hard. This day is the longest." He smiled and returned to the head of the column.

Alethea tightened the hood of her jacket around her face, tucked some flailing wisps of grey hair away and kept her head close to the perac's woolly flank. "Not long now. Not long now," was her mantra for the remainder of the journey as the wind and sleet strengthened their attempts to drive them from their path.

Hot food and shelter were priorities when they stopped where the track widened into a long, flat area that could comfortably take their large caravan. At the further end a stream gushed out, forcing its way down a narrow crevasse with hissing urgency, its origin high in the mountain forming the back wall to their camp. An overhanging ledge protected the site from rocks and debris.

"Please sit over here, Mlana," said Drathner. "We'll soon have your tent set up."

"I feel I should help," Alethea protested as he led her towards a covered crate next to a small fire.

"No, you have duties and burdens enough. Sit…please, and keep this blanket around you. Hot food will be ready shortly."

The rocky overhang kept most of the snow and ice from reaching her, although occasional flurries made it past. Alethea tightened the blanket around her and watched the cargo being unloaded and tents set up.

She sighed and felt herself falling into a Knowing. Her last conscious thought before giving herself to the Knowing was that she was too cold to ever wake up and would become part of the massive mountain above her.

She drifted in the winds driving the snow far across the mountains. At first she was pulled past the mountain peaks, then she rose higher. A different wind took her as if her sensory motes had body and purpose. The mountains diminished, the harsh colours of rock and tree barely distinguishable from the gathering darkness. The sun, now a pale orb low on the western horizon, had little impact on the grey dusk of the land beneath her.

She recognised Ean and the hills that hid Sanctus. These hills bled from the vast mountain range, the border between the two countries, becoming plains and leading to the artery of that country, the Great Southern River. The sun's dying rays caught the extensive Long Ranges in the east, acting as buffer to the desert beyond, where lay the source of the conflict that had drawn the Sutanite invaders to Ean generations ago: salt, a needful curse to the world and the cause of much turmoil and death.

Alethea found herself slowing, a need pulling her towards the land. *I require no prompting. The* Knowing *before I left was very strong. A force I have not felt for many years. A reminder of things not done, of tasks unfulfilled.*

A gust took her in a different direction to follow the course of the mighty river southwards. A town at the base of several hills, emerging from the mountains between Rolan and Ean, was only visible by the smoke of numerous chimneys and the occasional flare of fire. A powerful sense of foreboding filled her as she recognised it. A town with memories. A town from the past and much import for the future. A darkness filled her mind.

A soft smell infiltrated her nostrils, warm and wholesome—honey and herbs. Alethea opened her eyes to Boidea's concerned face, a steaming cup in her gloved hand.

"Mlana," she whispered, "please take this tea. I was worried."

Alethea took the cup and sipped. "Ah, thank you," she smiled. "Come, sit by the fire and I'll share what I've seen."

The camp had soon settled. Alethea was happy preparations and scent protection were in the competent hands of Drathner. Her weariness went more than skin deep. A small cup of soup, honey wafers and a draft of cordial shared with Boidea in their small tent were all the sustenance she could manage. The layers of travel mattresses and thick blankets could not prevent the cold filtering into her bones before she fell into a troubled sleep. The wail of the wind was an ever-present backdrop. Occasional noises competed but she was too weary to take notice. *Others have that charge*, she thought.

A gentle calling at the tent flap woke her. She pushed herself up on her elbow, noticing blearily that Boidea had already risen.

"Yes?"

"Sorry to disturb you, Mlana."

"Drathner, am I late?"

"We're almost ready, Mlana. Time for some food and then we must be on our way."

"I will be ready."

Alethea rose stiffly, pulling on her outer jacket and wool-lined boots. Boidea entered with tea and travel bread.

"Thank you, Boidea. Just about everything is packed? I do not like being idle."

"Do not think that. The mere fact you're on this journey is reward enough for any effort we make. We are all concerned you are not stressed."

Alethea smiled and patted her companion's solid shoulder. "Now, tell me of the noises I heard last night. Did they mean anything?"

"Well, yes," replied Boidea, a slight frown creasing her forehead. "Something was around the perac last night and they're not sure what. No damage was done but it managed to break through our scent guards. Drathner has his suspicions but didn't say what it could be."

"In that case it's nothing to worry us, until he says it is."

"Can I take your cup, Mlana?"

"Thank you. I will come with you since they're ready to depart."

Telpher stood next to her perac as she arrived.

"Should be an easier day, more down than up," he said as he gave her the lead. "Just be careful when you cross the crevasse. Follow Drathner's direction and you will be safe."

"I wouldn't dream of not doing what he tells me. He strikes me as a very stern leader." Alethea smiled with a twinkle in her eye and led the perac to the head of the caravan.

The wind of the night had died down to a stiff breeze; Alethea enjoyed the crispness on her cheeks. The sun was making an attempt to appear and the mist had risen above. The line of animals stretched out along the track.

She paused at a high point on the path and looked back to the eighteen perac making up the rest of the caravan. Each had an attendant man or woman in the greens of Rolan. They carried a staff in one hand and held the lead in the other. They were fit, healthy and competent. *Any one of them could lead the caravan through these mountains. Yes, I am blessed,* she thought as she turned and followed Drathner down towards the first of the trees fighting for a hold alongside the path. Gnarled and weather-beaten, they were nevertheless a pleasing sight since they gave some colour and life to their road. She shivered as she looked down the steep slope off the side of the road.

"Be of care," called Drathner over his shoulder. "Best you keep a firm hold on your animal, and stay on the upside. I never like travelling this section."

Alethea concentrated on their path, ignoring the steep slope as they came up to the trees. With rough bark and dark green needles on contorted stems, the trees fought for the sparse soil in the rubble of rocks, gaps appearing where a rockslide had pushed even these tenacious plants to their doom.

"Keep moving," Drathner called softly.

Alethea's perac pursed its lips, an echoing vibration grew. She could see it rolling its eyes and blew calming scents at it. The perac settled, although it tiptoed its way along the narrow, rocky path.

"Keep moving. Keep them calm," Drathner called. "Not long now."

Alethea took a breath and felt with all her senses. Trickles of distress circled the caravan. She could tell the people were calming their animals, but the stress of the dangerous track and nervous animals hampered their efforts. An unfamiliar scent mote drifted across her sight and was almost instantly swallowed. Despite herself she was intrigued, and she attempted to backtrack its passage. It had originated, she found, from an area they had already passed, amongst the trees. It came again but she didn't know it, couldn't recognise it.

A screech, the panicked bleating of a perac and then a harsh crashing echoed down the slope. She quickly looked back along the caravan. The strength and calming scents from the perac handlers had little effect; the animals were jumping, dislodging rocks as they moved. Alethea stopped, locked her own animal in a strong scent bond and hummed at a high pitch, drawing scents from wherever she could. The sound gradually filtered through the panicked animals, other handlers joining in her sending. Slowly calmness descended and order was restored.

"Be still," she called. "Hold yourself still."

"My thanks, Mlana, for averting a possible disaster," said Drathner. "Can you lead your perac into the thicket and tie it off with mine? I'll send the rest to you and then investigate what has happened."

"No," responded Alethea, "I'll have Boidea do that. I need to see what has happened. I sensed an unfamiliar force at work."

"Your wish, Mlana," said Drathner, "but I am merely thinking of your safety. Come with me, then."

It took time to move the animals up to their temporary holding area before Drathner and Alethea were able to edge past.

A young handler knelt on hands and knees looking down the slope. She scrambled to her feet as Drathner and Alethea arrived. "Oh, I'm so sorry. I had no way of stopping it…couldn't do anything." Her speech was punctuated by sobs.

"Calm, Undrea," said Alethea taking her hand and sending calming scents into her face, "Tell me what happened."

"My perac is down there, gone in an instant. I was lucky not to go myself."

"What happened?" repeated Alethea, stroking the distressed woman's hand.

"I was on the end of the line, since I was carrying food supplies and not goods." Her hand left a smear of blood as she wiped away her tears. "This thing came out of those trees and went straight into the side of my animal. I dropped the lead as it took her down the slope. Way down there." She pointed to a dark patch far below."

"Too far and difficult to get down, I think," said Drathner. "The fall would have killed it. I'm sorry."

"But the food…"

"We have enough for our journey. Come, best you have your hand seen to.'"

Undrea nodded and turned to walk up the path to where the others were waiting.

"What do you think it was?" asked Alethea.

"I've my suspicions," said Drathner. "That, and the fact it went for the food supplies."

At that moment a drift of the same unfamiliarity hit Alethea's senses. This time it came from above, not down the slope where the perac had fallen to its death.

"A moment, Drathner. There's something above in that thicket of trees."

"Be careful, Mlana, we know not what it could be."

"I'll be careful, but I do not feel threatened."

She stepped off the path. The leaves tugged at her clothing as she pushed through into the small space at the centre of three twisted boughs.

A pair of dark eyes looked up at her. A flood of scent gave her the strongest feeling she should look away, leave and not remember what she had seen. She backed away in surprise.

"Most unusual," she muttered. "How did it do that?"

Alethea looked back into the hollow. The animal hissed, showing sharp white teeth before turning its hairy brown back.

Alethea reached down with a gloved hand, all the while projecting calming scents over the creature. "Come, little one, I'm not going to hurt you." She touched its back and it flattened, leaving little space to get her hand under its belly.

"Come," she repeated, and pushed her second hand under the animal. She straightened, holding the wriggling creature tightly, and stepped back onto the track.

"Careful! That's a young voral," cried Drathner. "That must've been its mother that took our perac; it must've been killed in doing so or we would have heard. We cannot leave it to die. Give it to me. I will dispose of it."

"No!" Alethea turned her hands so that its white belly and four black, clawed feet pointed towards her, a long red tongue flicking from its flat, snouted face. "No, we will keep it; there may be others of its kind further down. We can leave the animal where they will find it."

Drathner looked at the elder, sensing her words did not reveal all.

"No one can ever make a pet of a voral; they're killers, and fiercer than a k'dorian lizard."

"It is coming with us." Her statement allowed no argument.

Chapter Five

"**A**rrgh! Cursed woman!" Sweat coursed down the furrows in his face. "Shall I stop, my Lord?" Nefaria's voice trembled.

"No, blast you!" He groaned as she heaved him into a sitting position against the backboard of the bunk. Waves of pain flared through him. He banged his head against the wood. "Higher...pull me higher! I need to stand."

"If you wait a moment, Lord Jakus, the cramping will cease," Nefaria whispered as she pushed healing scents across him.

"Do not," Jakus hissed through clenched teeth, "tell me what to do!"

"My Lord..." She eased Jakus's legs off the edge of the bunk and onto the floor. Removing the woollen blankets from his grip, she placed his hands on her shoulders and steadied.

"Now?"

Jakus panted, dark eyes staring fixedly into Nefaria's concerned face as if daring her to continue.

"Ah!" Her slim body bent backwards, straining against Jakus's weight. His fingers hooked into her shoulders as she continued to pull, slowly lifting him from the bed until he slumped against her brown-clad form.

"Help me to the wall," he demanded. "I'll be better once I've walked." Each slow step across the cabin was made more difficult by the slight rocking of the floor. Once there, he released his hold and leant against a wooden beam. Nefaria stepped back, rubbing at the red marks on her neck.

"You are a lot better than last time we were on a ship," she offered tentatively.

"Should be!" Jakus snapped, "I've had enough time over these years to get my body into some sort of condition. If it weren't for these cursed cramps... Get me my clothing."

"S...shouldn't you take it slo...?"

"My robe!"

Nefaria turned and removed the long, black, hooded robe and cord belt from the peg behind the rough wooden door.

She hesitated, holding the clothing before him. Jakus held out one arm and then the other as she settled the woollen garment over his gaunt, pale body.

"Ah, I feel alive again. Now"—his eyes narrowed at the young woman—"get the shaving gear."

Nefaria bobbed her dark head before edging around him and opening the cabin door.

"When you've finished my shave I will see the Captain."

"Yes, my Lord."

As the door clicked behind her, Jakus ran his hand over the stubble of his head and face. "Yes," he murmured, "there is a lot to achieve, and he will need to play his part."

"Come!"

As the thin man entered the cabin Jakus straightened in his chair, stifling a wince.

"Tibitus! Good you could find time to attend me." Jakus slowly ran his eyes up the boots, black trousers and green woollen shirt until he reached the lined face of the man.

The captain ran a hand through his lank hair, the vague cloud of scent about his head quickly dissipating as a gust of sea air blew through the cabin door.

Blood's curse. I can hardly see the colours, even read the man's scents. He's nervous but I cannot find it in his scent aura.

Jakus steeled his face.

"You are up and about early, Jakus?" His eyes were wide, hand gripping the door jamb.

"Should I not be?" Jakus raised an eyebrow.

"Yes. No. I mean…" He fell silent.

"Tell me how long to Port Saltus," Jakus snapped.

"Ah"—he shifted into the cabin—"we've had fair winds despite the long tacks, so it would be around two days out."

"Good," said Jakus, rubbing his chin. "I assume you've kept a lookout. No-one is following my ship?"

Tibitis nodded.

"It is time, Tibitis, to talk of that other matter, magnesa crystals. What supplies of it and its base material, magnesite, are to be had in the port?"

"Virtually non-existent, Cer. I…err…have tried our usual sources but since the war it's dried up. The crystals are not openly available. Any supply is limited and pricey. The Rolan mystics are making it hard for the normal trade to continue, probably controlling it with the rebel Eanite government, I wouldn't wonder."

"I've been out of action too long, it seems," said Jakus, rubbing a hand over his freshly shaven head. "You know the value I place on that substance."

"I do, Cer." Tibitis straightened imperceptibly.

Yes you do, don't you? thought Jakus. He'd enjoyed using his scent powers to control Tibitis.

"So it would seem our voyage is a necessary one? I need my remaining supplies from Ean. I assume you still have access to our old rooms in the port?"

"Yes, Jakus," replied Tibitis, "but where did you conceal the cache of magnesa crystals? I could have found them for you. I've shipped into Saltus on a few occasions while you were in Sutan."

"It is well hidden in a way that a scent master might use. You would never have been able to access it with your lack of skill," he sneered. "No, it is my need we fulfil this trip. Your role is to get me there.

"Attend me later when you have anything of worth to report," he said with a flick of his hand. "And send Nefaria to me. She's had enough free time."

Tibitis nodded and hurriedly left the cabin.

Jakus thought of the small supply left to him, a shiver of need running through his body. So much had changed since he had been forced to flee Ean. He was coming back in disguise; discovery would see him executed by the new rebel government.

But the risk is worth it. With magnesa I can be powerful again, my scent abilities enhanced. He bared his teeth. *I have a lot of people to repay.*

"You asked for me, my Lord?" Nefaria's slender figure stood in the doorway, her black curls in disarray, the shape of her lithe body outlined by the breeze, which was attempting to claim her gown.

"Yes, I need a distraction. Close the door."

"Cer, there's two of their ships heading our way. The Eanites have scent masters on board. They'll find you," Tibitis announced from the doorway.

"Enough! Just get back to the helm and sail. Do nothing suspicious. Give me time."

Jakus thrust the captain out of his cabin and walked to his bunk. Wincing, he bent to pull out a large brass-bound box from underneath, and concentrated. A thin spike of scent extended from his mouth and infiltrated the latch to dismantle the pattern of interlocking bonds sealing the box. He lifted the lid and smiled as he took out the hand-sized leather bag.

"Ah, precious to me, deadly to my enemies," he whispered, pulling at the drawstring. "Ahhhh," he trembled, taking a large pinch of red magnesa crystals with long pale fingers. "Too much?" Jakus wondered, thinking of the impact of the withdrawal symptoms, but his tongue extended almost without thought to take the substance.

The impact of the magnesa hit into the smell and emotional centres of his brain. The colours of the room were brighter, richer, as if a painter had used primary rather than pastel hues. Myriads of scents drifting through the room became opaque, their colours identifying their origin: the brown of wood, a yellow tinge of nervousness left from Tibitis, a grey tendril of resolve from himself.

This was the moment. Years of rebuilding his shattered scent abilities, keeping unnoticed and concealing his weakness from his brothers Brastus and Faltis…and others. Time to reclaim his power.

The taste of Targas when he had him at his mercy was locked in his scent memories. He had been able to infiltrate the foreign scent master's mind and unlock secrets that had made him such a worthy opponent. Jakus recalled the extrapolation of scent usage, the bonding of different motes from a range of scents that had aided the rebels in their conquest of Ean. *My Ean!* Targas's ability to "see" and bond scents over such a large distance with such tight control was a significant weapon.

The captains of the two Eanite vessels from Port Saltus closing on his ship should not be aware a much-desired Sutanite scent master, the former ruler of their country, was on board. Jakus, with his magnesa-enhanced senses, was a formidable opponent and he looked forward to the challenge.

And if they learn I am aboard then they won't stay alive to profit from it.

He resealed the box and stood with a slight wince. Focussing downwards, he extruded a dark scent flow from his mouth which thickened as it reached the large container, slowly enveloping it. Only a slight reddening of his forehead showed his effort as the box slid under the bed.

"Mmm," he smiled, the scent snake dissipating as he headed for the door.

Jakus took the several steps up to the deck, emerging in front of the rails that outlined the helm. He maintained a cloaking scent to ensure that his distinctive profile as a Sutanite scent master would not be obvious; he would appear to be an ordinary passenger.

The crack of the topsail caught his attention. A sailor high above him was shortening the sheets, with others doing the same to the square sails of the other mast. The jib and spritsail, tight in the wind, gave them manoeuvrability as they entered the channel leading into Port Saltus. One of the Ean ships suddenly peeled off, its bowsprit crashing through the waves as it tacked towards a distant sail. The other ship drew closer.

"One less to worry about," breathed Jakus, as he turned to watch the remaining small vessel.

"Where's Jakus? We're about to be boarded. He'll be found out," Tibitis muttered as he hurried straight past towards the bow, paying little attention to the disguised figure at the rail.

"You're not attending the helm," called Jakus softly.

"What?" Tibitis pulled up to peer at the figure. "You...Jakus?"

"You are a fool, Tibitis," said Jakus. "I'm not about to proclaim to the world who I am. And nor will you. If I am found out, you will not live to regret it." His tone froze the captain. "And remember, I am to be called *Bastin!*"

Jakus manoeuvred his way along the decking rail until he reached Nefaria near the bow. He reached a hand around her waist.

"Uh, you startled me, my Lord."

"I could not find you," he whispered. "You had left me at this particularly vulnerable time." He pushed his tongue into her ear. "It's not what I wanted, is it?"

Nefaria's neck strained as she tried not to recoil. "I'm sorry. It's just that I... ah…" She gripped the well-oiled rail.

"I need you now. Control yourself. Here." Jakus extended a finger, on the end of which glinted a single red crystal.

She bent forward and licked the finger, eyes half closing as the taste hit her.

"We have visitors very soon and you have a very important role as a trader's consort. So control your scents and show your respect," he hissed.

The calmer waters in the channel allowed the Ean vessel to launch a small rowing boat. There seemed little urgency from its four occupants as they caught up to their ship. Tibitus conferred with a sailor before ordering a rope ladder to be unrolled over the side.

Jakus's eyes narrowed and he pulled Nefaria against him, quietly strengthening his aura to be in keeping with his purported profession, projecting a calm exterior with just the slightest of scent bonds disrupting the profile of his face. He felt little concern, provided the others played their part. Should the worst happen and he be found out, then he would use his power on the hapless scent master about to come aboard.

I think I am going to enjoy this.

"Cer, uh, Bastin," called Tibitis, leading a short, plump scent master dressed in grey trousers and vest, a brown woollen coat flapping loosely across his shoulders. "This is scent master Grefnel, in charge of port protection. He wants to have a word with you and your lady."

Jakus smiled as he nodded to the man.

"I appreciate it, Captain." A frown furrowed Grefnel's round face as he glanced down at his sheaf of papers. "Now, Cer Bastin and...?" He looked at Nefaria.

"My consort, Nepryl..." he said, spelling her name helpfully. "We're here to enjoy a few days rest before our return journey."

"Hmm," Grefnel continued. "It says here you're after salt—as is virtually every trader—and woollen goods, too. Your trade is fine cloth, vintages and copper. Fairly straight forward. My men are currently assessing the cargo for taxes. No objections?"

Jakus maintained an outward calm, squeezing Nefaria's waist in a seemingly comforting gesture.

"Now…" Grefnel looked up from his notes. "We're required to check all passengers and crew for signs of Sutanites of the old regime wanted by our government. Do you have any knowledge of such?"

"No. Is there much of a problem now?" Jakus enquired.

"N…no, although you'd be surprised," Grefnel paused, looking closely at Jakus's face, "but you do have a look, uh."

"Of what, scent master Grefnel?" Jakus smiled as he manoeuvred a translucent odour over the man and tightened the bonds within the blanket of scent to hold his body immobile. *Yes, Targas, see how I can use the skills I took from you.* Grefnel's mouth was open, eyes wide as Jakus extruded a scent spike straight through the man's mouth and into the olfactory areas of his brain.

Jakus used his enhanced senses to sift through the man's scent memories and take his collection of Sutanite odours. Jakus reinforced his own scent as a trustworthy and important person Grefnel would be only too pleased to help.

"Hold on there," Jakus said jokingly, releasing the scent cloud and reaching out a supporting hand as the scent master staggered, "I thought you would have your sea legs by now."

"I…I don't know…" Grefnel raised a hand to his head. He looked at Jakus and continued. "I think I have all I require. You can be on your way to the docks." He turned and walked towards Tibitis at the helm.

"That went well," Jakus smiled at Nefaria, "very well indeed."

They had left Tibitis to the process of unloading, organising storage and transport, and preparing for return cargo to Sutan. No one took notice of the merchant and his consort as they manoeuvred their way through the activity on the wharves to the quieter streets away from the dock area.

Jakus forced back a burgeoning magnesa-induced headache to concentrate as he and Nefaria entered a narrow street running parallel with the waterfront. Wooden two-storey buildings rose on each side, blocking off the port and allowing little light to enter the small windows that broke up the weathered facades.

Jakus used a small brass key to unlock a solid, aged door, then pulled Nefaria through and locked it behind him. "No point in having a curious scent master finding us at this stage," he commented as he led the way up a set of steep stairs in the gloom. Nefaria felt for each step as she climbed after Jakus, not daring to ask for the wall candles to be lit. He banged open the door at the top of the landing.

"Little usage since I've been gone, I see," said Jakus as he breathed in the air filled with dust motes visible in the light of a small window high in the wall. "I thought the cursed Eanites might've tried to take it over."

"This was yours, my Lord?"

"One of mine," he grunted as he stalked around a small wooden table to a row of shelves lining the back wall. Jakus searched along the few books and old maps lying scattered along them, sniffing occasionally.

"Tibitus still uses it when in port. Apparently, he was telling the truth about the magnesite. Any trace that's here is old. Didn't think he'd try to fool me again.

"No, nothing here," he said, swinging around, and walked to the door. "We'll stay in Port Saltus tonight and travel to Nebleth next day. There I have some well-hidden supplies of magnesite."

"Won't it be dangerous, going back there?" asked Nefaria.

Jakus looked back at her from the head of the stairs. "The supplies are vital for my plans. Nothing will stop me, Nefaria." A cloud of dark scent rose from his mouth. "Nothing!"

Chapter Six

The rustling in the corner of the room brought Alethea out of an exhausted sleep. She moved and the rustling paused.

"What. Are. You. Doing?" she groaned, raising her head to look at her scattered belongings, light filtering through a pair of wooden shutters above the bed revealing a dark shape rummaging through the clothing.

She had argued against preferential treatment to the rest of her Rolan trading party but the Eanite scent masters wouldn't hear of it. They had given her the best room in Sanctus, large and tucked away in a secluded section of the vast, granite-composed complex. She admired Sanctus, which fitted so seamlessly amongst the hills forming part of the mountains near the joint border between Rolan and Ean. *No wonder,* she thought, *the enemy had not been able to find it during their long occupation of Ean.*

The rustling, followed by a scampering of heavy paws, ensured she couldn't fall back to sleep. Alethea smiled at the youthful enthusiasm of the voral as she thought about getting up. She had a full schedule of teaching ahead of her: the large school of acolytes who were training to become scent masters had eagerly accepted her offer.

"Little enough," she murmured, grateful she hadn't continued with the trading party taking their goods to the various towns and cities in Ean. "Far easier on me to stay here. Besides, I need to see Lan when he returns from Lesslas. Even more so now, after last night."

That night she had fallen into a light sleep after a day teaching a group of enthusiastic youngsters. Although exhausted, her essence was pulled into the dusky night sky, so reminiscent of her experience those few days ago that had encouraged her journey to Ean. She had drifted down the valley, following the dark grey ribbon of the Great Southern River.

She recognised the town backed by the huge western mountains separating Rolan from Ean and the darkness she had felt emanating from it, but was surprised she didn't drift there. Instead, she was drawn down the mighty Great

Southern River until she saw the Ean cities of Regulus and Nebleth spaced along it.

Then something happened. Whether it was the young voral making a noise in her room, or just her time to withdraw, Alethea found herself returning to her body with a dire feeling, a pressing need. Why her journey had shifted its focus past Lesslas to the cities was most curious. All she knew was the urgency of the Knowing was almost bursting out of her chest as she awoke, like the land's future depended on it.

"Hey!" she protested, jerking when a small, flat head poked over the side of the bed. Its black eyes briefly caught hers, white teeth gleaming, before it scampered over the covers and thudded back to the floor.

"Oh, you silly thing," she said. "Why do you have to play now? You're making me wish I hadn't kept you."

Indeed Drathner, the leader of their expedition, had tried to make Alethea leave the orphaned voral behind and not take him on to Sanctus, but she'd resisted, even though the voral had not made it any easier. He had hissed, bared his teeth at everyone and made a nuisance of himself by seeking out any food not securely locked away, the voral's strong claws and sharp teeth making short work of any container not made of metal or fired clay.

She smiled and lay back. There was something about this animal that was endearing, a feeling he was important, very important. She had learnt not to ignore such feelings.

Thrap! came a knock at the door. The voral stilled. Alethea sat up, recognising the scents.

"Come in Boidea, but mind the voral, he's in a playful mood."

"Playful?" said Boidea, carefully opening the door. "It's vicious, it is. Just don't let it go for my legs, or I won't come in."

Alethea sighed and projected calming scents at the voral, soon hearing him quieten. "It'd help if you brought him some honey. He'd be your friend for life."

"Yours maybe," growled Boidea as she entered the room carrying a tray. "It's hard to see where I'm going with the windows closed." She put the tray on Alethea's lap and threw open the shutters, allowing a stream of light to enter. "Make sure it doesn't snatch any of the food." Boidea took a small bowl off the tray, then bent over and put it on the floor. "Here, you…you creature."

The voral waddled over to the bowl, gave a tooth-filled smile to Boidea before plunging its muzzle into the honey.

"See?"

"Humph," she replied, standing next to the bed. "Just to let you know that Lan returned last night and is waiting for you in the common room."

"Good," said Alethea, wriggling up in the bed, "I need to see him."

"I can tell, Mlana, you have had a disturbed night. Don't you go overdoing it," said Boidea sympathetically.

"Thank you, Boidea, I'll take time with my meal. Can you take the voral outside for a while?" She looked up from under her eyebrows, a small smile on her lined face.

"Oh, you are incorrigible, Mlana," Boidea frowned. "Only for you, mind."

"Lan." Alethea walked over to the grey-robed scent master seated at a small table under a window in the common room. A number of long tables occupying the room were mainly empty, since lessons had already begun for the day. He rose with a smile on his weathered face.

A coruscation of scents rose and intermingled, Lan's dominated by blue green with pink and yellow, Alethea's more violet and silver with pinks gradating to red. They touched heads and inhaled. "It has been a long time, too long, Alethea," murmured Lan, holding her arm, "but you have much to tell, as have I, and I am most anxious to listen."

"Yes, Lan," said Alethea, "I had hopes during the war we would meet again, and fears it might not happen. Ah, would that we were but ten years younger."

"Our essences are the same, even if our bodies are not," said Lan. "Come, sit with me and we will enjoy each other's company again."

"With pleasure," said Alethea as he walked her to the table.

"Shall I get you some tea?" called Lethnal, poking her head around the kitchen door.

"Please," responded Lan.

Alethea nodded.

"Now, my dear Mlana," said Lan, "how shall we begin?"

"Lan," Alethea said, taking his hand, "start by not calling me Mlana. This is your country and we've known each other a long time."

"Of course, Alethea," Lan smiled, "but *Mlana* means much more to me than a title of address, you know."

"Hmm," Alethea smiled. "Now let me share some of my scents, some of my Knowing."

Lan's grip tightened as the two scent masters leant forward and a nimbus of scents circled around them. After a short while they broke apart. Tea was served and Alethea took a slow sip, eyes on Lan.

"Ah," he said, "I understand the urgency, what drives you. We will need to act as soon as we can in a matter most profound. Are you certain that the Knowing is driving this; that our very future depends on such an insubstantial thing?"

"It is a matter of interpretation, Lan," said Alethea, "I cannot be certain, but we must not neglect the portents. The growing dark fills me with fear."

"Then I imagine we have little time to waste," Lan smiled and shook his head.

"I had believed, or hoped, that we would have some moments together, to revive old times and enjoy what is owed, but it appears it is not meant to be. Another journey awaits, another challenge is before us and we must rise to it."

"Yes," murmured Alethea, "but perhaps we have a moment or two before we must depart?" She smiled into his eyes.

"I agree with all my heart," said Lan, rising to his feet. "Come. We'll take our tea elsewhere."

She placed her hand in his and they walked out of the room.

The grey granite boulders that made up the hillside on which Sanctus lay soon hid the *Centre for Scent Excellence and Training* as they travelled. Once it was a well-kept secret, a sanctuary for the resistance against the depredations of the Sutanite invaders, now it was open and the ultimate goal for Eanites who desired to enhance their scent talent. It also served as a training centre in the art of war, for though the enemy might be defeated they would not have forgotten.

Alethea felt her body falling into the perac's rhythm and smiled at the inquisitive head of the voral peeking over the leather bag strapped in front of her. Boidea had made half-hearted objections, but Alethea was adamant; Lan just smiled in his inimitable way.

She watched the straight back of the Eanite scent master leading the way and felt a wave of longing for him. She wanted more time with him, not just a snatched moment or two, and certainly not to be travelling on the journey to Lesslas and beyond after he had just returned.

Maybe, when this is all over we can be together; if we survive all that is ahead of us, she mentally sighed.

Alethea took a long look at the peaceful place they were leaving, just able to discern the scents that marked it out from the background odours. Boidea's tall figure near her attracted her gaze before she focussed on the fourth person of their small party. The fair-haired, thin-faced woman, clad in the grey and light blue travelling clothes of an initiate, waved her hand as she shifted uncomfortably on her animal.

Alethea thought about Lan's choice of Cathar to complete their group. *Another of the small pieces in the puzzle ahead of us.* She had initially been surprised at Lan's choice of a young, relatively untrained woman to accompany them, but when she considered it further, she'd capitulated: like his decisions, Lan seemed so inscrutable, but look deeper and you'd find a man whose brilliance shone from deep within.

"And what to do with you?" Alethea stroked the bristly head of the young voral, then smiled as it gave her a toothy grin. "Why do I need to bring you on this dash to the cities, when it would have been so much easier on us and the long-suffering perac to leave you behind?" The voral wriggled, put a clawed paw on her leg and shifted to get a better view. "And," she added, "if you keep putting on weight you'll soon be walking."

The track meandered down a rocky slope, scattered grass and straggly bushes leading to a small stream trickling and gurgling from the hills to their right. A line of flat-topped boulders provided an insecure-looking ford, but Lan headed straight for it without slowing.

By now the sun angling out of those hills meant that the night was not far off and Alethea knew that Lan would be seeking a campsite soon. The stream's chuckle was now overpowering any attempt at conversation, but they followed Lan's example when he dismounted and began to lead his perac across the ford.

The splash of the water attracted the voral's interest and it gazed avidly into the stream as if seeing prey of some sort. Then Alethea remembered that the haggar, a large worm-like predator, lived in the waters throughout Ean and her country and with the memory the faintest of scents came to her. "I wonder," she murmured, "whether there is more about vorals than we know?"

They continued following the track as it wound past clumps of small trees and thickets of bushes. The peracs kept attempting to snatch mouthfuls of grass as they rode, while Alethea had to restrain the voral each time he caught sight of lizards slipping away from their presence.

Dusk was falling by the time they led their animals up a slope to a flat area in the lee of a hill. A number of bushes were scattered about but the area was open enough to set up their camp.

"Been used many times before," said Lan as he looked around. "You can see where it has been cleared and the perimeter of salt to deter any crawling predators is still evident."

Alethea stretched, feeling a pop or two in her back.

"Can I help you, Mlana?" asked Boidea as she hobbled her perac.

"My thanks, Boidea. If you would tend to my animal, I would be most grateful."

"May I help, Mlana?" came Cathar's youthful voice. "Perhaps I…I can get the voral down for you?" She reached over to lift his bag off the saddle.

"Don't…" Alethea started to say as the voral snapped at Cathar's hand.

"Oh!" Cathar jerked back, her face pale.

"Sorry, but they are aggressive. No one has ever made a pet of one, uh, until now it seems." She shrugged. "I better handle him." Alethea projected calming scents at the voral before lifting him out of his bag and onto the ground. "I don't believe he'll go far, but he can forage."

"Hmm," Lan smiled, "you continue to amaze me, my Mlana. It is now my turn to amaze you with my cooking, if you and Boidea will let me."

Alethea went over to him and rested her head against his. "If it's all the same I think we'll let the young ones prepare the camp and do the cooking, don't you?"

It was a clear night with the leaping flames attempting to rush into the darkness and join the myriad of stars lying scattered across the sky. Boidea and Cathar were talking together in low voices and sipping Rolan cordial after a passable meal cooked on the campfire.

Lan and Alethea leant into each other watching the sparks and scents mingle on their journey skywards, the opportunity for a peaceful moment eagerly taken as they sifted each other's essences.

"Try some cordial," said Alethea, "it helps make times like this even more complete."

"I am not partial to such a sweet drink…but for you…" He smiled and took the cup she held out.

"Every advantage, even as seemingly insignificant as a sip of Rolan cordial, must be garnered if the peace of a night such as this is not to be shattered. I feel we are pieces on a game board being moved around to make a difference."

"Yes, Alethea, I am of like mind," he smiled, and touched her face. "And we must be in a position to make choices and influence all we are able, despite the weariness of our flesh."

A delightful laugh pealed into the night, causing them to look across at Boidea and Cathar talking avidly.

"She's an interesting choice, Lan," said Alethea. "Another piece of the puzzle?"

"Mmm," Lan nodded, "I have great hopes for her. There is a lot of hidden strength in her, and untapped potential. Get to know her, my Mlana, as you'll find it worthwhile.

"Look, here comes that creature of yours. By the size of his belly he will not need feeding."

The voral clambered over Alethea and settled between them with a huff.

"By the look of him," she said, "he's taken to you too—most unusual."

"Another piece of this extremely large puzzle," he laughed.

Chapter Seven

Jakus pulled his brown hood over his head, the chill autumn air blowing through the street giving him a logical excuse. He and Nefaria had left Port Saltus in the dark, pushing their perac hard to arrive at Nebleth not long past midday. Leaving the exhausted animals at stables near the large wooden entry gates, he hurried Nefaria through the streets towards the centre.

"Come," he grunted, tightening his grip on his companion's arm, "we have much to do this day."

Despite his tiredness, Jakus strove to disguise the limp from the many fractures sustained in his devastating fall years before in this very city. He hunched to lessen his height, a recognisable feature of the former ruler of Ean, as they hurried along the busy, stall-lined street of houses and trading establishments. He caught the odours of perac, traders, tradesmen, occasional barge people and salt carriers; every so often discerning the distinctive odour of an Eanite scent master, cleaner and crisper as if they were making the most of their new status since the Sutanites had been deposed. The odours also identified some people familiar to him from earlier times.

And I'll be needing to catch up with one or two, he thought, *including Heritis, my dear, weak cousin, still living well in Ean even though I had to leave. He'll be responding to my message even now.*

He stopped abruptly as he neared the large tower dominating the centre of the city. People following behind grumbled as they made their way around them.

"Look what they've done," he gasped, forgetting his distinctive profile with the aquiline nose might be noticed. "They've knocked down my balcony, destroyed the carved stonework."

"It is to be expected, Jakus," said Nefaria, shifting her bag on her shoulder. "They wouldn't want to be reminded, would they?"

Jakus craned his neck as if to see into the space where the balcony had been situated below a brick vent high on the side of the tower. He remembered leaning on the balustrade in happier times, observing the city from the position of power when his will was respected, his needs met.

He hissed as he moved on with a shuffle, half feigned, half real. "I want it back, Nefaria. I want my city back!"

They turned at a crossroads against the steady flow of people and into a quieter laneway running towards the river. Here the houses and shops gave way to low wooden buildings with fewer windows. The warehouses were easily identifiable by the stock they held, those closer to the docks mainly containing salt, wool, raw and milled timber and foodstuffs.

The odours buffeted Jakus, overloading his senses with smells from the past. He grimaced and forced himself to move through the thinning traffic towards the banks of the Great Southern River, the lifeblood of Nebleth. Here goods were received from the garrison city of Regulus, a day's ride to the north, before moving southwards for export from Port Saltus.

"Come, Nefaria," he snapped, pausing at a dark gap between two warehouses, "be ready." Jakus pushed back his hood to check if anyone was paying them undue attention before heading into the passage. He shoved at a small stone-coloured door set in a rock wall which formed the end of the alley.

"Stuck," he breathed with effort. "Needs a bump." He leant close to a small but solid latch and opened his mouth, absorbing the odours. "No one has used this in some time. Good."

Jakus extruded a dark, sinuous scent spike from his mouth. Like a living thing it dived into the small hole just beneath the latch.

Nefaria took a step back and looked up the alley; it was deserted.

"Got it," hissed Jakus, glancing to Nefaria, eyes glittering. "Good to have my strength, my powers, working, eh?" He forced the stone door inwards.

"Urgh!" Nefaria recoiled at the sudden gust of vapours and noxious odours she recognised from previous encounters with giant, wasp-like creatures. "That's hymetta stink, Jakus. Those foul things."

Jakus tightened his grip on her shoulder. "They have proven useful, Nefaria, and may do so again. *In!*" He pushed her into the darkness.

Nefaria stumbled into the room ahead of Jakus, who turned to shove the door closed behind them and allowed a few moments for their eyes to adjust. But their noses could not. To the aging scent master and his consort, the stifling odour of rancid meat and decay was almost overwhelming.

"You can almost hear the wings buzzing," he chuckled as Nefaria shivered.

"The hymetta, Jakus? I believe they're still here, in these caverns. The scent has a"—she shuddered at the thought—"a *freshness* about it."

"You think so?" Jakus snapped. "Hymetta still here with the Eanites in control? They would have destroyed them, every last one. There's no way they would have left them alive."

"But the stink's so strong."

"They were bred here, so what do you think? Now be quiet, I believe I'll need to dig up the keeper from wherever he's been hiding. His scent is around despite the masking odours from those creatures. "Torch!""

Nefaria reached into her pack and pulled out a wooden stave with wadded end. "Can you hold it, my Lord while I light it?"

Jakus fidgeted while she struck the firelighter and held it to the end of the torch. A flame grew, driving back the darkness.

"We have to move. I've a package to find."

The light struggled to overcome the dark as they descended into the caverns following a steadily strengthening odour.

The scrape of their boots on stone echoed eerily from the domed ceiling as they made their way into a large, open space.

"Yes, I remember. This was where they were. The stench is still here."

Jakus reached into his pouch, took a small pinch of crystals and put it into his mouth. He crouched to the floor, his shape dark against the vague light reflecting from the cavern walls and took a deep breath.

"The keeper's been here, Nefaria. And he may have some of his pets after all, hidden. Most useful."

Jakus rose to his feet amid a cracking of sinew and joints. He huffed heavily through his nostrils before hobbling off at a quick pace. Nefaria hurriedly followed.

The temperature warmed to an uncomfortable degree, the humidity cloying when they paused at a rock wall deep in the cavern.

"Are we there, Jakus?" Nefaria's voice sounded thin.

"Huh," Jakus grunted, feeling the wall with his hands. "Fool," he hissed. "It's broken down so any half-decent scent master could find it. But my trace is there, undisturbed, just as I left it all those years ago." He pressed closer to the stone and breathed loudly. "I was powerful then, wasn't I?"

"Pardon, my Lord?"

"Stand back! Steady the torch!"

Jakus pressed against the wall and began to delve deeply with his scent power. A shiver ran through the surface and stone fragments pattered to the floor, the sulphurous odour of freshly broken rock permeating the air.

"Ah," he breathed.

The side of rock crumbled, revealing a dark space, and the characteristic aroma of magnesa burst forth.

"See Nefaria, I've done it. Enough here to facilitate my plans."

He reached into the space and pulled out a small satchel that crunched as he lifted it. "Yes," Jakus said, slipping it into a voluminous pocket in his over-robe, "enough here to start a war." He chuckled as he swung away from the wall and snatched the torch. "Now come, there's the keeper to find."

Nefaria breathed in the familiar smell. So much of her life had been linked to the substance, from the time she had been taken by Jakus from Sutan to serve as an acolyte in Ean to now being his trusted consort. She had endured a peculiar relationship with the leader, putting up with his autocratic ways and sometimes irrational behaviour, always knowing he needed her. And, something she never felt she had to assess, her need for him.

She hurried after him, savouring his urgency and the richer flow of magnesa in his aura.

They burst out into the sunlight between the warehouses, still deserted although a curious lizard eyed them.

"The waterfront, Nefaria. The keeper's there, trying to drown himself in the tavern no doubt," Jakus smiled. "But we'll find him, won't we?"

The Hag's Tooth was a fixture amongst the wooden buildings along the water-front, the years softening its planking and collapsing it into its neighbours. The few attempts to bring light into the tavern by plastering greased parchment across small square holes gave the building an uncanny look, as if it were trying to emulate the haggar namesake.

"My lord?" Nefaria's hand squeezed his arm.

"Come!" Jakus ordered, crossing the irregularly-cobbled street and shoving at the door. It banged into the side of a table wedged in the small space behind the entrance.

Faces looked up at him standing outlined in the doorway. Jakus instinctively hunched and produced an obscuring scent, giving his audience little ability to recall his features. He hissed at his failure to anticipate the inn might be filled with people who would recognise him.

"In. Now!"

They pushed into a close atmosphere and a crowd of people; a smell of stale beer overrode the sour odour of vomit and unwashed bodies. "And I thought the caverns were bad," Nefaria murmured as she held a hand over her nose.

"There," nodded Jakus as he cast an eye around the packed room. "The table in the corner has a space."

"Someone's already there."

"Just the fat fool I'm after."

"Get food and decent drink, not that swill they normally serve," he said, giving her a handful of coins as he stepped over the outstretched legs of a snoring bargeman, whose grubby tunic was blotched and stained. Nefaria manoeuvred her slender form through the obstacles of tables, chairs and people to the bar while he slowly scanned the room.

Most at *The Hag's Tooth* were as they seemed: tradesmen getting a drink after work or having food with a companion; one or two tables included brightly dressed women. But in an opposite, dark corner sat a figure with obvious control, a cup of wine on the table. Jakus attempted to read the scent master but had no luck. *Hmm,* Jakus thought as he turned and made his way to the opposite corner, *no one would be expecting me here. At the very least they think I'm dead. But he's worth watching.* He restrained himself from touching the satchel hidden in the deep pockets of his brown over-robe.

Jakus stepped carefully around the clusters of people, avoiding body contact and holding a tight rein on his scents, *innocuous and non-threatening.*

He reached the hunched form of the keeper staring into his mug. Jakus kept emitting scents of amiability as he sat down on a battered stool. The keeper moved back as he tried to recognise the figure.

"Beer," Jakus muttered, and put a copper piece on the table.

The keeper kept blinking his crusted eyes in a bloated face. Wet spills of drink were on his loose tunic, which sagged around his large body. A rank odour filled the corner.

"No," said Jakus softly. "No more for you, yet."

The man's balding crown showed as he looked down at the coin.

"Uh," The keeper glanced up, his jowls shaking. "Uh?"

Jakus snapped a scent tendril around the man's neck, effectively gagging his response.

"Take a good look," hissed Jakus. He saw recognition flooding into the keeper's eyes. "Yes, it's me. You will keep quiet, and listen."

"Yess, Cer," the keeper muttered, shaking his head. "You was dead; yes, you was dead."

Jakus's face stilled as he tightened his hold. "I'm back from the dead, keeper. And I need information."

Chapter Eight

Kyel left Regulus through the southern exit where it opened below the castle tower having seen no sign of Nefaria during his brief travel through the city, but then he hadn't expected to. If she was in Ean she would be in the capital, Nebleth, a day's ride to the south. He had used his burgeoning scent skills to sift the air for any trace of her but found nothing.

"Some scent master I am," he murmured as he rode the perac down the well-made road. "As if I could really detect her scents and find her. I'm good, but not that good." He grimaced into the morning sun peeping over the Main Belt Mountains east of Regulus and lighting the river on his left. "The Great Southern, still grey and still huge." Then his face fell as he remembered travelling the same route with Jakus years ago.

While he tried to keep his quest in the front of his mind, he thought back to what he had left behind. The endearing face of his little niece, and his sister and her concern for him, even Targas. There were times when he could see the man was having problems, and it wasn't just with him. But he couldn't take on other people's issues. This was his time to prove himself and find the one person who'd befriended him and would surely be happy to see him again.

"Besides, she may need me. I helped her once when we saved Jakus. She may need me again."

When he tried to rationalise his thoughts, he couldn't concentrate, and slipped into the rhythm of the ride to Nebleth.

Nefaria placed the cup of wine in front of Jakus and a mug of beer at the keeper's elbow before squashing herself onto a small ledge at the back of the table under the dark, cobwebbed beam crossing the low ceiling.

She took a quick sip of the Rolan cordial from the small cup in her hand and half closed her eyes as the flavours hit her, taking her back to a time when life had been ordered and the dangers of being with a fugitive fleeing the country had not yet occurred. *Not as good as the red crystal*, she smiled to herself, *but it'll do, it'll do.*

"**N**o Cer, no! You can't be wanting me hymetta again."

"You have little choice," he hissed.

The keeper's voice had risen and she saw Jakus squeeze down to silence him.

"Here you are." The serving woman pushed two platters of stewed meat and vegetables onto the table, forcing the men to sit back. As the thick aromas rose, Nefaria suddenly realised how hungry she was. She smiled her thanks at the woman.

"Right, we'll go," said Jakus.

"My Lord, shouldn't we eat first?" Nefaria said.

Jakus frowned, glanced over his shoulder to where the unknown scent master still sat. "Be quick."

They stepped off the narrow verandah and onto the mud of the filthy street, the keeper supported between Jakus and Nefaria. It was late in the day with a chill in the air, shadows already lengthening. The few workers with their animals were going about their business, no-one appearing to notice them.

"Walk casually, towards the warehouses," Jakus urged, looking over his shoulder. "Ah."

"What, my Lord?"

Jakus quickened his pace, his limp barely noticeable. "Keep up." His grip caused the keeper to groan.

"I can't do this," he grumbled, "I'm going to spew."

"In here, now!"

They had reached the narrow entrance between the buildings and entered the empty alleyway.

Jakus bent to the narrow door, opened it and pushed the two of them through. "Keep moving."

He hurried them into the passage leading to the dark cavern, the light from the half open doorway enabling them to see. "Keep going to where you're holding the hymetta, keeper. Nefaria, stay with him. Leave the torch. Unlit."

"Can't see," the keeper wailed.

"Keep going!"

Jakus took a pinch of magnesa crystals from his pouch and placed it into his mouth. He heard their feet receding as he waited behind a bulge in the rough wall.

A vague change in the light caused Jakus to stiffen. He held his breath and tightened a scent shield over his body, flattening himself against the wall.

The light flickered and a soft scent came through the door. Jakus directed its flow away from his body as the scent stream manoeuvred down the passage towards the caverns. He remained silent until he heard the scuff of a booted foot.

He recognised the dark figure of the scent master from the tavern moving cautiously through the door. Jakus waited, suppressing an urge to reveal himself.

The man had thrown back his hood, revealing a shaven head and his native Eanite features. His head moved, mouth open, sifting the range of scents. Jakus knew he'd be picking up Nefaria and the keeper but would be puzzled at the absence of Jakus's scent.

Then he attacked, smashing a huge scent bolt at the head of the stranger. A hastily erected shield did little to prevent the force of the blow, and the scent master was knocked to the floor. Jakus jumped forward and forced out a scent snake into the man's defensive shield of interlocked scents. He could see the man's set face as he resisted Jakus's attempt to break the scent bonds.

The scent master countered, heaving Jakus back into the wall. Jakus forcibly tightened a blanket of scent around the stranger's shield. He struggled hard, almost breaking through, but Jakus locked the bonds of scent causing the very air motes to be excluded.

"You can thank your friend Targas for this trick," grunted Jakus as the man's face turned blue.

He held on until the scent master's body spasmed and all movement ceased.

Jakus sat on the body, rubbing at the small of his back. All echoes of the struggle had gone before he struggled to his feet and made his way back to close the door.

The darkness comforted Jakus as he kicked the body and returned, before casually lighting the torch.

"Keeper!" he called, walking down into the caverns, "I have fresh meat for your pets."

Chapter Nine

"I knew it," Targas grunted, binding a wide assortment of odours to leave a solid sheet of insubstantial-looking fog suspended in the dimness. The edge of the sheet tightened and solidified as he worked at pulling and tying the motes of odour together. "Stronger, more visible; I wonder how long it can stay up."

He stepped away from the structure hovering at eye level, its bottom edge caressing the floor.

"Ow!" Targas backed into the edge of the solid stairs, causing his concentration to falter. The odour rippled like clothing on a line, edges fraying as he watched.

"Wine-rotted place to experiment." Targas's eyes swivelled around the dark cellar. He had little room to move due to the steps and rows of wooden barrels lining the wall. The majority of the barrels contained beer to supply the patrons in Jeth's tavern but a number were smaller casks, now holding the slowly maturing malas spirit he had made. He briefly smiled before he heard the scrape of a stool from the floor above and the murmur of voices.

"No you don't." Targas's dark eyebrows creased his forehead as he concentrated to prevent the odour sheet from collapsing further.

"Why won't it stay, be more solid?" he murmured. "Different odours, more linkages? Hard to know."

A thump sounded from directly above his head and a square of light illuminated the space he was in.

"Finished yet, Targas?" came Jeth's voice from the open trapdoor. "I could use some help. Sadir left a while back."

"Why? Is there news?" asked Targas anxiously, but Jeth had moved out of sight.

He rapidly climbed the stairs into the noisy throng of patrons keen to slake their thirst after their day's work. *There must be news about Kyel. Has he come back home? Why didn't she let me know?*

Yes, he thought, *that must be it. I've got to go, find out. I'll just have to convince Jeth to carry on for a bit longer without me.*

Sadir and Anyar stood on the crest of a hill overlooking Lesslas. The wide roof of the town hall drew her gaze, its brown tiles almost turned gold by the setting sun, reflecting a value that had turned false over the last few days.

"Lan came, Kyel left and then Lan didn't stay either. I wonder if that means something. Everything's so unsettling at the moment. So now I'm here, on a hill by myself…and you, of course." Anyar looked up at her mother, then followed her gaze back to the town.

"So, is Targas better for all that? I don't think so. There's been no change I can see. He's still as irritable as ever. Why can't we be like we were, a family? Never had a real family before."

A gust of wind, cold and biting, blew across her. She grabbed Anyar's hand until a slight whimper made her loosen her hold.

"Sorry, Anyar," she murmured, turning away from the town and looking along the direction Kyel must have taken. "I know he's going to the capital, but why? He can't still think his Nefaria will be there, will have come back for him from wherever she went." But she knew, in her heart that he probably did, that he was probably off chasing a false dream in a faraway city. "No one seems to care, not Targas, nor Lan. But I do!"

Though Targas had never fully been the head of the household in her brother's eyes, he'd tried in his uncertain way. That uncertainty was an endearing quality which had attracted her, but lately it seemed irritationality had subsumed this part of his character. Even their lovemaking was infrequent, lacking the spontaneity of the early days. She still loved him, but her brother's and daughter's needs had to come first.

She bent down and hugged her daughter, shielding her from the wind with her body.

"We'll go and find my brother, even if your father doesn't care." Sadir felt her resolve strengthen. She was a veteran, a survivor of all the Sutanites had thrown at her.

"Come, my little one." She lifted her daughter onto the perac, trusting that the saddlebags and Anyar's innate disposition with animals would keep her safe. She pulled the reluctant perac from a succulent patch of grass and headed down the slope of the road that ran through the vast grasslands of the Great Southern River valley.

Targas entered and called for Sadir, even though the scents were stale and the cottage cold. He stood in the corridor, his mind racing. *She's left. Taken Anyar and left. No guesses as to which way they've taken,* he thought, shivering, gripping his shoulders with his arms and wishing they were his lover's arms instead.

"Should I go after them, help them find Kyel?" He shook his head. "No, I'd only mess it up, again. Best to stay here. She's better off without me. I'd only start another fight. Sadir will bring Kyel home."

Targas took off his backpack and removed a small barrel which sloshed as he placed it onto the table. He licked his lips.

He looked in the larder. Cheese and some roots were there, plus a chunk of stale bread.

A sudden rage began to rise, red and unreasoning. The smell of spilled body fluids and rank water filled his nostrils. The air grew thick in front of his eyes with ropey threads of scent. His jaw clenched and the air grew denser until all he could see were scarlet motes of blood. Anger and fear consumed him.

"Ah, damn!" he shouted, snatching out his belt knife and stabbing it into the barrel's bung, seeking the relief he knew would be there.

Chapter Ten

Sadir checked the girth on the perac and settled Anyar between her packs before setting off on the road towards Regulus. After a quiet night camping out, she led the animal down the gravelled road to the bridge crossing the Western Wash which led into the Great Southern River.

Even allowing for stops to relieve Anyar, it would still be a good day's walk to reach Regulus, find accommodation and seek news of her brother. If he was in Regulus, Sadir had a fair idea who to ask: a former enemy and now friend, Regna, the Sutanite consort of Heritis, Jakus's cousin. A skilled administrator for Regulus, Heritis had been allowed to remain in Ean and had proven a useful ally in the early days of the new Eanite government.

"Sorry, my love, but we will have to go a bit quicker while we can." Sadir pulled the animal into a faster walk.

"Yes, Mar," said Anyar, her light eyes—Targas's eyes—looking steadily at her.

"Where are the gates?" murmured Sadir as they entered the city. The wooden palisade was still there, protecting Regulus as it had during the rule of the Sutanites, but the northern entrance was open and untended, the gates pushed back against the walls. On her left, the width of the Great Southern River, bisecting the city, still impressed her. It seemed so broad and inexorable even here, halfway on its journey to the sea.

The noise of the city and its odours struck her at this late hour. The business district of Regulus was full of activity as hawkers and stallholders tried to make a late sale before night fell. Sadir smiled at Anyar staring wide-eyed at the mass of people from her perch on the perac. A wizen-faced woman was entreating them to buy small river fish, redolent with odour—she could see why the seller was trying so hard, with rust-coloured threads of early decay wafting around her. She shook her head and threaded through the crowd, keen to reach the castle, whose bulk overshadowed the city.

Sadir had never lost the habit of observation, and her increasing skills allowed her to sift through the scents rising from a myriad of locations along her route. She could ignore the dramatic scents, such as decaying fish or privies, and gently pick through the more subtle odours. The market added many local scents with the occasional thread of something more unusual or exotic: an imported spice, the distinctive smell of a mountain dweller from far in the hinterland, the tantalising drift of wine and even a mote of Rolan cordial— Sadir licked her lips at the thought of the liqueur. Suddenly a drift of scent caught her eye, half hidden, not meant to be seen—the signature of a scent master.

Ah, of course, Sadir nodded to herself, *they'd have to be guarding the way.* She felt a modicum of relief the city was still defended after what they'd been through in overcoming the Sutanite rulers. As she pushed through the thinning crowd she located the occasional scent signature of Eanite scent masters; once catching sight of a hooded figure sitting in a nook against the stone wall near the first bridge across the river, observing the passing traffic.

A guard barred her way at the steps up to the castle, the first time there had been any overt security. Sadir smiled at him, consciously projecting a companionable scent.

"I'm here to see Regna."

"Mmm, yes." The man's eyes passed over her dusty form, focusing on her face, then the laden perac behind her. Anyar looked gravely at him. He smiled before suddenly straightening. "You're *her,* aren't you? A hero of the revolution. Please, wait a moment, I'll let someone know. Your animal will be attended to."

Sadir looked over the side of the steps at the grey-coloured river flowing next to the castle, allowing her thoughts to reflect on Regna, Heritis's consort and now partner in the administration of Regulus and its surrounds. A fortunate decision, she thought, in leaving a former enemy in charge of the city. At least Heritis knew how to run a government and its many facets, and had proven to be a friend of the local inhabitants rather than clinging to his Sutanite roots. *Pity,* she thought, *that governing Ean was proving to be such a stumbling block for the country. It was one thing the Sutanites could do well, even if they were ruthless in enforcing their rule.*

"Sadir, so good to see you." The tall woman, dressed in flowing, dark robes, flung her arms around her, enveloping her with scents of welcome. "Let me look at you."

Regna stood at arm's length and gazed at Sadir with concerned brown eyes. "Hmm, you're looking well, but tired, and..."—she brushed her hand through short dark hair before touching a finger to her pointed chin—"sad. And there's something else, isn't there? I don't even need to see your scent to work that one out, do I?"

Sadir nodded. "Yes, I haven't come to terms with it yet. And Kyel has gone, left home. That's why I'm here, trying to find him. And there's Targas, of course...yes, Targas."

"Oh, my, I didn't see her hiding there. What a beautiful young girl. Anyar, isn't it? Come, let me look at you."

Anyar stared at the vivacious woman from behind her mother. "Mar?"

"Go on, little one. She is a friend."

Regna leant over and held out a hand. Anyar took two tentative steps forward.

"My, look at her eyes. Not yours? Targas's?" she asked, taking Anyar's smaller hand in hers.

"Yes, she has her father's Tenstrian eyes."

"Yes, such light colour is less rare in our homeland of Sutan than Ean. She is quiet, though." She gave a slight shiver. "I feel as if she's assessing me. Has she shown any scent talent?"

"N…no, not really," Sadir replied, "but usually talent doesn't show itself until the change of life, about thirteen or so."

"Hmm." Regna straightened, letting go of Anyar's hand. "But I am remiss. You have travelled a long way. Come inside and have something to eat and drink. You're staying here, of course?"

Sadir smiled, before following the slim shape of Regna through the corridors of the castle. She was around her own age, mid-twenties, and briefly wondered if she had ever considered having children.

"Come in here. It's comfortable and the fire's taken the chill off the air. I'll get what we need."

Regna gestured to a room with muted wall hangings, towards a low brown-covered couch a short distance from the stone fireplace, before continuing down the corridor. Sadir wandered slowly into the room with Anyar holding her hand, put her saddlebags next to a stone wall and went to the couch. She took off her travelling coat, looked down at the soft, comfortable cushioning before her eyes welled with tears.

"Come, Anyar, sit next to the fire and warm up." When her daughter was settled watching the flickering flames, Sadir reached up to a narrow mantelpiece above the fire and rested her arms on the polished wood. It was as if all her resistance had drained away at that point. She began to cry, laying her head on her arms to smother the sound.

Soft arms slipped around her waist and a chin rested on her shoulder. Regna's voice whispered into her ear. "Come my dearest, turn around and let it all out. There's only us here and you're safe."

The two women hugged until the heat of the fire became uncomfortable.

"Let's sit with Anyar," suggested Regna, and led her over to the couch. Sadir sat down and pulled her daughter next to her. Regna handed her an embroidered cloth. "Dry your eyes and we'll have some tea."

"Sorry, I don't know what happened," Sadir sniffed.

"I do, and you don't have to worry. Just eat something and we'll talk it all out.

Of course," Regna said, taking Sadir's hand, "I have something stronger to drink. A drop of Rolan cordial?"

Sadir took the small glass from the table and took a sip. The flavour pushed into her head, lifting her mood immediately.

"Thank you, Regna, this is good."

"Have a cake; helps soak it up." Regna offered a platter of small aromatic cakes. "Anyar, would you like a cake?"

The young girl nodded and delicately took one.

"Mmm," murmured Sadir, "they're delicious."

The fire crackled, spitting out a burst of sparks. Sadir eased her boots off and leant back. Anyar cuddled into her mother's side, watching the fire. Regna sat next to Sadir looking at the glitter of the cordial through her small glass.

"Lovely, this. It seems to heighten your senses, makes you feel more in tune with things, able to cope. It's even as if I can see the scents as Heritis and others can, though I've never known such a thing in my family."

"Yes, it does seem to give my abilities a boost, and it's calmed me down. Sorry about my outburst but things haven't been going too well, and it's having someone who cares that set me off."

"It's fine," said Regna, "and having a young one doesn't help matters."

"I knew you'd understand," responded Sadir, sitting up. "Men just don't see how hard it is. What responsibility and worry mothers have."

"You're to be congratulated, and I'm sure Targas has been a good father."

"Yes, he has, although lately it seems we're always fighting and I don't quite know why. He's changed somehow and although we both know it, he's not doing anything to get better."

"Surely you've got your friends. There's Lan for one. If anyone would know what to do it's him."

"He was with us a while ago, but Targas is still the same."

They took another sip of the cordial and watched the fire in silence.

"Regna, it's remiss of me. How is Heritis? I haven't noticed him here."

"No, Heritis and I are doing fine." Regna's smile was tight. "Running the city and having such close ties with Nebleth and Port Saltus doesn't leave us much time together. He's been away for a day or so. Always off on some mysterious mission or other. In fact… No, we'll leave that for another time."

Sadir yawned. "Sorry, Regna, it's so nice to be comfortable and warm."

"I think we need to let you two get some sleep," said Regna, "although Anyar's already nodded off."

"Ah, no," Sadir started. "I've got things I have to do. I must find Kyel. He must have come into the city several days ago, and I must find him."

"What about your young one? You're staying with us and I've a room already set up for you both. I'll check with the scent masters for any record of Kyel."

"Thank you, but I really need to look for him."

"Next day will be soon enough. Now come on. You can have a clean-up and then bed. Next day we should know where Kyel has gone."

Regna helped Sadir to her feet, as she lifted her sleeping daughter. "I'll bring your things."

Chapter Eleven

Kyel strode along the paved street of the capital as if he belonged, the hood of his worn brown travelling cloak half covering his face. He was nervous being so far from home, prey for the more unscrupulous in the city and relying entirely on himself. He tried to push that nervousness out of his mind, to bolster his courage and follow his purpose. No way would he slink home to Lesslas without proving he was worthy to...

He slowed and sniffed, relying on his enhanced scent powers as he had been trained to do. *A trace? Am I picking up a trace of her, of Nefaria?* he thought, feeling almost certain she was nearby, that she had returned. "Nah, it's impossible. Nefaria's really gone. She left Nebleth years ago. I'm a fool. She won't be back. But..." He shook his head. "Maybe it's my stronger scent powers picking up traces of her, so small that I don't realise it?"

Kyel moved out of the flow of people and turned into a side street, picking his way past some refuse in the gutter, heading into a quieter area.

He could see strong dark tendrils of odour rising and twisting, the slight breeze tugging them eastward into the darkening sky. The sun had gone but the bulky tower dominated the skyline of Nebleth. It glowed golden with the residue of the light, as if refusing to let it go. Kyel felt drawn towards the building, a memory of the time he'd spent training under the Sutanite scent masters, being confused by the ruler, Jakus. While he knew the man had used him, made him believe he was his friend, and Sadir and Targas were his enemies, there had been the euphoric pull of the magnesa Jakus had given him.

Then there was Nefaria, a stunning woman desired by most of the male acolyte trainees. And he had been closest to her. He smiled at the memory.

She had had time for him, as immature as he was. Even though Jakus had treated her badly, even though he knew she was tied to the former ruler of Ean in some strange way, it did not put him off wanting her.

A gust of chill air caused Kyel to tighten his travel coat around his long, slender body and wish his grey wool trousers weren't so lightweight. He hurried towards the river, where the warehouses had a number of alleyways and nooks a person with few resources could stay for the night. The foot traffic was thinning as he made his way down the slight slope of irregular cobbles, his nose assailed by the myriad of aromas from the stuff stored there. He half-heartedly assessed them, cataloguing the aromas with his enhanced scent powers, recognising the foreign spices, wools, timber and wine quite easily, the smell of the streets and the river providing a background.

He stopped as a mote of scent hit him, matching a scent memory as if it were a key to a lock. "Nefaria," he breathed. And then it was gone, masked by everything around it, hidden. *It's almost as if...* he thought, *as if someone's done it deliberately.* He leant against a wall, testing the air. Only then did he notice something strange in the bulk of scents surrounding him. *It's like a track, a snail's track of nothingness pushing through, making sure that certain odours are rubbed out, erased.* Something he knew a scent master would follow up on, if he had been looking in the first place.

"I better stay here," he murmured, gazing into the night sky. "First thing next day I'll look further." He found a narrow laneway that led to a dead end, took a perac wool blanket out of his pack and wrapped it around himself before lying against a corner where the rock met building.

"It'll be cold and I've gotta get food next day. Wish Tel was here," he smiled wistfully, remembering his lizard companion of many years. "But I suppose he's got a whole family to look after now." He pulled some clothing out and made a nest of it on the pack, then laid his head down and watched the sliver of stars between the building's corner and the rock face. Sleep came quickly.

They were sitting in an inner courtyard enjoying fresh bread, pastries and tea. The rising sun warmed the chill air, highlighting the raised flower beds. Several bees, smaller cousins of the pria, foraged amongst the blue flowers of the low-growing plants. Anyar, head tilted to one side, watched them gather pollen.

"You look better this day, Sadir. Did you manage to get some sleep?"

"I did, thank you. Ah, Regna, do have you any word of Kyel?"

"The scent masters are gathering reports, although it was somewhat harder to get them to move on it since Heritis is still away in Nebleth. Once I mentioned that the request was from you they put more urgency into it, so it shouldn't be long." Regna picked up her cup.

Sadir watched the swirls of the tea's scent around Regna's head. *She really is a beautiful woman,* she thought, *such a graceful neck and handsome face.* The sun slanted down, casting Regna's shadow across the red floor tiling. With it the spirals of scent could be seen, in shadow as well as in life.

Strange, it's as if I'm seeing double, like when my eyes are blurred. Yes, Sadir peered at the ground, *there are definitely two images in the scent's shadow.*

"Regna?"

"Mmm?" The taller woman looked up from her cup.

"How well can you see scents?"

Regna's brow furrowed. "You mean this, from the tea, around me?" Sadir nodded. "Yes, I can see them, but they're faint and lightly coloured. Like I was saying to you last night, it's something I've only recently been able to do."

"Fine, but can you see more than that, like they're double—the shadows seem to be showing double?"

"No, I'm not sure what you mean."

"Umm…I'm just wondering…" Sadir sat forward and rested her hands on the wooden table between them. "Do you have any more of the Rolan cordial?"

"Of course. Why, do you want some?"

"Yes please, if you'll humour me."

Sadir waited for Regna to return while squinting at the odours filling the courtyard. Now she was aware she could see the stronger scents had a slight blurring, as if a fainter duplicate sat just behind. She moved to a drain hole in the corner of the tiles to inspect a particularly vigorous, brown-coloured odour tendril coming from the pipe. "Yes," she murmured, "definitely something."

"I've two tumblers, Sadir, just in case you've got a thirst," said Regna as she placed the squat bottles on the table. She poured the liqueur from one into a glass. "I keep some here now that the horrid war has finished and supplies can get through. I first tasted it when we lived in Sutan, before we became part of the regime that ran Ean. Then it was just unavailable. So yes, I've kept a stock, just for me and my women friends."

"Thank you, Regna," said Sadir as she accepted a finger-sized glass. She held the liquid to the light before taking a sip. "It is so good."

"There's more if you want it, though it's a bit early for me."

"Oh, I'm sorry," replied Sadir, "I only wanted it to see if the effect of the cordial is as I suspect. And I think it may very well be."

The familiar rush of the liqueur drove through her, opening her sinuses and enhancing her smell sense. She carefully examined the solid tendril of brown scent.

Yes, it's different.

"Well," asked Regna, "what do you see?"

Sadir sat back on her seat and slowly pulled her eyes away from the scent. She saw the inquiring face of her friend. A bubble of excitement rushed through her.

"I think I'm right, Regna. I think I'm right. There appears to be another scent, a copy sitting just away from the one we can see, a sort of shadow scent. I've never seen it before nor heard anyone speak of it."

"How do you see it? Could I if I take some cordial?"

"Maybe," said Sadir, "although it seems to take a bit of effort. Just scrunch your eyes after you've had a sip, as if you're looking into the sun."

Regna took some time peering at various scents within the courtyard before shaking her head. "No Sadir, it's not working for me, probably because I'm not as developed as you. Anyway, what use would it have?"

"Not sure, but I'll have a try, see what I can do." Sadir looked at the water scum odour and extended her senses in the same way as Targas had shown her when he'd manipulated scent to work all manner of effects. Among other things, he was able to take apart the very bonds and link them to create a blanket of scent capable of supporting a person's weight. But she didn't feel it was the right way to approach this shadow scent.

She used her mind to push past the obvious odour notes and gently prise off the shadow, like a knife separating sheets of wet parchment. The shreds of scent tried to spill free and dissipate, so she linked them together as she built up a ball of the stuff, pinpricks of moisture beading her forehead.

"Ah, I've got it," she murmured, and gently nudged it to the table.

"I think I can see something," said Regna excitedly.

"Damn," gasped Sadir, "I can't hold it."

Suddenly a small hand reached up and poked the middle of the brownish ball.

"Anyar?" Sadir's concentration was lost and the ball of shadow scent broke apart, scudding wisps flying around them before disappearing. An overwhelming feeling of nausea hit them.

"W...what just happened?" stammered Regna. "What was that? And what did Anyar do?"

"I don't know. It was so strange—something to do with the shadow scent, I guess. And then Anyar..." Sadir shook her head slowly. "How could she see it?"

"Sadir?"

They looked up to see a tall, fair-haired man at the doorway.

"Oh, Jelm, is it really you? It seems so long since Targas and I were with you in Nebleth. You're looking well and handsome as ever."

Jelm strode forward and met Sadir half-rising from her seat. He pulled her into his arms.

"Not so hard," laughed Sadir, "I need my ribs."

"I'm sorry to be so enthusiastic but it's been a while." Jelm stood at arm's length, still holding Sadir's hand. "Yes, and your daughter too. She's a pretty thing, takes after her mother."

"You haven't changed, Jelm. Anyar, come here and say hello. This man is a friend of mine and your father's."

"Mar?" said Anyar as she came and stood by her mother's knee. Jelm leant forward and looked into the girl's eyes. She pressed into Sadir, keeping her gaze locked on him.

"There's strength there," he commented, "more than I would expect from a young child. But I suppose with a father like Targas, I'm not surprised. I think you need to watch her, Sadir, see how she grows and what she does."

"I'm sure you're right, Jelm," said Sadir, for some reason holding back on what had just happened. "I see the years have been kind to you as well. How is it you're here since I understand you govern Nebleth now?"

"Only as part of the governing body—that and the training centre take up most of my time. And governing is a thankless task, I'm afraid," he sighed. "May I, Regna?" Jelm sat at the table and helped himself to a pastry. "I've just come up from the capital in response to your need to find Kyel. I do have some news, but not as much as you may have hoped."

"Would you like a drink, tea perhaps?" asked Regna, lifting a mug.

"Mmm, yes," he said through a mouthful of food.

He swallowed, took a sip of the lukewarm beverage and looked towards Sadir.

"The good news is we know Kyel entered Nebleth last day and we're searching for him now. But that's all I have, I'm afraid. There is some disquiet in the city at the moment. One of our best scent masters has gone missing, but that's another matter. I'll receive a report soon so we'll know what there is to know, probably next day."

Sadir looked into Jelm's light grey eyes. "I guess we'll wait, then."

Chapter Twelve

"Mmph." Targas thrashed in tousled bedclothes, legs projecting over the side of the bed. "No! No," he yelled, sitting up and flinging an arm up towards the wooden beams supporting the ceiling. A coil of dark scent erupted from his mouth and crashed into the lime-washed wall of the bedroom, causing pieces of plaster to rattle to the floor.

"Get out! Leave! You're not wanted!" he gasped, panting, twisting, and slamming a hand into the wooden bedhead.

The sound reverberated into a series of thuds and continued into his head, behind closed eyelids.

"Damn!" He opened sticky eyes, the stale taste of malas in his mouth. The sound continued. "Who? Must be blasted Jeth. Why can't he leave me alone? He doesn't need me yet."

The banging continued.

"Wine's rot," Targas staggered to his feet and dragged on a crumpled pair of trousers.

"Where the fire, Jeth?" he growled flinging open the door of the cottage.

"Oh." Targas's mouth closed with a snap as he took in a group of people standing in the cobbled street. "Lan, what are you doing here, and your friends? I thought you had gone back to Sanctus."

"I suggest we come in rather than stay out here. Our journey was lengthy," said Lan calmly.

"Ah, oh yes," agreed Targas, moving back from the door. "You...you'll find it's a bit messy. I haven't had time to clean since...since Sadir left."

"We understand, Targas my friend, but we have not come all this way to worry about the state of your dwelling."

"You're here, about Sadir, Kyel? Do you have news?"

"We'll discuss that shortly," Lan said as he ushered in his companions, "but first I will be making introductions. Targas, formerly of Tenstria and hero of the revolution, meet Alethea, Mlana of Rolan, Boidea, her companion and confidant, and Cathar, acolyte of Sanctus."

Targas's eyes widened as he attempted to acknowledge the people now crowded in the main room of the cottage. He particularly noticed the diminutive woman before him whose scent aura overpowered those of her companions.

"Ah, tea, of course." Targas ran a hand through dishevelled dark hair as he hurried over to the stove. "Damn, it's out. Ah," he looked down to notice that he had nothing on other than a pair of trousers. "Could you start the fire while I dress? Wood's out the back."

"Take your time, my friend," said Lan. "We will prepare a meal while you make yourself presentable, as it is past midday."

"Allow me," offered Boidea, forestalling Alethea. "Come, Cathar, we'll get the packs in and light the fire. Mlana, you and Lan, please leave it to us. I'll even keep an eye on your creature, even though it's still asleep on your perac."

Lan opened his mouth, but Alethea placed a hand on his arm. "Let them take charge," she said, wafting a pleasurable scent.

Lan smiled, pulled some clothing off two of the chairs and sat down with Alethea.

The fire was crackling with a full kettle on the stove by the time Targas re-entered the room.

"Apologies for being so unprepared, Lan and uh, Alethea," said Targas, looking at Boidea and Cathar busy clearing the table and setting up a meal from their packs, "I've been worrying about my family and stayed at the tavern too late."

"Please sit," said Lan, "our friends have prepared a good meal and the kettle is boiling."

"Targas," Alethea smiled, "I am very glad to finally meet you and observe your scent aura. You are a most important part of the future of this country, and indeed of my own."

"What?" His jaw dropped.

"Now, I'm sure you're hungry?"

Targas looked up at Boidea who was handing him a slice of travel bread laden with meats and a pungent cheese. "What? Thanks."

"Tea, Targas, if I may call you that?" Cathar's voice was soft and modulated. A smile lit up her thin, pleasant face as she handed him a mug.

"Certainly, uh, Cathar."

"It's just that you're a hero of the revolution and some of what we learn at Sanctus has been developed from what you did. Forgive me for being forward, but maybe you could teach us, give us some lessons while we are here?"

"Cathar," warned Lan, "leave the poor man alone. He has enough to think about at the moment. Let him eat."

"Yes, Master Lan." She dropped her head, a blush staining her cheeks.

Targas sat at the table letting the chatter from the Boidea and Cathar wash over him as he ate. His head was spinning, but he was grateful for the space Lan and Alethea gave him. He knew Lan well enough to know he was up to something, and knew of Alethea by reputation. He wanted to ask but had to get his head clear.

"I need to wash my face." He stood. "Then you can say what you want to say."

The talk halted, Lan's light eyebrows lifted and he nodded.

Targas left the room for the temporary sanctuary of the washroom.

He paused when he returned, half-thinking that Sadir must have come home, since the living room was tidy, the scents warm and companionable. Alethea and Lan sat comfortably near the hot stove while Boidea and Cathar were looking at a parchment on the table.

"That better, Targas?" asked Lan. "You look almost presentable and rested. Come, join us?" He indicated a spare chair. "We're here to help, and I'm sure you have many questions, but first let Alethea have a look at you. I have appraised the Mlana of Rolan of yourself and what is ailing you as far as I am able, but she is of a different ilk to me. Her abilities with the mind and scent talent take a different direction."

"Oh?" Targas sat stiffly.

"Lan, stop scaring the poor man," said Alethea, "you make me sound unapp-roachable. It is true," she said, taking Targas's hand, "that my fields of study and experience differ from those in Ean. I have an insight into the ways the mind's scent system works and various methods for assisting resolution to any hurts."

"Yeesss," said Targas, trying to edge his hand away from Alethea's, "but why are you here, now? I only saw Lan a couple of days ago. What's so urgent that it couldn't wait? We've more important things to worry about." He pulled his hand back.

"Mmm," murmured Alethea, projecting calming scents which Targas angrily blocked. "I can see you require an answer. At the same time, I understand you are a man definitely in need. Please, come closer."

"Lan!" warned Targas, "Not this again. Don't treat me like an idiot."

"Relax, please. I'm not going to do anything now."

"No, Alethea, or Mlana, you're not." Targas sat back and held up a hand. "Just tell me: what's so urgent."

Lan slumped back, before looking over to Alethea.

Alethea took a sip of tea. "Bear with me, Targas. My explanation may of necessity be somewhat mystifying, but it is how it must be."

"A moment," interrupted Targas. He got up, put a log of wood into the stove, dragged his seat a little closer to the warmth and sat down. "Fine, I'll listen." He crossed his arms and fixed his gaze on the old woman.

"Rolan is a different country to Ean, its reaction to scents and how they manifest less straightforward," Alethea began. "It may be something to do with the magnesite deposits, particularly the extracted crystals, magnesa, used by the Sutanites during their time in Ean. The effects of its extended use in that form are still unknown and we endeavour to restrict its usage as much as possible. It may also be the reason womenfolk are of a more mystical persuasion, able to infiltrate the scent aura of the very country itself, foreseeing what may come to pass in ways not understood. We just do not know.

"The title of Mlana, with which I am blessed, is not just to confer leadership but also to recognise the development of that talent, the talent of the Knowing. It is this talent of foretelling that places a responsibility and indeed a burden on me. Through this I am aware of the importance of one such as yourself and indeed something of what ails you. I am also aware of circumstances and events that might come to pass in which certain players of the vital game of life are most significant.

"One such event is upon us. My Knowing is so urgent that it feels it will burst out of my skin. The factors impressed on me focus on the cities to the south and several important players. I know little more apart from this necessary meeting with you and the imperative urge to go south. Your partner, Sadir, with her unusual background, Kyel and what is happening with him, and your daughter, too. All are in the mix."

Targas looked around the room. Boidea and Cathar were sitting attentively at the table, while Lan sat back, eyes half closed.

"So that's what you're here for, to seek my family, go to Regulus and, ah, Nebleth? And"—Targas hesitated—"I'm to come as well to assist in the search?"

"Yes, Targas," confirmed Lan, "that is what we must do."

"Why me? What's so important about me? My, uh, affliction is driving me mad, so I doubt I'll be any help. I'm desperate to get my family back but I'm the main reason they left in the first place. And,"—his eyes flicked between Lan and Alethea—"I've got things to do here, a business to run with Jeth…"

"I think that deep in your heart you know the answer, Targas." Lan sat forward and looked into his face. "Your interests extend further than just the tavern."

"So this Knowing of yours is something to do with Sadir and Kyel, even my daughter?"

"And you, Targas. Definitely you," said Alethea.

"I…I…" Targas stood and shoved a hand through his hair. "Wine's rot!" he swore, "I was just coming to terms with things, and you come and break it all apart. Why can't I just be left alone?" He swung around and stomped out of the room, the door slamming behind him.

"That went well," murmured Boidea in the sudden silence.

"No matter," said Lan, getting up. "Please make ready to depart. He needs a moment or two to compose himself." He moved to the door and, opening it, followed Targas into the back of the cottage.

The sober group of travellers stopped to talk with Jeth at the tavern before they headed out of Lesslas and took the road leading south-easterly towards Regulus. The sun was already descending towards the line of mountains on their right as they led their perac through the vast grasslands of the Great Southern River valley.

Targas was in a sombre mood, walking in silence next to Lan along the gravelled road, their animals behind them. He had recognised the need to come, appreciating the group's commitment to people he cared about. His focus on the tavern and experimenting with malas had merely put off the inevitable: what was happening to him, causing the nightmares and making him difficult to live with, needed to be resolved, and the people with him were in the best position to help find the answers.

"Lan?"

The scent master looked over to him. "Mmm?"

"Something the Mlana said puzzled me."

"Just one thing?" Lan smiled and raised an eyebrow.

"She mentioned Sadir and her unusual background. What unusual background?"

"Ah, that." Lan looked away. "I fear I have neglected to tell you about her origins. Somehow it did not seem important amongst the many other events that have been happening in this country and to you, but Alethea has mentioned it for a reason." He looked back to where she and Boidea were walking.

"It relates to Sadir's past, her origins. Her mother was a foreigner, probably from a land like yours, but a scent master of unusual talent. She was brought in secret to Ean to aid the resistance many years ago but, sadly, did not survive. Sadir and Kyel were orphaned and adopted by a Lesslas couple. So Sadir is special too, as she is beginning to show in her healing talents."

"She could've told me," growled Targas, kicking at the path. "Another thing she's kept from me."

"Yes, you could look at it that way," acknowledged Lan. "But it is up to her to decide the relevance of it. You love her for who she is, do you not?"

Targas nodded.

"Then it is not a problem. Just be aware that Sadir and you are special people, and so is your daughter, Anyar. You do not need Alethea to say that, do you?"

A growl broke the silence. A low brown shape dashed past him and smashed into a thin bush just off the road. Several lizards sprang up into the air to begin gliding down the slope. The animal leapt up and grabbed the lowest-flying lizard by the tail, pulling it to the ground.

"What in Ean was that!" exclaimed Targas.

"That," said Alethea from behind him, "was our pet voral. Hadn't had the opportunity to introduce you since he was asleep when we left. So now you know."

"A voral? So that was the hint of unusual odour." Targas looked at the grass from where sounds of crunching were coming. "Aren't vorals untameable, being wild animals from up in the mountains? How do you happen to have one of those?"

"I found him as an orphan on our trek from Rolan and had a strong feeling I needed to keep him, despite advice to the contrary. He seems to have taken to me and is loyal, as well as betraying some unusual scent attributes."

"He seems aggressive, like most animals in this country," said Targas. "Just don't let him anywhere near Anyar."

"No, that I won't," she said, "although he responds to scent control, if it suits him. There's more to him than meets the eye, Targas."

"Come, my people," came Lan's soft voice, "we must make haste if we are to make camp before it is too dark to see."

Sleep came quickly, the best Targas had had for some time. As he dozed off he could hear the crackle of the fire from beyond the small tent he and Lan shared, and briefly wondered how the others were faring.

A vague unease infiltrated his dreams, but such was his exhaustion that it was soon forgotten.

Chapter Thirteen

"**H**ah!" A force jammed him hard into the unyielding surface. "You fool. Die!"

Kyel's body shook as he tried to move, his eyes bulging, face turning red, heels drumming on the stone. A blanket of tightly bound odours pushed hard on his body so his chest couldn't move. He saw the figure over him through a haze of red, hawk-nosed below small staring eyes, lips thin over clenched jaw. Then he heard a voice, a well-remembered voice urging Jakus to stop.

Air flooded into him as he took huge, sucking breaths. He struggled to rise. Soft arms pulled at his shoulders until he was able to rest against the wall. He looked up into a familiar face, wide hazel eyes surmounted by short dark hair.

No, it's her. It's her. His mind opened in euphoria even as his body recovered. *I knew she'd come back for me. I was right.*

"I…I knew you were here," Kyel puffed, "I knew."

"Take your time." Nefaria's arm looped around his shoulder, her scent flooding over him. "I'm sure Jakus won't hurt you."

"Jakus? Jakus! But he's dead. I know he's dead." Kyel pushed hard into the wall, the rough stone cutting into his back. "He can't be alive?" He looked up at the tall, lean figure silhouetted against a brightening sky.

"Dead? What are you gabbling about, boy? Why are you here, spying?"

Kyel shivered, caught between Jakus and the wall. He was different, head covered by dark stubble and his clothing brown—no sign of the shaven head and black robes of a Sutanite scent master. And he seemed well, yet Kyel had seen him broken and helpless.

"I'm not a boy," he muttered as he sought to avert his gaze. "And I was just looking around…"

"Spying!" Jakus's eyes narrowed. He looked into the rapidly brightening sky. "We must leave. Only one more thing left before we depart for the Port now my weak cousin has fallen into line. We must tie up any loose ends." He frowned at Kyel still on the ground, a blackening of scents building around his head. "The boy. We've no use for spies."

Nefaria glanced between Kyel and Jakus. "N…no, you can't mean… Please, my Lord, Kyel may prove very useful, depending on your wishes of course."

Jakus looked down his nose, eyebrows together, mouth tight. "You presume much, but you have pleased me this trip, Nefaria. And I am a generous man. He may yet have a role to play." He glanced up as an early trader walked a laden perac past the laneway. "Come then!" he ordered as he turned to limp up the narrow way.

As Kyel stood on shaky legs, an enticing drift of scent came from Jakus. *Magnesa. He has magnesa,* he thought, feeling a pull for the substance from deep within his brain. Buoyed by this he looked towards Nefaria, seeking warmth in her scents. He had come so far to find her and even the slightest hint of affection would be enough. *She's got to still care for me. Even though that black k'dorian's still alive, she's got to.*

He saw Nefaria's face soften even as his control on his scents failed.

"Come on then, Kyel," she said, her voice prompting him to obey, "my Lord doesn't like to be kept waiting." She turned and began to follow Jakus.

Kyel saw her slender form in front of him as he pushed his clothes and blanket into his pack. *I've no choice while there's a chance with her. If I had a choice, I gave it away when I left Lesslas. I've got to go with them.*

Nefaria paused, looked back and smiled hesitantly.

Kyel gulped, thoughts of his family driven from his mind, and began to follow.

Jakus, hooded, stopped where the lane met the main street. "If you don't hurry, you won't need to." His voice was low yet menacing.

"Move, Kyel," warned Nefaria softly over her shoulder, "if you value your life."

Kyel stretched out to catch up to her, biting down on a groan as his limbs reacted to his night on the ground.

They pushed into the busy thoroughfare leading through the city. Although early in the day, people were about and active, moving goods, setting up stalls in preparation for trading. A surprisingly orderly flow of animals and people moved through the streets and alleys.

"Hold! Control your scent," hissed Jakus. Kyel enjoyed being next to Nefaria as they waited in a small group for a stall being erected. The stallholder blinked at them before busying himself setting out his fruits. Kyel opened his senses to see what had attracted the attention of the Sutanite scent master, searching for a variation in the norm.

The scents looked normal for the time of day. The air was chilled as expected with the coming approach of the cold season, so no heat traces were evident other than from the people and peracs. Scents floated in a myriad of washed colours, principally showing as browns and greys from the surroundings. Occasional flashes of deeper colour revealed emotions where goods were spilt or an altercation had occurred. Kyel noted a trickle of cooking odours and fresh manure adding to the mix of scents, but nothing untoward.

Jakus flapped his hand in warning and Kyel edged closer to Nefaria. Then he noticed it. He had an inkling the day before where there had been an absence of scent, an area in the slurry of odours where a small section had been erased. He tracked it with a slight movement of his head.

A man, grey over-robe, hood up, sat on a wooden stool against a wall as if appreciating the warmth of the rising sun, holding a pipe. Kyel could see the smoke odours, see the normal scents moving around him, but could not clearly see the man. Something was blocking his smell, moving it aside so he wouldn't be noticed. Kyel looked at Jakus.

Ah, he thought, *that's what it is. A scent master is checking what is going on. No wonder Jakus is wary.*

"Boy," hissed Jakus, "we move normally down the street. Under no circumstances attract his attention. If you do"—his stale breath gusted into Kyle's face—"he will die. So will you. Understand?"

Kyel nodded, then looked at a tense Nefaria, her eyes large.

They moved into the street and along the row of stalls. Every now and then Jakus would pick up an item and inspect it before replacing it and moving on. Nefaria joined in, picking up several apples, paying the vendor and then giving one to each of them.

Kyel bit hungrily into his, savouring the juices and momentarily forgetting the game they were playing.

"Turn here, boy," said Jakus.

They moved into a quieter street that led to stables by the smell. "I think we have avoided him; at least I felt no interest. Now we pick up our animals, for we have a long ride to Port Saltus. You"—Jakus looked at Kyel—"will have to ride on the pack animal. And mind you look after the goods I am transporting. They're worth more than your life." A dark warning cloud of scent gusted from his mouth.

They paused just as they were about to leave the city. Kyel could see the large tower dominating the buildings around it. A flash of sunlight through the growing clouds, highlighted it like a beacon.

Jakus pointed, his skeletal finger hovering in the air. "That is mine. I will have it back, whatever the cost!"

Kyel shivered at the resolve in the man, remembering the lives which were lost amongst those who had ousted him from that very seat of power.

Jakus had already swung away and was kicking his animal, forcing it into a fast trot.

"Come, Kyel," said Nefaria, "we have a long ride and we don't want to anger my Shad."

Kyel climbed onto his perac, feeling Nefaria's steadying hand, absorbing her touch. "Nefaria," he murmured, "I...I so wanted to see you again, came all this way for you. And I'm not a boy anymore."

"No you're not, Kyel, but there's danger in coming with me, with us. You sure you want to? I'll try to help you get away if you like." She looked at the rapidly disappearing Jakus. "But it'll have to be soon."

"No, I'm coming. I've made my decision," he said, feeling a sudden sense of loss as Nefaria released his hand. *And I'm sorry, Sadir and Anyar*, he thought to himself, *I'm a man now and must make my own way.* He let his animal move into a trot to keep up with Nefaria."

"Good that Jakus trusts us to follow him," said Kyel, as his animal moved up alongside.

"Really? Would you expect my Lord to be lenient if we didn't?" Nefaria leant closer. "And please forget my offer now you've made your decision. I don't know what came over me." Nefaria straightened and urged her perac on.

Kyel bowed his head, pretending interest in a side street, knowing in his heart Nefaria was not as interested in him as he was in her.

The paved road running along the right bank of the Great Southern River was well maintained, recognised as a vital connection to the coast and the city of Port Saltus. While the river was crucial for the shipment of cargo, the road was used for faster travel between the cities of Regulus, Nebleth and Port Saltus.

Kyel recalled the power of Jakus when they had used the road years ago on the way to Nebleth from Regulus—when he was under the man's sway—and they had spent one foggy night in a way station. Jakus's response to an attack had left the attendants, a guard and several rebels dead.

An awful man, a ruthless man, a powerful man, not one to cross. *So what am I doing here, following him? Can't be just Nefaria, can it? She won't have me while he's around, but what can I do? What if*—his mind drifted back to the time when he was captured and training as an acolyte—*what if it's about magnesa?* His tongue ran around his lips and he shivered slightly. *Getting some will help me, make me more powerful, maybe even make her like me more?*

No, stupid to think that.

As the sun rose, clouds accumulated and the breeze stiffened, a steady number of travellers came from the direction of Port Saltus. They made the odd comment about the weather and travel conditions as they passed. Kyel noticed Jakus only gave a curt response.

The river traffic built up as they neared the port city. At times they had to avoid one or more perac pulling barges upriver. More heavily laden barges glided downriver with the current to the port city's docks, carrying their loads of salt, timber and wool. Sea-going ships waited there to take cargo destined for lands like Rolan and Tenstria; amongst them was Jakus's ship.

L ow mists were creeping in from the river by the time they reached the city. Traffic was still heavy as most travellers wanted to be safely settled down before nightfall.

"We'll head to the dock," ordered Jakus from the lead. "I want to be on board this night, for we sail first thing."

Kyel's ears pricked up at the mention of sailing. He hadn't thought much past the fact he was again with the woman he loved. The repercussions of this hadn't occurred to him. He had spent so much time thinking of Nefaria he hadn't really thought about his family. What would they think? Yes, what would they think? Would they be worried? Not Targas, of course, but Sadir and Anyar? Deep down he knew the answer, but at that moment he was with Nefaria and nothing else mattered.

"Come on, Kyel," said Nefaria gently over her shoulder, "not long now, and then we'll be able to eat and get some rest."

"Yes, Nefaria." He followed the gentle sway of her slim back on her perac.

Chapter Fourteen

"Mar. Mar, Par's gone," Anyar's voice shrilled in the dark room.
"Sweetling, what's the matter?" Sadir bent over her unsettled daughter and lifted her from tangled bedclothes. "Hush. Hush. Don't worry, you're safe with me." Sadir slipped back under the covers with Anyar and stroked her face. "Go to sleep my baby, go to sleep."

"Par's gone," she said, her eyes white in the dark.

"No, sweetling, Par's not gone. He had to stay home while we look for Kyel. We'll see him again soon."

"No, Mar, Par's gone. No smell of him."

"Well, he's not here, so you won't smell him."

"No, Mar,"—Anyar reached up and pulled the sleeve of the night dress Sadir had borrowed from Regna—"his smell is gone."

"Oh, I understand," Sadir smiled. "Don't worry, we'll see him again as soon as we can."

"Sadir?"

"Regna?"

"I thought I heard Anyar."

"You did. She's in bed with me. Come in. We're both awake."

Regna, in a pale nightdress, came into the bedroom carrying a candle in a holder. Anyar lifted her head and murmured, "Nice," before lying back in the crook of her mother's arm.

"Did you sleep well?" asked Regna placing the candle on a small table next to the bed.

"Yes, thank you. I didn't think I would with everything, but the long ride must have tired me out. Anyar didn't stir until just now. She was saying something about missing her father's smell."

"That's clever," said Regna, as she sat on the end of the bed.

"Yes, I think so, because she must have been referring to the clothes I was wearing before I wore the nightdress I borrowed from you."

"So, Sadir, you think she may have a touch of scent talent?"

"Maybe. It would certainly tie in with what she has been showing recently."

"Mmm," Regna nodded thoughtfully. "Might I suggest you come down and have some food and a hot drink? It is very near dawn and I'm expecting Jelm back with his reports."

"Yes please, just give us a moment to dress."

"Yum, flatcakes with honey," said Sadir, "it's got to be one of my favourites." "Anyar's too, by the look of it," smiled Regna, "though most of it's on her face."

"Do you want some more?"

"Uh huh." Anyar looked up at Regna, her pink tongue seeking dribbles of honey on her chin.

"Yes, she has a real liking for honey," added Sadir. "Do you have a cloth? I don't want any on her clothes—I've only got one spare top and pants."

"I'm sure we can find extras. There are one or two women who work in the castle with children her age."

"Thanks, Regna," said Sadir, as she accepted a damp cloth. She reached over to her daughter and wiped at the accumulation of food around her mouth. "You are as grubby as old Tel used to get, little one. Ah," she sighed, and sat back as she thought of Kyel's pet lizard and the trouble both had got into.

"What can I smell?"

Both looked up at the male voice.

"Ah, Jelm, we were just talking about you," said Regna.

"What news, Jelm?" asked Sadir from her seat at the kitchen table.

"Yes, I do have news, but don't get your hopes up. I'll explain it over some flatcakes," he said, his face red from the outside. "That is, if Anyar has left me any."

"Yes, Jelm," Anyar smiled at him.

"My, you're quick in picking up my name."

"I'm sure she won't mind you having some of her food, if you'll sit at the table," said Regna. "Tea too?"

"Yes, thanks." Jelm pulled out a seat and sat next to Anyar, who reached out a sticky hand and smeared part of her breakfast over his wrist.

"Honey as well? Thanks, Anyar."

"Sorry," said Sadir.

"Don't worry, Sadir. Now, I do have some news." Jelm put his elbows on the table and leant forward. "You remember how we had indications of Kyel entering Nebleth? Well now we have a very vague trace of him leaving, on the road that heads to Port Saltus. The strange thing is that it was concealed. What are his skills like, Sadir? Can he hide his scent motes?"

"Yes, he can, but I don't think that was a real focus of the training Targas and the others were giving him. They were more into the manipulation and bonding of scents. But why would he go so quickly, without staying for a least a few days? He can't be thinking of getting a ship, leaving Ean, can he?"

"Why would he do that?" Jelm's forehead furrowed under his fair hair.

"He's always been going on about that woman, a Sutanite, Nefaria. He thinks she loved him or some-such. But surely he wouldn't leave us for someone he hasn't seen for years. He was only a young teenager when he knew her." Sadir took a sip of tea.

"Don't know. Teenagers get some funny ideas, and Kyel was going through a harrowing time."

"Jelm, you want cake?" interrupted Anyar.

"Mmm, these are good, Anyar." He took a big bite of flatcake, winking at her.

"The other thing I mentioned last day is the unexplained loss of one of our best scent masters. Despite our efforts to locate him, the only conclusion we can come to is there's foul play involved. The scent traces of the man have vanished so thoroughly we can only conclude there's a talented person of the ilk of Septus or Jakus involved, but that's impossible. Even Heritis, who joined the search, agrees."

"Is he due back soon, Jelm?" asked Regna.

"I think we should see him any time now. He had left Nebleth late last day and no doubt overnighted at a way station."

"So," said Sadir, "what can we do? I need to find Kyel."

"Yes, I understand." Jelm reached over and took her hand. "What it will mean, I'm afraid, is a long trip to the Port, since that's where he seemed to be heading."

"When can we start?"

"If you'll give me time to do justice to this beautiful food, we can travel to Nebleth. The weather is cold, but no rain is likely, so if you're well clothed you should be alright."

"I can look after Anyar, if you like," offered Regna.

"Oh, no," said Sadir hurriedly, "I'm not leaving her." She saw Regna's look of concern. "Anyar's very resilient and only happy with me. Thank you for your kind offer."

S adir was in her bedroom packing up when there was a tap on the side of the door.

"Oh," she gasped as she turned and saw an unfamiliar figure wearing a dark over-robe. He was tall and imposing, with the beak-like Sutanite nose and dark eyes under cropped, greying hair. He had a tight smile on his lined face.

"Heritis, you startled me."

"Greetings, Sadir," he said, looking her up and down, "it is a long time since

I've seen you. How is that man of yours?"

"Targas? He's well, in Lesslas and quite involved in the local tavern, brewing and so on." Sadir felt flustered but didn't know why. Heritis seemed pleasant enough and his scents were normal.

"I saw your girl in the kitchen. She's a pretty thing. Really takes after you."

"Thank you, Heritis," said Sadir, picking up her saddlebags and coat, "but I better go to her now. We must journey to Nebleth this day."

"Ah?" Heritis's eyebrows rose. "Then let me help you." He took Anyar's small bag, stood aside as Sadir moved out of the room, and then followed towards the kitchen.

"I found her," he announced to Jelm and Regna, "getting ready to leave after such a short time here. I know you're taking her to Port Saltus, Jelm, but it is really a fool's errand. The indications her brother Kyel has gone that way are tenuous at best."

"Nevertheless, I must go," said Sadir firmly. She went over to Regna and hugged her. "Thank you for everything," she murmured into her ear, "especially for being my friend."

"A pleasure," said Regna, hugging her back. "Call in on your return, please."

"Thank you," said a little voice.

Regna bent down to receive a pair of arms around her neck. "You're welcome, little one. Now, you will look after your mother?"

Anyar nodded solemnly.

"Come, you two. It's time to get on the road," said Jelm.

"Keep an eye out, Jelm," warned Heritis, "I'm sure there is some villainy in the countryside. Just because our Sutanite regime was ousted, it doesn't mean it is safe for the traveller, especially with such a pretty little one in your group."

"Heritis!" snapped Regna.

"Just saying the obvious," said Heritis, his arms outspread.

"Thanks for the advice," said Jelm as he bent down and picked up Anyar. "I'll bear that in mind."

Sadir's eyes widened at her daughter's lack of protest at being handled by a relative stranger. "You have a way with children."

"Ah, remember I was one once," Jelm laughed, "although it was some time ago. Thank you for the meal, Regna. I'll look forward to the next batch of honeyed flatcakes on our return."

Clouds scudded across the sky, giving a wintery feel to the day. The wind whipped at them like a living thing, trying to burrow under their clothing and causing their eyes to water. Even the peracs were jittery despite their thick woollen coats.

Sadir kept Anyar sheltered from the worst of it, but her daughter sat upright between her legs in a cocoon of clothes, keeping her gaze fixed on Jelm's broad back leading the way along the paved road towards Nebleth. On their left was the Great Southern, a wide, grey river moving inexorably along its path. The road came close to it at times, often serving as a tow path for pulling the long, low-profiled barges that carried cargo up the main artery of Ean.

Sadir remembered the barge people both she and Targas had become good friends with during the war against the Sutanites, where many had perished in the fighting.

"Sadir?"

She looked up to see Jelm waving towards a way station just off the right side of the road.

"We'll stop there. Give Anyar and the perac a rest."

They took a leisurely break to eat the supplies they had brought when Jelm suddenly shook his head before looking at Sadir.

"I just heard a rider pass at speed and thought I caught a mote of Heritis's scent. If it was him, I wonder why he was going to the capital in such a hurry, especially after just returning home this day."

"I'm sure he has his reasons," Sadir said, her hand reaching down to stroke Anyar's head. Lifting her arms, she pulled Anyar onto her lap.

"We must be going," said Jelm, standing.

The gates of Nebleth were welcome. Sadir was having trouble keeping warm and was stiff from riding and holding a sleeping child. Jelm slowed to ride alongside.

"An uneventful journey, despite Heritis's warnings," he said. "The sooner we're out of this biting wind and in the tower the better. How is Anyar?"

"Asleep," murmured Sadir, looking down at her face just visible in a swaddle of blankets. "I think she could sleep anywhere."

"An admirable trait. Still, we'll be inside by sundown and be able to relax. I have rooms available for visitors and guests."

They made a fast pace through the main street to the tower. The stallholders had already packed up and few people were abroad in the unpleasant weather. Sadir found herself drifting off as they entered the tower's yard where they could leave the animals.

With Anyar being carried asleep in Jelm's arms, they entered the side door and climbed the stairs to the main rooms.

"I'm sure there's a fire where we can warm up," said Jelm. "It will be good to relax."

They had come to the main dining room and saw a tall figure seated before the fire.

The man stood and turned toward them.

"Uh, I thought so," said Jelm, thinking of the whiff of scent he'd caught earlier.

"You made it safely, then," said Heritis.

Chapter Fifteen

Kyel sat on the small bunk in the cabin he shared with Tibitus, the captain of Jakus's ship. The motion of the vessel caused his stomach to twist and lurch; he'd had a sparse meal with Jakus and Nefaria earlier, but he was concerned he might lose what he'd eaten.

Tibitus was at the helm as the ship sailed on the second day out of Port Saltus on its return voyage to Sutan. The trip, he had assured Kyel, was likely to be relatively smooth since the ship would be travelling with the prevailing winds and the seas were usually mild before the storms of winter.

It was of little matter to Kyel. The euphoria of reuniting with Nefaria had faded. The sense of loss of his family and friends, exacerbated by sea sickness, hit hard and he could do little more than stay on his bunk, except when he had to dash for the head.

At least I've avoided Jakus this way, he thought. *He can't get rid of me or throw me overboard now. So what use am I to him? He hasn't asked me about Targas. And he wouldn't be doing it for Nefaria, would he? If she were my girlfriend, I wouldn't let her go, wouldn't be so...cruel to her.*

Thrap, thrap.

Kyel's body reacted to Nefaria's scent even before the door opened.

"Sorry, Kyel, I know you're not well, but my Lord wants you on deck," came her soft voice.

He groaned and slowly got to his feet. "He wants me?" His voice shook.

Nefaria came to help him up and he leant into her body, revelling in her closeness and soft scents.

"Come, Kyel, you'll feel better in the sea air. And my Lord is in a good mood."

She led him up the several steps to the aft platform where Jakus and Tibitus stood at the short railing forward of the wheel. A sailor had the helm. The three square-rigged sails on each of the two masts were taut, driving the vessel through a low swell. The motion of the ship made Kyel feel queasy but the feeling quickly left him as he looked at the scent master's stern face.

"If the winds hold and we're able to keep this westerly heading, I would anticipate being in sight of Sutan late next day," he heard Tibitus say.

Jakus, a tall dark shape, shaven head gleaming in the overhead sun, stood on the prow looking out across an empty blue sea, his black robe whipping in the wind, a sound that could be heard over the billowing of the sails. He turned, gave a curt nod and beckoned Kyle to him. The younger man grasped the rail to steady himself.

Jakus kept his gaze on the horizon while Kyel waited tensely. Wisps of cloud to the east indicated a possible change in the weather, but with the sun highlighting patches of green in the blue depths he was able to appreciate his first trip to sea, even though his mind was roiling.

"I haven't had time to speak with you, assess your role in my plans, Kyel." Jakus's voice was calm and measured. He paused, watching a shoal of small fish leaping out of the waves, flying on long transparent fins before re-entering the water.

"I am not a vindictive man, at least not in your case. I am aware of your assistance when I was not in a position to argue after that cowardly attack by Septus some years ago. Fortunately, I have recovered and, indeed, my powers have grown in the interim.

"Now, what to do with you?"

Around Jakus's head, Kyel noticed a slight fog of scents which built up but did not dissipate with the sea breeze. He automatically began to build a blocking wall before thinking better of it and relaxing his defences. He recoiled as Jakus infiltrated his olfactory centre.

"Shad, er, Jakus, what are you doing?"

"Seeing where your loyalties lie, boy," said Jakus. "If you are to be of use, as Nefaria assures me you will, then I must determine this. I am satisfied you will have some value. Now you will tell me all Targas is doing, his plans and, of course, about the rest of your family. We will move into my cabin, where I can relax."

"I'm not, uh...I mean, he doesn't tell me anything, or do anything except... do his blasted drinking and argue with me and my sister."

"Ah?" Jakus looked sharply at Kyel. "Nefaria, bring food and drink. We will be below."

"My Lord." Nefaria went off to the galley while Kyel followed Jakus down into the ship. A blackness of despair rose over him. He didn't want to be the author of harm to his family but saw little way to avoid it. *I don't know much,* he thought, *but if I keep my answers simple I should be alright. Not that they care what happens to me.*

A strong headache built on his seasickness as Jakus grilled him unmercifully. His thoughts were confused, making him uncertain if what he told the Sutanite scent master could be used against his family. While he was answering the questions, Jakus deliberately ate and drank, allowing the scents to add to his nausea. He was relieved when Jakus finished.

"Nefaria," called Jakus through the door, "you better take this boy. Let him recover."

"Uh," said Kyel, staggering to his feet and gratefully accepting Nefaria's arm.

"Come," she said, "I'll let you stay in my room while I attend to my Lord. It will be more calming than the captain's cabin."

Kyel nodded his thanks and was soon lying on her bunk bed. He breathed her scents and let his mind drift.

A sudden change in the motion of the ship woke him and he sat up. The light through the small window was dimmer, as if the sun was lower in the sky. He looked around and saw a jug secured on a small corner cabinet.

"Water," he murmured, "that'll help." He stood and poured a mug. The room was small and sparsely furnished. Besides the bed, a narrow cupboard and the cabinet were the only items of furniture. He opened a small drawer in the cabinet and found several pieces of jewellery and a small leather-bound book. Nefaria's Journal was written on fine parchment inside the cover. Kyel had few qualms in turning the page and reading.

I think it important that there is some record of the events leading to my Lord's fall from grace and his decision to recapture his former power against all odds, thereby regaining the status he once enjoyed as the ruler, the Shada of the land of Ean.

My chronicle begins on board my Lord Jakus's ship when we were forced to flee Ean from the Port of Saltus. That traitor, Septus...

Kyel glanced at the door to the cabin, half expecting it to open and to be caught reading Nefaria's personal thoughts. He continued:

...had cowardly attacked my master, severely injuring him—all because of the extraordinary scent powers of their captive, Targas. This man, this foreigner, was the cause of so much disruption to the land that Jakus needed to understand him and the extent of his talent. But the timing was poor and the damage Septus inflicted on my master catastrophic. At that time we weren't aware the city of Regulus had fallen to the rebels, or that they were then moving on the capital, Nebleth. We had little time to flee but fortunately we were able to sail from Ean with minimum difficulty.

Even then I was only concerned with healing my master. I never realised the extent of his injuries though...

Kyel's heart skipped a beat when the ship shuddered as it hit a sequence of waves.

...he recovered quickly in the days we sailed back to Sutan, until he was able to walk upon the deck and hold himself as upright as he had once done. His short temper was in evidence since he seemed to blame all, including himself, for what had happened. I think Septus, had he lived (although we didn't know, or care) would have borne the full brunt of Jakus's anger if he could have been found, but I digress. My Lord Jakus refused to let his weakness be evident. Fortunately we had a supply of magnesa so any time he needed a show of power we used that. Although I was not a scent master in my own right, I had training as an acolyte and was able to support him, aided by this wonderful crystal. At least the captain of the ship, Tibitis by name, never knew of our situation and remained subservient to Jakus.

We took some slow time sailing to the land of his birth, Sutan. I understood this was at my Lord's directions so that he could gain in health and power before he had to report to the Shada of Sutan, his father.

"So that's what happened." Kyel nodded to himself, aware that Jakus had seemed almost as he used to be. Yet he remembered seeing the former leader of Ean lying smashed and broken without his scent powers. "Still, it doesn't explain it all," he murmured, and continued reading.

His family is a formidable group with conquest and inbred power. Jakus, the eldest in a line of three males, had been charged with holding Ean in the name of Sutan and increasing the output of the much-needed salt, a commodity with which Ean was blessed. All had been well, the locals kept under control by the scent powers of Jakus and his seekers, bolstered by the practice of bringing newly developed scent users into the ranks of the seekers or scent masters.

Why, I myself was a third-year acolyte, though from Sutan, not Ean, at the time of all the unrest. I achieved a lot as I trained in using scent for messaging, weaponry and healing. I never would have become a seeker, as they were hunters of men, but a scent master was right for me.

He looked up as loud voices came from just outside the cabin. They faded and he continued:

The family was unaccustomed to defeat and abused poor Jakus terribly, forcing him off his estates to a smaller property in Hestria, a considerable distance from the capital city, Sutaria. Out of sight, and a lesser punishment than his brothers were arguing for—at least his ailing mother showed some feeling for her son.

I remember the day Jakus reported the loss of Ean to the Shada, his father, Vitaris. Even relating the turncoat Septus's attack on him failed to elicit any sympathy. The screaming from Faltis and Brastus was overwhelming and would certainly have resulted in them destroying Jakus where he stood had they not believed he still retained his powers. Again magnesa came to our rescue, its importance not understood by his family. His brothers had only been mollified by Vitaris, the Shada, old but fully in control of his scent powers; the roiling emanations of purple and scarlet towering above Vitaris had made everyone cautious. His decision to send Brastus to re-join the Sutanite armies overseas to ensure completion of their campaigns before organising the recovery of the gem that once was Ean, is all that kept his brothers from Jakus's throat.

Now, Jakus and I have had a number of years to live a quieter life away from the influence and expectations of his family.

"They are planning to retake Ean, of course," Kyel murmured. He stood, put the book into the drawer and crept to the door, but all remained quiet. "No, I have to finish this." He returned to the cabinet, took the book back out of the drawer and sat on the bunk.

During our time in Sutan my Lord has been working assiduously to regain his powers, recruiting scent masters to his cause and above all developing what he sees as his secret weapon, that crystal, magnesa. I have only had it in limited quantities but the effect it has on opening the senses and allowing one's limited scent powers to blossom out of all proportion is amazing. However, the downside, which my Lord ignores, is the craving for it, the bereft feeling when it is used to excess, the headaches and weakness of the body it induces. It affects me to a lesser extent, even so.

"Ah," gasped Kyel, looking up, "I never thought… Is it affecting me, too? Is that a reason why I came? Left my family?" He reflexively licked his lips before reading on.

I understand why Jakus sees this as the means to regain what he has lost. And I feel his ambition is to reconquer and be Shada of Ean again before his family can. The slow process of Brastus finishing the campaigns in other lands, before retaking Ean has played into his hands in this.

So, if the truth be known, Jakus's fixations are twofold. The first is the magnesa crystal, for with this he can not only be more powerful and have a distinct advantage over his family, for they know not of the importance of this elixir, but he can also make a limited army very effective and formidable. The second, and I know not why he is so intransigent, he wants to recapture Targas to, he says, keep his talents out of others' hands. He doesn't listen to reason in this second goal and, for my part I have to be very careful if ever I broach the subject.

"Why Targas?" Kyel pondered. "Why is he blaming him? Is that why…why he wants me close?" He shook his head as he read on.

As I continue my chronicle, I suppose I should refute any thought that I am foolish to stay and support my Lord, despite occasionally being treated harshly by him. One might think it is for the drug, ready access to the red crystal, that I stay, but I would dispute this.

It is an unfortunate failing of great men that matters such as relationships and companions fall well beneath the lofty ideals their minds aspire to. However, I can put up with it as long as I can be there for him. My use on this earth is to provide succour for him when he is in need. I've stood beside him when he's been attacked by his family, I've saved him from death at the hands of Septus, I've given him a body when his needs have been great, and I've done all this willingly.

For I need him too, and will be with him when he achieves his destiny to become the Shada, the greatest ruler our world has ever seen.

"Ah," breathed Kyel, "she really does love him, and doesn't see him for the abuser he is. But if that's so, where does it leave me?"

Kyel tore at his hair. "Why did I ever come, to this? How can I get home?"

His jaw tightened as he flipped back several pages, rereading portions, all the while shaking his head. The floor creaked outside so he shut the book and made a conscious effort to dissipate his scents before slipping it into the drawer. A chill had grown over him as he thought how naive he had been in chasing after Nefaria and the situation he now found himself in.

"What have I done?" he whispered as he headed to the door. He waited for a moment before silently opening the door and easing through.

Chapter Sixteen

A scud of scents floated above the bulky Great Southern keeping pace with the flow, reminding Targas of clouds of small insects in their mating flight. The sun reflected off its surface, turning the river into bronze fire with the scents swirling like embers above it. That river had played a big part in his life, stretching his scent talents to the limit while life and death warred on its unforgiving surface; a time when his friends were relying on him to save them from the Sutanite rulers, and a time when his love for Sadir had been new and pure.

Targas shook his head, causing his perac to look inquiringly over its shoulder as it continued its slow, rolling gait along the well-maintained road towards Regulus. He scanned his companions astride their animals, Lan and Alethea ahead, Cathar behind him and Boidea at the rear. A small brown shape scurrying from one clump of reeds to the next along the river's edge made him smile, its antics reminding him of a similar animal in his native Tenstria.

"He is very entertaining," said Cathar, as she came up to Targas's shoulder. "I never thought I'd say that about those ferocious beasts. When they're full-sized it is said they can easily take down a perac."

"I've heard they prefer honey."

"And mud, it seems," she laughed.

The peal of Cathar's laughter struck a chord in his heart and he looked at the young woman.

"If you don't mind me asking, Cathar, but how old are you?"

"Not at all, Master. I'm in my seventeenth year."

"Please," Targas said, holding out an arm, "don't call me Master, just Targas, as we agreed. I'm not that much older than you and don't feel aware enough to be a master of anything. Now, tell me about yourself. How is your training going?"

"I'm from Telas, a small village in the far north, fairly close to where this great river begins. When the call went out to scent-talented youth for the future defence of Ean, my parents sent me to Sanctus.

"But training's been hard. I never realised that I had so little knowledge—you think you've got some skills but then the masters show you just how much you have to learn."

"So why did Lan pick you for this trip?"

"I really don't know," she smiled, her brown eyes focussing on the river. "Maybe it is because I'm a woman with some vague link with Alethea. We get on. Boidea's a delight and Alethea is a very deep mystery that pulls at me, making me feel I'm only scratching the surface of my own talent. There, you've made me sound like I'm full of myself, and in the presence of such a mastery of the scents."

"No, Cathar," said Targas, "what you've done is start me thinking less about myself and what is happening to me. I can't resolve my problems for the moment so being active and seeking my family is something positive. So, for that I am grateful."

She reached over and put a hand on his arm. "You know, your scent aura is so inviting I can understand what your…Sadir…sees in you. Oh, look." She released his arm and pointed at a low silhouette on the river; the reflection from the sun's rays adding a copper gilt to the shape.

As Targas puzzled over Cathar's words, he automatically looked in the direction she was pointing. A large, heavily laden barge, pulled by the Great Southern's current, was slowly overtaking the group. A figure, dressed in dull colours but with a bright yellow scarf, had an arm raised in greeting even though the vessel was too far away for them to recognise it. A woman and several children came onto the large, flat roof and began to wave. He waved back.

The barge folk were a resilient people who had fought and died alongside the rebel fighters. A pulse of sadness showed itself as a light grey-green cloud in his scent aura when the memories of loss came flooding into his brain.

With it came a red-tinged blackness—Septus, taut white face floating across his vision, blood-filled mouth laughing at his control; Targas chained to the rocks in the caverns of Nebleth, helpless to prevent Sadir's exposure to giant carnivorous hymetta living there.

Targas closed off his mind, like Lan had taught him, blocking off the despairing memories forcing themselves into his psyche.

The light filtered back in, the movement of the perac comforting, the backs of his companions ahead of him on the road seemed as it had moments ago. He glanced back at the river and caught Cathar's face looking at him, eyes wet, hand to her mouth.

Blast, he thought, *she'll think I'm mad.* "Just caught in some bad memories of the times when we went with the barge folk—nothing to worry about." He attempted a smile. But the smile was only shallow; the memories were deeper and the impact of Septus deeper still.

I can't let it be so, I can't. I can't. He shook his head and pointed up the road.

"Not long now, Cathar."

She looked along the road. "Yes, not long now."

Targas didn't have to see her scent aura to know she was concerned for him; the very thing that irritated him, the concern of others. Then, when it got too much he lost his temper and took it out on himself, and Sadir.

I've got to fix this, somehow.

They walked their animals through the wooden palisades of Regulus, the river flowing quietly on their left, many river barges temporarily moored against the stone wall protecting the city from the river.

"Better get the voral into the saddlebags," said Alethea. "No telling how he will react."

"Come here, you," called Boidea. She lifted the small animal with a grunt and he dived headfirst into the bag on Alethea's perac. "You didn't tell me how muddy he was," she said, looking at the streaks of dirt on her travel cloak, "or how heavy."

Alethea and Cathar laughed.

"Straight to the castle," ordered Lan. "We need to speak with Regna and Heritis to determine Sadir's whereabouts, and whether we stay or need to travel on."

They pushed through the traders and stalls, and the flurry of scents that came with it. Occasionally Lan and a scent master exchanged recognition scents without pausing in their journey to the castle. It was almost a relief when the party met the guard near the stables on the lower steps.

"We will take our packs from here," said Lan nodding to the guard who took the leads of the animals.

"I'll carry yours for you, Mlana," said Boidea, "for the voral is a weight."

Targas carried his saddlebags over a shoulder and briefly assessed the odours around the castle's entrance, looking for the familiar scents of Sadir, Anyar or Kyel. The mix of odours was complex, but nothing stood out as he followed the others into the building.

"Lan!" exclaimed Regna, coming downstairs from the main hall. "I'm pleased to see you."

Targas smiled at the tall, slim figure of Regna approaching him, scents with light yellow and pink dominant, showing her joy. His eyes narrowed at a thread of unease in her scent aura.

"Targas," she said after she had greeted Lan, "it is lovely to see you. I have just had a most pleasant time with Sadir and your beautiful daughter. I'm sorry, but they left for Nebleth two days ago, following her brother's trail."

"And Kyel? Has he been found?"

"Not that I know of, Targas. Let me tell you more when you've had time to rest and clean up." She placed a hand on his arm as she turned to look at the others.

"Please forgive me, as I haven't introduced myself to your companions; I am Regna, consort of Heritis."

"I am happy to introduce you to my companions," said Lan. "Please meet a long-time friend of mine, Alethea, Mlana of Rolan. The two younger people are Boidea, her friend and confidant, also from Rolan, and Cathar, acolyte of Sanctus."

"Welcome to Regulus," said Regna, "on behalf of Heritis and myself. I'm sorry he is not here, but he had a hurried journey to Nebleth and has not returned."

Again, Targas noticed the thread of unease in her scents, a dark line she quickly suppressed. By then Regna had turned and was heading up the stairs to the living areas. He shook his head and followed Boidea, with Cathar next to him.

Suddenly a small brown head popped out of the saddlebag Boidea was carrying and grinned white teeth at him.

"You'll have to tell Regna what she's letting into the castle before too long," he murmured, "or he'll make sure he's noticed."

"I'll leave that task to Alethea," said Boidea over her shoulder. "This is her youngster, weighty though he is." She heaved him into a more comfortable position as she climbed the steps.

Targas wandered into a room with hangings on the stone wall opposite a hearth where a fire was already settling into coals. A low table held steaming mugs, several platters of small pastries and bunches of small, dark-coloured fruit best enjoyed when turned into wine. He took a mug and sat on a brown-covered couch while assessing the room for scents.

He paused when his gaze came to a narrow mantelpiece above the fire. There he recognised an old scent of Sadir's, particularly on the polished wood. It hadn't yet merged into the background odours, and sadness pervaded it.

"Targas," said Lan brightly as he entered the room, "I trust you are feeling rested? What is it?" he asked, seeing Targas's face.

"Sadir." He got up and walked towards the mantelpiece. "And she's been here, crying."

Lan focussed on the scents. "Yes, you are right, but I don't detect a strong grief. I would suspect she was able to express herself more freely in Regna's presence, and I"—he glanced at the door—"would allow it is more of a female way, such a release of emotion. Now do not tell Alethea I said that" he winked. "Ah, Regna, it is pleasant to see you." Lan swung around as she entered. "This is a most convivial room."

"Thank you, Lan. It's a refuge from the day-to-day bustle of living." She smiled when she saw Targas standing near the fire. "I see you've found the refreshments."

"Yes," he said, raising his mug. "I noticed that Sadir was here recently, and she wasn't happy."

Regna frowned. "Really? Oh, yes, we had a quiet moment or two in here. I think the troubles of home overcame her; you, in particular."

"Fine." Targas raised an arm in acknowledgement. "I know I haven't been easy to live with. But I'm here now."

"Yes,"—Regna's lips pursed—"we have to be thankful for that."

At that moment they heard Alethea, Boidea and Cathar coming along the corridor. "Please," said Regna, lifting a platter and offering it to Lan, "have a pastry."

The moment Alethea entered the room the atmosphere changed. It was as though her presence brought a gravity with it, reminding them of their purpose. As they exchanged pleasantries, Alethea smiled at Regna.

"Although we do not know each other, I am aware of your role in making Regulus a much more secure place, a place of comfort for the people of Ean." Alethea rummaged in a small pack she had with her. "Ah, here they are." She pulled out several small bottles and placed them on the table. "A gift, for you."

"Why, Alethea!" cried Regna in delight, picking one up and rolling it in her hands, "Rolan tumblers; how wonderful. These have a better finish than those I've managed to get before."

"Yes, they have," said Alethea. "Being Mlana does have its small privileges. You'll find it slightly more potent, too."

"Sadir liked a drop of that," commented Targas. "Said it was what women preferred. Felt my malas was too strong for her taste."

"I suppose it is more of a drink for women," said Alethea. "Some of its effects are more suited to female ways. Now"—she looked pointedly at Lan—"I am going to ask both you and Targas to leave us while we have a talk."

"But you were going to tell me more." Targas looked at Regna.

"Come," said Lan to Targas. "We shall head to the kitchens, where we may find a beverage more suited to our tastes."

Targas looked at Lan, eyebrows raised.

"What was all that about?" he asked as he followed Lan along the corridor.

"A useful time for the women to get to know each other, and"—he turned to look Targas in the eye—"to find out what is troubling Regna."

"Oh, I see," said Targas, shaking his head.

"It is good to have some time to ourselves," said Alethea, looking at the women. "Men can so stifle conversation."

"I agree, don't you Regna?" said Boidea, putting an arm around Cathar. "It's rare to get some time together. Do you have any cordial open, Mlana?"

"I have a supply," offered Regna, "and of course there's what you brought today."

"No, no," said Alethea. "If you provide the glasses, we will use the cordial from our supplies. Boidea?"

Soon they were sitting comfortably around the table with a small glass of cordial each.

"Please accept our wishes for you, Regna," said Alethea, raising her glass. "It is good to be here."

They took a drink, then sat back. Alethea watched the scent auras of her companions changing as they relaxed, responding to the impact of the cordial. She sighed and looked closely at Regna. She could detect a reticence in her scent aura, as if she was holding her breath; a dull green shadow hovering closely against the composition of scents, where only a trained eye could see it. Normally it would be hidden by a person's will, but this night it was exposed.

Alethea reached forward, picked up a pastry and took a bite, "Ah, it is some time since I have tasted flour this good. In Rolan it is usually a coarser grind, flavour certainly but not melt-in-your-mouth. What do you think, Cathar?"

"Mmm." Cathar was looking into the fire, her scents showing her weariness. "Yes, I agree this is a good pastry but my mother back in Telas makes excellent pastries too."

"Where is it from, Regna?" asked Alethea.

"I believe it comes from the arable lands near Nebleth," Regna said softly, "although we had good grains back in Sutan. Oh, forgive me for bringing that name up." Her scents gave a brief flash of red.

"You are amongst friends, Regna, and have proven yourself," murmured Alethea. "You will notice your senses are heightened, that there is a certain clarity to your scent aura, an effect we believe is due in part to the Rolan cordial. I am able to tell something is worrying you, that you are torn between raising it here but have a duty not to. Please"—she pulsed a gentle, encouraging scent towards her—"I think you should tell us."

"Oh," Regna said, burying her head in her hands, "you're right. Something has been troubling me. Sadir, and her Anyar were delightful. I had hoped they would stay longer but she had to go once Heritis brought back reports that her brother had been in Nebleth. When Jelm, who oversees Nebleth's administration, went with her I had some misgivings. These grew when I found out that…my… my partner had left not long after them. He'd only just returned from the capital and had no reason to go, that I knew." She stopped, took a gulp of drink and reached for Alethea's hand.

"And…?" Alethea patted Regna's hand. Boidea and Cathar both leant forward.

"And I am worried Heritis might be up to something, something not in the best interests of Sadir, and…Ean."

"Surely there's no evidence he is other than a competent administrator of

Regulus?" asked Alethea. "It has been some years since the overthrow, and Heritis and you have proven your loyalty to Ean."

"Y…yes," Regna nodded slowly, "but there have been little things I can't put my finger on, and I…I'm worried."

"You are right to raise your concerns. Let us hope this can be easily resolved," said Alethea. "And it is clear we must follow Sadir to Nebleth early in the morning, if only to keep those fears at bay."

Chapter Seventeen

Sadir woke abruptly and sat up as Anyar, in rolling over, drove a small elbow into her mother's stomach. She drew a large breath and sorted through the various odours. A female trace still lingered, despite the efforts to launder them out of the bedclothes. She must have noticed it when they went to bed, but she'd been too tired to consider its meaning. *Ah*, she thought, *Jelm has a woman, even though he's very discreet about it.*

"Mar," came Anyar's sleepy voice.

"Quiet, sweetling," she murmured as she stroked her daughter's head. Jelm had given her the adjoining room to his in his Nebleth tower.

It was Jakus's consort's room, all that time ago. *Nefaria was her name*, she remembered. As if she'd forget since her brother, Kyel, had been so infatuated with the woman he never stopped talking about her.

Little point in sleeping in, despite Kyel's shipping out from Port Saltus, as Heritis thinks. We must find him even if he's chasing his dreams. She smiled sadly.

Her muscles protested as she stood. She put slippers on before walking to the window and pushing open the shutters. Light from the sun already made its presence felt, as she combed fingers through her short brown hair.

Sadir looked back to Anyar, whose feet were moving under the bedclothes, meaning it would only be a short while before her daughter was up. She went to a wooden door set in the middle of an internal wall and knocked quietly. After waiting for a moment, she twisted the iron latch and pushed the door open.

The large room, dominated by a huge bed with a mess of untidy covers, was empty; nor was Jelm in the nearby washroom.

A bang on the door to her room made her swing around. It opened to reveal that very man, carrying a large tray with several steaming plates on it.

"Ah," he said quietly, "you're awake. Is it alright if I come in?"

"You're already in," Sadir smiled, closing the adjoining door, "and it's time Anyar woke. Just give me a moment to put on a robe." She walked to the bottom of the bed and took up a light cotton garment, while Jelm placed the tray on a table near the window.

"Sit and eat while I give you the latest news."

"Mar, I'm hungry."

"Oh, Anyar, how about you let me take you to your mother?" He bent over the young girl and lifted her. "That's a good girl." Jelm gave her a cuddle. "You're still sleepy, aren't you?"

"I think she hasn't adjusted to all this travel. Come here, Anyar," said Sadir. "Sit and we can see what your nice uncle has brought. If I don't miss my guess, it has a lot of honey on it."

"Heritis's contacts have come back to him," said Jelm, sitting on a stool near the table. "I'm afraid that Kyel does appear to have left the port, on a trader's ship."

"Oh no!" exclaimed Sadir, rubbing a hand through her hair. "So it's true what Heritis said last day?"

"Yes, it does seem so. I have no reason to doubt Heritis's source since mine haven't come through, although more detail would be useful."

"Jelm, I need to know. We need to get to Port Saltus and find out."

"Uh-uh, Sadir," warned Jelm, raising a hand, "it is a long way to the port and too far for a mother and child to go, particularly just to gather information on a fairly certain fact."

"But we have to make sure."

"I agree," said Jelm. "That's why I will undertake the journey myself. I'll make it fast if I change mounts along the way. I should be back late next day if the fates are with me."

"Lizards' teeth!" Sadir swore. "No! I must go. I must know."

"I'll be as quick as I can," said Jelm, placing a hand over hers. "You have to stay. You and Anyar. Rest, see more of the city and meet up with some old friends."

"Blast!" She snatched at a piece of toast. "Have your way then! We'll be fine. Here. Waiting. Not much choice anyway," she said under her breath.

"I heard that," laughed Jelm, leaning toward a honey smeared Anyar. "Your mother is cross at me."

"Huh." Anyar stretched out a hand. "Jelm, you're going?"

"I'm afraid so, young one." He stood and placed a hand on Sadir's shoulder.

"Stay here and look after yourselves. I'll be as quick as I can. If you need anything just ask the cook, or one of the housekeepers," said Jelm. "I think you know your way around, although be on your guard as we still have the unsolved mystery of a missing scent master."

Sadir chewed mechanically through the food until her daughter's restlessness stopped her thinking.

"Come, sweetling, let's get dressed. I think you and I will see some of the city today, since there's little else we can do." She took Anyar's hand and led her into the washroom.

Before long they were heading out of the tower and through the gates. The sentry on duty nodded as they passed.

Jelm's let them know I'm here. He's efficient, I'll give him that, she thought as she moved out into the busy thoroughfare, taking in the sights and smells of the capital. They headed through the movement of people and animals to the traders' stalls, where Anyar soon caught a sweet scent.

"Oh, Mar?"

"I think it's time for a treat, even though you've just had a meal."

A row of honey-glazed apples on sticks made the young girl's eyes widen. "Mar, look."

"You must have been a voral in your previous life, since you love honey so much," Sadir smiled. "Either that or a pria."

"May I?" came a familiar voice. Sadir turned around, steeling her face as she recognised Heritis, a slight smile touching his lips. She felt like stamping her foot as she realised she had not detected him, letting the familiarity of the place relax her guard.

"Why, Heritis," she said lightly, "I had thought you were returning to Regulus."

"Still some work to do before I go back," he said, running a hand over his shaven head. "But you haven't answered my question."

"What? Oh, yes, you may get a honey apple for Anyar. I don't believe she's ever had one before."

"My pleasure," said Heritis, reaching past her with a coin in hand.

Sadir felt Anyar move back and put an arm around her trousered legs, her familiar scents having a troubled air, as if she had withdrawn into herself.

"What's the matter, sweetling?" she asked.

"Here it is," said Heritis, proffering a glistening red apple.

"Thank you, Heritis," said Sadir, "I'll pass it to her as she seems to have gone shy."

"Just enjoying the sights?" he asked as they walked along the lines of stalls, Anyar nibbling at her apple.

"Yes, I have quite a few memories of this place, and it's good to see it without the shadows once here." She looked up into his insincere face.

"I understand," he nodded, "since I was involved too; a small run-in with your partner, Targas, in Regulus if I recall."

Of course you recall. It was when Targas bested you during the war. Sadir kept her scents under tight control.

They wandered in silence, Sadir thinking how a nice walk in the sun had been spoiled.

"I must be getting back, Heritis. Anyar will be tired, and I have a few things to do." She felt a cold shiver run down her spine, as if a cloud had gone over the sun.

"Ah…Sadir," Heritis spoke hesitantly, "I thought you might…uh…like to see where we detected a few traces of your brother?"

Sadir glanced at the man, his head silhouetted against the bright sky, but there was nothing untoward in his scent aura. "Yes, I would." She looked at her daughter, who was still eating her apple. "Is it far?"

"No. Just several roads down towards the docks." He took her elbow and led her along a quieter road with a rougher surface where some of the cobbles needed repair. "Must tell Jelm to get his roadways in better order." Heritis gave a barking laugh.

"Now, down here." They entered a narrow alleyway between two warehouses. A lizard basking in the sun scurried into a crack.

Sadir could smell the odours of trade: wool, timber and the acridness of salt, but it seemed as if they lessened in the short alley, which ended at a stone wall.

"We think he may have slept here"—Heritis pointed to the ground—"and then he met someone, maybe…further down." He walked towards the end of the alley. Sadir followed, opening her senses to the widest.

Something not quite right. Heritis's scents are almost non-existent. "What else?"

"We found an item." He paused. "I think it was left just inside this warehouse." He patted the wall forming one side of the alley. "Uh, wait here. I'll just be a moment." He disappeared up the alleyway, leaving them alone.

Sadir bent down to test the air, catching a slight trace of her brother's distinctive scent. "So, he was here, though a time ago."

As she stood, a vague sound caused the hair to rise on the back of her neck. A sticky hand grasped her side, and she began to turn.

Her head suddenly shook with a massive blow, breaking through her hastily erected scent barriers. "Mar!" came a high-pitched cry as Sadir lost consciousness.

A foul smell assaulted her senses, gagging her awake to pitch darkness. A hideous vision of large creatures, all jaws and wings came unbidden and her stomach rebelled. She bent forward to retch.

But Sadir found she was restrained, held against a wall, arms secured above her body, manacles clinking as she moved.

"Mar? I'm scared."

"Anyar! Where are you?" she asked, her voice breathless.

"Mar?" A pair of thin arms wrapped tightly around her middle.

"Oh, Anyar, you're safe," she gasped. "Stay here, with me."

She thrust her concern for her daughter to the back of her mind and, opening her senses, filtered the thick odours around her.

Sadir knew with a horrid certainty where she was: the caverns below Nebleth. A place where the Sutanites' hymetta, large wasp-like creatures, had been kept. Her fingers scrabbled at the rock behind her as the iron manacles clinked dully.

The smell of the hymetta was everywhere, *but not nearby*, she thought. Sadir shuddered at a sob from Anyar. "Just stay with me, sweetling. I can't get to you but just stay. Hold onto me." She gritted her teeth to prevent a scream building up and bursting forth.

Who? Why? She should have listened to the vague feelings she'd been picking up from Heritis. She should have taken account of her daughter's reticence around the man, but that's what she *should have* done, not what she did. She felt a momentary pang of disquiet, thinking if Regna's partner was a traitor maybe Regna was too. *No, I can't believe that. But why has he done this? Why?* She pushed her head back, crunching into the stone. The flash of pain was blinding, threatening her consciousness.

Her eyes slowly became accustomed to the dark, a soft glow from a nearby opening revealing a large, open space in a high-roofed cavern. A flood of scents rolled through, dominated by the rancid, musty odour of hymetta. *The caverns were supposed to have been closed down, the creatures destroyed, yet here they are, alive and multiplying under the streets of the capital itself.*

She firmly filtered out their odour and sought beneath it into the mix that lapped around her. The normal smells of the cavern confirmed where she was, but there was more. People were noticeable, one a strong scent, several others weaker. She struggled with her scent memory.

Ah, I remember him, the Keeper's odour overrun by sweat and ill-health. He's near. Did he do this? But there are two other scents. Whose are they? A waft of recent death floated above, like a thin blanket seeking to disperse. She shuddered at its nearness as she tried to block it from her mind.

Another, softer scent trace broke through, feminine and familiar from a time ago. It reminded her of the bedroom they had left this very day, a previous occupant of that bedroom, from years before. "Nefaria!" she whispered to herself. Immediately she cast about for Nefaria's lover, the Sutanite leader, Jakus, but couldn't detect even the merest mote of his scent. "He must've been here. She wouldn't have been here without him, but he's left no trace, nothing," she murmured.

"Mar, I afraid," whimpered Anyar, pulling on her mother.

"Oh Anyar, my poor baby," she groaned, heaving at the restraints. "I can't get to you. I can't. Please stay. Hold my legs." She projected a calming scent at her daughter and heard her whimpering quieten.

"I've got to get out," she muttered. Then she remembered that Targas had managed to break up iron by attacking the very odour bonds in the iron itself, weakening them, like rusting sped up a thousand-fold.

How did he do it? She thought of his explanations of how he was able to bond disparate odours together, causing solid structures to form. The opposite of that would weaken those bonds. Sadir began to draw on her scent memories, focussing on the iron, pushing, feeling, driving into the material. "Ah!" She drew a relieved breath as she heard flaking particles hitting the stone floor.

She worked hard, desperate to break her restraints and hold her daughter. As she concentrated, she wondered why she was here, and why no one was keeping an eye on her. They must know she had scent talent and of her association with Targas, the greatest scent master in Ean. "No, stop it," she breathed, "I must concentrate and not worry. I must get free."

Then a musty, rancid odour began to infiltrate, driving into her awareness. At the same time she heard a rustle, a scratching coming from the opening. Something was coming.

"Mar, something bad coming!" yelled Anyar. Sadir could feel her daughter standing, back, pushing into her legs. "Mar!" she screamed, her fear ripping through her.

"No!" Sadir shut her eyes, trying to block her thoughts. She jerked hard at her restraints, feeling the harsh edges ripping her skin, and just stifled a scream.

Shaking her head, she looked towards the opening.

She knew what was coming.

Chapter Eighteen

Jelm entered the gates of Nebleth at a canter, the perac blowing hard. He caught sight of a guard standing by the entrance waving frantically, so he quickly dismounted.

"Jelm—uh—Cer," said the guard, his weathered face creased with a frown, "I was told by Heritis to catch you the moment you returned, but we weren't expecting you until sundown."

"No, I'm returning earlier than anticipated since I found what I was after," responded Jelm, thinking back to a fortuitous meeting on the road with the commander of the garrison from Port Saltus. "Tell me why Heritis is so concerned to contact me. I only saw him around dawn."

"I am to inform you that...ah...Sadir and her daughter have gone missing," the guard said.

"What! When?" exclaimed Jelm.

"Before midday, I understand, Cer. We've been scouring the city ever since. I..."

"Where's Heritis? I must find out what has been happening."

"He'd be out, Cer, looking."

"Enough! Take care of my animal," he ordered as he ran off along the main thoroughfare into the city.

"Quiet, sweetling. Quiet; hold tight. Let Mar get ready," Sadir said, keeping her voice soft to control her fears. She took a moment to pulse soothing scents over her daughter before working at her iron bonds, while continuing to watch the tunnel entrance.

The scents grew thicker, as if the creatures knew their prey was trapped and were producing saliva in abundance.

I can't attack them with scent, she thought, *it would only make them mad. We wouldn't survive. No, I've got to try something else. Getting free would help.*

"L…lady," called a voice from a distance away. "I'm sorry, I really am."

"The keeper," she hissed, remembering the nervous man from years ago, the man that Targas had cowed completely. "Keeper!" Sadir yelled. "How dare you chain me here. My daughter, too. How dare you! Let me loose this instant. Take your creatures away!"

"I only do what I'm told, lady. I'm sorry." His quavering voice faded.

Sadir screamed until her voice was raw, but the keeper didn't reply.

A scratch of stone caught her attention. There in the entrance was a creature standing thigh-high on six thin legs, the faint light glistening off its shiny carapace. The hymetta hesitated, yellow mouthparts working beneath large black eyes, wings buzzing. A second, then a third creature appeared. The first lifted a long, spindly leg and, wiping a droplet of drool from its mouth, moved into the cavern.

Anyar's fingers gouged into Sadir's legs.

"I fear we must hurry," puffed Alethea, dismounting as they pushed into the crowds along the main street of Nebleth, "I believe this moment is crucial to the future of our lands."

Her urgency hastened the group towards the tower. Even the voral appeared agitated, panting as it peered from the saddlebag against her leg.

Targas used his size to push the compact group of people and animals through the crowd along the busy road. "Straight to the tower. Jelm and Sadir should be there, I hope. Whatever it is, we should be there in time."

"You know, Alethea, don't you?"

"I…I do know it relates to your partner and…and your daughter, Targas, but…more than that…I…I cannot ascertain," gasped Alethea. She grasped Boidea's strong shoulder to keep up the pace.

"Targas!" called a strong voice, "Thank Ean you're here!"

Targas looked over to see Jelm pushing his way through the crowd of traders and shoppers. "Hold up," he called to his companions, "it's Jelm, administrator for Nebleth. He'll know what's happening."

"Ah, Targas," said Jelm as he approached. "And Lan, too?" Most fortuitous that I've found you." He grabbed Targas's arm, his concerned scents coiling in dull greens, yellows and browns. "Sadir's missing. We've everyone searching."

"Anyar? Do you have her safe?" Targas felt like shaking the tall man.

"No. She was with her mother." Jelm's eyes took in the other members of the party and suddenly jerked his head. "Let's go to the tower. We may find Heritis there since he's co-ordinating the search. Follow me."

As they rushed off, Alethea caught the eyes of Boidea and Cathar, and gently shook her head.

They passed their animals to the several handlers at the entrance to the tower and followed Jelm up the steps, Boidea again carrying the voral. "He's getting no lighter," she grumbled to Cathar as they entered the building.

"Raitis!" yelled Jelm. "Where are you, man?"

"Here," puffed a wizened man, stooped with age. "I didn't expect you back so soon, Cer."

"What's the situation with Sadir? Has she been found?"

"No, Cer, no word. Ah...ah, we have most of the tower out looking for her and her daughter. A seller in the markets sold them an apple, not long before midday, but no one remembers seeing her since."

"And?"

"Not sure where Regulus's administrator is though; Heritis was one of the last with her. He raised the alarm and is out looking for her."

"The tower's been searched thoroughly?" Jelm asked his advisor.

"First thing we did, Cer," Raitis replied. "No trace of her, and her last scents are stale."

"Right, arrange for our friends' things to be taken to guest rooms and we'll get out there." Jelm suddenly looked at the group standing behind him. "Sorry," he said, rubbing a hand through his fair hair, "I haven't been introduced."

"Understandable, dear friend, understandable," said Lan softly, raising an arm. "Alethea, Mlana of Rolan"—Lan smiled towards her—"then Boidea, also of Rolan, and Cathar from Sanctus."

"Welcome to Nebleth." Jelm gave a short bow of his head.

"Please! We must go," said Targas, turning to head back down the steps.

"Yes," agreed Jelm, moving after him, "let's go to where she was last seen."

He caught up to Targas and hurried down the steps towards the markets, the others trailing in their wake.

"You go on," Alethea whispered to Boidea. "Take Cathar with you, but leave the voral. Lan and I will follow."

"Can I?" said Lan, reaching for the bag. "I won't have a problem with him."

"Thank you, Lan. I'm just not as strong as I used to be." Alethea hooked an arm into his after he had placed the bag's strap across his shoulder.

"Best let the younger ones go on. We'll do what we are good at: examining the scent traces. I know Sadir's scents well, and young Anyar's, so if there's a trace we will find it."

They could soon see Jelm and the rest talking with a trader not far ahead, so they began sifting the scents.

"Allow me to share your scent memories, Lan. Sadir is a woman and I may be able to find her traces easier than you."

Lan leant his head towards Alethea. A thickening of the air was momentarily visible as she extracted essences of Sadir and Anyar from him in a matter of moments.

Alethea's eyes fluttered and she sighed. "Very strong, Lan. You have grown over the years." She gripped his arm and looked around the street. "Now we must begin."

The creature edged into the cavern in small, stilted steps, keeping to the rough rock wall, the black eyes of its fellows watching from the entrance. Each movement was captured by Sadir's horrified gaze.

She had given up trying to free herself, worried the slight patter of falling particles might attract attention sooner. Her mind worked frantically, knowing there were only moments before the hymetta reached her on its circuitous route. Anyar's head pressed hard into her thighs, her daughter's fingers restricting the blood flow.

How did Targas stop them before? she thought back. *Something about a familiar smell, but I can't do it; no time. Didn't he block them out, cause a wall or barrier to form by joining odour bonds? How did he do that?*

A rustling, like dried leaves blowing along a path, broke into her awareness. Anyar whimpered. The sound stopped. Sadir's eyes straining in the dim light saw the creature only a short distance away, its head raised, jaws moving, black eyes on her.

"Lizards' teeth," she hissed. "Anyar. Stay. Quiet. For pity's sake."

It took a tentative step towards her.

Sadir began to pull frantically at the odours around her, trying to force them to bond and create a wall between the creatures and themselves. She could see the air thickening, a slight darkening of the dim light, but was uncertain her skills were enough to stop this scent-based predator from breaking through and attacking her.

The hymetta took another step, which motivated its companions to follow across the cavern floor.

Sadir's heart was beating rapidly, sweat pouring down her face while she tried to call on all her experience and scent memories to find a way to stop them. A slight shift in her focus allowed her to detect a secondary scent behind the first, a shadow scent like she had seen while sitting in the sun with Regna, but they hadn't really worked out what it did.

The hymetta was so close she could see its drool dripping to the floor. Sadir kept thinking, remembering how she had scraped the shadow scent away, pulled it together into the odour ball that had become so powerful in its effects. But then she had the cordial to help her; now she was on her own. Desperation leant strength and she peeled away the shadow scents from the odours she had collected. She was certain the strongest scent, the hymetta scent, would form the basis of the ball she was accumulating.

The creature reached out a leg and pushed into her protective odour wall. She felt it give. *No time left,* she thought, releasing her control on the ball, collapsing it, breaking it apart, exploding the odour in one powerful burst.

The hymetta reacted as if stung. It jumped back in a thrust of its legs, crashing into the other two behind it. The three tumbled in a frenzied ball of legs and bodies until they hit the far wall.

Sadir sagged against her restraints.

"Mar!" Anyar screamed and released Sadir's legs. She pushed away, breaking through the scent barrier Sadir had put around them.

"Mar, gotta go!" Anyar's cry echoed in the cavern as she ran into the darkness.

"Anyar, come back! Please!" Sadir screamed.

The hymetta picked themselves up, heads turning towards the receding sound of the young girl.

They followed.

"**H**ere. A distinct trace down this alley," urged Alethea. She and Lan hurried down to the end and stopped by the blank wall.

"Argh!" yelped Lan as the voral scrabbled out of the pack and hit the ground with a thud. "What is your hurry?"

"Violence here," stated Alethea, ignoring the animal's antics.

"I agree, and not too long ago. Sadir's scent is strong."

"But where...?"

A flurry of gravel spat into the air as the voral began to dig urgently where the stone wall met the path. Lan backed off, all the while studying the rough wall.

"There!" he said, pointing to where the outline of a door was just discernible. "We must get it open!"

The combined power of two scent masters quickly overcame the lock, and the door swung inwards. The voral pushed through and disappeared into the darkness.

"I believe we had better follow him," said Alethea. "He obviously knows where he is going."

"Be ready," growled Lan. "There has been recent death and, by Ean!" he gasped, "I can detect hymetta. Here. In Nebleth."

"Come," said Alethea. "Whatever is there, it is where the voral is heading. We must hasten."

The sounds made by the animal faded as they moved into the tunnel. They focussed on the scent path of hymetta odour, its strength increasing.

"I can sense Sadir," said Lan. "She is in distress."

"Lan? Lan!" echoed Sadir's panicked voice. "Help me, please! Anyar! They're chasing Anyar."

By the time they reached the cavern, Sadir was pulling at the manacles holding her to the wall. She sobbed when she saw them. "Get me out! I must find my baby."

She pulled hard, blood darkening on her arms. Lan and Alethea wasted no time, diving scent spikes into the rock around the manacles, attacking the bonds that held the substrate together. Rock spurted out in clouds as the wall crumbled. Suddenly Sadir yanked hard and her hands, wrists still in their iron bracelets, came free.

"That way!" she screeched. "That's where she went. The creatures are after her."

With Lan and Alethea behind, Sadir ran down a long tunnel lit by a natural phosphorescence, the scents they followed enabling them to navigate the dimness.

Where the tunnel widened into a wider, high ceiling section the odour of the hymetta overwhelmed any traces of Anyar.

"I can't find the scent," yelled Sadir, "I can't find her. They've caught her!"

"No, Sadir," said Alethea, puffing soothing odours over her, "I don't believe they have. I would know."

"You? I don't even know who you are," she said, swinging around to Lan. "What do you say? Is my daughter alive?"

"Sadir, I know that the hymetta have not taken Anyar," he said, holding her arms. "Their scent path leads on, and they are not hunting. They are merely seeking to get away from an unpleasant experience."

"Them?" huffed Sadir. "I'd destroy them all if I could. If...if they haven't got Anyar, where is she?"

"Sadir, my name is Alethea, from Rolan, and I agree with Lan. We must have somehow passed where she turned off the path, although I do not see how she could have eluded us. We must backtrack."

"She must be here?" Sadir gasped. "We traced her. We've gotta go back." She turned and headed along the way they had come.

"Come on, Lan," murmured Alethea, "something is not adding up. And where's the voral? I can't detect him at all."

"We will return and see if we can find where Anyar's scent trail disappeared. That will give us a starting point."

The scent filled the voral's nostrils, overwhelming him with the rightness of the trail he was following.

Danger. Danger. An inherent memory told him the predators following the same trail were dangerous. His tongue flicked out, licking his snout, tasting the threat the creatures posed, and he snarled. He knew he could attack, probably win against them, but the scent pulled at him. That was his priority and he had to protect it at all costs.

The forest of spindly legs appeared out of the gloom and he doubled his speed, rushing through, giving the wasps no chance to bite down with their powerful jaws. They weren't his concern.

The delicate scent, overlaid with fear, drew him on. It tasted good, right and fulfilling. He had to reach it to feel complete.

Sound overcame the scent, and he could hear the child's breathing, her breaths coming in gasps. She was at the end of her endurance and would soon collapse, an easy victim for the predators following her trail.

He put on a spurt and reached her side, pushing his head under her arm, projecting calming scents. A desperate hand reached down and grasped his fur. The voral slowed and the young girl kept hold.

He pushed her with his firm body into a slight recess in the wall of the darkened cavern until she hit the rock and slumped to the floor. He lay heavily across her lap and concentrated on quietening his breath, slowing his racing heart. The girl followed his lead, her gasping fading as if she realised noise would attract attention.

The voral lifted his head, listening for the hymetta. A moment later he dipped his head and stilled. A calmness emanated from him, influencing the girl he was with. The light faded and nothing impinged. They were in a cocoon, alone and isolated. Nothing bothered them. Nothing saw them. The voral huffed, content, enjoying the soft stroke of a small hand through his neck fur.

S adir re-entered the cavern where she had been held captive, searching frantically. She glanced back as Alethea and Lan came into view.

"Didn't you say the creatures hadn't caught her?" Sadir yelled. "Where is she then?"

"Alethea," echoed a woman's voice, "are you in there?"

"Ah, Boidea," called Alethea, "Lan and I are not far from you, with Sadir too. Who is with you?"

"Jelm, Targas and Cathar," Boidea replied, "although..."

"Targas!" screamed Sadir. "Anyar's missing. You must find our daughter!"

Lan caught a flicker of movement in the tunnel they had just come up, the dim glow highlighting two small figures. "Look," he whispered. "Anyar."

Sadir swung around at Lan's whisper, following the direction of his gaze.

"Mar," called the young girl as she stumbled into the cavern, hand firmly gripped in her companion's fur. "I safe with my friend."

"Get away from that thing," she yelled, running towards her daughter.

Anyar slumped against the voral, arm around its neck. It hissed at Sadir, showing its teeth as it pushed back into the girl.

"No, Sadir," called Alethea, "it's friendly. It won't hurt her."

"What? That animal?" she said, slowing down. "Oh," Sadir said, crouching and holding out her arms, iron manacles ringing faintly, "come to me, sweetling."

Anyar looked up, streaks of tears on her dirty face glistening in the dim light. She got to her feet and staggered towards her mother, the voral following closely.

"Oh Anyar, my baby." Sadir flung her arms around the small girl and hugged her to her chest. "What happened to you?"

A large shape suddenly enveloped the pair, strong arms encompassing them. "Sadir. Anyar. I'm so glad you're safe."

"Targas, my love," murmured Sadir into his shoulder. Anyar whimpered and buried her face into Targas's leg.

"Here," hissed Alethea to the voral, clicking her fingers, "come here."

The animal looked at Anyar cuddling her parents, waddled over to Alethea and climbed into the bag that Lan held open.

"There is a mystery with the animal that bears investigation," she murmured to Lan.

"Thank you, Lan, Alethea," said Targas, looking over Sadir's shoulder, "I'm thankful that you got here when you did." He coughed several times. "C...can we get out of here? This place and the stench hold bad memories. I feel it."

"Yes, let us go. Can you two help?" Lan asked of Boidea and Cathar, who were standing close by.

"Certainly," said Boidea. They both moved over and gently assisted Sadir to her feet–Anyar holding tightly to her mother's neck.

"I...I've got to leave," Targas coughed. "Hurry."

At that moment the manacles on Sadir's wrists clanged together. Targas grabbed at his ears, hunching his head into his shoulders, dropping into a crouch. "He's there! He's back, inside. I...I can't get away from him," he screamed.

"Take Targas outside. At once!" ordered Alethea. "Lan! Help me!"

They gripped Targas by the shoulders and hustled him forward, pouring calming scents over him as they went. The others hurried with them.

Chapter Nineteen

"**M**ake way!" Jelm ordered as he rushed the party through the scattering of guards and officials and up the tower stairs. "Raitis," he said to his advisor puffing alongside, "ensure the search parties are notified we've found Sadir and Anyar. And find Heritis urgently. Get him to me."

"Cer?" Raitis hesitated.

"Now, man!"

"At once, Cer." The older man stopped, letting the group pass. He looked at the figures of Lan and Alethea supporting Targas as they swept by, while behind them the two young women had their arms around Sadir and her daughter. Raitis shook his head before hurrying down the steps.

Sadir found herself back in the bedroom she had left only that morning. So much had happened. It seemed long ago when she had woken to a pleasant meal with Jelm, Anyar still sleeping in the large, soft bed.

The room was full of people doing other things, ignoring her. She noticed Targas and Jelm nearby.

"Targas, what's happened? Tell me!" she implored, her voice rising. "Have you found Kyel? Did he leave Ean? Or did Jakus kill him?"

"What?" Targas snapped as he stepped towards her. "Jakus? He's dead."

"No! It was him, or at least that woman of his, the one Kyel was chasing. They did this! They tried to kill me. And they've got Kyel, if they haven't killed him."

"Sadir," Lan said, joining Targas and Jelm, "we did find traces of Nefaria, and the merest mote that could indicate Jakus, although he would be adept at hiding his spoor. The Keeper was obvious, but we have been unable to locate even him for now."

"If it was Jakus, why did he trap Sadir, lure her into the caverns?" asked Jelm. "It doesn't make sense, to reveal himself for so little gain."

"No, it does make sense," said Targas softly. "Jakus was, or is, a vindictive man and would blame me for being defeated, for losing Ean. What better way to get back at me than by destroying the one I love?"

Sadir reached up and gripped Targas's hand.

"Come, Targas, Jelm," said Lan. "Enough thinking, we must get the manacles off, then leave Sadir to get cleaned. Talking all this over now will not help."

Targas smiled tightly as he released her hand and followed the men through the central door into Jelm's room.

S adir could hear water being sloshed into the large bath in the washroom while a flurry of hot scents drifted in.

A bath, anything to clean the filth off me and Anyar. She shuddered at the memory of the hymetta's alien face as it prodded her scent barrier and held her stained, abraded hands over her face.

"My dear," said Alethea coming over, "we need to take care of you." She beckoned to Boidea, and together they began to remove Sadir's dirty clothing.

"Come," murmured Alethea, "I think it is time for you and Anyar to enjoy a hot bath." She helped Sadir walk into the welcoming warmth of the washroom.

The water was steaming gently, with the waft of a fragrant herb dominating the scents. She stepped in, leaning against the back as the water rose to her chest.

"Mar."

A pale, wriggly girl was placed on her stomach, water from her feet splashing into Sadir's face.

"Sorry," said Cathar, "I couldn't stop her. I'd hoped to give you at least a few moments to enjoy the water alone."

"No, don't fuss," murmured Sadir at the grimy face looking into hers. To the woman, she said: "She deserves it as much as me with what she's been through."

"We have some perfumed soap, too. Let me clean you," said Cathar. "Oh, your poor wrists. And your head's bloody."

"Mar. Mar," shrilled Anyar, squirming in her mother's arms, "Vor. There's Vor."

"What?" Sadir pulled her head away from Cathar's massaging fingers to see where her daughter was looking.

At first it was hard to discern the dark figure wedged under a small wooden cabinet, but then she saw a grin of white teeth and the gleam of black eyes.

"Oh, it's the voral," chuckled Alethea. "You cannot keep him out of things."

The animal suddenly dashed to where Anyar's arm hung over the side of the bath, and a long red tongue licked her hand.

Anyar giggled.

"Is he safe?" Sadir looked at Alethea who raised an eyebrow. "Guess I'll have to get used to him then."

"I think we will let you get a good relaxing soak while I get food brought up into the bedroom. Now you"—Alethea bent and picked up the voral—"will have to go out."

He hissed and looked pleadingly at Anyar.

"Vor." She held out an arm as Alethea took him out of the bathroom.

"Come, little one," said Sadir, "let's get clean."

She was enveloped in a soft perac-wool gown, hair still wet from the bath. Anyar, in a pale green coverall, was sitting on the floor at her feet, brown head bent over as she rubbed the voral's stomach.

"Eat some of these pastries while they're hot," said Boidea, lifting a platter.

Sadir took a small pastry-covered pie and bit into it, her eyes focussed on the white belly of the animal.

"Now that you are settled and Targas is in your bath, I thought we could talk about the mystery of that creature at your feet," said Alethea as she sat, bent forward, a steaming mug in her hands.

"Uh huh," Sadir agreed, raising her eyes to meet Alethea's earnest gaze.

"You are aware of my role in Rolan, and the long relationship between our two countries, one that the occupation did a lot to hinder?'

Sadir nodded.

"I had a Knowing," Alethea began, "a foretelling if you will, to come to Ean. Your partner Targas and yourself, your daughter and Kyel, were part of the Knowing. There are unusual links there.

"On our way through the mountains we fell in with an orphaned voral, who exhibited some unusual and inexplicable traits. He has accompanied us on the journey and been an interesting travelling companion with a mind of his own.

"That may have been all, except for what has just happened. The voral, or *Vor* as Anyar calls him, led us into the caverns and suddenly disappeared, obviously on the trail of your daughter—why or how I have no idea. What I do know is that he has an ability to…obscure or hide himself—he did it when I first found him, and I surmise he did this when those creatures were after Anyar. It was so effective that even we experienced scent masters couldn't locate the pair of them."

"Well then, I'm in Vor's debt," said Sadir pushing at him with her toe, "and he is cute."

"I'm sure he is," added Boidea, "but they are known for their ferocity, and I've never known one kept as a pet before. Still, he and your daughter seem to be firm friends. Apparently you were right, Mlana, as usual–I was all for getting rid of him."

"Have you left any pastries for us?" asked Lan as he came out of the washroom with Targas.

"Sadir," said Targas, his clean face lighting in a smile. He came over and took her face gently in his hands, "it's good to see you looking well. And you too,

Anyar," he added looking down at his daughter. He came over and sat on the bed next to Sadir, putting an arm around her waist.

She leant into his shoulder. "It's so nice to be clean and safe, and to be with you." She looked into his eyes.

"I'm sorry to have put you through all this, and…and not coming to rescue you when I should have."

"Targas, we are all here. And we're safe. That's all that matters," said Sadir. "I just hope Kyel is well, if you're sure he's left Port Saltus on a ship." She looked up to the sympathetic nods of Lan and Alethea. "And he's definitely…alive?"

"Yes, Sadir," said Lan. "The only confirmed sighting we have was that your brother was riding away from Nebleth with two others, one being a woman. There seemed no sign of coercion."

Please, please be safe, Kyel, she thought, and squeezed Targas's hand.

"So if we can't follow Kyel, what do we do?" she asked. "I'm sure you've got something planned?"

"Food first," called a cheery voice from the doorway. "I'm sure we are all hungry, even Anyar, if she can stop playing with that pet of yours."

Jelm pulled a large table from the wall and stood back as two serving men brought steaming platters to the table; another of the staff brought in two jugs, while still others had mugs and dishes.

"Even honey for the voral," said Jelm placing a deep dish on the floor. "I believe he's been a hero and should be rewarded."

The silence was only broken by the sounds of eating until Sadir sat back against Targas and glanced up at him with sleepy eyes.

"Heritis, Jelm!" she suddenly gasped, jerking forward. "What of him?"

"Ah, yes," said Jelm, reaching into a cloth bag suspended by a strap crossing diagonally over his shoulder, "I was coming to that. Do you recognise this?" He pulled out a shirt and passed it to her."

Sadir took the woollen garment and placed it into her lap. "Yes, I do. Did Heritis give it to you?"

"Yes. He said he was going to get something of Kyel's from a warehouse, but when he returned you had gone. That's when he raised the alarm."

"Do you mean,"—she waved the shirt in the air, her eyes beginning to fill with tears—"you believe him? That's his excuse for leaving me to be taken to those…those creatures?"

Targas's arm came around her and she pressed her head into him.

"Jelm," his voice broke in, "where is he? It would be best if he could speak for himself."

"I'm afraid that's impossible, Targas," Jelm replied, "since he has already left for Regulus."

116

"What!" he growled.

"Jelm," said Lan, "we needed to talk to Heritis, get to the bottom of this whole unfortunate incident. There is also the disturbing matter of his cousin, Jakus."

"I apologise, Lan, Sadir, but his story seemed reasonable to me and he was in a hurry to get back to Regulus once he heard that you were safe," said Jelm, looking at her. "After all, he is the administrator of Regulus and essentially my equal in rank."

"I think we need to have a long talk with him," said Lan, "which means we should head back to that city now that our urgency has been met." He looked at Alethea, who gave the smallest of nods.

"So, I suppose that's all, then? For Kyel. You're not going after him?" Sadir's voice was small.

"No, Sadir, that's not the case," said Lan. "While we have no way to chase Kyel, we will have all our vessels look out for him, and any news of him. He won't be forgotten."

"Fine!" She stared at Lan for a long moment. "Now I'm tired, so I'd like some time alone with my family."

Targas looked down at Sadir and Anyar, who had snuck up onto the bed. The rest moved out of the room and the door closed.

Chapter Twenty

"Back on this road again. Always on the go. Leaving Kyel to the mercy of that beast. He's still young and shouldn't be alone." Sadir looked at Targas as they walked their animals alongside the river.

"I agree, love, he shouldn't," Targas said, watching the road, "but take a little comfort in your brother's strength. Sure he has the impetuousness of youth, but beneath it all he is strong. Consider what he's been through. How he's come out of all that. I don't think he'll come to harm if he keeps his wits about him."

"I suppose you could be right, but..."

A pealing laugh from their daughter in response to the voral interrupted her train of thought.

Targas lifted his face to the sun as it broke through the Long Ranges in the East, feeling the slight warmth that it brought. Sadir smiled at him and reached for his hand as they walked the peracs along the road, the sounds of the river ever present.

"I don't want this to end, Targas. We've had nothing but trouble for the last long while and it's taken this horrible thing to bring us back together."

"Me too, Sadir. For some reason I've managed to block what's going on inside my head, almost like a blanket pressing down over the...the..."

Sadir squeezed his hand and looked up at his darkened face. "I think Alethea will be able to help us. She really does have some unusual abilities."

"I'll be happy for that, I think," said Targas, looking over at the group of women accompanying them, Anyar trotting at their feet. "I've had enough of this...this evil that won't leave me alone."

They had left their overnight stop to continue their slow journey northwards to Regulus, where they would catch up with the men who had gone earlier.

"Sadir, Targas," said Alethea, coming alongside them, her perac trailing her. "Do you mind if we talk as we go? There are some things I think we should discuss."

"Targas?" asked Sadir.

"Mmm. Why not?"

Alethea looked away from the two walking next to her. Far off were several barges travelling together down the Great Southern River. The bronze water reflected the brightening morning, and their distance made them seem like dark logs floating languidly through an azure sky. A slight breeze coming from the west ruffled their hair, bringing the hints of the coming winter cold. "I will be making a late trip through the mountains to Rolan if I don't miss my guess," she murmured.

"What's that, Alethea?" asked Sadir.

"Nothing, just thinking ahead is all." She shook her head and changed the subject: "Now Sadir, let us talk through your experiences with what you have called the shadow scent. We know of this in Rolan, although we don't name it. Tell me what you know."

"I don't really know much…but I think it's something to do with Rolan cordial. The first time I experienced it was when I was with Regna and I had a sip of the cordial. I started to see an extra scent layer, almost like a shadow. I was able to separate it and form a ball of strong scent. I didn't have a chance to do anything more." She frowned. "When I was in the caverns I was desperate, and it took a lot of effort to bring up a shadow scent to stop the hymetta, but it worked. I don't know why."

"How did you do that?" asked Targas, leaning closer.

"I used any scent I could find," Sadir continued, "and it was hard in the dark of the caverns. It was you, Targas, what you've done that reminded me of using the creature's own scent against itself…and it got so close." She shivered and wrapped her arms around her chest.

"And it obviously worked, Sadir." Alethea placed a hand on her shoulder. "What we have found is that the cordial is an enhancer, enabling the smell centres of the brain to develop more fully, and it appears to be gender-linked."

"Really?"

"Yes, Targas. We have found men don't benefit from it, but they tend not to like the sweetness of the liqueur anyway."

"I prefer malas, thanks."

"And it is a fine drink too, Targas, from my limited experience," said Alethea, smiling. "However I have a further question for you, Sadir." Her bright eyes looked intently from under floating wisps of grey hair. "Did you, at any time, feel that you had an…an inkling of what might be going to happen?"

"You mean a sort of premonition?"

Alethea nodded.

"Funny…" said Sadir, hesitating. "I did, more than just a hunch, when Heritis was leading me to where I was taken. If only I had listened to it."

"Ah," Alethea nodded, "I have hopes for what might be happening, then. For a significant attribute in the more, shall we say, *gifted* women in Rolan, is their ability to understand what might or will be. It is that which brought us to Nebleth with such urgency."

"Just that?" Sadir asked sharply. "Targas needs help too."

"Sadir! I'm not sure I want to talk about it now."

"Forgive me, Targas, but we do need to talk," said Alethea, "for you are a vital part too."

"Alright! Do you believe you can rid me of this…this parasite I'm carrying in my head? Lan couldn't."

"Straight to the point, Targas?"

"Sorry. I haven't the patience I once had."

"As you have said, Lan has tried to resolve what ails you with limited success, but I have other skills which may be effective. I suspect Sanctus will be the logical venue, with its natural ambience, but we shall see."

"So, for Targas?" asked Sadir. "What do you foresee for Targas?"

"Ah." Alethea slowed her stride as she thought. "A Knowing is never specific, never precise, and it would be presumptuous of me to say so. I do know our journey will not be simple, with many trials. But we all have a role to play and mine will be to assist both of you, and Anyar."

"What about Kyel?"

"No," said Alethea, "I have no role regarding him, I believe."

"Mar, Mar," shrilled Anyar, breaking into their conversation, "Vor's been naughty."

Sadir looked over at the smiling faces of Boidea and Cathar. "No, Sadir," said Boidea, "it's just that your daughter has worn the poor animal out and he's slipped into the saddle pack to rest."

Targas bent over and picked up his daughter. "I think it's time you rode as well, my girl, don't you?"

"Now she is one we must watch," said Alethea. "Something about her is intriguing, and significant."

Sadir watched her daughter snuggling into Targas's shoulder as he walked to the perac behind them. A shiver ran down her spine and she looked away.

They entered the tunnel leading under the castle dominating the southern approach to the city of Regulus. The sun was setting behind the Sensory Mountain range, and all were tired and looking forward to their rest. Sadir was apprehensive at what they might find out when they met up with Jelm and Lan.

"Welcome back," said a tall robed man standing at the first series of steps inside the castle, a gloomy figure in the dusk.

"Oh!" Sadir gasped, taking hold of Targas's hand.

"I am so glad that you are safe," said Heritis, pulsing welcoming scents. "Please forgive me for not speaking with you sooner, but I had to get back to Regulus urgently. Come, everyone"—he stood back to allow the group to continue on up the steps—"your friends wait for you by a warm fire.

"And Sadir, I'm pleased to see you and your daughter safe. It has been a most distressing time for you, I imagine."

Sadir increased her pace beside a silent Targas, tightly gripping his hand.

Regna greeted them just inside, her manner more restrained than before. "Welcome to you all, especially you, Sadir." She came and gave her a hug. "I'm so sorry for all you've been through. Come into the warmth. I've set up food and drink next to the fire. And let me have your bags taken to your rooms." She signalled to several of her people waiting nearby.

Sadir kept her pace along the corridor, hoping the fire would remove some of the chill in her bones, the feel of Heritis behind adding to her discomfort.

They entered the familiar room and went straight to the sofa. Targas put Anyar on the end, whereupon she jumped to the floor.

"Par," she squeaked, "where's Vor?"

"Coming, young one," said Boidea as she entered. "I think he's as eager to get down as you were." She bent down with the wriggling bag and the voral made a beeline for Anyar. They immediately tumbled in a heap, the girl's laughter echoing in the room.

"Still got that animal," observed Regna. "I see Anyar is very taken with it. No hope I could put it outside then?"

Sadir smiled at her, then looked around the room. Boidea and Cathar were helping themselves to the food, while Alethea was warming her hands by the fire; she could see no sign of Heritis.

"Jelm and Lan are coming," said Regna, as if in response to Sadir's unspoken question. "I'll make sure we have enough drinks to go around, and something for the voral, of course." She hurried out of the room.

Sadir moved up next to Targas and leant against him. He handed her a small pie.

"Something's not right," he murmured. "The sooner we're on our way the better."

"Ah, Lan," his voice brightened as the aged scent master entered. "Come, sit with us. Have some food."

"It is good to see you, my friends," said Lan, his lined face breaking into a smile as he came over to them. "No, no food for me, but I wouldn't mind a beer if there is one going."

"I think Regna is having some brought in," said Sadir. She looked around before lowering her voice. "How did you go with…you know?" Her eyes flicked to the door.

"Ah, not very satisfactorily," Lan said quietly. "He…has remarkable resilience and on the surface it was as he said, merely an unfortunate incident. But"—he held up his hand to forestall Sadir's question—"there is more to it than meets the eye. Enough to bear watching.

"Here's Jelm," Lan said, as the tall man came through the door. "He has had more added to his workload, I am afraid."

"Just enough room for you to sit too, Jelm," said Targas.

"Thank you," Jelm breathed, taking a cup of wine. "I am due for another early departure next day. I have several things to follow up: the existence of hymetta beneath the city, and why there are traces of Sutanites in our city. I see that Lan is filling you in on what little we've learnt from our…ah…*discussions* today."

"Yes, Jelm," Lan nodded, "to some extent. I'll have more time to talk as we travel back to Lesslas."

"The drinks are here," called Regna from the doorway. "I believe yours would be a beer, Lan? Targas?"

Targas nodded and took a large mug from the tray.

Sadir noticed how Targas inhaled deeply before drinking. It reminded her of all those years ago in the Lesslas tavern when she had first met him, and he'd shown his liking for the beverage. She looked contentedly at her daughter sitting next to the fire with the voral's head resting on her lap and smiled.

If only it could stay so peaceful, she thought, *but it won't, I know it won't.* She briefly wondered whether this was a premonition, a *Knowing* that Alethea had spoken of earlier. *I'll just have to take it one day at a time and hope I'm wrong.*

Chapter Twenty-One

The smell after so many days at sea was overpowering, a ripeness of decaying fish, sewage and animal odours backed by a myriad of scents: from baked stone, rotting wood and tar to hints of strange spices and alien smells. Surrounding it hung a dry, acrid substance reminding Kyel of those times when a wind blew from the deserts east of the Long Ranges in Ean.

He shifted his stance at the bow of Jakus's ship, straining to see Southern Port, his first sight of Sutan.

They had passed a number of ships on the way in, generally of a similar build to theirs, two-masted and narrow, with main and spritsails. One larger, three-masted, broad-beamed ship sailed by, riding high, a whiff of coal coiling from its empty holds.

Before long he saw rows of wooden piers projecting fishbone-like from a broad stone causeway joining a mass of warehouses and buildings. Most piers were occupied by ships, ranging from two-masted, narrow vessels to squatter, two- and three-masted transports. Smaller vessels, including fishing craft, occupied most other spaces. There was much activity around the ships. Carts pulled by cantankerous animals, like peracs but with bobbed horns spreading sideways from above their eyes, were moving between the ships and along the causeway. People loading or unloading the vessels were everywhere. He could see scent users but they were in the minority. The main workers were men, poorly dressed in one-piece, ochre-coloured clothing tied around the waist. They were barefooted with black hair, although Kyel noticed the odd person of lighter colouring. It was readily apparent they were slaves or servants from a mix of races.

Kyel looked into the sky, seeing thick and oily odours forming a blanket about mast high, too intertwined to even decipher. Beyond stretched a conglomeration of buildings eventually giving way to a vast brown land where only the broad swathe of a river broke the monotony

Their ship continued with just a topsail providing the impetus from the inshore morning breeze until Kyel could see the individual buildings, aged brown and grey stone structures jumbled across the backdrop of the port, red-tiled roofing dominating. A sailor at the bow threw a length of rope to several fellows lounging against the bollards. They snapped to work and quickly tied the vessel to the pier.

He felt the delicate waft of Nefaria's essence as she came beside him.

"Your first taste of Sutan, Kyel?"

He nodded and gripped the rail, still affected by the revelations in her journal.

"We will have to stay on board while the cargo is unloaded," she said.

Kyel could see her profile out of the corner of his eye as she looked over the warehouses; he admired the small nose, determined chin and wide forehead with her short, dark hair ruffling in the breeze. When she leant over the rail to watch the unloading, he felt he could take her small waist and make her want him, but the moment quickly passed.

"Nefaria," he asked, "where are we going once we land? Jakus wouldn't say."

"My Lord is somewhat busy at the moment," she said, turning to face him. "There are some big issues underway and if he'd wanted you to know he would have told you."

"Oh, I know that his brothers are a problem for him, especially Brastus, but…"

"How!" Nefaria's hand flew to her mouth. "How do you know about them?"

"I…I…just heard talk."

"Ah," she said, leaning closer. "Just don't mention their names, as Jakus is not a forgiving man where his brothers are concerned."

Kyel's jaw closed with a snap. He stared, unseeing, at the workers moving bales from the ship, while the slop of muddied water next to the ship's hull sounded clearly.

They remained at the rail until the captain called them.

"The Shad left orders that once the unloading was completed you were to follow him, bringing what you need," said Tibitis. "I'll have one of the men accompany you."

"Come on, Kyel," said Nefaria, "we'll just pick up my writing materials and be on our way."

"Writing materials?"

"You'll see," Nefaria said over her shoulder.

Once they left the gangway, the bustle of the docks made him raise a scent shield around himself. At one stage when he bumped into one of the draught animals and sought to avoid its horns, the handler yelled at him.

"Stay with me!" Nefaria hissed. "It won't do to be attracting attention."

Kyel slowly calmed down while relaxing his shield He noticed her scents of concern and was about to ask why when he saw scent masters, strolling in pairs through the crowds, their dark clothing different to the more subdued colours worn by the servants and traders. They seemed at home, but a space was left around them as they moved through the people.

"Don't look around," warned Nefaria, "just keep your head down and walk with me, like we are close companions."

"Why?" Kyel couldn't help asking.

"There's a lot of unrest at the moment. We can't tell whose side they're working for so it's best not be noticed or appear out of the ordinary. The sooner we're off the docks and into the business area, the better."

The sailor leading them looked around and frowned before continuing along the main thoroughfare. He turned at a narrower, quieter street where there were no scent masters and few people. The buildings lining the cobbled road were mainly of wood, interspersed with occasional stone facades. A number had their shutters open, taking advantage of the sea breeze despite a chill in the air.

Kyel staggered as his boot hit an uneven stone and he felt he was still on the ship. His stomach grumbled.

"Can we eat soon, Nefaria?"

"Mmm," she nodded as she looked along the street. "I've rarely been in Southern Port, but I think it's a tavern we're going to."

"We could ask our guide," he said.

"No, I think that's the building ahead of us. Jakus will want us there now."

The structure was of a darker wood than those around it, as if it had absorbed years of grime. A distinct scent hovered around its door, reminding Kyel of the tavern in his hometown of Lesslas. A wave of longing rushed through him. He wondered about his family and how Anyar was growing.

"In here, if you will," invited the sailor, opening the door.

Kyel allowed Nefaria to enter first, feeling the brush of her travelling cloak against his hand. He followed her into a dark entrance, the odours of stale beer and wine rushing out to envelop him. He noticed the creak of the floorboards as he extended his senses, pushing through the overlapping smells of the building.

He gasped as it stung his nose, singing along his nerves, exploding into recognition, and building an unwanted euphoria in his memories. *Magnesa, in quantity;* he shivered at the thought.

Kyel bumped into Nefaria as she hesitated in the long, gloomy corridor lit by only two lanterns. "You feel it too?" he whispered.

"Yes," she said quietly, "and my Lord is here, with others, many survivors from the troubles in Ean. You would also have noticed the guards in the alcove?"

Damn, he silently admonished himself, *I should have picked that up. Fine scent master I'll be.* "I suppose he'll know we're here by now?"

"Certainly," she murmured. "The last years in Sutan have made him even more wary than before, and you wouldn't have got far if you'd been unwelcome."

They entered a room thick with visible scent traces from a multitude of people sitting at four large, rectangular tables. The walls were lined with a pale panelling extending from the wooden floor to the low-beamed ceiling; lanterns on regularly spaced sconces lit the room. A long, black wooden counter was inset into one wall, behind which were stacked kegs and clay flagons; an open door led away into a darkened space. A brick fireplace containing red coals occupied another wall.

Jakus, his back to the fire, pointed to a spare seat nearby without taking his attention from the people sitting around him.

Nefaria nodded towards a low stool jammed in the corner before going over to Jakus. Kyel kept his head down as he skirted the people to the stool, his grumbling stomach forgotten as he felt the pressure of the occupants of the room—they were scent masters of varying capability.

These were confident men and women, he decided, dressed in more colours than he had seen so far, ranging from deep purple to dark greens and blues; one woman even wore a yellow tunic with matching leggings trimmed with red. He glanced to the travel coats hanging near the door, noticing that they were less flamboyant, more of the innocuous browns and greys. Most of the people had close-cropped hair, many with a tinge of grey, although Kyel was surprised to notice several men sitting together had short beards, which wasn't normal in scent masters. Cups containing wine and a few plates with the remnants of meat and bread were scattered across the tables, but most obvious was the evidence of recent magnesa use.

Jakus sat where he had a clear view of each table, a dominant dark scent cloud hovering above his head. Kyel could see the deference shown to Jakus and how he was controlling the conversation, recognising there was little hope it would end soon. He wriggled into a more comfortable position on the stool, trying not to think of his missed meal. He noticed Nefaria was already writing on parchment in her large wood-covered folder.

He soon realised the people in the room were representatives of various regions within Sutan. He had only a rudimentary knowledge of the country picked up on the voyage and understood the capital was Sutaria, situated several days' journey north on the river he had seen from the ship. Further north still were marshlands and the forbidding steppe country. The river marked the edge of the extensive deserts spreading eastwards, while to the west was another large river on which the city of Hestria was located. Both rivers wound their way from a vast plateau in the north-west which surmounted a rough, untamed country of ravines and gorges spreading south and south-west to the sea.

Kyel found it difficult to place where the people were from but thought Hestria, Sutaria, the far northern steppes and the coastal ports of Southern Port and Semplar were represented.

He noticed various individuals were reporting on disputes and small disturbances across the country, with Nefaria writing it down. Jakus appeared pleased as each speaker added their details.

Kyel's ears pricked up when the colourful woman with a flamboyant scent cloud stood to speak.

"I think, after having heard what everyone has said, the plan is working, and with the opportunities your magnesa presents, we can finally see some unexpected hope in a land where the rule by your family has been oppressive, to say the least"—her eyes flashed from under short, reddish hair—"and I make no apology for saying that." Several others nodded, while Jakus appeared relaxed.

"Go on, Sharna," he said.

"We wouldn't be here if we didn't have issues with the rule, particularly Brastus. While you have been isolated in Hestria, he has been raping the country to provide for his armies both here and in the overseas campaigns. Now Ean is said to be his ambition, his jewel in the crown."

"My crown," muttered Jakus, his face darkening. "What do you say, Festern?"

A tall, heavily built man in dark brown tunic and black trousers stood. His close-cropped hair was peppered grey while his short beard stood out against his tanned face. "Brastus's reach is long, even in the Steppes," he growled. "We have provided many fighters for his wars, yet he still bleeds us dry. This latest push for Ean is overstepping his authority. It rightfully belongs to you, and those of us who have had to leave the land where we had many links. If, as we've just experienced, this magnesa is the weapon to give us the edge then I, for one"—he looked at the bearded men on each side of him—"will support you, Jakus."

"My thanks for your words, Festern, Sharna," said Jakus, standing and leaning on the tabletop. He looked slowly around the room, his eyes flicking to Kyel sitting quietly in the corner. "Do any of you disagree with those sentiments?"

Even from where he sat Kyel could feel an increase in the pressure of the scents, as if the scent masters feared that Jakus was personally inspecting the truth in each person's scent aura and didn't want to be found lacking. He noticed flares of nervousness escape from several people, especially the other woman in the room, a pleasant-faced, slim woman in sombre colours.

"What do you think, Poegna?" Jakus asked. "For you have a difficult role to play."

"Uh, Jakus," she said hesitantly, "being situated in Sutaria, with estates adjoining your brother Faltis, does make my position in supporting you somewhat precarious. Both your brothers are astute and of suspicious mind. But I am pleased to inform you that things are looking more promising of late. Could I ask we go over this in more detail later?" She sat back, her scents showing the dull green of anxiety, with a flicker of yellow.

"Hmm." Jakus watched her for a long moment, until she shuffled uneasily on her seat. "If you will stay afterwards."

She nodded.

"I notice a few of you are uncertain how we are progressing, but let me assure you the fomenting of unrest within Sutan should not only continue but increase, limiting damage to property, of course.

"My destiny," he said forcefully, "is to assume my rightful place as leader of Sutan and Ean. This requires seizing the sources of magnesa in Rolan by our expeditionary force. We therefore need to keep my brothers' eyes firmly distracted by the internal struggles rather than focussed towards Ean. What I am proposing will lead to the attainment of all our goals and reward those who support me. My way will ensure a return to a world ruled by those with our interests at heart. But we will need to be discreet; we will need to not let word of our intent leak out. And."—his eyes scanned the room—"believe me, I would know.

"My own abilities are so well developed that no mind is restricted to me. Death is the only way to escape my will, as I"—Jakus slowly scanned the faces before him—"am sure my brothers' interests will learn.

"It is time to return to your homes and continue the operation." Jakus shifted and rubbed his back. "We will meet here in nine days' time and communicate only by word of mouth or letter, not scent messages, lest they fall into unfriendly hands. I expect your forces to gather at Hestria over the next while, but discretion is vital, as your lives will depend on it.

"Good fortune and remember your oaths. And the rewards."

Kyel, Nefaria and Poegna remained seated while the room had emptied.

"Now Nefaria, I trust you have a record of what was said as we need to keep apprised of where we have activity to keep my brothers occupied. Next, we must travel to Sutaria and pay my respects to Father," he said amiably. "It wouldn't do to have him, or my brothers, think that I am merely sitting out time in Hestria while others prepare to retake my Ean.

"So, young Kyel, why don't we have the tavern keeper get you a meal? No doubt you are hungry. Yes, you too, Nefaria."

Jakus turned and looked at Poegna. "Lady, would you sit with me by the fire?"

"I wonder what that's about," Kyel whispered.

Nefaria shook her head and pushed him through the door.

"Please," said Jakus, enveloping Poegna in encouraging scents, "tell me how our little project is developing, or should I say how my nephew, young Bilternus is performing."

"Jakus"—Poegna looked around the room before leaning forward—"I think we may have our insider. I have carefully laid the groundwork and there is no love lost between Bilternus and his father, your brother Faltis. I believe the right approach will see him firmly on our side."

"That is pleasing," he said, taking her hand. "I think it is time to make that approach. Arrange for him to be at your estates the day after your return. I will meet him then." Jakus smiled into her eyes. "I will trust your discretion in this."

Chapter Twenty-Two

"Shad," a tall man in a dark brown cloak addressed the Sutanite leader emerging from the tavern, "all is clear. We're travelling to the compound?"

Jakus gave a curt nod as he pushed past, Poegna following. "Keep the unit spread out, Kast. Arrange escort for Nefaria and the Eanite."

He strode down the street towards the main arterial road leading from the wharves, the hooded woman hurrying beside him as scent masters emerged from the side streets and gaps between the buildings to follow.

Dusk had fallen, obscuring normally visible scent traces, the way lit by lanterns set high on regularly spaced wooden poles.

"Keep up, Kyel," hissed Nefaria.

"Where are we going? And with this...army?"

"You'll see," she said, grabbing his elbow. "My Lord has a compound in Southern Port, large enough to discreetly hold many people."

"So are these scent masters coming as well?"

"Of course," said Nefaria. "Did you expect it's safe for Jakus to walk here? Didn't you listen? My Lord is in the middle of a campaign to ensure he can regain his influence in Sutan and prevent his brothers from usurping Ean.

"You know about his brothers, don't you, Kyel?"

"Not really. What are they like?"

"Well, Faltis, the youngest, is cruel but weak..." She looked around, then leant closer, "but Brastus, he is not only cruel, but powerful. You wouldn't want him ruling Ean. And of course there's Vitaris, my Lord's father. His power over his sons is waning, but he's still a force in Sutan."

"So Jakus has all of them against him," said Kyel. "With that and what we heard, there's some trouble going on in Sutan. Hope we don't get caught up in it. What about elsewhere, outside the country?"

They crossed an intersection to move into an area of wider streets and low, extensive buildings. Pools of light pushed back the shadows except where dark clumps of trees and bushes grew. The sea breeze whispered through their branches, creating moving edges to the ominous pools of blackness.

Kyel shivered, imagining hidden figures watching them pass, waiting for an opportunity. He almost didn't hear Nefaria continue.

"Sutan isn't a peaceful place, and part of what they do best is be aggressive, make war. Ean's not the only country to suffer under their rule. Others, most of which you've probably never heard, are fighting to prevent Sutan taking them over. Tenstria is one—that's where Targas comes from, doesn't he?"

"Yes…he does…" Kyel noticed the road narrowing into a dark section of buildings spreading back against black thickets of vegetation covering a low bank.

"And there's several, expeditionary-style forces attacking countries a great distance away, far to the south. It's a long sail, but apparently rewarding enough to attract Vitaris's attention."

"Are we near Jakus's compound now?"

"Quiet," said Nefaria. "We'll talk more later."

The breeze had dropped, leaving a vague chill in the air, the mournful *grunk, grunk* of a lizard, and water trickling nearby the only noises breaking the silence.

They continued walking, senses on high alert. Tension seemed to build around them.

A scent master in front of them hissed as a strong scent command broke across them and they froze. Minute motes of magnesa came to Kyel's nostrils, telling him Jakus was preparing for action.

He crouched to build a scent shield, taking odours from around him and his olfactory memories, linking the bonds, tightening them, preparing for any attack in this unknown land. He could see the shadowy figures of scent masters around him, heads cocked, absorbing scents.

Kyel felt Nefaria leaning into him, her scents bonding into his in a strange way. He briefly wondered whether his newly taught skills were responsible for this. Suddenly his attention was snatched away.

A cascade of light rippled from the vegetation on the bank and along the watercourse. With it came crashing thumps and several of the dark figures around him staggered or fell. Kyel shuddered as something hard clipped the side of his shield His immediate worry was that Nefaria had been hit—he could feel her crouch by his feet as the noise grew.

Wood splintered and the thickets on the bank exploded into shreds, disappearing against the last remnants of twilight. The screams of wounded resounded through the repetitive thumps of scent bolts.

Kyel flattened against the ground with Nefaria, eyes wide, breathing in any smells that weren't filtered out. His stomach suddenly twisted with the enormity of what was happening, and all he could do was wait it out and hope Jakus would be able to deal with it.

"Move!" hissed Nefaria. "Into that ditch!"

He followed her in a sideways motion, edging off the road surface and into a gutter. A flicker of movement, black on black, gave a second of warning before he was enveloped by a smothering weight. Kyel rolled with it but in his fear his concentration lapsed, and he felt the bonds of his shield unravelling. The gleam of a long blade coming towards his stomach galvanised him and he twisted, shoving with his legs, flinging the weight away.

Kyel jumped to his feet, shielding in tatters, in time to meet the slash of the blade across his palm. He yelped, backing away, at the same time pushing at the large man attacking him. Without thinking, he solidified odour motes in the air, automatically recalling Targas's instructions on how to keep them suspended.

A smattering of scent bolts sizzled past, deflected by the solid push of bonded odour. He heaved harder across the broadness of the man's chest, lifting him off the ground. The knife struck Kyel on the leg without penetrating. Despite the noise around him he kept lifting, holding the solid scent bonds, blocking the man's air. The attacker's legs flailed, hands held to his throat.

A sudden scream broke through his concentration, and he let go. As the man fell with a crash, Kyel swung around to see Nefaria fighting a dark figure. He thumped a scent bolt directly into her attacker's back.

Nefaria heaved the body away and staggered to her feet. She grasped Kyel's shoulders, gasping with the effort. "Ah..." she puffed. "J...just came from nowhere. Couldn't keep him off."

"Is...is he dead?"

"Ah..." She looked down at the still body. "Yes, I think so, though yours is not."

He followed her gaze and saw the man lying groaning in the road.

"Oh," he said.

"I think we're right now. I'm not sure how everyone else is. I'll have to find my Lord." She began to move off. "Stay there, Kyel. I'll see what's happened."

Kyel sank to his haunches, his heart still racing, his head splitting from the effort and his stomach churning. The man lying nearby gave a final gasp and lay still.

He had killed someone.

It was quiet. He heard an occasional groan and saw people moving, but he seemed to be in a pocket of calm, the world going by him. He wanted to throw up, felt the churning in his stomach, but he held it at bay. Inside his own skull, he heard the words, incredulous but with an unexpected matter-of-factness: *I've killed someone.*

He felt a touch on his shoulder and almost jumped.

"Kyel," came Nefaria's soft voice, "come. Jakus wants you."

Dark blood streaked Jakus's thin face and his cloak was ripped.

"Report!" he snapped, eyes wandering across the litter of bodies and injured lying on the road and amongst the shadows of broken vegetation.

"I was attacked by someone," began Kyel nervously.

"I know that! What happened?"

Kyel related the events as he saw them, and what he had done to save himself and Nefaria. Jakus appeared to half listen as he continued scanning the area and buildings around him.

"Why did they target you then, hmm?" Jakus leant over, forcing Kyel to step back.

"I, ah, don't know," he said.

"You have some future use…for me. But for anyone else…?" Jakus swung around. "Kast, we'll head to the compound. Bring any prisoners that we can interrogate. The rest, dump in the watercourse for the scartha."

"What does he mean, *future use*, Nefaria?" asked Kyel as they started off. "What plans does he have? And what are scartha?"

"W…what?" she asked, eyes on Jakus's back. "Let's get to the compound now."

Kyel looked across the dark waters to their right, hearing the splash as bodies were dumped in. A much louder splash further off made him jump and seek Nefaria's side.

"Don't worry. It's scartha coming in." Her hand held his shoulder. "You'll be safe on the road. Come on."

"What do they look like?"

"Scartha?" Nefaria hesitated. "Huge, scaly, with teeth. Like those big lizards in Ean but they live around water."

The screaming began as guardsmen and scent masters ruthlessly tossed the remaining captives into the river. Their pleas and cries tore into Kyel's mind as he ducked his head and hurried after Nefaria.

Jakus's compound was set back from the road across flat, featureless ground. The long grey stone building had a low profile with small narrow windows set into the thick walls. The compound squatted in the darkness like some large creature waiting for prey.

The troop of scent masters and guardsmen straggled across the stony ground, some supporting others, with several on makeshift stretchers. A strong scent of tension filled the air as they sought safety after the dangers of the night.

"The sooner inside the better," whispered Nefaria. "It's too dark. Too quiet."

Her words shivered down Kyel's back as he remembered the pleasure of home and the fire, and the feeling of safety. Now he was in a foreign land, having survived an attempt on his life, with an uncertain future. Not for the first time, he wished he hadn't been so strong-willed to search for a dream. His face tightened as he looked at the woman next to him.

"Would you and Kyel assist with the wounded, my lady?" Kast asked Nefaria as they went through a narrow doorway into the building.

She nodded and, taking Kyel's hand, guided him along a narrow, dimly lit corridor, following the stretcher bearers.

They entered a narrow room. Camp beds were lined along each side, allowing only a restricted walking space between. Some of the beds were already occupied and several people in light blue robes were attending. Scents of pain and blood competed with an aroma of herbs.

Nefaria sent Kyel to fetch bandages and water for the first patient, a young scent master who'd been hit by a scent bolt. When he returned, he stared at the open wound, the edges of the skin peeling away, blood covering the white skin from chest to groin and struggling to coagulate. The groans of other patients, the thickness of the odours around him, only made it worse. The patient shuddered uncontrollably.

"Help, damn you!" growled Nefaria, as she tried to staunch the bleeding. "Try some soporific scents, a relaxant, anything. I can't work with this constant movement."

"Uh." Kyel had lost focus and his ability to delve into his scent memories as the contrast of red blood on white skin overwhelmed him. A realisation was pressing into his mind amidst the confusion in the room as he looked past the wound to the body before him. *It's a woman. Not a man, but a woman.*

"Kyel!"

He shook his head, squashing down his thoughts, and began drawing on his scent memories. A drift of odour containing the essences of sleep flowed over the body of the scent master, soon causing a noticeable lessening of the thrashing.

"More! At her head, not at me. Then help with the binding of the wound," ordered Nefaria.

Kyel concentrated the scents for a moment or two and then moved closer, next to Nefaria. He could see the movement of the bloody internal organs and Nefaria's efforts to seal the wound. The odours were thick enough to easily begin bonding together, like the shield he had used during the attack. He drifted it down onto the wound. Nefaria lifted her hands as it fell into the opening.

"Help me close this hole in the intestine," she ordered. "That's right. Now we'll seal the wound with thread. More permanent than scent bonds."

By the time they had finished he was exhausted and felt like washing.

"Don't even think of going somewhere else," said Nefaria, "we still have others to see to."

"I wasn't..." he began when he saw a guardsman coming towards them.

"Jakus wants you. Now!" he ordered, looking at Kyel.

"But I…" He glanced at Nefaria.

"No, you go. I'll make do," she said.

"If that's what you want," Kyel muttered as he followed the man.

They moved down a series of steps dimly lit by flickering lamps on the rough walls. It was a momentary relief to leave the wounded and retreat to the quiet, odour-free atmosphere. The guardsman pushed open a wooden door and went in. Kyel followed.

He saw two dark-clad people held to a wall by iron manacles before noticing Jakus.

"Just in time," Jakus snapped. "This filth is about to die on me." He reached over and gripped the slack jaw of a thin-faced man sagging in the restraints, wrenching his head to face Kyel.

"What do you know of this youth?" he hissed. The man's eyes focussed briefly, before his head dropped to his chest.

A dark scent spike coalesced from Jakus's mouth and penetrated the man's nostril. His head jerked up, eyes widened as he gave a gasp of pain. The scent master leant forward, palms pressed on the wall either side of him as he scoured the scent memories of the prisoner.

The man stiffened, tendons cord-like in his neck, then his body slumped, held up only by the iron manacles.

"Blast, an underling!" Jakus cursed. "Little use.

"And you?" He turned to the remaining prisoner. "Are you going to give me trouble?"

The man pulled back, face white, head turned away.

Jakus looked around and smiled at Kyel's expression. "No, it isn't pretty, but it's one of the things you do if you're a leader. Accessing scent memories is an almost infallible way to gain information otherwise denied you, and there are other benefits as well, particularly if the subject is young."

Kyel froze, trying to supress a shudder.

Jakus's mouth thinned, eyes hooded. "Step closer, let him take a good look at you."

The prisoner's feet suddenly drummed on the hard clay floor, his face turning a bright red, foam pouring from his nose and mouth.

"No!" Jakus screeched, and grabbed the man's shoulders, "No. You fool. You cowardly fool!" He leant forwards, exuding a dark spike of scent, and began to work it through the foam-covered nostrils.

Kyel moved back from the scene in front of him. The body of the prisoner was spasming, Jakus trying to hold him steady while working his scent magic on him. Kyel made it to the door and stopped, afraid to leave, yet afraid to stay.

The prisoner's body collapsed, slipping out of Jakus's grip.

"Arrgh!" he screamed, and drove a scent bolt into the man's head, exploding it in a bloody spray. Kyel crouched down, arms over his face.

Only the sound of Jakus's harsh breathing broke the silence. He kicked at the body slumped against the wall, arms pulled high by the restraints, before walking towards Kyel.

Kyel peeked at the dark-robed figure before him, and at Jakus's grim face.

"Not a good example of control for you, boy," Jakus shook his head. "And a prisoner who is talented enough to take his own life rather than face interrogation. It raises the question, doesn't it?" He sank to his haunches to look into Kyel's face. "What was so important that he didn't want me to know? Was it loyalty to his master, my brother Faltis? Or was it something else?" Jakus leant in until his nose just touched Kyel's. "Was it something that I brought from Ean? Was that something *you?*"

K yel was shaken by the devastating ambush, Jakus's ruthless interrogation of the prisoners and the Sutanite leader's conviction Kyel was a target for the forces belonging to his brother, Faltis.

Why would *he* be important enough to be a focus of the enemy's attack? No one would have been aware of him arriving in Sutan until very recently, and he had limited powers and little worth to Jakus.

No, he thought, shaking his head, *Jakus is paranoid, wanting to link me with the attack. I'm just a nobody in the scheme of things. Just a nobody.*

He looked over the sleeping men scattered across the large room from where he sat on his thin mattress against a wall. *Unless he's right,* Kyel shuddered, remembering the prisoner dying in front of him.

Chapter Twenty-Three

"You are a fool, Faltis, the least of my sons," growled Vitaris, supreme ruler of Sutan. "Did you think to impress me by attacking Jakus? Did you think he would be unprepared? You don't know your brother, you fool.

"Wait." He held up his hand before Faltis could answer. "Xerina!" Vitaris's voice echoed in the vast hall where huge, carved columns supported the dim roof high above and wide perac-wool rugs spread across the grey slate floor relieved the monotony of the sandstone walls. Vitaris, a large man with stooped shoulders and shaven head pushed back into his carved wood chair with padded arms, stretching the purple and gold robe that he wore. He drummed long fingers on the dark-wood table before him as he looked to a distant shadowed side door.

Faltis, tall and thin, shifted from one leg to the other, lips tight in his hollowed face, dark eyes glittering and fists clenched against his sides. He looked like a paler imitation of his brother, Jakus, with less of the presence of the former ruler of Ean.

"Where is that woman?" Vitaris flicked a hand towards one of the shadowy figures standing in the alcoves along the walls before turning to his son. "While we wait for Xerina to be fetched, give me your explanation for causing yet another rift between my sons. I am only glad that Brastus is sorting out our Tenstria campaign; otherwise he would no doubt be standing here with you. I would not trust any of you to behave when there's an opportunity like Ean waiting.

"Well? Answer." Vitaris's eyebrows lifted into a lined forehead.

"Wait for that ancient soothsayer of yours if you want an answer," said Faltis, inwardly wincing at the high pitch of his voice. "I only acted in response to her foretelling, that is all. In your best interests, I might add."

"My best interests, hmm." Vitaris's scent aura took on a dark aspect, causing Faltis to stiffen. He knew that his father was still a formidable opponent, and one to be wary of.

"And so the chance to remove your brother from the race didn't occur to you as well?" He smiled up at his son's tight face. "Although I'm beginning to think you may have some of the necessary attributes to rule, despite my earlier misgivings."

A clatter in the back of the hall caught their attention. Soon the click of a stick and shuffle of feet were heard as the bent shape of Xerina hobbled towards them. Faltis's lip curled, waiting for the wheeze of the soothsayer's voice, knowing the reliance his father put on the words of the old woman.

"Y…you requested my presence, Shada?" puffed Xerina.

"What have you said to cause my son to attack Jakus on his return from Ean? Which of your foretellings said he should do this?"

"Shada?" The old woman straightened her worn grey robe as she lifted her head. "Am I to understand Faltis has acted upon something I have said? Or is he merely interpreting one of my foretellings to suit his ambition?"

"Xerina," said Vitaris, "I am asking whether your latest foretelling regarding Jakus carrying the possible seeds for the destruction of Sutan from Ean, is a prediction worthy of note, whether it has the remotest chance of occurring through his auspices."

"My Lord Vitaris, I am in the unenviable position of receiving foretellings that come to me on the scent winds, or Knowings occurring to one of my ilk. By their very nature they are general, uncertain things depending on interpretation.

"Since my removal from the land of my birth to Sutan I have served as advisor to your family. Over my lifetime of servitude I have been responsible for many foretellings that have proven of benefit, and in all this time I have never had such a Knowing as this. In fact, it was so vague, so much into the future that I hesitated to advise you of it, my Lord Vitaris." Xerina paused, shifted her weight as she leant on her stick and looked directly into Faltis's eyes.

"But my duty came first, and I told of the potential of the Knowing, not thinking your son would act upon it."

"Why would you say it then, you old crone?" said Faltis forcefully. "Why would you say an Eanite was coming to destroy Sutan? My spies told me Jakus had brought a youth who had been involved with his debacle in Ean, a youth closely associated with the leader of that rebellion.

"So I acted, in my father's best interests, to snuff out a possible threat to our land. So what?"

Xerina gave Faltis a long stare before looking back to Vitaris. "My Lord, did you call me to argue the point with your unrepentant son, or to request further interpretation of the Knowing?"

Faltis opened his mouth, but his father silenced him with a look. "Xerina, it is apparent I require more work on this Knowing of yours. I need to understand whether this young Eanite is a danger to Sutan. And if we have anything to fear from him or his associates, and when.

"And Faltis, you may soon meet and assess this youth yourself. Jakus will be with us within the next few days, and you'll be able to explain your position to your brother then."

Faltis stiffened, glared at his father and stamped off through the side door.

"Xerina, you may go, and"—Vitaris stood to tower over the diminutive woman—"don't keep me waiting too long."

"My Lord." She gave a perfunctory bow of her head and turned to hobble back to the doorway.

As the sound of her steps faded, Vitaris waved his arm at a large figure standing silently against a wall. The man stepped forward into the light and removed his hood.

"Shada," his voice rumbled, dark eyes looking from under a bony brow ridge, his shaven face and scalp showing a few age lines.

"You have been witness to the discussions, Dronthis?"

The man nodded.

"You will undertake the necessary preparations for my son's visit. We must be ready for a certain display of bravado from Jakus," said Vitaris. "Knowing him, I expect he will be more than a little upset."

"I thought Jakus—ah, the Shad—wanted to get to Sutaria?" Kyel asked the tall scent master next to him as they sat eating their early meal at the long table in the internal courtyard.

Kast slowly mopped gravy off his plate with a chunk of bread before looking at him. "In a hurry to go, are you?"

"Uh, no…" Kyel hesitated under the scrutiny of Jakus's commander. "I…I didn't think the Shad would be delaying after last night."

"Good point," Kast nodded, "but our Shad has his reasons which in this case should not be too hard to work out." He looked at Kyel's plate. "Enjoying the meat?"

"What do you mean?" Kyel frowned down at the scattered remnants of his meal. "It had an unusual flavour."

"Your first taste of scartha, then?"

"That!" He pushed his plate away. "That was a scartha? But they eat people."

"Yes, they do, but they provide a lot of meat, too, when you can kill one. Anyway, I have much to do now the reinforcements are arriving, young Kyel." Kast stood up and joined the general exodus of people leaving the courtyard.

Kyel sat for a moment before leaving the table to find Nefaria.

His route took him around the back of the compound and past a line of dark-robed scent masters, and guardsmen dressed in tunics of lighter grey and brown. They were occupying a wide, gravelled area bordered by a perimeter of scrubby bushes and trees. Kyel saw Kast and Jakus with a group of people, and noticing Nefaria's scent trace amongst them, decided to keep out of their way.

He walked along the back of the sleeping quarters until he smelt a delicious aroma of baking bread coming from a separate building. He entered through a wide doorway into the cooking area, standing against a wall as a sweating baker hurried past with a tray of hot buns, then several serving girls rushed by carrying dirty plates towards a large, steaming sink amongst racks of drying dishes. He let the moment wash over him, half closing his eyes in the warmth of the room.

"Cer"—a tug on his sleeve made him look down into a smiling face—"Cook asks if you'd like somethin' to eat."

He recognised a serving girl from earlier as she handed him a bun. "Uh, thanks," he smiled, "it might help to get rid of the taste of scartha."

"Scartha?" she queried. "Didn't you like it?"

"Not really. Never had it before."

"You're from Ean?"

"How do you know I'm from Ean?"

The blue eyes smiled at him. "It's the talk of the compound, Cer. It's not often that a handsome man with a pleasing accent comes here."

Kyel blushed. "Uh, you needn't call me *Cer*, I'm Kyel. And you are…?"

"Sencia. I've gotta go," she said, turning away. "Maybe we could meet later? I have a break before midday."

"Yes, I'd like that," he said, "but I better go, too." He smiled to himself as he saw Sencia wipe her hands on her long apron before talking with an older woman who had called her. *Handsome, huh? It's the first time anyone's been nice to me since I arrived here.*

"Hisst!"

Kyel lifted his head from where he was resting on his sleeping mat to see Sencia beckoning him from the doorway. He rose to his feet and hurried over.

She reached out a small hand and took his, leading him down a long corridor. Kyel began to blush as he saw her strong red and orange scents of desire. They took several turns and ended up at dead end where two doors were set in the walls on both sides.

"Quick, Kyel," she said, opening a door, "in here."

He followed her into a small room lit by a slit high on the wall. He could see a wooden bed on one side and a chair and small table on the other. Sencia reached behind him and closed the door.

"What?" He shook his head, confused by her flurry of scents. "Er, is this your room?"

"I've heard that you'll be leaving for Sutaria and there's little time." Her eyes were large in the poor light. "And…and I thought you might like…me."

"Oh." Kyel tilted his head, feeling a warm reaction throughout his body.

"Yes, I…I'll be leaving soon. And d…do you mean what I think?"

"Please"—she took both his hands, yellow scents joining the orange and red—"you look so lonely and far from home. I thought you might like some comfort."

"I…" Kyel could feel the pressure of Sencia's grip and a slight trickle of sweat running down his neck, his body reacting to the scents of this pretty woman. "I really should go back. Someone will be looking for me."

"No Kyel, no one will notice if you're gone for a little while. They're all still out on the marshalling ground. Besides, I think you like me?" She let go Kyel's hands, stepped back and pushed one side of her smock over a shoulder, and then the other. The garment slithered to the ground.

Kyel's mouth fell open at the sight of the naked woman in front of him. His eyes travelled down her shadowed form, taking in the dark-nippled breasts, the slightly rounded stomach and the darker shadow at the top of her thighs. She smiled and stepped forward, lifting his shirt before he could think. As it moved over his head he reacted, grabbing at his pants before Sencia's hands could begin on them.

"Come on," she whispered, "I can see your need. Please." Her hands pushed past to his trousers.

He gasped as the material snagged on his erection. "I don't think…"

"Come on, Kyel." Her hands ran down his flanks as she pushed the trousers to the floor. "Let me, please." Sencia rubbed against him before taking his hand and leading him to the bed. "Sit, here," she ordered, pushing him back until his legs hit the side.

"Now…" She stood in front and took hold of his head. Her breasts pushed into Kyel's face and his hands automatically took hold of her naked waist before slipping down across her smooth buttocks.

"Ah," he groaned.

"Yes," Sencia said as she straddled his body and eased him back on the bed, "just let me do this for you. We have plenty of time."

Kyel gasped as he felt her softness on him, and a hand grasp his erection to push it into a warm, moist place. He focussed on the exciting sensations her body was giving him, forgetting anything else, holding onto her firm waist with his hands, letting himself go with the movement of their bodies and revelling in the pleasure it gave. The rhythm grew in a rush until he felt his body explode, before Sencia fell forward across his body and sought his mouth with her own.

Soft lips pressed on his. "You'll have to go." Her breath tickled his ear. "They'll be leaving soon and seeking you."

Kyel ran a hand across the smoothness of her bottom and sighed as his body reacted.

"No, we don't have time." Sencia lifted herself off him and stood up. "Although I wish we did. Maybe, on your return, you beautiful man?" She looked down his body before picking up his shirt and trousers. "Put these on. You'll have to be quick."

Kyel took his clothing and began to pull on his trousers, all the while watching Sencia standing unselfconsciously, arms under her breasts. She smiled as he pulled his shirt over his head and put her arms around him.

"Come back again, Kyel," she said kissing him. "Now go."

He clasped her to him briefly and then opened the door and slipped out of the room. He touched his lips as he walked along the corridor, his mind awhirl with his first sexual experience.

"Kyel, there you are," said Nefaria, coming through the doors from the marshalling yards. "We have time for a quick meal and then we are leaving."

"But it's only midday. Aren't we leaving at dawn next day?"

"No. The Shad has decided to make for the ford this night, then travel on to Sutaria next day."

"Oh." Kyel's face fell. "I'd hoped...we'd have more time here."

"Ah," Nefaria nodded as she reached him. "I think I know why. You really must control your scents, you know. Now come along."

Kyel clamped down hard on his betraying scents as he blushed. *Of all the people to catch me out, it had to be Nefaria. Now she'll dislike me.*

He followed her into the meal area, his mind in turmoil.

"Sit with me," said Nefaria. "You look exhausted."

Kyel sat, eyes down, hoping his scents wouldn't betray him.

"Would Cer like the meat dish, for strength?" a familiar voice said next to him.

His ears went red as he looked up into Sencia's smiling face.

"Hmm, I think I'll bring you some of the casserole. And you, Nefaria?"

"The same. And thank you, Sencia."

The girl nodded to Nefaria and grinned at Kyel.

"Truly my pleasure, Nefaria." She hurried away to the kitchens.

Kyel hid his face in his hands and groaned.

Nefaria smiled broadly.

Chapter Twenty-Four

A chill wind blew from the Steppes of Stone in the north of Sutan. In its drive southwards it picked up the dank smell of the marshlands and river, bringing an unpleasant combination of odours to Kyel's nose. However, he didn't care. Night had fallen and still they moved. Jakus had pushed the contingent of guardsmen and scent masters relentlessly in his efforts to reach the ford at the Grosten River. From there it was less than a day's journey to the city of Sutaria; his urgency caused by the attack the day before and his vulnerability in the open, between cities.

The euphoria of Kyel's experience with Sencia had quickly evaporated during the rush to Sutaria. He was jammed in a knot of scent masters, Jakus at their head, and the pace they set their peracs drove columns of dust into the air, caking his body and mind. His rear ached from the ungainly gait of the animals and he feared his exhausted perac would soon collapse, driving him into the hard gravel.

I t was some time before he was leaning against his pack in front of a large fire, eating a stew. Kyel didn't care if the meat was scartha, it was all he could do to keep his eyes open. Nefaria had gone to share a small tent with Jakus, while he was camping between two scent masters.

He thought briefly about her, then about Sencia and his first experience of lovemaking. Something had changed. He ought to have been upset by Nefaria leaving him to go to Jakus, but he wasn't. For once, she wasn't on his mind, her place taken by Sencia with her smiling eyes and...

His thoughts turned to the Sutanite leader, puzzling why he had been ignored since, according to Jakus, he was important. But that importance had not been evident after the attack, and he was consistently left to his own devices. Kyel had thought about offering to help with food preparation or cleaning, but everything seemed to be done so proficiently that he kept to himself.

He looked at his companions: Kast grunted occasionally when he tried to initiate conversation, and the scent master on the other side ignored him, although

Kyel knew he was aware. He rolled his blanket tightly around his body and lay back, seeking familiar stars from the dark skies of home. The wind blowing continuously over their heads dragged wisps of cloud that gradually thickened until most of the stars disappeared. He could see the odd sentry moving past the camp and thought he heard a clattering of rocks before he fell into an exhausted sleep.

The crunch of Kast's boots on the gravel woke him. Light filtered through thin grey clouds, and the wind had dropped. He got to his feet with a groan and followed several men moving away to relieve themselves behind a low scatter of scrub.

When he returned, he managed to grab a mug of hot tea and a slab of travel cake. The camp was astir, and Jakus was talking with Kast and several others. Kyel noticed Nefaria walking towards him and gave a tentative smile.

"I won't ask if you slept well, Kyel. A saddle blanket is not the most comfortable," she said, answering his smile.

"I'm very stiff but fine, thanks."

"We are leaving shortly," Nefaria said. "Jakus wants to reach Sutaria this day, so we'll be travelling quickly."

"I don't think I'm keen on Sutaria." Kyel shook his head.

"Really, Kyel?" She turned her head on one side. "Missing Sencia already?"

Kyel turned to hide his blush, fiddling with his gear until he heard Nefaria walk away.

Spits of rain fell as they formed into a column and moved at a quick trot across the ford and along a wide gravel road leading into the lowering grey of the sky. Sparsely vegetated hills gradually rose on each side to meet the rain-filled clouds, colourless in an already dull day.

Kyel remained near the back of the column, knowing that this day they would reach Sutaria, meet Jakus's father, and he would learn what they had in store for him.

He knew he was a pawn in Jakus's plans. Nothing he could do would stop what was going to happen, even with his improved scent powers. He would have to get through the time ahead and be ready to use any opportunity.

The rain grew heavier as the breeze strengthened, forcing Kyel to form a scent shield using the very motes of rain odour to prevent the water reaching him. At first it was relatively easy to keep dry, although the increasing wind made it more difficult, but when the perac began to slip on the muddy road his attention wavered. He soon gave up his efforts, his hooded coat and tunic becoming as wet as his surroundings.

This day was long and exhausting, with no slackening of the wind-driven rain, Jakus maintaining a punishing pace. Soon Kyel noticed buildings through the misty rain, grey and indistinct, but still Jakus showed no sign of slowing. Relief came when the column pulled into sparse shelter provided by some large, heavily leafed trees.

After grabbing cold tea and travel cake Kyel searched for Nefaria, but she was in a knot of people, all scent masters. He eased closer to catch a few words of conversation—it was plain they were discussing their entry into Sutaria. He noticed Jakus placing something in their hands and came nearer.

"Nefaria!" Jakus snapped, swinging around to face Kyel. "Take the Eanite with you when we ride out, behind my scent masters. I don't want him noticed by those we meet."

"Yes, my Lord," Nefaria nodded. "Kyel, come with me, now." She led him back to his perac.

"What was Jakus giving everyone?" he asked.

"I think you'd be able to work it out, Kyel. We're in the outskirts of the city and about to meet Vitaris. Jakus needs to present a powerful front after the events in Southern Port."

"Ah, but I thought he didn't want to waste any of his precious magnesa."

"Kyel," smiled Nefaria, "it sounds like you're disappointed."

"I suppose I am," he said. "It's like he never trusts me."

"Then it's to be hoped you'll have the opportunity to earn that trust." Her eyes hardened as she turned away.

Kyel stood for a moment before following Nefaria, realising his hopes of returning home depended on one person, himself. If he didn't work things out then he would never see his family again.

The opaque scent shield flickered scarlet and deep purple, reflecting off the clay walls of the buildings, turning their earthy hues a sickly colour. The menacing scent aura of Jakus and his scent masters preceded them along the cobbled street, compounded by audible crunching where their combined shields clipped the buildings.

People, their scents reflecting their awe, lined the route, keeping back against the sides of the houses and homes delineating the main thoroughfare into Sutaria. No danger appeared in the alleyways or from the rooftops of the blocky one and two storey buildings. The cobbles were slippery from the recent rain, piles of refuse and animal droppings littering their path.

Jakus kept them to a steady pace, eyes fixed firmly ahead, concentrating on holding the shield. Kyel knew magnesa had augmented the scent masters' odour control so that the populous had to be impressed. Their ride continued up the long road towards the dominant building situated on a small rise, with the palace's light sandstone walls contrasting against the deeper browns of its neighbours. Large gates stood open at the end of a white paved strip.

Kyel thought he recognised Vitaris in the group of people waiting. He wasn't the tallest but had a powerful scent aura even from a distance. He could see steel-grey colours showing resolve and determination. He detected a slight flash of red reflecting unease, quickly quashed. A taller man next to him, with the look of Jakus, had less control, his aura showing the dark red of alarm with yellow flickers of anxiety.

Ah, Kyel thought, *Faltis. He has reason to worry.*

Kyel shifted on his saddle, noticing the scent auras reflecting differing levels of control, but one was significantly different, softer yet with strength and a violet cast to it. A small, old woman stood to one side, dressed in subtle greys and blues. She seemed innocuous, yet her scent aura was strong.

She nodded slightly to him.

In a short while Jakus had led them through the gates and then dismounted. His scent masters and guardsmen quickly stood in a formidable block facing Vitaris and his troops. The air was filled with tension, shields tight. Jakus slowly extended his scent higher, expanding it until it covered the whole group. A slow pulsing of scarlet and purple hues added strength to the display, with each scent master contributing.

Vitaris's stern face suddenly relaxed and he dropped his shield. He stepped towards Jakus, open arms highlighting the gold and purple of his robe.

"Welcome, my son. Welcome," his voice boomed gruffly. "Come in. Let my people take care of your animals. It has been some time since we last met and there is a lot to discuss.'"

"Greetings to you, Father," answered Jakus, his voice tight. "Is it appropriate to lower my shields or should I prepare for another attack from my brother?"

"No. No. No. A significant misunderstanding. Nothing will happen here. You have my word."

"Your word? Hmm." Jakus rubbed his chin, stepping towards his father, his scent aura dissipating. "Your word has always been good, unlike the word of other members of the family."

Faltis gradually lowered his shield while glowering at his brother.

"Come. Enter. Refreshments await." Vitaris clasped Jakus's arm and turning, led him through the doorway.

Kyel followed, several rows back from Jakus, feeling the stare of the old woman and Jakus's brother. He kept a shield hard against his body, trying to remove its tell-tale outlines as he stepped between the white columns and into the vast entry hall. He gasped, looking up into the high ceiling criss-crossed with curved beams ascending from regularly spaced pillars along the sandstone walls. Torches flaming along the walls made the alcoves between the pillars dark and ominous.

A clatter of people and servants echoed in the huge space as they headed towards a long dark-wood table set with food and drink.

"Come, Kyel," said Nefaria, taking his arm. "You will soon meet the rest of my Lord's family. I doubt you would have expected that when you left your home in Ean, eh?" Her smile didn't reach her eyes.

"That's true, Nefaria," Kyel answered. "Many things have happened since we met up in Nebleth. It's just that it's taken me a while to adjust."

Nefaria hesitated before leading him to the table.

"So this is the Eanite, Jakus, the one causing so much fuss," said Vitaris, eyebrows raised. "Come closer!" he ordered.

Kyel stepped towards the supreme ruler of Sutan, legs feeling like jelly. Vitaris was a big man with more presence than either Jakus or Faltis, eyebrows dominating a lined face and wrinkled scalp. He stood a mere arm's length from the man, sweat breaking out across his forehead.

"He's just a stripling. I can't see why your foretelling would include such a one, do you, Xerina?" Vitaris said to the old woman standing near his shoulder. "And hardly worth your rash reaction, eh, Faltis?"

Faltis's thin face tightened, and he glared at his father. Kyel watched the woman shuffle forward. She placed a hand on Kyel's shoulder, bent her head on one side like an inquisitive lizard and looked into his face.

Her eyes were bright and assessing, and they seemed to peer into his soul.

"Hard to tell," Kyel heard her voice rustle. "I would need more time to understand whether the Knowing relates to this one, my Shada."

"So, we need more time?" Vitaris snapped his fingers. "Dronthis!"

"Yes, Shada." A man, taller than any around him, came to the ruler's side.

"Take him away so we can investigate this. With your permission, Jakus?" Vitaris looked at his son. "He will come to no harm."

Jakus glared at his father, then relaxed. "Any harm will be answerable. I have not finished with him."

Kyel was gripped by the huge man and pulled away before he had time to resist. He sought Nefaria's eyes as he was hustled away.

"Xerina, you have my leave to depart." Kyel heard Vitaris say. "Between you and Dronthis we will see whether this Eanite has the potential in him to influence the future of Sutan."

"Lizards' teeth," hissed Kyel as he realized there was nothing he could do, helpless in Dronthis's grasp, in the enemy's palace and with no options.

Chapter Twenty-Five

Sadir led them into her small cottage, wrinkling her nose at the stale odour. *I left in a hurry after Kyel, but Targas was still there. He could have left it tidy, but*...her thoughts trailed off as everyone began carrying their gear and supplies inside, their animals having been left at the tavern's stables.

The clomp of Anyar's footsteps and skittering of Vor's claws on the tiles brought a smile to her face. *Oh how I envy the resilience of youth.* Sadir dropped her bags in the corner and headed through to the back to collect water from the well. Targas busied himself setting the fire in the stove.

By the time the fire had removed the chill from the air the cottage felt lived-in. Targas was sitting at the table in discussion with Lan and Alethea, while Cathar chased Vor into the back of the cottage to the sounds of Anyar's squeals.

"Let me help you, Sadir," said Boidea. "We'll leave the others to their talking and get this place tidied. Now what can I do?"

Sadir smiled gratefully at the pleasant face of Alethea's companion, a quiet, reliable presence in the party.

"Thank you, Boidea. We will need to get everyone fed and then see if we have enough bedding. I'm sure some airing of the blankets would be useful, too."

"Why don't I put some of that energy Cathar and Anyar have to good use? They can find and spread the bedding. Then I'll start peeling vegetables." Boidea eyed a pile of dusty tubers dumped in the corner near a small table.

"Please," Sadir said quietly as she went outside to fetch more fresh water.

The crackling fire gave a pleasing ambience to the room by the time Boidea sat to peel the tubers.

"Can I help at all? Make tea perhaps?" asked Alethea. Lan and Targas looked over.

"My apologies," added Lan. "We're getting carried away letting Sadir work."

"No. No, everything is under control," said Sadir. "Better to keep the rest of you from crowding me."

"You sure?" asked Targas.

"Yes," she said firmly, turning to her chopping board and unwrapping some fresh meat. "Boidea, would you mind filling the kettle from the bucket and putting it on the stove?"

Sadir thought about the pleasure of having the cottage filled with people once more. Her concerns about Kyel and Targas faded as she relaxed into the routine of preparing a meal. The companions were fast becoming friends, helping her overcome her fears, and giving hope for the future. She was feeling more confident, able to cope with her concerns and even accept the horrible experience in the caverns.

And her scent power was improving. Since her first experience of the shadow scent and its dramatic use against the hymetta, she had taken every opportunity to experiment. Even along the road to Lesslas she worked adapting the scent until it became an instinctive thing. She noticed the accepting smile of Alethea as she saw what Sadir was doing and appreciated the offer of Rolan cordial when resting from the day's riding.

Not that it's difficult to accept, she thought. *The cordial is very moreish, even if its attributes are a well-kept Rolan secret.*

"Mar!" Anyar's pull on her travelling cloak broke through her thoughts. "Vor is gone. He's run away."

"What? I'm sure he's around somewhere." A crash of breaking crockery came from the back room.

"Oh!" yelped Cathar, "that animal's into something. I had better find out."

A short time later she returned holding the voral in her arms. He lay there unconcerned, pale belly exposed, licking at his black-clawed paws with a long red tongue.

"I think," she grinned at Sadir, "there was some honey there. I'm afraid he's got into it."

"Mmm," Sadir frowned at the relaxed voral.

"Vor not bad, Mar?" asked Anyar.

"No, Vor's not bad. But you must look after him."

Vor hiccupped while still licking a paw, and Cathar chuckled.

"Come on," Sadir laughed with her, "the kettle's boiled and we need to get the vegetables on."

They had eaten a filling meal and taken to the bedrooms and spare spaces in the living area. With the aid of riding gear and blankets everyone was comfortable, and Sadir enjoyed Targas in their own bed.

She woke in the dark. Something had changed. She listened above Targas's heavy breathing but nothing seemed unusual despite so many people in the cottage. Sadir began to roll over, when she realised Targas's breathing was different somehow. She was used to his restlessness over the past months as part of his increasing irritability.

His breathing had changed. No longer a grumbling rumble but lighter, as if ending in a wet-sounding chuckle, it struck a chord. She had heard it before. Somewhere. Long ago. Sadir found herself listening to each breath but couldn't place it. Sleep took her before she puzzled it out.

"Mar." A small figure clambered onto the bed. "Mar, can we go now? Vor wants out."

"Fine, Anyar," Sadir mumbled. "But let him out the back."

"Hello, my love." Targas's stubble prickled her face. "No rest with our daughter here."

"Targas!" Sadir pushed up on her elbows. "How did you sleep?"

"Huh?" He rubbed his eyes. "Not so good, even though I was tired. Why?"

"You were breathing heavily and in a funny way. It...it reminded me of..."

A soft knock came on the half open door. "Are you awake?"

"Cathar?" said Sadir. "Anyar's been in, so yes, we are. She's taken Vor outside."

"I'll light the fire? Put water on?"

"Thank you," Sadir answered through the door.

"No privacy, I'm afraid." Targas smiled, rubbing sleep from his eyes.

"No," she agreed. "Now, about what I was saying. I don't feel we should gloss over it."

"You mean my breathing?"

"Yes, Targas, your breathing, or rather what's behind it."

The noise of Cathar making the fire came through the door as Targas slumped back on his pillow. "I don't want to go there. I...I feel I have a lid over what may be causing it and I'm afraid to open it. If I do, I won't be able to control what comes out. You've had enough worry with the way I've been, so I'm loathe to cause you more concern." Targas smiled and put an arm around her. "Lie back while we have a moment."

Sadir sighed and lay with Targas's arm around her. "Yes, just for the moment. But we can't let it go."

"No," he agreed, "we can't."

The topic didn't come up again until they were sitting around the table eating boiled eggs and toast. Curiously, it was Boidea who raised it.

"Still looking tired, you two," she said over a mouthful of food. "Heard a bit of noise during the night." She saw Targas and Sadir exchange a look. "Oh!" Her hand flew to her mouth and her face reddened. "I didn't mean..."

"No, Boidea, I know you didn't," said Targas, "more's the pity. It was the normal issue I've been having, but according to Sadir it's something different now."

"You mean the blockage is beginning to manifest itself in a different way, my boy?" said Lan.

"I'll leave it to Sadir to explain."

"It's hard to tell, and I don't know if it's related to any blockage." Sadir took a sip of tea. "There's something different in Targas's breathing just now. Last night there was a…an extension to his breath, a wetness that rattled." Sadir noticed a darkening in Targas's scent aura and hurried on. "It brought back memories. Memories of the last time, in Nebleth." She raised her hand to her mouth. "Oh no, not Nebleth."

Sadir remembered what had happened in the capital between herself, Targas and Septus, the evil Sutanite scent master. How he'd captured them both and it was only through great courage Targas had managed to save them.

Septus was a man who liked to gloat and reinforce his power over his captives, and she remembered his phlegm-filled voice, his cackling whisper, his vindictive words.

"It's…it's Septus! That's what it reminds me of. Septus!"

"Septus?" Lan asked. "But how? He's dead." He looked from Sadir to Targas.

Targas had covered his eyes with his hands, and Sadir lifted Anyar onto her knees and hugged her.

Alethea put a hand over Targas's and squeezed it. "I can see there is more to this than it first seemed. It may be at the limits of my experience but there is much to be done, and soon."

"What do you think, Alethea?" Lan asked. "Is it something like being overwhelmed by scent memories?"

"It may well be, Lan," she replied, "but I'd be happier at Sanctus where we can look into it further."

"Well, Targas"—Lan touched him on the shoulder—"what do you wish to do?"

Targas raised his head. "If I'd learnt to hate anyone for what he did to me and mine, it would be Septus. There is no way I want him to still influence me and my life from the grave. I'll do whatever it takes to destroy any memory of him." He stared into Lan's eyes, while reaching out a hand to Sadir.

Sadir sighed as she closed the cottage. *No sooner home than gone again. And with no time to get it homely for Kyel.* She shook her head as she realised how unlikely that would be. *Why did he do it, leaving Ean with Jakus and Nefaria? Surely Targas and I weren't that bad.* Her worries for her brother were always in the back of her mind but she realised that he had made a choice in life and whether it would prove right or wrong it had been his choice. She closed her mind to the ramifications of his being influenced by the enemy.

"Come on, love." She felt Targas's hand on her arm. "We'll meet up with him again. And when we do he'll be older and wiser, and better able to cope with what life throws at him."

Of course he had known what she was thinking, she thought. *That was another thing that made their being together so special.* She smiled and followed him outside to the street where the others were waiting.

After picking up their animals from the stables, they followed the cobbled road leading to the northern exit of Lesslas.

The road was filled with herders, traders and workers coming in from the grasslands surrounding Lesslas. Targas assessed the scents drifting in the air and looked at his companions, a pleasant array of scent auras surrounding them. The soft pastel colours reflected companionship, loyalty, resolve and love. He could see flickers of unease in Sadir's scent aura, a trickle of dull yellows and greens that suggested her thoughts might be lost in memories of something unpleasant, like their hurried flight from the town years ago. He smiled as he noticed his daughter holding his partner's hand, then concentrated harder. Anyar's scent aura showed a domination of steely grey, as if she was controlling her scent projections. *Surely not,* he thought, *she's just a young girl. Wouldn't it be too soon for her to have such control?*

Then Targas almost stopped walking as he noticed the bundle in the saddlebag on Sadir's perac. He could see the flat head and long snout of the voral peeking out, but there was something different about him. *No scent? That's impossible. How can he do that?* He puzzled over that until he noticed another strange thing: the voral's lack of scent seemed to extend across to Anyar so part of his daughter's scent aura was obscured. He shook his head at the strangeness of it all and resolved to raise it with Alethea later.

The sun was descending to the western mountain ranges when Lan headed the party to the low foothills from the plain. They stopped at a site where the tree cover was thicker on the rocky soil. Targas felt Sadir's hand on his arm and smiled at her as he dismounted. He took hold of Anyar and lifted her down. The voral scrabbled out of the saddlebag and was away, Anyar following.

"Don't go too far," Sadir called after her.

Targas watched her small figure as she scrambled over the rocks projecting through the soil. Soon she was hidden by the thickets of trees and bushes.

"Shouldn't we go after her?"

"Cathar's following," said Sadir. "Besides, Vor will look after her."

"You have a lot of faith in that animal. I hope it's as good as you think" Targas pulled the saddlebags off his perac.

"Yes," added Alethea from nearby, "I believe that he is."

Sadir gave her a quick smile as she lifted Anyar's small pack.

Chapter Twenty-Six

Kyel's feet dragged on the stone floor as the huge Sutanite hauled him out of the great hall. He attempted to seek some help, but Jakus was focused on discussions with his father, Vitaris and Nefaria was out of sight. Then he gave up when he noticed Faltis avidly watching his progress.

"Don't damage him, Dronthis!" said the old woman hobbling at his side, her stick clicking on the floor.

Don't damage him. The words echoed in his befuddled mind, while his legs attempted to keep up. *Why are they doing this to me? What Knowing was the old woman talking about?*

Kyel was hustled through a shadowed alcove, along a corridor and towards a descending flight of steps.

"To my temple, Dronthis!"

"The Shada will want him in the interrogation room, Xerina," growled Dronthis, descending the steps.

"My temple. I need him in my rooms," puffed Xerina, struggling to keep pace with the strutting soldier.

Dronthis ignored her, continuing along a dark passageway, pushing through some wooden doors and shoving Kyel to the floor. "Wait here."

"No!" Kyel, yelled scrambling to his feet and building a solid, defensive wall of scent. As quick as the thought, he fired a scent bolt at the big man's back, which bounced off but caused Dronthis to stagger and almost collide with Xerina. The soldier swung back, a visible dark scent aura forming around his head, and he drew a long dagger from a sheath at his side.

"Lizards' teeth!" Kyel gasped. "It didn't even stop him." He crouched down and rapidly strengthened his scent shield, pulling on all the training he'd had from Targas and Lan.

Kyel stiffened, pulling the bonds together as the Sutanite swung his dagger at his head. It drove deeply into the scent shield before rebounding, ripping the weapon from Dronthis's hand.

"Blast!" Dronthis bellowed, wringing his hand as the weapon hit the wall with a clang.

Kyel kept his head down, concentrating, holding the shield tight.

Dronthis kicked at Kyel, his foot rebounding from the elasticity of the scent barrier.

"Dronthis!" came a firm voice. At the same time, the man's body was stumbling backwards. "Control yourself!" commanded Xerina.

The man swung around, fists raised. "Stop interfering or I'll—"

His fists froze in the air, his eyes bulging and face rapidly darkening with blood as he strained to move.

"A little control is all you need," Xerina said calmly before turning her back on him. "Now, Kyel, I am sorry about that unnecessary roughness. Dronthis is prone to using brawn rather than finesse."

Kyel looked from the old woman in front of him, her arms folded, then to the frozen Dronthis. He could see a slight shimmering in the air emanating from Xerina, but the absence of scent colour surprised him. *How is she able to do that?* he thought, even as he released his scent shield.

"Now, this isn't much of a place to talk," she said, gazing around the stark room lit through slits high in the stone walls. Aside from several wooden chairs and a small table, there were several ominous metal rings and chains fastened to the walls and some timber beams leaning in a corner. "Still, I do not want to irritate Dronthis any further, so it is best we sit down and have a chat.

"Dronthis," she said over her shoulder, "you may go. Perhaps have a servant bring us tea and cake." She winked at Kyel out of a lined face.

Dronthis growled and shifted, a dark rush of scent building around him. He moved half a step towards them before shaking his head and turning away. "I'll be back!" he snapped and hurried off.

"H…how did you do that?" Kyel asked. "I…I've never seen anything like it, keeping him under control, without any effort."

"Ah, Kyel," smiled Xerina. "I think you'll find that there are many things you don't know, and this will be one more. Suffice to say that my ability comes from another land and another time."

"But…?"

"Now, I have a job to do. Why don't we move to that table?"

He did as asked, and she collapsed tiredly onto a chair opposite him.

"That's better," she gasped. "Too much activity for one of my years. Now,"— she reached out and patted him on the knee—"we need to talk before we are interrupted." She smiled. "You have some scent talent, my boy. A very good shield to defeat the likes of Dronthis. But that is not why we're here. I must determine whether you are a potential threat to Sutan."

"Threat! Me!" Kyel shook his head. "Is that what this is about? The attack, the...the torture..."

"Down to me, I'm afraid," she smiled grimly. "At least to those who think my words are accurate enough to act upon." She gazed around the stone walls before continuing. "I have a skill, a talent for foretelling. It is an ability linked to women of my race and can help predict future events. Usually it relates to simple things like the coming season, a successful birth, who should best lead on a council and so on. Occasionally they stretch further and become vaguer. One vague Knowing was hard to interpret but it held such an air of warning I felt it my duty to communicate it to the Shada.

"It warned Sutan of a danger linked to Ean. One interpretation was that an individual had the seeds for the destruction of this country. Your arrival, particularly your background, has led to some taking no chances, hence the recent attack on you."

"But I'm nobody special," Kyel protested. "I have no particular skills, nor want to fight anyone."

"That well may be true, my boy," said Xerina, "but there are those who will not take the chance. Therefore it is best we try and determine what potential you have, to diffuse any concern that may be around. Otherwise..."

"Otherwise?" Kyel gulped.

A clattering of boots came along the corridor. Dronthis burst in, followed by a slim young boy carrying a platter of breads and mugs.

"Here, crone. Your food and drink...as requested."

Xerina smiled coldly at Dronthis while the food was placed on the table. The boy bowed quickly, then hurried from the room.

"Help yourself, Kyel. I've no doubt you are thirsty and hungry with the lack of hospitality you've been afforded since your arrival."

He hesitated as he saw the large man fold his massive arms and lean against a wall, watching him. It was only when Xerina lifted one of the mugs that Kyel took a slice of bread and a hot mug.

Xerina slowly sipped her tea. "Now, where were we? Oh, yes... Kyel, I hope you will trust me. I certainly do not think the other method, shown by our friend here, is an appropriate means of ascertaining the truth.

"So, if you've had enough to eat for the moment, we might begin."

Kyel put his mug on the table and clenched his hands as Xerina moved her seat forward until their knees touched.

"Try to relax," she said. "It won't hurt but will be a bit uncomfortable. Please trust me."

Images of Jakus taking hold of him by scent and ruthlessly invading his smell centres flooded Kyel's mind. He shuddered and started to rise.

"Please, my boy. Please." Xerina pleaded, pushing him down with soft hands. Kyel could feel her calming scents and controlling strength infiltrating his mind. *No, I can't,* he thought but the realisation this was a better way to endure the ordeal made him settle and accept Xerina moving into his smell centres and his mind.

He remembered Jakus driving into his nose with a harsh scraping within sinuses—a pain like the worst toothache driving into him, pinning him down, leaving him helpless against the agony. Xerina was much more subtle. Her probing tickled like the skittering of a lizard across his arm, and he felt no danger. A few sections were blocked against her, and he felt her pause and investigate.

He opened his eyes to her smile.

"There, that was not too bad, was it, Kyel? And informative, too." She leant back and rubbed her chin. "But will it satisfy the Shada?"

"What did you find?" Dronthis grated, now standing above them.

"Interesting," Xerina replied, "interesting. But not, I think, a matter for you, although this man is not the threat that has been intimated. If the Shada is free I would best report to him." She slowly stood to her feet.

"The prisoner stays here!" ordered Dronthis.

"If he must, he must," she conceded. "I'm sorry, Kyel, but I'll be as quick as I can. Do no harm, Dronthis!"

As soon as Xerina left the room, Dronthis grabbed Kyel's shoulder and squeezed hard. "You've had enough babysitting from the old crone. Stand over there against the wall. We'll make sure you can't escape."

Dronthis pulled him to the pair of rings fixed in the wall and fastened each wrist to them by the attached chains. Kyel was left with his arms in an uncomfortable Y-shape above his head.

He tugged at them, then screamed as Dronthis punched a huge fist into his stomach. He attempted to double over but just hung, open and vulnerable.

"You traitorous Eanite!" snarled Dronthis, punching him again, the pressure causing Kyel's nose to bleed profusely as he gasped for breath. "What did that crone find out, eh? Not such a big man without her."

Blood began to splatter on the floor as Kyel hung from the chains gasping for breath. The big man moved back, paused for a moment then left the room.

Kyel attempted to get air into his lungs while his stomach screamed from Dronthis's blows. He leant his head forward to avoid more blood spilling onto his tunic top and woollen trousers, getting his breathing under control. Each breath forced out a groan. He wondered whether he was dying, his insides ruptured, never having experienced such pain.

"So, what did you find out?" Vitaris asked Xerina as she entered the leader's sitting room.

"My Lords," Xerina nodded to Vitaris, Jakus and Faltis. "May I sit?"

Vitaris pointed towards a cloth-covered seat at a low table where they were sitting. He waited as she settled, poured a cup of water and took a sip.

"Well!" said Faltis. "Hurry up."

"Patience, my Lord," said Xerina. "I do have some news to report but not, I fear, very informative.

"I have investigated the young man with my usual thorough techniques and have found little hidden. I would say he is very unlikely to be the possible threat to Sutan the Knowing suggested. There may be some facets of him linked to it, but I cannot be sure.

"For the benefit of Shad Jakus, I should advise this Knowing indicates an individual from Ean could lead to the complete breakdown of Sutan—when was uncertain. It was therefore imperative to ascertain whether your Kyel might have been that person."

"So, Xerina," said Jakus, "if you're saying this Eanite has a vague link to this deadly doombringer, who could it be?"

"I don't know," continued Xerina. "The Knowing is so vague. At a guess I would think it could be an Eanite Kyel has encountered. Do you know of such an outstanding warrior?"

"I say get rid of the threat anyway," said Faltis, glaring at Jakus.

A scent cloud grew swiftly above Jakus. "Again?" He looked at his brother and raised an eyebrow.

Faltis looked away.

"In answer to your question, Xerina, I don't know of any such warrior. Targas, the Eanite's leader in the rebellion, wasn't a native anyway. The self-styled leader, Lan, is a doddering old fool. Although…?" Jakus rubbed his chin for a moment, then shook his head. "No, there's no-one else."

"Well, I've done my best, my Shada," said Xerina to Vitaris. "I should go back and see how the young man is."

"No, you've done what we asked," said Vitaris. "Go to your temple and work on the Knowing, see if you can find out more."

"Very well." Xerina stood, bowed her head and left.

"We will have a banquet in honour of your return this night, Jakus," said Vitaris. "Until then you may retire."

"As you will, Father," said Jakus.

"Jakus, my Lord." Nefaria met him as he left the room. "I'm glad I've caught you. Poegna is waiting in the hall to see you."

"Poegna," repeated Jakus, remembering last meeting the scent master in Southern Port. "Ah, good, I wonder what she has for me."

He walked out into the hall and, seeing her, took her elbow and drew her to a darker corner.

"Welcome, my Shad," she breathed.

"Just keep it to Jakus at the moment," he said. "What news of young Bilternus? Is he on our side?"

"Yes," nodded Poegna enthusiastically, "he is now. Apparently, he and his father have had a falling out. Bilternus tried to find out details of the attack on you at the garrison, but Faltis was suspicious.

"He'll be at my estates next day, so if you need to talk to him I'll be happy to arrange it."

"Yes, I'll be there," said Jakus walking her towards the door of the great hall. "I think we need to discuss a few things but now is not the time, nor the place."

"I'll look forward to it, my Sha...Jakus."

He watched her hurry off through the door to where her serving man held two perac, before he turned and re-entered the hall.

He stopped as he saw Dronthis cross ahead of him and head down to Vitaris's quarters. *I wonder where the Eanite is*, he thought.

A sound woke him and he lifted his head with a groan, pain coursing through him. A dark shape stood before him, tall, thin and menacing.

"Trussed up and helpless? This will be easy," said Faltis, showing a long, thin dagger to Kyel's wide eyes. "I think a careful insertion of this blade through your ribs will remove any danger you might pose to Sutan, despite what the crone says."

Faltis lifted the dagger and stepped forward.

Kyel tried to form a scent shield through his pain, then merely closed his eyes.

Chapter Twenty-Seven

The rolling gait of his perac allowed Targas to settle and enjoy his daughter's constant chatter. The girl sitting between his legs, and thus between the reins he held loosely, laughed gaily at the antics of the voral loping alongside their small party.

The sun rose overhead and began its descent towards the line of hills and their goal of Sanctus.

Soon, familiar grey boulders began to erupt through the soil, making the track meander as it ascended the slope. Groups of shrubs and trees became more infrequent. Targas noticed a strong drift of scent from a stony outcrop some distance away and recognised the K'dorian lizard.

It was odd, he thought, that he hadn't noticed any of them around for some time. The huge beasts were dangerous, but at least you knew where you stood with them: they had their own territories where they hunted, and you only needed to keep clear. *Unlike the haggar*, he thought, *those revolting river worms.*

He looked down on the brown head of his daughter and hugged her.

"Par," said Anyar, lifting her head. "Where Vor?"

Suddenly the voral scrabbled down from where he had recently been riding in Sadir's saddlebag and bounded away into the rocks.

"Vor!" called Anyar.

"Let him go," said Targas. "He'll be wanting to forage before we get to Sanctus." *And find something to eat*, he thought. *I hope he avoids those large lizards.*

They rounded a bend and saw a tall woman in a long, grey robe standing on the track holding out her arms, a rainbow of scents rising from her.

"Lan, and Alethea, welcome," her voice rang out. "Cathar and Boidea, too. And, if I'm not mistaken, Targas and Sadir."

"Greetings, Lethnal," answered Lan. "It is good to be back."

"Come," Lethnal called. "It is almost time for the sundown meal, so we'll settle you in as quickly as possible." As she turned, the voral crashed out of the bushes. "Oh, he's still with you, I see."

"Vor! Vor!" yelled Anyar.

"What? You've your daughter with you, Targas? How wonderful." She smiled briefly at Anyar. "Now please follow me." Lethnal began to walk up the track.

They soon dismounted at a group of huge boulders dominating the hillside and disguising the entrance to Sanctus. Cathar and several acolytes took their animals away while the others followed Lethnal inside.

Targas held Anyar's hand as he walked into the large common room, where grey-robed scent masters, acolytes and other students occupied the tables filling most of the space. The chatter ceased and scents of welcome filled the air. The smell of the meal made Anyar's eyes widen.

"Par, I'm hungry."

"Yes, Anyar, we'll be eating soon," he replied as he remembered the room with unadorned granite walls and window slits providing light, doors framed by thick wooden supports and a smooth rock floor.

"Follow me and I'll get you settled," said Lethnal to Targas and Sadir, "then we'll have something to eat. Now where did that voral go?"

"I'll take him with me before he gets up to mischief," laughed Alethea as the animal wandered towards the kitchens. "He's familiar with my room."

Lethnal led them down a short corridor of grey granite walls and ceilings, past openings leading into small bedrooms, before turning into a larger room lit with a small slit window. "This should do the three of you. One large bed and one small bed that'll suit Anyar. If you want to wash off the dust of your travels, you know where the washrooms are. Then come into the common room." She smiled and left.

"Back in Sanctus, Targas," sighed Sadir, sitting on the bed. "I don't know about you, but it feels safe, secure."

"Mmm," agreed Targas, as he dropped his bags to the floor.

"Mar. I'm hungry."

"I guess our first priority, after a quick wash, is food?" said Sadir. "Come, Anyar, let's get cleaned up." She led their daughter from the room.

Targas lay back on the bed, hands behind his head, and looked at the granite ceiling, noting the clean scents circulating around the stone. They seemed crisp and uncomplicated, unlike that bubbling behind his eyes. The journey brought a lot back to him and every so often a knife-like stab had echoed in his mind. He knew it had to be confronted and that he couldn't be in better hands, but he was frightened of the consequences. *What I wouldn't give for a drink of malas right now,* he thought, *just one cup.*

Targas preceded Sadir into the common room with Anyar tight against his side, eyes wide at the bustle around her. Sadir enjoyed the normality of the scene and the welcome from the friendly people. Several already surrounded Targas and were admiring Anyar, since children were infrequent visitors to the Sanctus centre of learning. She noticed a vague puff of scents from her daughter, with a link of control showing, and shook her head—Anyar was rapidly growing up.

"Sadir!" She saw a thickset woman coming towards her, a mop of short, greying hair drifting down to her eyes, arms held out.

"Rasnal!" She hugged the woman, who was one of the friends she had made during the campaign to free Ean from the Sutanite rule. "How are you? Still in charge of the tina?" Sadir said, recalling the giant scent moths that were the focal point of the resistance communication.

"Oh, yes," said Rasnal solemnly, "they are more important than ever with the running of Ean. I'm always sending and receiving messages, although I have several of the young people training to handle and care for them."

"Perhaps you might like to take my daughter, Anyar, to the caverns some time?"

"I'd be pleased, but don't let me hold you up, as I can see you have a meal waiting." Rasnal stepped back.

"Thanks," Sadir smiled and followed Targas, recognising Brin, the leader of the river people, and Zahnal, the healer, as they approached their table.

Lan and Alethea were in a conversation at one end while Cathar and Boidea made room for Anyar and Targas.

"Well, what would you like?" said Cathar as Anyar leant towards the laid-out food. "Something hot, perhaps? Fish, casserole, mushroom stew or egg on deep-fried bread. Or maybe something sweeter? Dumplings in honey?"

"Cathar," said Sadir as she sat down, "don't give her too much choice, particularly sweets. Could you just give her some egg on bread, and she can come back for more?"

"Mar, I'm big enough to help myself." Anyar looked at her mother with large eyes.

Sadir smiled and helped herself to casserole. "Targas, how are you feeling?" she asked, noticing the stress lines across his forehead.

"Fine, at the moment," he nodded through a mouthful of food. "There's something calming about being here. Remember how it was when we were here before?"

"Yes." Sadir recalled how Targas had learnt to refine his scent talent in Sanctus and then prepared for the expedition to ultimately retake the country from the invaders. Memories of this place were good. "Maybe we can get an early night?"

She saw Targas's eyebrows rise and a slight smile creep across his lips. "If Anyar sleeps soundly enough," he said.

"Oh, I don't think we'll have too much worry with her," said Sadir. "She's had a long journey and is tired."

"Yes," yawned Targas, "I'm tired myself."

"Huh?" Sadir woke to a cold nose pressing her cheek. Targas's arm lay across her chest and the room was dark. "Vor, what are you doing in here?"

She heard a giggle from the bed that lay at the foot of theirs. "Come on, Anyar, don't encourage him."

The voral bounded away from their bed and bounced onto Anyar. A peal of laughter erupted from her.

"What's all that noise?" growled Targas sleepily. "It's still night." He rolled over and pulled the pillow across his head.

"Come on, Anyar," said Sadir. "Let's take Vor outside. We'll leave your father to sleep." She rose and pulled on her tunic and leggings before helping Anyar dress into similar clothing. They slipped out of the door, along the corridor and through a wood-framed doorway into a long, narrow room where several rock sinks were filled with steaming water. A grey-clad woman, sleeves rolled above her elbows, smiled up at them as they entered.

The voral loped out of the door, which stood ajar. Anyar ran past with a squeal and Sadir waved at the woman as she followed them out.

She looked out into a crisp, pale sky from amongst jumbled grey granite boulders surrounding the entrance to Sanctus. The sun pushing up from the long ranges competed with the wisps of wintery cloud filling the air. She shivered and rubbed her arms.

Anyar's excited chatter came from nearby, and so she hurried along the lightly defined track towards the sound, remembering it led to the caverns a short distance away.

"Anyar, wait for me," Sadir called.

"Blast that voral," she swore as she manoeuvred her way between the boulders and found her daughter looking down into a narrow ravine where a small stream splashed its way to a ledge, before tumbling into a long drop.

"Mar, Vor's gone." Anyar glanced back at her mother.

"Just stay there!" Sadir held out a hand. "Not another step. Vor can wait."

"Sadir? And Anyar?" Rasnal's grey-gowned figure emerged from around a huge wall of granite that fronted the ravine. "You're up early."

"It's that pest of an animal. Once he's up, we all are."

"Well I haven't seen him," said Rasnal. "I've been in the caverns checking the tina for messages." Her face brightened as she leant down to Anyar, "Why don't you come with me and see my friends, the tina? They're all settled in now it's daylight and they're rather special."

"What about Vor, Mar?"

"I think that's a good idea, Rasnal," said Sadir. "Vor will be fine out here. It's probably better that he doesn't come with us, as I'm not sure what he'd think of the tina." Anyar nodded gravely and took her hand.

They followed Rasnal along the narrow trail across a wooden ramp bridging the stream and through a small, dark opening in the rock face. Their feet crunched onto coarse sand as they walked into a dimly lit cavern. The tina keeper took a burning torch from a wall sconce and led the way, light flickering on the high ceiling.

Anyar pressed against Sadir's side as they walked so she pulled her closer, murmuring softly. "It'll be fine, sweetling. It'll be fine. This is a nice place."

After a time, they reached a series of smaller caves The dark seemed to press on them, thick and cloying.

"Don't worry about the feel, Anyar," said Rasnal softly, "it's only the tina. They like it here and their scents add to the atmosphere. Can you detect their odour? It's a...a *musty* smell with flowery overtones—very pleasant."

"Mar! It's dark. Like before!" The girl shivered against Sadir.

"No, Anyar. The smell's good. This place is good and we're with a friend. You'll like it." Sadir nuzzled her daughter's hair.

"Now we'll go in," continued Rasnal. "You'll like them, you'll see."

A slight breeze wafted the musty smell into their faces as they entered, and a faint rustle of living creatures filled the small cave. Rasnal set the torch onto the wall and walked into the darkness. "Come," she encouraged.

The flickering light of the torch showed the far wall crammed with large insects, wings folded flat across their backs, feathery antennae sprouting above compound eyes, thin legs gripping the rock, vibrating bodies creating a movement of air.

"Come closer, Anyar," she said, noticing the girl's hesitation.

"Come on, sweetling," encouraged Sadir, edging her forward, her hand holding the girl's. Anyar crouched on her haunches and put her hand out to touch one of the creatures on the back.

"It's soft, Mar."

"Yes, it is."

"It's best not to touch them, though, since they are covered with a fluff to help them fly. Now, I'll show you how I get the messages off one." Rasnal gently stroked the sides of the large, thigh-thick creature, and pulled a small strip of a soft, flexible material from amidst its thorax fluff. She held it in front of Anyar's nose. "Have a smell, little one. Each of the scents means something, and it is the way we send messages around the country."

"Smells funny," said Anyar, pulling away.

A loud growl echoed in the cavern, and a dark shape came scrabbling through the fine sand into the cave.

"No!" screeched Rasnal and Sadir, but the voral ran straight for the tina on the wall.

Anyar reacted immediately, stepping in front of the animal and holding out a hand; a rippling flash of scent lighting the dark.

The voral skidded to a halt, dropped to its belly and slunk to Anyar's feet.

"Vor." She clasped the animal to her legs.

The voral rolled onto its back, exposing its pale belly.

"How did you do that?" questioned Sadir.

"Just as well your daughter has good control on that animal," said Rasnal with a relieved laugh. "I think vorals eat most things, including tina."

"Can we go out, please?" asked Anyar.

"Yes, Anyar," said Sadir, "we've had enough of caves for now, and your father will be wondering where we are."

They followed Rasnal back through the caverns, the voral slinking along at Anyar's heels.

The rising sun had broken through the thin cloud, warming the surrounds as they came up the path. Lan stood at the entrance framed by several towering monoliths of granite, his scent aura a whirl of pastel pinks and blues. "Thought I would catch the pair of you on your return, Sadir. Targas, Alethea and Boidea have gone on ahead."

"Sorry, Lan, but where have they gone? I want to get Anyar inside and have something to eat."

"They are down the hillside amongst the warming boulders. They have a basket of food and hot drink, so your needs will be met. If you will follow me."

"Thanks for everything, Rasnal. I'll see you later," Sadir said as she and Anyar followed Lan down another path.

Targas saw Sadir and Anyar with Lan and smiled as he noticed his daughter holding a fistful of the voral's fur. The sun warmed the east-facing nook, and he was sitting back against an angled section of granite with a hot drink in his hands.

"Par!" Anyar broke into a run, the voral at her heels.

He placed the drink on a flat rock and pulled the excited young girl onto his lap. "I can tell where you've been," he murmured, nuzzling her hair. "In the caverns, and I can smell tina."

"Par, I didn't like the cave, and Vor was naughty too," she said, looking at him out of big, solemn eyes.

Targas raised an eyebrow at Sadir. "Still too soon after the caves in Nebleth?"

"I think so, and Anyar averted a near-crisis. We were in the caverns with Rasnal seeing the tina when Vor found us and decided the creatures were either food or a danger. He ran to attack, but strangely, Anyar was the only one who could stop him. Our words and scent had no effect. I'm not sure how she managed it, Targas."

"There's something more to it," added Alethea. "I've felt that all along, ever since I first laid eyes on him. I believe it's a mystery to be solved, but in its own time. But come, sit, eat." She patted a flat rock next to her.

"I've some honey and bread for Vor, on the off chance," said Boidea, reaching into the basket. "Would you like to give it to him, Anyar?" She passed a bowl to the young girl.

"I admit it's very pleasant out here, Lan," said Sadir, sitting next to Targas on a blanket-covered rock, "but why all the mystery?"

"No mystery, Sadir. We felt that this place would be a nice area for a meal."

Targas nodded at Lan's words, the sun warming the left side of his face as he gazed towards the south along the wide valley where the foothills of the Short Ranges pushed in from the west. It was some years since he had last sat near here with Sadir, trying to come to terms with his maturing scent ability.

They ate in companionable silence, each in their own thoughts. The warning trills of Conduvian lizards arose as the voral, having finished his bread and honey, wandered off.

"I think," said Lan, "Alethea might outline our suggestion to attempt to treat this malady of yours, Targas."

Targas stiffened and Sadir sought his hand.

Alethea smiled at Lan and looked at Targas. "We've had some time to consider what might be happening to you and while it is not clear what it is, we are certain there is at least some residual echo of a traumatic event within your scent memories, which may extend into your mind."

"I could have told you that," grumbled Targas.

"Please." She held up a placating hand. "It may be that you know this, but there is some impediment, a blockage which is most unusual. Lan has investigated it and so have I, and we are of the opinion an attempt to remove it should be made using the resources of Sanctus—the people and the caverns."

"It would be a similar procedure to what you experienced before," added Lan, noticing Targas's stony expression. "That is if you are willing."

"And Targas," added Alethea, "my feeling is that we may need to complete the cure in Rolan, if necessary." She smiled sadly.

"What choice do I have?" Targas said quietly. "It's either that or keep him in my head."

"Septus?" whispered Sadir with a shudder.

Targas gripped her hand.

Chapter Twenty-Eight

Kyel sagged against the restraints holding him to the wall, eyes closed, breath oozing from his lungs, heart noisily pumping its last beats.

He felt the prick of the dagger edging its way through his blood-covered tunic. He could feel the finesse of the wielder as he tensed for the final thrust.

Then silence. The pain eased and the sodden thump of a body hitting the floor caused him to open his eyes. He saw a dark shape on the floor and heard feet. He recognised Jakus, dark with odour, before he noticed Faltis standing shakily.

"You tempt my patience again, brother!" Jakus fired a scent bolt which Faltis instinctively deflected.

"So! Try this!" A dark scent billowed from Jakus, reaching out in long fingers. Faltis pushed back with a scent shield from his position against the wall, face set, veins cording in his neck.

Kyel watched through a pain-filled haze as they fought in front of him. He could see the effect of Jakus's magnesa-enhanced power. Tendrils of scent manoeuvred their way around Faltis's shield, until the bubble of the scent shield was criss-crossed with dark lines. Then they tightened, constricting the barrier, forcing it back upon its creator. He could dimly see Faltis's face, eyes bulging, gasping mouth open.

Faltis staggered and fell to one knee, gulping for air.

"Do you yield, brother?" Jakus snarled.

Faltis collapsed to his knees, scent shield faltering. He grabbed at his throat and held up a hand in surrender.

"Hah!" Jakus shouted, dropping his attack while Faltis drew in long, shuddering breaths. "So you seek to test me again, despite your agreement to leave my property alone? If it weren't for my promise to our father, I would be justified in killing you. Now get out or I might regret my leniency." He moved closer to Faltis, eyes glittering while his brother got slowly to his feet.

Faltis glanced to the dagger lying on the floor.

"Leave it as a reminder of your treachery!" Jakus snapped.

Faltis grimaced and hobbled from the room.

Jakus watched him go before he relaxed and rubbed at his back with both hands. He stretched with a groan, knuckled his temple and then turned to look at Kyel.

"You fool. What kind of scent wielder are you to end up like this?" Jakus's harsh breath gusted into his face. He reached behind Kyel and released the chains holding him to the rings on the wall.

Kyel collapsed to the floor.

"Make your way to Xerina's temple when you are able," Jakus ordered. "Get her to treat you since she allowed this to happen. I mean to have words with Vitaris."

Jakus walked away, his boots echoing loudly on the stone.

Pain wracked his body as he crawled to reach the chair, his stomach threatening to spill its meagre contents. He didn't know whether to feel relieved or disappointed he'd been saved from a quick death. He was still in Sutan, surrounded by enemies who wanted either to use or kill him. And why did Dronthis attack so viciously? Why did Xerina, who had been friendly, leave him with that man?

No, he thought as he struggled to sit upright on the chair, *it's all too much to figure*.

He heard a light footstep before he recognised familiar scents.

"Kyel, what's happened to you?"

He felt Nefaria's arm go across his shoulders and the brush of her short hair as she leaned down next to him.

"Your poor face. And all that blood. My Lord said that you had been mistreated, but I had no idea. I must get you to Xerina."

Kyel groaned as she attempted to pull his arms away from his stomach.

"Come on, Kyel," she urged. "You're too big for me to manage by myself. You'll have to help." She gently pulled on his arm, draped it over her shoulder and then straightened with a grunt.

He rose shakily to his feet, hissing with the pain. Each shuffling step was agonising as they moved out of the room and down the corridor.

Kyel had no idea how long it took to get to Xerina before he was laid down on a hard bed. A cold, wet cloth gently washed his face as the tunic was eased from his body.

"Dronthis will pay for this," muttered the old woman as she viewed the bruising on his torso. "He had strict orders. Kyel, where does it hurt? Just the stomach?"

He grunted.

"And look at this," she said to Nefaria, "there's a small cut, just above his heart—it's very recent. Do you know what caused it?"

"I'm not sure, but Jakus was very upset with his brother," she answered, and then walked over to a large window overlooking a shallow pond filled with flowering plants. "Xerina, I will leave Kyel in your safe hands.

"You'll stay with Xerina in her temple this night, Kyel," whispered Nefaria, placing a smooth hand on his forehead. "I must go."

Kyel heard her leave and relaxed onto the bed.

"I must see to your hurts, my boy," said Xerina. "This may not be very comfortable, since that man has inflicted some damage."

Kyel kept his eyes closed, gritting his teeth as she gently palpitated his stomach.

Nefaria waited at the living room entrance where Vitaris and Jakus were seated, their scent auras flickering with the reds and purples of their emotions.

"I offer no excuses for Faltis, but it does seem that he is overzealous about the foretelling."

"No excuses indeed," said Jakus. "But it does bring into question the worth of the word of the ruling family, Father."

"As you have said." Vitaris stood. "Now that Faltis has been suitably chastised and agreed not to act rashly, I would hope that you won't take matters into your own hands."

"That I have agreed to do, but I will react with full force if my brother is foolish enough to try anything," Jakus answered as he rose.

"We'll meet at the banquet, my son," said Vitaris dismissively.

"Until then, Father," agreed Jakus.

Jakus beckoned to Nefaria as he left the room. "That blasted father of mine defends my foolish young brother," he growled. "And I imagine he wishes his favourite son, Brastus, was here to take care of things instead of on campaign overseas. Of course Brastus would be able to sort things out as my father's choice for the future leader of Sutan and Ean, wouldn't he? My father has little trust in me, but he'll learn, if he survives long enough."

"My Lord?"

"Nefaria, ignore my ramblings." Jakus glanced at her. "Now, how is the Eanite?"

"Not well, my Lord. He is with Xerina, being treated," she said. "His injuries are mainly to his stomach—it seems he was punched several times. And curiously, he had a knife cut in his chest."

"Ah, it seems I was just in time," he muttered as they walked towards their rooms on the far side of the palace. "Now we have some moments before my father's banquet." He smiled at Nefaria, the orange and red of desire rising around him.

"**N**efaria." Xerina looked up from tending Kyel. "It is a pleasure to see you. You no doubt want a report?"

Nefaria forced a smile and nodded as she came up to Kyel's bed.

Kyel straightened with a groan and attempted to rise.

"No you don't." Xerina put a hand on his shoulder and pushed. "You wait; you're not fully healed."

She turned back to Nefaria. "I think Kyel is recovering well. Dronthis knew how to place his blows to create maximum pain with minimum damage—some skill, hmm? Now…" She looked at Nefaria's scent aura. "You don't look too healthy yourself. Has Jakus been misusing you?"

"Please, Xerina"—Nefaria put up her hand—"it is a matter between my Lord and myself."

"If you say so, my dear. But don't let him abuse you. He and his brothers are too used to getting their own way."

"Thank you for your concern, Xerina. Now I must leave." Nefaria smiled at Kyel. "Stay here for a while longer, Kyel. I'll be back later in the day."

"I do worry where that family is leading us." Xerina shook her head as she watched Nefaria leave. "In all the time I've been here I've seen little I am truly comfortable with."

"You're not one of them, Xerina. Where do you come from?" asked Kyel.

The grey-clad back of the old woman stiffened for a moment before she turned to face him. "You are inquisitive, despite all that's happened to you." She tapped her teeth with a fingernail as she looked out of the window at her pond. A beetle buzzed into a white multi-petalled flower floating on the water.

"I've a mind to tell you," she murmured. "In fact I've a feeling, or should I say"—she gave a barking laugh—"a Knowing to tell you.

"A soothing tea first, young man?" She began to pour from a pot on a small table. Xerina pushed a cup near Kyel's hand and sat back in the bucket-shaped seat next to the bed.

"I have been in Sutan for so long now I've almost forgotten where I came from. I was young then, full of bravado, and talent, if I may say so. I had been recognised for it, my talent I mean, and a future had been planned for me. But I rebelled, unwilling to fit the life chosen for me, and ran away. Away from the mountains and down to the sea, down to the port city to see the ships that came in, to hear where they had been and where they were going. To see if there might be a place there for me.

"Ah yes, some say youth is no excuse for lack of wisdom, but in my case it was." Xerina smiled and took a sip of tea.

"I was pretty then. Long curls of black hair and an air that made men look twice. I was flattered by all that attention until, one morning, I woke up aboard a trading ship, a Sutan vessel. It appeared the captain had recognised my talent and the price I might command in his homeland. And he was right.

"I had no choice but to endure a miserable trip, being forced to do things I'd rather forget, until we arrived at Southern Port. I was then sold to Vitaris's father, Baremis, to be one of his foretellers.

"A long time ago now, young man. And in all that time I have served the family, providing Knowings as they occur." Xerina sighed and put down her cup. "And I will die here; never to see Rolan again."

"Rolan!" exclaimed Kyel. "You come from Rolan?"

"Yes. The country that adjoins Ean," she answered. "Where I had the potential to become one of the wise women, even the Mlana herself. The events that shape one's life, eh, Kyel."

He struggled to a sitting position, eyes wide. "I didn't know."

"Xerina," said a soft, feminine voice, "I have your meal." A young woman dressed in a light robe carried two platters. She placed them on the table, looking at Kyel with large, pale eyes.

"Thank you, Empha. That will be all."

"I'm at your service," Empha bowed, a shock of dark hair falling across her forehead.

Xerina smiled at Kyel as he watched the girl walk away. "Now you and I have something important to do. Take some food and I'll tell you."

Kyel picked up a slice of soft bread smothered with jam and took a bite.

"It's all to do with two Knowings; the one that has caused all these problems, and the other I had last night."

Kyel stopped chewing.

"When I investigated your scent memories, I determined you didn't have the level of ability to be a danger to Sutan. However, I noted you might have an influence. I advised Vitaris and thought the matter at an end, but I'm afraid Faltis took the view your removal would solve the issue. It won't, but that is not satisfactory from your point of view.

"Keep eating, Kyel," she said. "I will now tell of the second Knowing. You're the only person I will tell, and I'm of a mind the Knowing only occurred due to your presence here.

"Look out of the window at a view of tranquillity, a pond filled with floating plants that flower profusely. Their scent and colour draw any manner of insect and give me much pleasure. Can you see the drift of scents surrounding the flowers?"

"Yes," he nodded.

"Describe them to me."

Kyel bent forward with a wince before leaning his elbows on the stone sill.

"The scents are pale in colour, a mingling of greens, blues and yellow—even pink. They are thickest around the flower heads until broken up further away.

You can see where the bees have pushed through, even a touch of their scent trace, darker, like thin lines."

"Now concentrate on a stronger colour, around one of the flowers, and tell me what you see."

"R…right," he said. "It's a deep green, but very small. I can't see much of it. The other scents are confusing, slightly obscuring. I…I don't really know what you want me to say."

"No, Kyel," Xerina said softly, "what I'm trying to show you is that you are seeing what any scent master worth his salt can see."

Kyel sat back with a groan and rubbed at his short, sandy hair. "What's the point, then?"

Xerina reached into a pocket of her faded grey robe and placed a small pottery bottle on the table.

"That's…that's one of those drinks we get back home, a tumbler," said Kyel. "Sadir has them, but Targas thinks they're too sweet, not a man's drink at all. Hey, they come from Rolan, don't they?"

"Yes, Kyel, they come from my home country," she nodded, a smile lighting her eyes. "Hard to get here in Sutan, and well recognised as a drink preferred by women. Rather clever, don't you think?"

"What are you getting at, Xerina.?"

She laughed. "The point I am making is that these cordials contain an attribute that aids gifted women of my country to see scent differently, to see an *other* scent lying behind the normal scent you perceive. What you saw was what you expected to see. What I can see, and use, is that extra scent."

"So what?" grunted Kyel.

"It is best seen by observing." Xerina pointed out of the window. "Look at the same flower."

Kyel watched her concentrate. Other than her stillness, she exhibited no sign of scent use; no colours disturbed her normal scent aura, and the scents of the flower appeared undisturbed. A beetle buzzed into the bloom, breaking the haze of scent, but nothing else happened.

Xerina slowly turned her head. "Watch…this…now."

The air darkened before Kyel's eyes until a floating ball was clearly discernible against the light. It grew larger, separating into tiny filaments that appeared to have a life of their own. He reached out a cautious hand and poked it. All at once they swarmed up his arm and over his face, tightening across his skin. As he jerked back in astonishment, they disappeared in an explosion of overpowering flower aroma.

He shook his head, blind, deaf and panicking. A moment later it dissipated, and he saw Xerina's smiling face.

"What…happened?"

"I have just allowed you to experience part of the *other* scent no scent user can normally see. It is a scent sitting behind the normal scents and is discerned by those who have talent and use the cordial contained in this tumbler. I know of no male who can see this, even with cordial use, so I assume it has some sex-related attribute."

"So the *other* scent has something special about it? I've never had that happen before," he said.

"Yes, Kyel there are several special things, things rather innocuous at first but different. The most obvious is the scent power; in concentration it can have a significant impact on one's target, blinding, even deafening a person or animal. The second is an unseen but tangible scent which can physically tie up or immobilise an opponent—you might recall how I was able to restrain Dronthis very effectively?"

"Yes," Kyel nodded, "I do."

"There are other aspects to the scent, but the main thing is I want you to be aware of it. The Knowing was very specific, which is rare in the vagaries of foretelling."

"So," Kyel mumbled though a mouthful of food, "I must remember the *other* scent. But you're uncertain why?"

"Yes, Kyel, you do," agreed Xerina. "You must know about the scent as you have a role in assisting someone close to you in time to come. Who, I'm not sure—it is lost in the vagaries of the Knowing. But it will be well into the future and will have consequences for Sutan."

"I don't think that'll help my future at all if you tell them." He leant towards Xerina.

Her eyes drifted away to focus on the flowers, and she slowly shook her head. "No, I don't think I will, young man. I don't think I will."

Nefaria stood with Kast and the remaining guard under the shade of very tall trees, higher than double-storied houses and covered in large leaves that rattled in the breeze.

Jakus had met Poegna inside a white-columned gate leading to a large, spreading house of sandstone surrounded by lush greenery. As they slowly walked down the gravelled path, a tall man in light tunic top and dark pants came from the side of the house and greeted them. Even at that distance Nefaria noticed a flash of unease in the man's scent aura as he addressed Jakus.

Jakus spoke with him for a few minutes and then beckoned her. She gave the reins of her perac to Kast and hurried towards the trio.

"Nefaria," said Jakus as she neared, "I want you to be part of this conversation as you may have to be my go-between with Bilternus."

The young man had a thin face with a squarish jaw, the hawk-like nose of the ruling family and dark eyes. He turned his attention to her. "Are you sure, Uncle?" he asked in a neutral voice.

"I may not always be available, and Nefaria is my consort. Your place in my government will be firmly entrenched if you prove your worth, which means speedy information. You are no use to me if you fail to keep me informed, or if your father finds you out."

"Yes, Uncle," Bilternus said. "I want to be part of your regime. Anything I can do to help you will be my pleasure."

"That is well, nephew," said Jakus, "for I don't tolerate failure." He turned to Poegna. "Your assistance in arranging this is appreciated. I will speak to you later, at the palace. Come, Nefaria." He nodded to Bilternus and walked back up the road to his guards.

As she followed she heard Poegna's whisper: "Just do as Shad Jakus says and you'll do very well, Bilternus, very well indeed."

Chapter Twenty-Nine

Lan half stood as Alethea came into his room. "Welcome. Share my freshly brewed tea."

"You must have been expecting me," she said, sitting down as Lan poured the sweet-scented liquid from a pot into a spare cup.

"It is near time, Alethea." Lan took a sip of his drink and looked through the steam at her. "I think all who are involved in the ceremony of renewal are prepared."

"Agreed, Lan. I have also included Anyar for the ceremony, despite her age."

Lan nodded as he gazed through the thin slit of his window overlooking a field of tumbled grey boulders.

"And the cave of cleansing; are you quite sure you are ready for your role there?"

"I am, but will be reliant on you when we do this with Targas. As much as I'm afraid to admit it, I am feeling my age." Lan's face tightened as he took her hand in his. "But I must not be sentimental. There is work to be done, and we cannot shirk our responsibilities."

"You're doing the right thing, Targas," said Sadir, leaning against him as they watched the interplay of scents through the valley against the hazy backdrop of the Long Ranges mountains extending southwards.

Targas idly played with a section of scent rising from a group of trees down the slope. Stronger and thicker colours revealed the presence of life: he recognised numerous small lizards, and even a faint trace of the large predator, the k'dorian lizard. He dragged a spiral of scent closer, spreading it, feeling its bonds stretch. He smiled as he saw Sadir influencing what he was doing, tying additional scents into his work, making the blanket of scent stretch and thicken until it cast a shadow across the rocky ground. He pushed it away further, down the slope, reducing his ability to retain control. Sadir followed, showing just how far her ability had developed. By the time sweat was beading on Targas's forehead, her influence on the scent blanket faltered and she slipped away.

"You're becoming a scent master in your own right, Sadir," said Targas. "But I suppose that's to be expected with your background; and with your experience in the Nebleth cave." He felt Sadir stiffen, and mentally kicked himself.

"We've never really spoken about where you came from," he pointed out, staring unseeingly into the distance.

"Never really seemed important, love." Sadir leant into him again. "I never knew my mother, my natural mother, but understand she had some real scent talent, and the Resistance were looking to her for help. Then she died when I was a young child, well before your time though."

"Might help to explain where Anyar gets some of her talent," Targas mused.

They sat quietly for a few moments looking down the valley.

"Um, I'm not looking forward to this night. Alethea and Lan want to work with me first though." He squeezed her hand. "You'll be able to come too?"

"Yes, I will. Anything to try and get you back to normal." She rubbed a thumb across the back of his hand and pushed into him.

A few moments later, Targas noticed minute scent flares of dark red and yellow coming from various places around them.

"The local lizards sense the voral," said Sadir.

A black snout pushed into her side and Vor was there, grinning toothily at them.

"Mar! Par!" called Anyar.

"Sorry. Tried to give you some time," puffed Cathar, as she followed Anyar into the small clearing.

"It's not a problem, Cathar," said Targas, hugging his daughter. "I think we were ready to be interrupted."

Targas and Sadir, followed by Lan and Alethea, crossed the coarse sand of the expansive cavern, its smooth, concave walls lit by Lan's torch.

The walls of the cavern contained a few large "pockets" along its length, scoured out by a persistent stream over the ages and Targas, gripping Sadir's hand, followed Lan through an opening into one of them. The almost spherical room was one he remembered as he stepped on the fine white sand, the small pool fed by a trickle of warm, clean water.

"Are you ready, Targas?" asked Lan as they settled cross-legged onto the soft sand.

Targas looked around the enclosed space. "I think so."

"If Sadir could shave you to remove the scent-trapping hair?"

"I'm happy to, Lan." Sadir smiled fleetingly at Targas.

Alethea and Lan sat quietly as Targas removed his tunic top, washed his head and torso in the warm waters of the pool and sat on a convenient rock near the pool. Sadir brushed his skin with a scentless lather from a large earthenware bowl before applying a shaving razor.

Targas tried not to think, keeping his mind as blank as he could, not going where dark things waited, feeling curiously detached as Sadir moved the razor across his skin.

He ran his hand over his face and scalp, feeling a fuzz of stubble where his hair had been.

"Now Alethea…" said Lan

"Could you sit on the sand before me, Targas?" Alethea said gently. "And Sadir, could you sit behind him? I may need to use you, so be prepared."

Targas settled into a cross-legged position with a slight wince. He watched Alethea as she breathed slowly and the scents of her aura thickened.

"Now Targas, this room is special. It consists mainly of neutral scents and allows us to better investigate our scent abilities and how and where they are situated within our heads. Make yourself as comfortable as you can and try to feel a part of this space. Let yourself go. Trust me."

Targas concentrated on the soft sand and the feel of the room as he tried to relax to the sound of Alethea's voice.

"Open your mouth slightly and close your eyes. Relax. Don't worry if you sense me."

Targas forced himself to relax, allowing his thoughts to drift.

He was on a long, curved balcony, one side a low balustrade that disappeared into the darkness, the other a wall. He followed the sounds of someone ahead, someone screaming. He recognised the scream, but he couldn't see anyone. He pushed himself, always the curve of the wall prevented him from seeing ahead. He went faster, body aching with effort. The screaming grew louder.

When his heart felt about to burst, another wall blocked his way. He crashed his fist against the stone, again and again. His hand cracked painfully, blood smearing the bricks. He hit his head on the hard surface in frustration.

The screaming now came from his side. He turned towards the sound. A stream of blood was running from his hand to the edge of the balcony, towards the darkness. He looked down.

It was pitch black, but he could still see the blood scent, pooling in the air, spinning into a whirlpool of dark odour. The screaming was ear-shattering as the whirlpool rose to meet him, forms swirling within it. Targas strained to make them out.

The blood coalesced into a face, bloodied teeth and staring eyes. They looked directly into his soul. The screaming swept over him until the voice he recognised died away. The face leered, laughed wetly and disappeared into the darkness.

He was drawn to follow that face into the void but something whole, something pure, prevented him. His shoulders heaved. He coughed and fell backward. He felt hands on his shoulders as he lost consciousness.

Targas's eyes flickered open. He was lying on the soft white sand, his head pillowed in Sadir's lap. The concerned faces of Alethea and Lan watched him closely, calming scents drifting across him.

"What...?" he asked, jaw feeling disjointed.

Alethea looked quickly at Lan. "I...ah, that was...most instructive."

Lan nodded, his face wrinkling. "One way to put it, Alethea."

"I never want Targas to go through it again," Sadir said firmly.

"Nor I, for that matter," gasped Targas.

He closed his eyes, using the softness of Sadir's lap to help slow the headache threatening to rip his skull apart. The face revealing itself, threatening to take over his mind, had come loose from wherever it had been hiding. The man wasn't dead, despite Targas having witnessed his terrifying end. Septus had survived somehow, inside his head, inside his scent memories. And he wasn't about to let go.

Targas felt rather than heard the others talking above him, coming to terms with what had happened, but he didn't want to know. The pain was pulsing in waves through his head as he realised...*the screaming*. The screaming wasn't Septus's, it was his victim's. The victim was Sadir, and the sound was her pain as Septus had dragged her away from a helpless Targas.

"Come, love," said Sadir softly, "we must get you back." She shifted his head and pushed him to a sitting position. Lan's rough hand gripped his and he got slowly to his feet.

"My head..."

Sadir helped on one side and Lan the other as he shuffled through the sand towards the entrance to the cavern. Alethea smiled encouragingly while they manoeuvred him through the opening and onto the path.

"Keep walking, Targas," Alethea murmured as they climbed. "We need to get you something to eat and drink to help you over this experience."

"Hah!" he snorted, and then immediately wished he hadn't as the pain began afresh.

The sun was directly overhead as they climbed the last few steps and entered Sanctus.

"To the bathing rooms, I think," said Lan. "The waters will be therapeutic."

The bathing rooms were set side by side farther back in the complex, with one normally used by men and the other by women. Each had several pools of varying temperatures, stone seats set against the granite walls, and two massage tables. The warm waters trickled into the pools at one end and fed away through a large drain hole. The humid air was filled with distinctive, sharp odours.

"We'll take him in here," said Lan. "It will be quiet and relaxing."

Sadir helped him to a seat. He felt fuzzy headed, with the headache receding as he drew in the sulphurous scent of the water.

"Come on, love," said Sadir, as she pulled off his trousers, "you'll be better for it." She and Lan walked him to the low steps, but he wobbled slightly as he felt the slippery stone under his feet.

"I best go in with him," said Sadir, knowing that it was not unusual for men and women to share the pools. "I wouldn't trust him to keep his balance."

Alethea took her place while Sadir removed her clothing, then taking his hand guided him into the water.

The water immediately warmed his body as Sadir led him to a seat set below the surface.

Targas sat and leant against the stone edge of the pool, enjoying the feel of the cloth as Sadir washed his face and chest. His eyes began to close as he felt her skin on his, and he felt more at ease than he had for a while.

The benefits of the bathing rooms and the afterglow of a massage kept the disturbing memories at bay. They were dressed in warm robes and sitting in Lan's room drinking hot, spicy perac milk.

"Now you'll tell me what you found," said Targas grimly.

Alethea glanced at Lan, who gave the merest nod.

"Why don't you tell me what you experienced?" asked Alethea. "We have our opinions, but it will be of benefit to hear yours."

Targas rubbed his hand across his bristly scalp shaking his head, face muscles tensing. "I suppose I must." He related what had happened, how his nightmare of the tower at Nebleth had been crafted by Septus, in his head. "But it was the screaming that pulled at me. Sadir's screams."

"And you, Sadir? What did you experience?"

"I felt fine at first," she said softly, "watching, seeing how you and Lan worked the scents, how Targas reacted.

"Then I was pulled in somehow, my head hurting so much that I was yelling." She looked at Alethea's understanding eyes. "At least I think I was."

"We heard nothing, Sadir," murmured Lan.

"So it was in my mind? He came in a red fog into my mind, too?" She took a quick gulp of her warm milk. "It went on. I…I think I was there, with Targas. And it hurt. Then the pain faded. I felt you both, and Septus had gone."

"So what do you think?" asked Targas curtly. "Have we gone through all this for nothing?"

"No, no, my friend." Lan raised his hand. "We have learnt a great deal. You are most fortunate in having a vastly experienced scent master here. Not only is Alethea well respected in Ean, she is the Mlana, the head of her country back in Rolan."

Alethea nodded, eyes bright in her lined face. "Yes, we have learnt from your experience, Targas. We do know you have been severely affected by the evil of that man. We also know he has infiltrated your scent memories, and your mind, in a most inexplicable way.

"The cleansing in the caverns enabled me to investigate your being in such a way that I could see the intricate web he has left in you. And together, Lan and I managed to force his essence back, away from affecting your life as he has been doing. His influence on Sadir should also have been reduced."

"So, I'm cured?" Targas ran his hand down his arm as if pushing off water. "No more Septus."

"Uh, no," said Lan. "But we do know more of what we are dealing with."

"Great!" Targas stood suddenly. "Just great."

"A moment, Targas." Alethea stood as well. "I will not be letting this go. My priority is to seek a cure for you. My Knowing is that I must do this."

"Seek a cure? Surely you mean *cure* me? I don't know if I could keep going if there's no hope."

"Targas, it would be wonderful if the Knowing was that specific, if it said you would be cured. But it doesn't. It is just that I should make every effort to try."

"So that means me, too," Targas growled. "And with no guarantees."

"As you know, my friend, you mean too much to Ean for us to desert you now." Lan came over and put his arm on Targas's shoulder. "Now you two may care to have some moments alone to ready for this night and the ceremony of renewal."

"Ah, the ceremony. Won't it just give...*him* an opportunity?"

"No, I doubt it," said Lan. "With the presence of our scent talents and what the ceremony brings to us all, nothing but good will come to you both."

"Thank you, Lan, Alethea," said Sadir, taking Targas's hand. "We'll go and find Anyar, have some family time."

"We'll have to be getting up now." Sadir gently shook Targas. "Anyar, little one, we'll get Vor his food and then we can go down to the caverns with everyone else. Can you make it on your own, Targas?"

Targas opened a bleary eye and watched Sadir take his daughter out through the door. "Ah, damn, that wine-rotted headache's back." His rest had been anything but restful, and he felt unprepared for the renewal ceremony. He sat at the end of the bed with his head in his hands, trying to push the ache away. "Not much use, but maybe it'll improve."

He slipped on his robe and sandals before shuffling out of the door towards the common room.

He joined the flow of grey-robed people walking through the dusk down the path amongst the tumble of granite boulders. When they reached the entrance to the cavern Targas slipped through the narrow split in the rock into the dark, still atmosphere. He immediately heard the murmur of those ahead of him as the sand crunched under his feet.

The cavern was lit by smokeless torches set at intervals along the rock walls and a familiar sweet smell filled the air. Moonlight filtered in through the opening in the ceiling.

"Par!" A small pair of arms wrapped themselves around his waist and as he ruffled Anyar's hair he saw Sadir next to him.

"I'm glad you're here, Sadir," he said, seeking her hand with his free one. "How's Anyar taking it, the dark I mean?" His daughter's grip tightened on his waist as he attempted to move further in.

"I think she'll be fine," whispered Sadir. "It's a problem that there are no other children at Sanctus. If it wasn't for Alethea, I would have preferred her back in the rooms."

Targas bent and kissed Anyar on her hair. "I think it's too late now. Lan's getting ready."

They followed the general movement of ghostlike shapes forming a large circle towards the back of the cavern. It quietened as the scent intensified to a cloying, vanilla-like aroma. An odd vibration added a sound, causing Anyar to stiffen and point at the sight of the large moths flying in and out of the man-sized hole in the ceiling.

The torches around the walls were snuffed out, leaving only the pale glow of the moon shining into the cavern. Alethea and Lan waited in the centre of the circle, directly under the hole.

"Targas, Sadir. Would you come?" gestured Lan, his robed arm held out in invitation.

"Can I take Anyar for you?" Boidea's voice near his ear caused Targas to jump.

"Sadir? Is that alright?"

"I think so, Targas," she said. "I think this is more about us, and she would be better off with Boidea."

He waited while Anyar reluctantly settled next to Boidea, before taking Sadir's hand and walking over to Alethea and Lan. He tried to push his concerns to the back of his mind. The ritual in the small cave had not given him hope things would get better. Last time he had everything to gain. This time he had more to lose.

Everyone stilled, waiting, the glow of the moon through the hole perceptibly brightening as it moved overhead.

"Now, my friends, it begins!" Lan's voice broke the quiet. "We replenish. We renew."

The soft rustle of clothing followed as the people within the cavern removed their robes and settled on the sand, linking hands. Targas briefly wondered whether his daughter would be comfortable with what was happening, before he disrobed and sat with Sadir and Alethea. Lan was opposite him, a ghostly shape in the moon's glow, part of a small circle in the centre of the large ring of pale bodies.

The noises ceased.

"Link hands," said Lan quietly.

The moon's light appeared like a solid beam, illuminating the four of them.

The vibration began, so familiar, so surreal. Experiencing such an event, when the people came together to bring psychic healing through their scent abilities, was the best of experiences, and Targas began to drink it in, adding to it in his own way. The atmosphere became heavier as the scent thickened to become visible in the light, the vibration allowing the scent to drive deeper into his body, into his head. He opened to it, feeling the people next to him, the steadfastness and love of Sadir, the depths of the Mlana of Rolan and the purposeful serenity of Lan. All were adding, contributing to the experience, making him feel part of a greater whole.

He felt his senses opening, allowing the scent influence to push and prod him, working through his memories, smoothing the way, making him feel complete. He sought to follow the light into the myriad of pathways that made up his scent memories, allowing the vast network of scent-talented beings to push him even higher into the cleansing ritual.

The sand on his skin began to irritate. He wriggled his buttocks to get more comfortable, to rejoin the experience, but a blockage was across his sensory memories. He felt a darkness where there should have been light, a tightness that should not have been there, but he could not move. He reluctantly pulled out of the joining, feeling he was unable to finish, feeling exhausted and unfulfilled.

The light slowly diminished as the moon moved on. He saw Sadir blink and turn her head, her eyes dark in a pale face. She smiled sadly and squeezed his hand.

After some time, the others began to move and get dressed.

"Come, Targas," murmured Lan, "it is time to leave."

Targas cursed silently as he stood. It had failed. Septus had won.

Chapter Thirty

Faltis kept his hand on his replacement dagger as he limped along the corridor leading from his rooms in the palace. A dark scent aura hung over his head when he flung open the doors to the courtyard. The guards straightened, keeping their eyes fixed ahead.

He hurried across the cobbles towards the stables, his dark robe flapping around his gaunt form.

"Where's Siluser?" Faltis yelled at the stable master, causing him to snap to attention.

"He was here earlier, Shad, but he went with the rest of your guard, just moments ago," the stable master said, edging towards the side wall.

"Damn him!"

"Y…your mount is ready, saddled and packed, Shad. Siluser has made sure of that."

"Hah!" Faltis pulled at his perac, causing it to jig sideways. "Well, take it outside then!"

The stable master slipped around him to untie the reins and lead the animal away. Faltis took a quick look around the building that held a long line of stalls containing merely a few perac. "Jakus is out, I see."

The man paused at the door. "Yes, Shad. He left earlier."

Faltis followed him, just as a wiry man in a dark cloak, brown trousers and black boots clattered out of the palace doors.

"Siluser! Where have you been?"

"Readying the guard at the gates. The men are awaiting your orders." He gave a disarming smile as his eyes registered the colour of Faltis's scent aura.

"We ride to my estate, as well you know. We have much to do."

They turned out of the gates and rode along the main thoroughfare of Sutaria, their rising dust swept away by the strengthening breeze.

They followed a wide side road leading towards low hills, the only feature of prominence in the flat plains around Sutaria. A wide, shallow river, waters brown and thick, lay a short distance to the west of the hills. A favourite home of biting insects and the deadly scartha, the river meandered through extensive marshlands from its origins on a vast plateau in the north.

Faltis's eyes tightened as his gaze swept the river, noting the shimmer of scents rising into the hot air. It was not the first time he was glad his home lay on the cooler slopes of the hills and away from the pest-ridden waters bisecting the city.

The brown brick buildings of his estate were squat and extensive, cut into the rocky slope, leaving a low, defensible profile. The surrounding ground was stony and barren, with wooden dormitories and stables on one side flanking a wide, gravelled area.

A number of servants rushed out when the troop of men clattered up to the stables. Faltis dismounted, flung the reins at one of them and hurried towards the house, Siluser in close attendance.

"Methra!" he shouted as he entered a dark hallway.

"Yes, my Lord." A tall, heavy-set woman wearing a long beige dress, dark hair tied behind her head, stood in a doorway holding a large cup in her hand.

"Prepare food!" he ordered. "We'll eat in the planning room." He grabbed the cup as he strode past. "A cold towel, too—it was a hot ride."

He continued past her, limping slightly as he headed down the hallway towards a bright, open doorway.

"Your side, my Lord," Methra called after him, "you're injured."

"Just do what I asked!" he snapped.

"Yes, my Lord Faltis," she murmured to his retreating back.

"Ah, Methra. You are well?"

She swung around as Siluser entered the house.

"Yes, Siluser, I am." A tentative smile crossed her face. "He went into the planning room, if you care to follow."

"My thanks." Siluser gave a slight bow and kept walking.

He entered a long, sunlit room where he saw Faltis bent over a large parchment spread on a low wooden table.

"Here, Siluser," Faltis beckoned. "Look at this map. Tell me where you think my brother is going. Tell me what your spies say."

He stood back as his captain leant over the parchment. Siluser took his time, tracing his finger along the line of the Grosten River from the plateau and the Steppes of Stone, down to Southern Port, along the coast to the port city of Semplar and up the Westforth River to Hestria. He tapped the map in thought, and then looked up into Faltis's impatient eyes.

"My information is that many of the greater families are in league with Jakus. You'll recall his meeting in Southern Port, and how cloaked in secrecy that was.

Unfortunately, our losses at that time prevent us from knowing just who they were, but we can hazard a guess." Siluser looked back at the map, pursing his thin lips.

"Your support is still extensive, but…"—he glanced sideways at Faltis's scent aura—"his display of power and this scent enhancer crystal Jakus has mean more are on his side than first evident."

Faltis stomped to the window before crashing his fist onto the ledge. "This is one time when I wish my brother Brastus was here. As loathe as I am to say it, he could always stand up to Jakus better than I. And together we could easily take him, even with his damned crystals."

Methra walked in quietly with a tray of food and a towel in a dish, which she placed on the table.

Faltis swung around at the slight noise, waved Methra away and came back to the table. He picked up the damp towel and wiped his face. "Your thoughts on what he will do and where an opportunity might be?"

"My Lord Faltis?" Siluser looked up with a slight grin. "You want my thoughts on strategy?"

Faltis barked a laugh and picked up a pastry. "As ever, Siluser, as ever."

Siluser placed a well-manicured finger on the location of Southern Port. "My guess is his expeditionary force to gain this supposed magical crystal from Rolan will either depart Sutan from here, or the Port of Semplar. Logical, since they are the only two ports, but it would depend on what secrecy he needs and from where most of his force is sourced, since Brastus has the pick of the troops with him on the Tenstria campaign. Again, we could surmise that apart from those loyal to you here in Sutaria, most of our opposition will come from the northerners and those in the west. Unfortunately, when Jakus was living in Hestria, he managed to make several alliances."

"So,"—Faltis dropped a crumb of pastry on the map—"it's nothing we don't know."

Siluser wiped off the crumb and pointed at the middle of the parchment. "The point where your brother will be with the least support and most vulnerable is here, at the Hestrian Pass."

Faltis leant forward, eyebrows drawing together. "Hestria. But what makes you think he'll be at his most vulnerable then, or even if he'd go there?"

"Could be, my Lord Faltis," Siluser said with an irritating half smile, "that I've surmised it is the most logical place for him to go. Or could be that not all my spies were killed in the Southern Port battle."

Faltis shifted impatiently.

"Yes, limited intelligence from that time revealed a small gem; they are gathering in Hestria in the near future."

"And the Hestrian Pass?"

"What better place, Faltis? One of the foulest holes in Sutan, with overwhelming scents and suitable terrain, the Pass gives the best opportunity to defeat your brother."

Faltis walked back to the window with another pastry and chewed slowly. "Yes," he said, "it may work. This plan may work." He pointed at Siluser. "Follow it up. Keep me informed, especially when your spies report. Now you may go and work with the men. Send Methra to me on your way out."

"My Lord Faltis," Siluser said, noticing the oranges and light reds of arousal clouding the man's scent aura. He inclined his head, took a pastry and walked out of the room.

"Kast!" Jakus snapped as the troop travelled the main road of Sutaria. "Did you notice anyone paying undue interest in our meeting?"

"Yes, I believe so, Shad," the tall scent master moved closer to Jakus's mount. "He was trying to use a scent camouflage to blend in with the background but the magnesa enhancement saw through it."

"As long he was far enough back not to see young Bilternus." Jakus stared at Kast.

"Yes, Shad. We were careful to block his view without appearing to."

"Hmm, that had better be so, Kast. There is much riding on this."

The troop entered the side gates flanked by twin sandstone columns on one side of the palace. Jakus's eyes narrowed at the sight of fresh perac dung scattered across the cobbles. He saw the stable master waiting at the doors to the stables and beckoned him over.

"This?" he pointed to the dung as he swung down off his animal.

"Yes, I apologise, Shad," the man began, his florid face reddening, "I'll…"

Jakus held up his hand. "I don't want to know your cleaning arrangements. Has Faltis left recently?"

"Yes, Shad. He and his guard left around midday."

"Take my perac to the stables," Jakus grunted. He dropped the reins and snapped his fingers at Nefaria. "We best go in and check on your Eanite. Won't want anything to have happened to him while we've been gone, eh?

"Kast," he continued as he walked towards the palace doors, "we'll meet after the sundown meal. There is much to do. See that our rooms are secure."

His boots rang on the stone floor as he strode into Xerina's rooms, his gait betraying his healed injuries from the battles long ago in Ean. Jakus stopped and glared at the small woman.

Xerina kept her eyes on the pool, watching a dragonfly hover over the water, the angled sun reflecting off its wings.

"I know you are there, Jakus," she said softly. "And I know you are impatient. Rest assured your charge is as well as can be expected. He is in my sleeping room, still recovering." Xerina turned her head, her eyes glinting. "I suggest you leave him for another day, at least. The abuse to his system requires that."

"Hmph." His scent aura darkened as he returned Xerina's stare. Then he turned and walked off. "Nefaria, check the old woman's not lying. Then report to me," he said loudly as he disappeared down the corridor.

"Not a likeable man, your lord, is he?"

Nefaria didn't answer.

Nefaria entered the main living room situated in the suite she and Jakus occupied. The noise increased in volume as the shreds of the barrier broke across her skin, the almost invisible scent bonds reforming behind her to continue providing some protection against eavesdropping.

Jakus looked at her and signalled. "Serve wine, then record our discussions."

She walked to the bureau at one end of the long, wide room, past the crackling fire and the narrow table, nodding briefly at Poegna and Kast before noticing Festern of the Steppes, whom she'd last seen at Southern Port.

She enjoyed being at the forefront of the planning for the coming campaign. Jakus's trust in her and involvement meant a great deal, allowing her to forgive his authoritarian ways.

A pottery jug of red wine sat on the bureau; a dozen cups of rare-traded glass around it. It took her several trips to bring them to the table and pour wine for each person.

Jakus took a glass without withdrawing his attention from the parchment spread across the table. She sat at a vacant place, took up the pen that lay with several sheafs of blank parchment and waited.

Jakus looked up. "My friends, it is now we can plan the next stage of our campaign. Faltis has been revealed as the current enemy within Sutan and as my father is content to leave matters where they fall, we need to take steps to negate my brother's effect on what we do.

"All scent masters and guardsmen should be in the Hestrian region soon with adequate supplies for the voyage to Ean and Rolan. So," he smiled at the people gathered around him, "we will be sailing to Rolan and to the very site of magnesite. Once we acquire it in quantity, we'll be able to achieve much, including the renaissance of Sutan as a world power.

"The future looks promising."

Nefaria sipped her wine and dipped her pen in the inkwell.

"Now for reports. Festern?" Jakus watched as the big man stood.

"I made this journey in haste, Jakus, for I wanted to be here at the planning of the next stage," said the bearded man. "My sons are gathering the contingent

I promised, those your brother, Brastus, left us when he was conscripting for his campaign. And there is certainly no support in the Steppes of Stone for your other brother, Faltis."

Jakus smiled, his scent aura glowing red and green. "The strength of the northerners is well known, Festern. Your contribution to the planning will be of value."

"You already know my position and of those I have readied to travel with us," Poegna added.

"Yes, I do," said Jakus. "I look forward to seeing how all the arrangements work out. Now, as I outlined in Southern Port, our initial marshalling of our expeditionary forces will be in Hestria. Festern, I assume your sons will bring the Steppe people directly to Hestria via the Westforth River?"

Festern nodded.

"I will be taking three ships stocked with additional troops, animals and supplies. We will be leaving Sutaria in several days once certain arrangements are made."

"You plan to discuss the tactics for dealing with the Rolanites when we arrive in Hestria, Shad Jakus?" asked Kast.

"Yes, in Hestria and while on board. There will be time for my scent masters to become well acquainted with techniques for dealing with them. One thing we must not do," Jakus smiled grimly, "is underestimate our enemy. They may not be known as a warlike people, but they have the use of magnesite and the effects of the magnesa extract, and it would not do to be complacent despite our knowledge of warfare."

A shiver ran down Nefaria's spine as Jakus spoke, and she hoped her reaction was not a premonition.

Chapter Thirty-One

"**P**ar, Par, Par," Anyar shrilled, bouncing on Targas's stomach. He grabbed at his daughter.

"Anyar! What in Ean's name are you playing at?"

Anyar stopped abruptly. "Par's cross?" she asked in a small voice, eyes wide in the dim light of the bedroom.

"Grrrrr!" A dark face, with sharp white teeth, came close to his neck.

"Lizards' teeth!" he yelled sitting up, still holding onto his daughter.

The voral stretched his clawed front feet onto the bed, looked at Anyar, and then dropped back to the floor.

Even in his rough awakening Targas could see a scent aura around his daughter, initially with yellow flashes of panic, now calmer with pastel blue and green.

"Sorry Anyar, I've had a hard night. But you really must try not to wake your father up so...so forcefully." He kissed her on the forehead and pushed her off the side of the bed.

"Par," the young girl said, winding her fingers into the fur of the voral's back, "Mar's eating, so you can come now?"

"Alright, if I must." Targas heaved a sigh and swung his legs over the side of the bed as Anyar and Vor scampered out. He sat with his head in his hands, thinking through the previous night. It hadn't gone well. The anticipated euphoria and sense of wellbeing had fizzled out in the ceremony in the caverns. The blockage in his scent sense had come to the fore and stopped his joining with Sadir and their friends.

Things were not going well despite all they had tried. The parasite in his brain remained.

Targas slowly stood to his feet and slipped on his robe before finding the sandals, kicked under the bed by an over-energetic voral. He half smiled at the bond between it and his daughter.

He heard the babble of people reliving the excitement of the previous night as he moved down the corridor and hesitated at the entrance to the common room. Several people looked up as he entered, and he saw the dull grey of disapproval in their scents.

"Targas, over here." Sadir waved from the usual table at the window. Lan pointed to a spare place.

He wove his way through the tables and crowd of people until he reached them. Sadir smiled, although next to her Anyar was busy slipping bread and honey under the table. He resisted the urge to look and rubbed at his eyes.

"Welcome, my friend," said Lan. "I trust you managed some sleep last night?"

"Very little. And I could have slept longer if…"

"Don't blame Anyar, Targas," said Sadir. "I sent her in. Now sit down and eat. I've got you tea as well."

"Stop nibbling my toes," Cathar squealed, looking under the table.

"It's that voral," said Targas. "Anyar and he are inseparable."

"Particularly with honey around," laughed Cathar, eyes bright, thin face flushed. "He's made my feet awfully sticky. Maybe best to feed Vor outside next time, Anyar?"

The girl glanced across the table at Cathar before ducking back under the table.

Targas took a bite of toast as he looked past Boidea and Lethnal, who made up the last of their group at the table, before noticing a number of strangers sitting nearby, dressed in similar green clothing to Alethea. Several were watching him and one nodded, clear eyes in a competent, weathered face. He raised an eyebrow at the Rolan Mlana.

Alethea followed the direction of his gaze. "Members of my party who brought me to Ean, Targas. They have returned from trading to Regulus. We will meet up after you have eaten."

He nodded and took another bite, followed by a swallow of tea. Targas didn't feel sociable and knew there would be more talk on the way. He felt Anyar push past his legs, followed by the voral. They ran past the people moving between the tables and scampered out of the door leading to the outside.

"More energy than I've got."

"It's wonderful to see," said Sadir. "There are no other children here so we should be thankful she's found a friend in Vor, now that Kyel's…" She put a hand to her eyes and wiped away a tear.

"I best follow," said Cathar, smiling at Sadir. "Never know what mischief those two'll get up to."

Kyel, thought Targas, watching the slim young woman follow Anyar's path, *how easy it is to forget what's happening to him.* Cathar was around the same age, a trainee scent master and safe, while Kyel was away from Ean with the enemy. He had no illusions of what Jakus was capable of.

"Best see where she's gone." He stood and took Sadir's hand. "I'll catch up with you later, Alethea."

Alethea nodded.

A group of them crammed into Lan's room to discuss the night of renewal. As Targas suspected, there was little outcome for him from the event. The best he could hope was more working with Alethea to try and fix the demons inside him, and that meant returning with her to Rolan, anything relating to Kyel and his Sutanite companions further away than ever.

He wondered at the loyalty of Sadir. As difficult as he had been, she had agreed to come with him—indeed Alethea said it was meant to be—but she had an almost greater motivation to stay. He looked at her and their eyes met, her scent aura showing the greys and pastels of sadness and loyalty. Targas breathed a supporting scent towards her.

"Before we involve Alethea's trading party," said Lan, "we have discussed who should go with Targas, Sadir and Anyar to Rolan. We must remember that time is against us. The weather is turning, and the passes become almost impossible during the time of snows."

"Oh, you're not coming, Lan?" asked Targas.

"No. There is a lot to do in Ean, my friend," he grimaced. "A lot, if we are to believe Alethea's Knowing and recent events. The Sutanites will not be leaving Ean alone and the attack in Nebleth, and other unexplained incidents, means we need to prepare."

"And you are the recognised leader in Ean, Lan," said Lethnal empathetically.

Targas stiffened. "Of course. It hadn't occurred to me, not with the time you've spent with us."

"I think, Lethnal, you are being a bit dramatic. Ean is really a collection of cities and towns, and each tends to control its region. Once the Sutanites were ousted, we have operated like this." Lan rubbed his chin. "I suppose I have responsibility for the northern region, along with Lethnal; Heritis is in charge of Regulus, as he was during the previous regime; Jelm has Nebleth and Port Saltus is controlled by a collection of merchants and barge people.

"But Lethnal is right to raise it. The time for a more cohesive control is now, and if that needs more leadership then it must be done. So"—Lan raised his hands, palms up— "in answer to your question, I will not be going."

"It's been a straightforward decision, Targas, Sadir," said Alethea. "I am blessed, or some say cursed, with the responsibility of Knowings or foretellings, and the interpretation of such. When you get to my age it's as easy as slipping into another set of clothing. Other than the unforeseen Knowings, I normally receive direction, and this trip is to include the three of you and the current minder of your child, Cathar. No one else from Ean is indicated."

Targas watched the flow of scents in Alethea's scent aura, a complicated mixture of regret, sadness and inevitability. He saw her take a quick glance at Lan and noticed a mirroring of her scent aura in his.

"One other thing if you wouldn't mind, for Sadir and myself. Do you have any feelings about Kyel, such as how he is, or where he is?"

Alethea looked into her hands. "I'm sorry for not talking to you on this very important issue but I have little to say. No Knowings have included him, at least not in a definite way. All I can say is that his journey is part of a greater scheme." She met Targas's eyes. "Kyel controls his own destiny, and I would hope to know if it were to end prematurely. Small comfort, my friends."

"Now, would you like to meet the other members of our party?" she asked brightly.

The air was still and chilly with the moon a golden globe far to the west, the sun still too low to make an appearance. Wispy fingers of cloud over the mountains behind Sanctus promised a change in weather.

The perac were restless, piled with traded goods of wool, salt and crafts from Ean. Anyar looked like a green ball in padded Rolan clothing, with Sadir fussing over her. Cathar spoke with one of the traders, a broad-shouldered man named Telpher, while the leader, Drathner, was tightening a load.

Targas felt a sense of regret as he looked around the rocky surrounds of Sanctus, the spill of huge boulders covering the hillside and into the darkness filling the valleys. It had been a sanctuary to both himself and Sadir during his time in Ean, and was aptly named.

A pair of figures separated from near the entrance to the Sanctus complex. He recognised Lan and Alethea.

"Targas," said Lan, "a lot is riding on you, more than you might realise. Please make every effort to get well and evict that which lives inside you, for it is vital for both of our countries. If I do not see you again, go well, my friend." He leant close and touched Targas with his nose.

"What? Surely not. We'll be back, won't we?"

Lan's face was inscrutable as he met Targas's gaze. Suddenly, Targas turned and walked to his perac, moisture welling in his eyes.

"Help me get Vor into the saddlebag," said Sadir. "Anyar insists."

He could see his daughter's face, pale under a hood in the darkness, as he began to look for the voral. A pair of clawed feet landed on his thighs, so he reached down and lifted him.

"In here, Targas." Sadir held open the flap, and the voral wriggled out of his arms and in.

"Phew, he's grown heavier," said Targas, grateful for the interruption to his misgivings.

"Travellers and friends," called Lan, his voice echoing, "The Mlana and I wish to send you off in our traditional way."

Lan and Alethea stood together against the granite entrance to Sanctus. They raised their linked hands and began to hum. The sound was quickly joined by the people in the clearing and those standing inside the complex. The vibration grew, building into a rhythm until the air seemed full of scents, thickening the twilight. The scents appeared to flow through everyone, bringing a sense of belonging and oneness.

Slowly the sound faded, leaving a feeling of peace. Targas looked over to Lan and Alethea, who remained linked, faces touching, their scent auras light in the early dawn. For some reason he sensed a final farewell.

No one moved.

Lana and Alethea broke apart and faced their audience.

"Come!" ordered Alethea, her voice cracking, "we have a long way to go this day."

Drathner helped her into the saddle before mounting his perac. He took the lead of a goods-laden animal and urged them into a walk.

The rest of the party followed, Targas behind Sadir. The soft, shuffling gait of the animals quickly moved them up a narrow trail leading into the hills behind Sanctus.

Targas looked back but couldn't see the figures in the dark. He had a feeling he would never see Sanctus and those he left behind again.

The sun had risen over the mountains, revealing the ruggedness of the countryside. They were walking their animals now the terrain was steeper. Tall trees with fine dark green, needle-like leaves covered the slopes, although jagged boulders and falls of scree made gaps in the vegetative covering. A small brown fern covered the ground, growing thicker in gullies and depressions where moisture remained. The track soon narrowed further, forcing everyone to walk in single file, Anyar sitting strapped on the perac.

Targas grinned as he watched his daughter fighting the urge to fall asleep. Sadir caught his eye and smiled back.

"It's not as unpleasant as I thought it might have been," she said. "It's certainly unlike any other country I've seen."

"You're seeing it at its best," said Boidea, from behind Targas. "A still day, sunshine and an easy incline make it pleasant, but the mountains have a habit of making people regret liking them. And I don't like the look of those clouds—there's snow in them."

They both looked up and saw dark grey fingers of cloud from dawn extending further. The sun had outrun them in its travel across the sky, but the threat was there and growing.

"I think we'll have to make it a long day if I'm any judge, for next day may be hard, especially where we're going," Boidea grumbled.

Drathner held up his arm, signalling a stop. They had moved into a wooded clearing where a small stream ran off to one side. The gnarled and woody trees were mainly the same needle-leafed variety, but barely reached a man's height. The undergrowth now consisted of large mosses and a low, prickly bush. Ahead, the trail continued upwards towards a V-shaped gap between two weathered mountains, the taller of the two having a dusting of snow on its crown.

"We'll have a break here. Water your animals and remove their packs." Drathner turned to assist Alethea, but Boidea already had settled her on the ground with a pack as a seat.

Targas helped Anyar down and Sadir took her to the stream to wash. He removed the packs off both animals before leading them to the water.

The perac suddenly reared and backed away at the sound of Anyar's laughter. She was giggling at the voral splashing in the water just off the bank. He bounded down the stream, plunged deep with both paws, lifted a large pinkish worm and ate it with relish.

"Get that animal out of the water, Anyar. We have to let the perac drink."

"Wasn't that a haggar, Targas?" asked Sadir.

"It might have been," answered Targas, certain that it was. "It seems vorals have their uses."

"Tea's ready," called Cathar. "I've got Anyar some cake and fruit."

Targas walked over to the small, crackling fire and took a mug of hot tea and a chunk of traveller's bread. He sat next to the trader, Telpher.

"Your first time in these mountains, Targas?" Telpher said, jerking his head towards the way they were facing, black hair flopping.

"Mmm, yes, although we have big mountains back in Tenstria, where I come from."

"Tenstria, now there's a place I'd like to go. Heard they have a powerful drink there." Telpher smacked his lips.

"Yes, that they do, called malas. I used to make it, and well, too. We'd get a range of qualities depending on how long it had aged and based on its characteristics—it's sought after all over the known world. I've tried making it in Ean but there's something lacking here."

Telpher swept his eyes across the mountains in the distance and took a gulp of tea. "Of course we have the cordial. You know of the tumblers that we trade, but they're more a female drink made with strong spirit and fruit. I prefer a more bitter taste. We also make something like your malas, but it's never had the impact of the cordial. Then there's ale…"

"Yes," nodded Targas, "then there's ale."

The next stage of the journey was under darkening skies with cold gusts of wind. The encroaching bulk and apparent menace of the mountains grew as they approached, adding stinging particles to the wind that whipped around them in ever-increasing frequency.

Targas pulled the hood of his padded Rolan jacket further down his face to deflect some of the wind and made sure that Anyar was well covered. Sadir held the perac's bridle tightly as they walked as fast as they could go across the broken ground, while the sun gradually sank in the west.

Soon the sides of the valley rose around them.

"We'll be stopping soon?" asked Sadir in a querulous tone.

"Yes," said Boidea. "We used the same camp area on the way over. It's well protected from rockslides and out of the wind to a degree. Won't be long now."

The group entered a narrow defile where the sounds of their party were overwhelmed by the ferocious wind hissing along the sheer sides. They turned past a large wall of rock and walked into a region of quiet. Drathner ordered a stop.

The space was a *u*-shape, as if a giant spoon had taken a scoop out of the mountain, leaving a well-protected area large enough to accommodate their party. Targas helped Telpher set up their tent, made of strongly woven, untreated perac wool with pockets along all sides and supported by light, but strong, wooden poles. They filled the pockets with as many rocks as they would hold and tied the front flap back before putting all their gear and blankets inside.

"It'll be cold this night," commented Telpher as he tested the set of the tent, "but I reckon it'll get colder before we get out of the mountains."

"How long before we get through to Rolan?" asked Targas.

"Another night, if we make good time next day, but the weather's not looking the best, it's not." Telpher shook his head. "Get some food into you and settle in. I reckon we'll need all the rest we can get."

Targas looked for Sadir and Anyar and found them eating with Alethea, Boidea and Cathar near the Mlana's tent. He wandered over.

"Welcome," said Alethea brightly. "Join us, please."

He sat on his haunches and took up a chunk of travel bread filled with cold roast meat and a spicy relish. He ate while looking around at the camp all set up, with the animals tethered in a small alcove out of the wind and the travellers eating in small groups.

"Targas, we will not have a smooth crossing of the mountains," said Alethea, "but this is truly the latest we could attempt it and still be able to reach Rolan." She cast a quick glance at Sadir and Anyar. "You will need to be resolute, my friend."

Darkness fell with amazing speed while the wind howled unceasingly. Occasional swirls of sleet whipped into the relative calm of their campsite and rattled the sides of the tent.

It took Targas a long time to doze off, cramped with Sadir, Anyar and Vor in their small tent. He had given up worrying about the animal and had to let things take their course. The voral lay alongside his thigh, its head protectively close to his daughter.

Something woke him, a change in the atmosphere. The howling of the wind had faded to a light whistling

He struggled to rise and move towards the tent flap. A shape was there, large and black. His heart jumped in his mouth, until he realised it was Vor, facing toward the tied-off opening.

"What's up, Vor?" he whispered.

The animal turned and came towards him, teeth white in its open, panting mouth. It eased past to lie alongside Anyar.

As Targas watched, the voral shimmered in a pulse of scents before it, and his daughter disappeared from view.

Chapter Thirty-Two

"Hah! Where have you been?"

Bilternus stepped away from the sheet of parchment on the table, taking in the red face and dark scent aura of his father standing in the doorway.

"I…I was interested in your planning," he stammered, glancing briefly at the map. "It's not as if you've involved me much; spending time with *her* again."

"If you were here more often, you'd get to know Methra better." Faltis thrust his chin forward and took a step into the planning room. "I said, where have you been? Spending the night with those dregs in the city instead of supporting me, your father?"

"No…I was delayed somewhat." He ran his hand over his forehead, nervous scents of dull greens and yellows showing.

"I haven't time for this, Bilternus. There's much to do and I have to rely on others to perform when you, by rights, should be the one taking responsibility." He huffed and strode over to the small table, lifted a clay pitcher and poured a glass of red wine. He looked over the rim as he drank, and his eyes narrowed. "Your scents betray you. What were you doing?"

Bilternus straightened and stepped back to the table. "I was looking at your plans. After all, if you want me to take responsibility, then how about involving me more?"

"Hmm." Faltis placed the cup down and walked to the map. "Very well. This is an outline of Sutan, at least as good a map as the drafters can make. Easier than those damn scent maps, and portable, too. Although I wonder if you have enough experience to be involved with planning, you soon could be my right hand, if Siluser and I agree."

"Siluser? Always Siluser. He's not family, yet he gets to be part of everything. Wine-rotted Siluser."

"Enough!" Faltis's dark scent aura flecked with crimson. "Leave me. Come back when you're less likely to argue."

"Aah!" Bilternus slammed his hand on the table and stormed out of the room.

Faltis watched the empty doorway for a moment before he turned back to the map, running a finger along the route he knew his brother, Jakus, would have to follow.

"Methra!"

He waited, drumming his fingers on the parchment.

"Yes, my Lord?" She stood inside the doorway, unkempt hair framing her face.

"Tell Siluser I want him here. And see if you can make sure my son stays on the estate. He may run off again."

"You are a bit hard on him, my Lord," Methra said softly.

"What!" he snapped. "Just go find Siluser, then tidy yourself."

"My Lord." She bowed her head and slipped out of the room.

Bilternus made his way to the gravelled troop exercise area where a number of men and several women were sparring with long knives. He found a shaded area against the side of a shed and leant back to watch.

"Aah, there you are."

He jumped at Siluser's voice, immediately drawing his attack scents together. He slowly let his breath out as the man joined him in the shade.

"Just wondering how you got on with your father, although I hardly need to ask." Siluser smiled sideways at Bilternus as he relaxed against the wall.

"You ought to know. You're in his pocket!"

"Hardly fair, young Cer. I merely provide advice and support to Faltis."

A loud clashing of weapons caught their attention. "You should be out there, practising with the knives." Siluser nodded towards the activity.

"What's the point? We've got sufficient scent powers to beat a weapon any time."

"That may well be, but a good scent leader doesn't just rely on his powers to win. He must be able to use any weapon if he needs to."

"Siluser!" They heard Methra calling from the house.

"It seems I'm required," he commented. "Anything you want me to say to Faltis for you?"

"Surprisingly, I wish I was going with you."

Jakus pulled his gaze from the broad field in front of him filled with troops and animals to look at his father. "What?" he asked, raising an eyebrow. "Wanting to go out to fight, at your age? And with your detested son? You're becoming senile."

"I suppose I deserve that but consider my position." Vitaris held out his hand towards Jakus. "You had the plum of Ean in your keeping, sending the salt of that land to Sutan, all the while seeming to get richer, more secure. Your brothers were envious of you and what you had. They've had to fight for favour, even more than you, for that is the way of our world. And I have sought not to show any favouritism, while supporting each of you.

"And with this lack of favouritism I have let you develop in your own ways, with your own strengths and weakness, seeking not to influence where I might otherwise be tempted.

"So, each son has made his own way, moulded by what they've experienced. Then you lost Ean, coming back to Sutan in disgrace. But I let you live. Let you slink off to Hestria and lick your wounds. Kept your brothers from challenging you, defeating you."

Jakus's eyes narrowed, his scent aura darkening.

"Yes, I knew," Vitaris continued. "I knew you were damaged and needed time to recover. But I allowed you that time. Let your loyal consort support you and bring you back from that damaging defeat, to see what you were made of.

"Now we stand here, this day, watching you prepare for your expedition to Rolan, showing more confidence and more power than you have ever revealed. And if you succeed and gain what you seek in the mountainous land of Rolan, you will come back better able to expand Sutan's might. So the Knowings, and my own gut, tell me."

"You have more, old man?" Jakus had turned to face his father.

"Little more, my son," the stoop-shouldered man replied, his face haggard in the light. "I have done what I can. Brastus is overseas and not likely to return for a time, while Faltis is now doing what he does best, planning and scheming. I will not stand between you two again.

"All I ask is that you don't kill him if it can be avoided."

"Hmm." Jakus gazed at Vitaris for a long while, until he saw Kast in the distance. "I will be leaving next day, Father," he said, and strode off to meet his second-in-command.

K yel swung his leg up and down while balancing against a wall in Xerina's room, the regular movement easing the stiffness of his wounds.

He felt, rather than heard, the young woman enter with a breakfast overhung with thick odours. He stopped his exercises and walked to the low table, admiring her pleasant figure.

"Xerina insisted you had a solid meal," she said, putting down a large platter of fried eggs, thin cured meat, sliced red fruit and bread, together with a mug of hot milk. "Will that be all?" she asked.

"Yes, Empha," said Xerina, walking in. "The young man, pleasing though to look at, needs his food."

"Yes Xerina, I am at your service," Empha said as she left.

"I know you would have preferred to talk with my young temple acolyte than an old woman, but that is how it must be." She pointed to the food. "Now eat while I speak."

Xerina watched him for a moment, then nodded. "I think you are as well as you might be. I will have no excuse to keep you from those who have a grudge against you, not that I think you will be attacked again. Too much is happening and soon you will be on the move."

She leant forward and rested her elbows on her robe-covered knees. "I had another Knowing last night."

Kyel stiffened.

Xerina sat back and looked out to the pool. "You know, this view is so restful. Enjoy it while you can, young Kyel, for you may never see it again."

"What?" Kyel stopped eating and sat up. "What are you talking about?"

"Sorry," she said, "I do have a flare for the dramatic. If you think it through you would realise it is what you'd expect anyway. You are leaving with Jakus to return to Ean, while I am old and quite ready to pass on."

Kyel watched her for a moment before taking a bite of bread and egg. "Hmm. So the Knowing… What did it say?"

"It was like a usual Knowing, vague and somewhat contradictory. In essence I believe that if you return to Sutan, you will be much changed."

"In what way?" He gulped milk to wash down the bread. "Does it mean something happens to me? Or do I die?"

"No, I shouldn't think so. It seems you have a task ahead of you, but not here, not in Sutan, although…it's somewhat related. Possibly"—Xerina cocked her head to one side, her eyes glazing over—"it may be the original Knowing, but no, it's not about you.

"You see, they are vague, troublesome things, aren't they? But I do believe we'll keep this one between ourselves, don't you?" She leant forward and patted him on the knee. "Now, time to get ready, as your sanctuary is almost at an end."

As Xerina stood with an effort, Kyel heard a vague rustle down the corridor that led further into the temple.

"You fit enough to travel?" Jakus barked the question at Kyel when he entered with Nefaria.

"Yes, Jakus." Kyel looked around the long, wide room, the fireplace and the bureau at the far end. The narrow table held scrolls of parchment, and several people were standing about it with glasses in their hands. He vaguely recognised a solid, bearded man from his time in Southern Port, along with Poegna and Kast.

"Festern, you'll remember Kyel, the young Eanite causing such a fuss? I'm hoping he'll defend himself better than last time. It seems he has some value after all." Jakus laughed and helped himself to a wine off the bureau.

"Next day we ride out. It will take two days to reach Hestria. Time enough to meet with the Steppe contingent." Jakus looked at Festern, who nodded.

"Poegna, my thanks for coming out in open support at this time. That should put paid to any vague thoughts Faltis might have to assert himself. Your troops will meet with mine at dawn in the palace marshalling yards. We may as well make a spectacle of the expedition."

"Kast, I leave the organisation in your hands."

"Yes, Jakus," the big man nodded. "Then I'll go and prepare."

As he left, Jakus turned to Poegna. "Any reports as yet?"

"No, Jakus, but I will hear more this night." The slim woman in a form-fitting robe inclined her head.

"Nefaria, we'll have food in here. Please see to it. Kyel, keep the wine up to my guests."

Kyel took up the jug of wine and poured himself a glass. *I've more than earned this,* he thought.

B ilternus stood outside his quarters looking across the flat expanse of the Grosten River, glistening bronze from the sun setting across the Steppes of Stone.

He rubbed some dust off his boot with a cloth before walking around the side of the house, pausing as he heard a fast-travelling perac arrive.

A young woman in a grey riding cloak leapt off the animal, leaving its reins loose, and hurried to the side door. He strained to recognise her but she kept her hood up, making it difficult. "Ah," he breathed, "her scent aura, I've seen it before. From the palace, but which one is she? One way to find out."

Bilternus entered the house through the front door and walked along the hallway. He heard a murmur of voices and went past the doorway to the planning room and on towards the washrooms that led from the side door.

"There you are, Father," he called.

The murmuring stopped and the hooded figure brushed past, hurrying out of the door she had entered. He heard a brief clink of coin and drew in that familiar scent. *Ah,* he thought, *the temple. From the temple.*

"What are you out here for?" growled Faltis, coming into view.

"Just looking to clean up before the meal. Who was that?"

"That?" Faltis questioned as he went into the planning room. "Someone with a message for me."

"What about?" Bilternus kept his voice light-hearted.

"My business. But we will be leaving well before dawn next day." Faltis hesitated before looking to his son. "I think it is time for you to be involved. Eat with me and then we'll meet up with Siluser and the other commanders of my force."

"As you wish." Bilternus kept his face calm, knowing any chance he had of reaching Jakus with the news of a traitor in his camp had vanished.

K yel sat on his perac near the head of a large army, one of many scent masters wearing the brown and black riding cloaks, dark tunics and trousers. Nearby was Festern, the leader of the Steppe people, dealing with a fractious animal. Jakus was off to his left with several scent masters and Kast was slowly riding around the outside of the baggage train. Nefaria was further back amongst the guardsmen and army followers. He was essentially alone.

He felt a wave of sadness for Xerina, for what she had said and her kindness to him. Her words had been encouraging, enabling him to think about the role he had to play for the future of Ean. If he was to believe the Knowing, he should come through this unscathed and most likely be reunited with his family.

Kyel rose in his stirrups and looked past the army to the palace. Vitaris and his advisers stood watching the preparations where the rising sun cast shadows across the sandstone walls. He fancied he saw Xerina with them, her scents too far away to make out.

Jakus yelled an order from behind him, and he sat back in the saddle waiting for the army to move and take him to Hestria and beyond.

Chapter Thirty-Three

Targas had slept fitfully after the incident the previous night. He breathed a sigh of relief when he saw that Anyar was still asleep, safe, beside him. He pushed back the flaps of the tent to find a carpet of white over the rocks and the track they were to follow. The wind had died and even the slightest noise reverberated amongst the boulders. He checked for tracks in the snow, finding few—most likely someone who'd left their tent during the night to relieve themselves—though close to some hardy vegetation at the lip of their campsite, he saw indentations in rows of four spearing through the snow. When he mentioned it later, Drathner said he suspected adult vorals.

They were on the move early, leading their perac carefully along the snow-covered track. The locals kept looking at the sky, making him feel all the more nervous for their safety. Vor covered the ground in his gambolling gait alongside Anyar on Sadir's perac.

Targas knew the bond between his daughter and the voral was something special, and that this wasn't the first time they had done a scent-based disappearing trick.

He subconsciously released calming scents for his perac as he walked along the undulating trail and reflected on the sharp outlines of the series of mountains ahead of them, how the white softened the rough, raw nature of their path.

The persistent hiss of the wind was rising, and the previous crisp outlines were becoming indistinct and fuzzy. He looked up the line to Drathner and saw him hunched against the lightly falling snow, doggedly pushing through the drifts covering the path. Boidea supported Alethea as they kept up with the leader. A number of the trading party with one to two peracs each were ahead of him and Sadir. Cathar had followed just behind, while the tail of the party was brought up by Telpher and two other Rolanites.

Targas concentrated his efforts on ensuring Sadir and their peracs continued without mishap during the long and exhausting day.

"We will work…with each other…link our scents…form the best barrier we are able. For without it…we will fail." Althea's breath puffed in white clouds, her face wizened and pale as she held on to Drathner's arm.

The wind gusted and howled, snatching at their party, trying to fling them down the side of the mountain. They had formed a tight circle wedged into a depression formed years before by a landslide. The path they had taken was treacherous in the icy conditions and with night falling, Drathner had decided to go no further.

Targas, bone-weary after a day's hard march through the mountain passes, concentrated with Sadir to join Alethea's attempt to form a defensive barrier around their precarious position.

Targas manoeuvred Sadir and Anyar deeper into the group huddled in the depression. He and Sadir joined in the bonding ritual, realising their survival this night would depend upon it.

Icy tentacles lashing their backs broke through his concentration as they attempted to build their connection. The animals had become living walls on the outside, their accepting nature reinforced by the Mlana's scent control. The influence of the howling wind slowly lessened as they built the scents into a flexible blanket, forming a barrier to the elements. Targas could recognise the presence of each individual as he tried to use his ability to take the scent bonds and set them hard into the scent mix.

It would be a long night; warmth, safety, and holding the protective barrier were all that mattered. As he relaxed, he noticed a strange aspect to the shield, a second layer linked intimately to the bonds, adding strength and form. He traced the individual strings, finding that most went to Alethea, though a good proportion went to Boidea and lesser amounts to the other women in the group. Sadir also projected a small number, but Anyar had none. *This would bear investigating but not now,* he thought, hearing the noise of the wind grow in strength, and he fell into the togetherness of the moment.

The whiteness whirling about them lost form and colour as the night progressed. Anyar and the voral were still and quiet in the relative warmth at their feet, and most of them had passed into a doze-like state. Several times, tumblers were passed around and he took a mouthful straight from the bottle before passing it on to Sadir. The cordial, though sweet had an invigorating lift to it, unlike the harsh bite of malas, and towards the end of the night Targas was looking forward to the next serving. Finally the whiteness stilled, the wind fell away and the sun rose.

They had survived.

A flick in his consciousness alerted him just as he heard a rumbling sound and felt the ground vibrating. He joined with everyone in strengthening the barrier they had held all night. A few panicked bleats were quickly suppressed as the vibration shook their insecure perch high in the mountain pass.

As the noise grew, Targas felt boulders adding their weight to the avalanche descending on them, and he crouched against Sadir with Anyar and Vor pressing hard into them. The vague light filtering into their shelter darkened with a rush, increasing his concern for the strength of their scent barrier.

He held tight as the barrier was pummelled by the fast-moving snow. The strain on the barrier was immense but held until, with a panicked bleat, one of the perac was snatched away. The scent barrier began to unravel as the remaining animals' fear infiltrated the group. Targas's mind was pulled painfully. An overwhelming sense of loss battered his senses, and he felt a slow slide towards the lip of the slope.

With a last shudder, the avalanche tailed off, dramatically easing the pressure, and the scent barrier snapped back into place. Targas gripped his family in relief and waited for his heart rate to subside.

"The Mlana!" cried Boidea. "It's been too much for her. She's failing."

The scent protection dissipated in an instant as they reacted to the plight of their leader.

"No time!" called Drathner, with a pulse of power. "The whole slope is unstable, and we need to move. I will lead; break the trail. On my signal Telpher, Undrea and those of you who lead the perac will follow. Boidea and Targas escort the Mlana. Until we get to safety, there's little we can do for her."

Drathner eased his way through the people and animals before edging past the lip of the overhang. He held a light pickaxe and a thin rope trailed behind him, tied to an outcrop of rock in their shelter.

Targas forced away the implications of the Mlana's condition as he watched Drathner stoically pushing through the jumble of snow covering the track until he became an indistinct figure in the growing light. The slope eased not more than a short distance from where they had spent the night, but there was still no protection from the elements. Drathner turned and waved his arm, accompanied by a burst of scent which flared yellow against the white of the snow.

"Right," said Telpher, "we follow."

It wasn't a simple matter bringing people and frightened animals out of the shelter and along a narrow, icy track. The perac, ears flattened against the sides of their heads, eyes rolling, needed strong control. Fortunately, the experienced traders kept them calm and one by one they followed Telpher along Drathner's path. Targas held Anyar tightly in the saddle with his arm and kept his scent control firmly on his animal and the Mlana's. Boidea kept an arm over Alethea's slumped body, infusing a light blue scent of healing while controlling her own mount. Sadir followed closely.

A haze of scent covered the line of people and animals, the grey of control interspersed with brief flares of yellow and blood red. Everyone was filled with a sense of urgency and a need to tend the Mlana.

The track climbed towards another set of lower mountains, with several cliff faces evident.

"Ah," breathed Boidea, near Targas. "I recognise this place. It's where we stopped on our way over to Ean. A good camp. If only we had made it last night, instead of where we were."

Targas strained his eyes, watching Drathner's distant form climb a short rise and finally disappear near the first low rise.

Their breath was coming in foggy clouds as they forced their pace, pushing through the piles of snow clogging their path. Boidea kept stroking Alethea's recumbent form and hissing in frustration, her light blue scent aura interrupted by red bursts of panic. It took a concerted effort for them to reach crest of the rise and come onto the flat, protected area that had previously formed a Rolanite camp.

"Quick!" yelped Boidea. "Get the Mlana down and into the tent."

Targas took hold of Alethea's still body and lifted her into Boidea's and Telpher's waiting arms. Drathner opened the flap of the newly erected tent and they pushed inside. Sadir, leaving Anyar with Cathar, followed them in.

Boidea crouched by Alethea and pulled at her clothing as she looked around, eyes flicking from Sadir to Targas to Drathner.

"Warmth," she screamed, "if we have any hope for her!" Telpher went back outside and began to shout orders.

Targas stayed where he was, assessing the scents at work within the confined space. He could see the urgency in the strengthening of the healing threads coming from Boidea, Drathner and Sadir.

"She can't be dying. Not the Mlana. It's not her time." Boidea's control began to slip. Drathner put his hand on her shoulder and Sadir knelt next to her.

No, thought Targas, *this isn't right. If the Knowing is correct then she's got to survive, otherwise I'll never get Septus out of my head.* With that thought he acted instinctively, using the techniques he had used and developed years before. He took the strongest scents from everyone in the tent, those of sweat, breath and exertion, and compressed them around Alethea, infiltrating through her loosened clothing, tightening them against her body in a pulsating blanket. Tighter and tighter he pushed, flexing and releasing. He felt Sadir understand and joining him as Alethea's body shivered with the pressure. Before long, Boidea and Drathner were contributing.

The effort forced her sluggish blood to move, a slight pinkness coming to her cheeks but still no further sign she was reviving.

Then Targas took one of the foulest scents from his memories, those when the giant k'dorian lizards marked their territory, and released it under her nose in a small, explosive puff.

"Enough," he called, just as Telpher came into the tent with a bucket of steaming water. "We can't do any more."

"Where do you need this?" asked Telpher. "It's already warm in here."

"Bring...it...to me," gasped Boidea. "I'll clean her face if it's the last thing I do for her."

Sadir turned and looked up at Targas, a sad expression on her face. "I think we've done the best we could, love."

"Mmm," he nodded, watching Alethea's chest in hope. "Is there...?"

"I'm not sure," said Sadir. "Boidea?"

"No," she shook her head, "I..."

"M...my friends," came a small voice.

Everyone froze for a moment before they yelled in relief. Targas sank to his knees as Boidea placed her hands on Alethea's frail form.

"Mlana," Boidea gasped. "We thought we'd lost you, but you're alive."

"So it would seem, Boidea," whispered Alethea. "I...still have much to do before...I go."

"We've done it, Targas," said Sadir, grasping his shoulder. "We've done it."

Targas sat on a saddle by the substantial fire, sipping a warm broth. Telpher and several other traders were with him eating and drinking. The overhanging cliff face forced a sense of stillness throughout the camp, although the black rock had a brooding presence he could feel as he recovered from the ordeal.

Sadir had stayed with Boidea, nursing Alethea. Drathner was pacing the camp, checking on the animals, looking out to the mountains they had come through. Every so often he would stride to where the path continued down to the east, stand and shake his head.

"In a hurry to go, he is," commented Telpher. "Still a fair trek to get to Rolan. Wouldn't want to be here for another night like last."

"Don't blame him," said Targas. "Can't wait to get out of these mountains myself."

"Don't we all, though I don't like the way Drathner's shaking his head. More bad weather on the way, I suspect." Telpher stood and tossed the dregs of his tea onto the rocks. "Better see what I can do."

Targas scrubbed out his bowl with a handful of snow and looked around for Cathar and Anyar. They were sitting by the fire, the voral a flop of dirty fur next to them. Targas rose and walked over, before crouching down.

"Hello, little one," he said, scruffing his daughter's dark hair. "Feeling better?"

"She is, Targas," said Cathar, "it's been hard on her, these last days."

"Thank you for looking after her, Cathar. It's been a great help."

"My pleasure." She looked over to the tent. "I suspect we will be on the move again soon. I don't think Anyar will stay awake much longer, so she'll have to go in a saddlebag."

"I'll check with Drathner." Targas stood with cracking knees, fastened his wool jacket and negotiated the rocky ground to where the leader stood with Telpher, gazing eastwards along the trail.

"Not looking good, Drathner?" he asked as the tall man spun around, a grim expression on his thin face.

"Ah, Targas." He looked back down the trail. "Our way lies through several passes to those mountains in the distance. At a good pace we can make it by nightfall, but we have the Mlana to consider. And *that*." He pointed at a thin, dark cloud that appeared to be wrapped around the peaks like a black stain.

"It won't make the last of our journey any easier," added Telpher tiredly, "but the further we can go the less we'll have to put up with what is coming."

"I suppose we must get ready to travel again?"

"I think we must," said Drathner. "And with all speed."

Chapter Thirty-Four

Kyel watched the swaying backs of the guardsmen in front of him through slitted eyes, a dirty rag over his mouth. Dust caked his face and, despite the mask, filled his mouth. He tried to spit, but moisture had long since gone. He reached for the water sack hanging off his perac's saddle, then lifted his hand back to the reins. The next stop was still some time away and he had to save water.

A chill wind hissed across the land, bringing a swirl of dust and another reminder of his thirst. He pulled the neck of his riding cloak tighter and huddled down, falling back into the rhythmic stride of his animal.

Another hacking cough irritated him, so he jammed his heels into the perac. It bleated and leapt forward, pushing past its fellows. Kyel's mouth tightened and he kept urging the animal on, a ripple of discontent spreading through the slow-moving army in his wake.

He rode up to the tall, black form of Jakus, Kast and Festern on one side and Nefaria and Poegna slightly behind. Kyel's arrival caused Jakus to turn his head, his scent aura darkening.

"Boy. Back to the rear," he said quietly.

Kyel took a deep breath and deliberately darkened his own scent aura before looking across at the leader. "I prefer it here, with people I know. Not always at the back."

Jakus frowned and turned his body towards Kyel, small flashes of red infiltrating his scent cloud.

Kyel tensed and strengthened his shield. A scent bolt leapt across the distance between them, hitting his protection, sliding him back into the saddle. The perac rocked back on its haunches before straightening. Kyel grimaced, looking at Jakus through narrowed eyes.

The grizzled Festern reached over and placed a hand on Jakus's arm. "It's good to see the lad show some spirit. Reminds me of a young Jakus, if you can remember that far back."

The dark scent aura lightened in an instant, and Jakus laughed. "Festern, Festern. Always the diplomat. A handy talent to have at the college of learning, I recall. You are right, of course. A bit of spirit wouldn't do the Eanite any harm. Might help him cope better than his last effort with my brother." His focus changed, and he half-turned in the saddle. "Move behind, Nefaria. Don't let me catch you any closer or I may not be so accommodating." Jakus's attention swung back to a scout riding in from broken land to the north.

Kyel showed no outward sign of his inner turmoil as he urged his animal behind the two women. A curious glance from Nefaria appeared to see through his rash act, noticing his quailing heart, but he had needed to prove he wasn't a spineless nobody, and taking on Jakus was a calculated risk. He was now away from those individuals who had been keeping a discreet eye on him, and to where he could hear more of what was going on. Just as well Jakus hadn't been using magnesa.

The wind had become a strong, steady force from the north. It brought the feeling of snow, but no rain. Several low hills gave limited shelter. The trees were bent and thinly leafed, the tallest being just over man-height. A small stream running between deep pools gave enough to refill waterskins and water the animals.

Kyel had placed his saddle and groundsheet near those of Festern and his Steppe companions on elevated ground, upwind of the low cooking fires with a backdrop of vegetation. No tents had been erected and the camp was quiet as daylight gave way to night.

Kyel sat near the northern leader eating a skewer of meat, a strong-tasting hot drink in his hand. Festern's eyes glinted as he took in Kyel.

"You'd like something better, lad?" He held up a loose waterskin.

Kyel hesitated before reaching for the offering. "Thank you." He raised it to his mouth and took a long drink. The liquid was pungent yet warming as it rolled down his throat. His eyes watered.

Festern nodded as he took it back. "Good in the Steppes, this is. Braknish, we call it."

"Tastes like malas."

"Malas?" Festern took a swig. "Yes, I've heard it called that, but not from around here."

"It's called that in Tenstria," said Kyel. His throat caught as he remembered Targas and his sister.

"Tenstria?" Festern looked into the fire. "Some of my men are in Tenstria, with Brastus, Jakus's brother. Just were conscripted and taken away to a useless war."

"Festern," said Kyel, "can you tell me where we are? I know Sutan somewhat but it's hard to know."

"Don't blame you, lad. It's a fairly plain country around here. No real arable land. Not much lives here. Some lizards. A legless one as well–has a poisonous bite, too."

"So, where are we?" Festern rubbed some spilt braknish from his beard. "You will have seen Jakus's map? What we are doing is travelling from east to west, from Sutaria towards Hestria, although that city is closer to the sea. Two days' travel through very average land and we'll be there. Rough ground, nothing to see, except the pass. The ground bulges there, as if the land had a gut-ache and couldn't get rid of it. It comes with filth, too. Stinks, has boggy ground and parts that never see the sun. Don't like going there myself.

"But that's next day. Something to look forward to," he chuckled, and took another swig.

"Something to look forward to," Kyel murmured as he lay back and watched the stars. A dark shape obscured them at one stage and he couldn't work it out, wondering whether it was a Knowing. Xerina's wizened face came to mind, shaking her head.

"You!" A boot crashed down and Kyel saw one of Kast's offsiders next to him. "Git to the cooking and help with the cleaning."

Quelling an angry response, he gritted his teeth and slowly pushed himself up before rolling onto his feet. After relieving himself in the trees at the back of the camp, he wandered to the fires, following the smell of cooking.

"Ah, help." A skinny man in a grey apron grinned at him. "Grab a bite of oaten, then help clean. The Shad wants to be on the move." He shifted to a pile of dirty plates.

Kyel gobbled down some unappetising, partially cooked watery oats before cleaning the plates. "At least I'm doing something useful," he rationalised.

The camp was quickly struck and they moved off. Kyel took his perac to the front and his position near Nefaria. She smiled at him and began talking with Poegna.

The sky was covered by watery cloud, giving a grey cast to the land. The army with their browns and greys, relieved only by the scent masters' black cloaks, fitted into that landscape. Kyel occupied his thoughts with how Hestria would look. It was a place where Jakus and Nefaria had spent some time, and apparently a power base for him. He remembered Nefaria's journal and how she seemed to have enjoyed her stay there.

Around midday the terrain changed. The hills grew taller but were severely eroded into a craze of jagged shapes, deep ravines and sheer cliffs. An odour grew, thick, with a greenish cast forcing Kyel to breathe shallowly.

Jakus raised an arm and the army stopped. Several men rode on ahead while they waited.

"Take a break here!" ordered Kast.

Kyel led his animal to a flat area surrounded by cliffs. A thin trickle of water came from ahead, but the odour kept the thirsty animals away.

Bilternus was frustrated as he slipped away from the group surrounding his father, using the excuse of seeking to relieve himself. He moved back from the cluster of rocks and stretched out the kinks he'd developed during the journey to the escarpment lining the Hestrian Pass. The way had been long and they had travelled at breakneck speed, for Faltis's force needed to be at the pass well before Jakus and his army arrived.

His scent masters had ensured their scents didn't drift on the breeze towards Jakus travelling the regular trade route towards Hestria. This necessitated locking down the natural movement of scent following the south-easterly winds. Faltis needed the element of surprise to keep their progress well hidden.

Bilternus had to find a way to warn his uncle Jakus. The worst outcome would be his father winning and then seeking Vitaris's favour for retaking Ean. But Bilternus had a lifetime of living with the man and knew Faltis was not the stuff of conquerors. Jakus was a man going places and would be happy to take a willing nephew along with him. That was his option, and he wasn't going to lose it.

He walked past a group of men tending the animals, one nodding as he passed. *Got to find a way,* he thought. *Got to get a message to Jakus. No point in being a spy otherwise.*

The weather was grey with filmy cloud as he walked further back towards a small knoll where the baggage animals were tethered. No one was paying attention as he ascended the broken and eroded rock until he could see over the spread of Faltis's army lined along the ridge forming the northernmost edge of the Hestrian Pass. The gap to the southern side of the pass was substantial but the height gave Faltis a real advantage. If Jakus's army was caught unawares, it could be severely decimated by boulders and scent bolts. The thick coils of scent in the pass were easily adaptable to an attack if the opponent was caught unawares.

Bilternus needed to send a warning.

He pondered sending a scent message in a broad enough swath so that it would be picked up by Jakus and the other scent masters. But that would be open to detection, and his usefulness, let alone his life, would be forfeit. *Not a good outcome for an ambitious man,* he thought.

It came to him in a moment: Poegna, his go-between with Jakus. She owed him and now he might make that connection work.

He recalled the scents making Poegna unique: the slight floral perfume she used, the vague perspiration with sexual overtones and the hint of the aromatic herb that abounded on the slopes of her property. That should do it.

No one was looking, either attending animals or preparing light meals. He slid behind a rough chunk of decomposing granite and drew on his scent memories. He kept it thin and concentrated on a broad band, pushing out and into the stiffening breeze. He concentrated pushing more and more out until he heard raised voices and then a boot scrape nearby.

Bilternus cut off the scent, dissipating it abruptly as the steps came closer.

"Off hiding, I see!" came Siluser's nasal voice. His shadow fell across Bilternus. "What are you doing?"

"Just getting some space to myself for a moment, Siluser. Why? Is there a problem?"

"Ha!" Siluser looked around suspiciously. "Your father wants to discuss the attack plan, now Jakus's forces have been sighted. Though why he wants you, I don't know." He turned and walked down towards the escarpment.

Bilternus stood, heart thumping, fully aware he'd done little enough and was unlikely to succeed. He mentally shrugged and followed his father's second-in-command.

K yel had made a habit of staying upwind since the days of eating dust. He could see the colour of the pass ahead as the army began a gradual descent towards it. The land was covered by low scrub, relief being provided by outcrops of rock breaking through the vegetation.

He caught a vague scent, making him think of the Conduvian lizards of Ean, then heard a smashing of branches up a slight rise to his right.

"Lizards' teeth!" He gasped at a huge reptilian face looking at him, its long tongue dragging in his scents. It was larger than the k'dorian lizards of home, more scartha build, and easily able to take someone his size.

Crunch! A scent bolt hit its scaly side, yet it waited for a moment before turning away into the bushes.

"The next one who does something like that is scartha fodder!" Kast's voice was low and threatening.

Kyel could see the dark scent aura over his and Jakus's heads, and was thankful he hadn't been the one to draw their attention. He kept his senses extended after that, while focussing on the noxious-coloured scent oozing out of the pass a short distance away.

He drew in a stray scent, recognising its familiarity. He smiled briefly before something struck him as unusual. The breeze was coming over his right side, from the north-west, but Poegna was on his left a distance off. The perac continued for a few more paces as he wondered. *No,* he thought, *something's not right. The scent's too personal.*

He eased his animal towards Nefaria. "Nefaria, I've just picked up something unusual. Poegna's scent, but strong and from along that ridge ahead of us."

Nefaria raised an eyebrow, before nodding. "Poegna," she called softly. "Come and hear what Kyel has to say."

She moved over as Kyel explained what he had experienced. "That means Bilternus is here, or at least nearby." She stiffened before riding over to Jakus.

"I think," said Nefaria quietly, "that Bilternus will be with Faltis, and I don't imagine they're here for pleasure. That pass"—she looked ahead—"is not going to be easy to get through. You'd best be prepared for whatever my Lord's brother has in mind."

The army had halted. Jakus beckoned to Kyel.

"Picked up a scent, eh?" Jakus grunted.

"Yes," Kyel said and took a breath to give some detail, but was immediately gripped by Jakus's scent bonding.

"Let's see, shall we?" A thin scent snake exuded from Jakus's mouth and drove up Kyel's nostrils. He shuddered as he felt the invasion of his scent memory, the scrape of the scent probe along his nasal passage.

"Ah." Jakus withdrew abruptly. "Bilternus bears fruit."

Kyel felt like vomiting, but he gulped, holding it in.

"Kast!" ordered Jakus, "get the scent masters to come to me. Quietly, discreetly, in case we're being watched." He held out a pinch of crystal. "Take this."

The big man put the crystals on his tongue and left to carry out the order.

Jakus continued taking pinches of magnesa from his pouch and passed some to Poegna and Nefaria. Then he put a small pinch in Kyel's hand. "You seem to be proving your worth."

Kyel looked at the red crystals on his palm, remembering what he had seen in Nefaria's journal, the effects of this substance. *No*, he shook his head as he placed them in his mouth, *I've nothing to lose.*

While he had had magnesa years ago, in Ean, he was now an accomplished scent user and could employ the effect differently. His senses expanded as the drug took effect. The natural scents surrounding him became easier to see and handle. He could reach out and manipulate them, tying them together, use them with ease. His own scent memories were easier to extract and use. He tried pulling out the essence of malas and was able to bring it powerfully to the fore. *Yes*, he thought, *this is worth having.*

"Move!" ordered Jakus. "We have an enemy to meet in the pass. We can't keep them waiting."

A small party of guardsmen with several scent masters disappeared into the scrub while the rest moved towards Hestrian Pass.

The pass was like a raw gash in the earth. Little grew along the rough, eroded walls apart from lichens and a slime-like algae. All around the torrid scents swirled, the lime greens and yellows dragging with them other duller colours, so deep that they appeared almost black. The hooves of the peracs made little sound, allowing the noise of a brackish stream trickling alongside the track to dominate.

Kyel tried to appear unconcerned as ordered, but he couldn't help looking to the edge of the escarpment, where the light of the angled sun attempted to push through the grey sky. He imagined faces peering down, preparing weapons to crush them.

"Be ready with a scent barrier," hissed Nefaria. "Jakus has seen something."

He looked ahead, noticing a growing scent shield around the leader and a flicker of red in his aura. With little warning, a black flurry of scent bolts exploded amongst them. The scream of wounded animals followed as he joined in forming a solid barrier of interlaced scents above the party. The scent bolts fired from the right-hand ridge soon began to bounce off or disperse harmlessly.

Rocks and boulders tumbled down, bouncing off or partially penetrating the vast scent shield covering Jakus's scent masters. A number reached the guardsmen and baggage handlers at the rear of the column, where they were not protected. Their screaming and shouting penetrated Kyel's consciousness as he concentrated on supporting the scent shield. But he couldn't let go, even when the attack lessened.

Kyel felt Jakus and others like Kast, Festern and Poegna pull out of the protection scent and begin something else. It took him a short while to recognise it, but in a vastly different way to what he knew. A blanket of transparent scent, containing strong soporific odours, was slowly moving up the wall of the pass, lifting to the top of the ridge where their attackers were massed. It drifted over the top in vast quantities, replenished continuously. Soon all activity above them quietened.

"Enough!" ordered Jakus. "Now move!" The scents rapidly dissipated and he dug his heels into his animal's side. Kyel followed, splashing along the slushy path with everyone else. They came to several narrow tracks leading up to the escarpment; Jakus took the right-hand one, forcing his animal up the slope. The last of the track was steep, making them dismount and walk their panting peracs to the top.

By the time Kyel came out of the chasm, he saw guardsmen and scent masters who'd left earlier now picking their way through a large number of people lying unconscious where they had fallen.

"Tie them! Sort the traitors out!" shouted Jakus. "Find me the ringleaders. Find me Faltis!"

Poegna dashed past and began looking into the sleeping faces of the men and women who'd attacked them.

"Where is he?" she called, her face creased in concern.

Kyel found himself holding the reins of a number of blowing perac as the bodies of the attackers were bound and pulled together. Poegna soon came over supporting a tall, young man who was still recovering from the effects of the soporific scent.

"This is who sent the message you picked up, Kyel. Meet Bilternus."

Kyel nodded to this scrawny version of Jakus, before his attention was distracted. Jakus had the sleepy attackers lined up in front of him. In the middle was Faltis, struggling to keep his eyes open while next to him was a smaller man, more alert. He shook his fist at Bilternus.

"That's Siluser, my father's right hand," whispered Bilternus when he saw Kyel's puzzled look.

"Explain, brother!" Jakus's voice rang out. "Explain why I shouldn't rid myself of you now."

Faltis straightened his clothing as he looked over his captors. He blanched as he saw his son.

"You know why I did this. I am still certain the Eanite must be removed!" he pointed angrily at Kyel. "Yet you won't believe me. Even now you turn my own son against me."

"I think your reasoning is known only to yourself, Faltis. You always were weak and now want what I have. I did warn you I wouldn't tolerate you attacking me again."

Faltis took a breath as Jakus snapped a scent shield over him and exerted pressure. His brother's face turned red before Jakus released the shield and turned to face the prisoners.

"I am known as a firm but fair man," he said loudly, looking along the line of men and women, "and I want to give those of you who would support me in assuming my rightful place as Shada of Ean and other lands, a chance. There will be only one."

"A chance?" huffed Siluser. "Since when have you been a fair man?"

Jakus's attention snapped back to Siluser. "Ah, my brother's personal scartha, yapping when it should hold its tongue. You'd never change your mind, would you?" His eyes narrowed and a dark scent snake formed at his mouth and quickly dove across and into Siluser's nose.

A stifled scream shook Siluser as he put his hands to his throat. His body rippled, expanding. Blood sprayed out of his ears and eyes. His head snapped back, neck tendons cording. He staggered back two steps before disappearing over the edge of the chasm.

Jakus gave a grim smile and looked along the line. "Well? Remember, I will find out if you are lying."

A ragged line of prisoners stepped forward, leaving only a few remaining.

Jakus waited, then nodded to his guardsmen. "We will keep only those who will serve."

He kept his smile as his men dragged those who hadn't moved to the cliff edge and threw them over. The screams quickly ceased.

"Now, Faltis. It seems I must decide whether to let you live or die. What will it be?"

Kyel saw Bilternus stiffen, start to speak, then close his eyes as Jakus moved towards his father.

Chapter Thirty-Five

Drathner and Telpher led the column along the valley floor, using several of the larger male perac to push through the heavy drifts of snow covering the path. In the middle of the line, Sadir and Targas led their perac through the slush left behind by many feet, and their trousers and boots were wet through. Targas checked on Anyar, making sure she had her soft wool hood pulled up. The voral, only its head protruding from a saddlebag, gave what might have been an appreciative purr, or even a warning growl, when he rubbed a hand over it.

"I think he's starting to like me."

"He can see the real you, my love," said Sadir.

The track through the pass was arduous, with the Rolanites frequently changing lead animals as the snow exhausted them, making the ascent even slower. The sky above was blue and clear with no hint of bad weather.

"Ware the wind!" came Drathner's voice as they neared the top of the pass. It took only a short while before Targas and Sadir found out what he meant. The moment they were on the level a cold blast took their breath away, stinging bare skin and making their eyes water. It whistled along a barren wasteland of broken rock, lifting and driving snow before it.

"It's normal for this time of year, the coming of the cold," called Boidea from behind them. "But it means we're nearly there."

"Ean be thanked," gasped Sadir.

The howling of the wind made conversation impossible, so they kept their heads down and trusted in their guides.

The wind suddenly dropped and they were able to see the tall spires of granite as the path meandered along between small, fragrant bushes. Targas heard Alethea speak excitedly to Boidea before a burble of voices reached him.

They entered a large clearing, animals already milling around. Many people in the greens of Rolan were surging amongst them, taking their perac, offering greetings in the strong local accent. Hot mugs were thrust into their hands, and they were enveloped in scents that brought warmth and comfort.

"Hold!" Targas heard Drathner's voice boom. "We give thanks."

Clasping Anyar and Sadir tightly, with the voral sitting firmly against their legs, Targas relaxed into the feeling. He noticed Alethea being supported by Boidea and several locals as it began.

A resonant humming grew in volume, filling the spaces, enveloping their bodies, pulling them into a rhythm so they swayed in unison. Targas tried to give himself to it, recognising the same feeling from Sanctus where everyone belonged and supported each other. The scents darkened and flowed, infiltrating and pushing his senses.

It happened. Again.

Targas dropped out of the communal experience, slipped out to feel alone and unwanted while everyone, including Sadir and Anyar, took part.

A dark rage overtook him, and deep in his mind, something laughed.

"What happened?" asked Sadir, as they joined the procession of people moving out of the clearing, Anyar walking alongside, her fingers entwined in the voral's fur.

"The same as in the caverns of Sanctus: *Septus*," Targas answered through gritted teeth. "Choses his time to make his presence felt."

"Oh, Targas." Sadir linked her arm through his. "At least we're in the right place."

"You must be Sadir and Targas. I'm Xerrita," said a buxom woman in a padded coat and loose skirt. She moved her face close in greeting. "And this is Anyar, with the voral? So it is true, what Boidea says, a real voral."

"Don't touch him," said Sadir as Xerrita bent down. "He doesn't like strangers."

"Oh." Xerrita straightened, pushing back a lock of hair. "Never mind. Can you come with me? I'm to take you to where you'll be staying in Mlana Hold. Do you have any bags?"

"On our peracs, wherever they've been taken," said Targas. "We would appreciate a place to wash and rest."

"Easily done," she said. "You're staying with the Mlana, in the cavern. There are hot springs for washing. I imagine you need it." Her eyes strayed to the voral as it pushed protectively against Anyar's legs. "What about the animal? Is it safe to be with the child?"

"He's not a problem. They're the best of friends," said Targas. "Now where did you say our quarters were?"

"Look, Targas!" said Sadir, gripping his arm tighter. "That's different."

They'd rejoined the line of people and animals down a trail into the head of a wide valley extending over a vast distance towards the south. The rocky bones of the mountains erupted in numerous places all down the valley. With little vegetation to soften the immediate area, the buildings spreading away from the arms of the slope were the dominant feature, built of rock with timber or slate roofs. Several were large, obviously used for gathering or storage, and the remainder appeared to be dwellings.

High rock walls built at an angle to the side slopes seemed to have a defensive purpose. A paved road led through them to follow a narrow river along a straight course into the distance. The high sun picked out green and brown fields before a slight haze obscured the view.

"You're up this way," said Xerrita, "in the Hold itself."

They turned to where she was pointing and gasped. A low cliff extended a distance from the path across the head of the valley to where the river emerged. An extensive man-high opening bisected it, like a large, partially ajar mouth.

"That's got to be the biggest cave I've ever seen," said Sadir. "It doesn't seem real."

"It is, though it's man-made," smiled Xerrita, "and it goes deep within the mountain. Mlana lives there, plus many scent adepts and, of course, important visitors. It is where we're going, so follow me."

The scale of the cavern became more amazing as they neared. "How is it held up?" asked Targas.

"It's been there for a long time," said Xerrita. "There's a thick ledge of very hard rock, which forms the roof, and with occasional columns it is strong and safe. You'll like it once you've adjusted. Now come, your daughter looks very tired."

As they followed her up a winding path, a pervasive background scent filling the air tickled Targas's memory. Soon they were standing in front of a bustling open area, behind which were brick-walled rooms. Small flickering lamps on the walls lit dark openings between them. Xerrita led them down a side corridor and through a wooden door into a wide room with light brick walls and a small door to one side.

She waved them towards several beds and a table and chairs in a room lit by several wall lamps. "You should be comfortable here. The side door leads to the bathroom and privy. I see your bags are already here," Xerrita smiled. "I'll leave you now and give you time to settle in. Food will be brought shortly."

"A bed!" shrieked Anyar. She ran and jumped on the small one, Vor following.

"No you don't," called Sadir. "Look, Anyar, there's a mat and bowl for Vor in the corner. Let him go and have some food. I'm sure he's hungry."

"Well I could do with a clean-up," said Targas. "Let's see the hot water Xerrita mentioned."

"We'll need Anyar washed first; she's ready for bed," said Sadir.

With Vor satisfying his hunger, they opened the side door and went in. A cubicle to one side held a smooth wooden bench with a hole, its purpose obvious, a trickle of water in a channel to one side showing how it flushed. Another waist-high door led into a water-filled tub large enough for their family, with an overflow leading off. Steam rose from its surface, with a distinctive, familiar scent.

"Water!" yelled Anyar, and she began pulling at her clothes.

"Hold on," said Targas. "It may be hot."

Sadir put her hand in. "No, it's not, it's pleasantly warm. I think the invitation is too good to miss. Come on, Anyar. Use the privy and then you can wash."

Soon they were all in the water, Anyar splashing and showing no signs of tiredness.

"This is nice, Targas," said Sadir, leaning back on him.

"Yes, I can feel it doing me good. Didn't know I had so many sore places." He slung his arm across Sadir's shoulder and held her to him. "I'm wondering what that background scent is. I noticed it when we first came in. It's certainly stronger here, in the water."

"Yes. And I know it," replied Sadir, "just hadn't thought about it. It's the cordial, the Rolan cordial. It has the same smell."

"So it does," agreed Targas. "Worth asking Alethea about. Hey!"

A long snout and furry head with black eyes peered over the edge of the tub, pink tongue lapping at the water.

"Vor!" exclaimed Anyar delightedly. "Vor can swim, Par."

"No you don't!" Targas growled.

"Let him sit there, at least," said Sadir.

"Humph," he grunted and settled back, watching his daughter's wet hands stroking the voral's snout.

They left Anyar asleep with Vor curled up alongside and headed out into the main area, the bright daylight through the vast entrance to the cavern harsh on their eyes after the dim light of their room. After a moment they could make out activity around them. Cooking facilities occupied one side a distance away, and long tables and benches were dotted around the area. Everyone seemed involved in something, so Sadir and Targas walked to the entrance and absorbed the scenery.

Long shadows were already edging their way from the mountains and tree-covered hills to the west of the valley, the sun lighting parts of the river and leaving other areas dark. It was apparent harvests were over in some of the fields on the limited arable area of the vast valley. Others showed tinges of colour: the earthy browns of fallow fields, the muted colours of cold-growing crops in others. Smoke already permeated the air, drifting high until broken by wind. Beside the background scents Sadir had identified as the cordial, the odours of rock, sharp astringent vegetation and river competed with perac, lizard, and, strangely enough, honey."

"Peaceful," murmured Sadir. "But it will get cold this night."

"Yes," said Targas, his arm around her, "but at least we'll be warm for a change."

"Targas, Sadir, isn't this something?" Cathar approached, her thin face alight. "I never believed Rolan would be like this."

"Mmm, it's good to get here at last," said Targas. "How is Alethea faring?"

"Better, I believe, now she's home. Anyar and the voral asleep?"

"Yes, finally," said Sadir. "The moment she saw the hot water she forgot all about being tired."

"The people here are very welcoming," said Cathar. "I hear there's a banquet this night in our—or rather, I mean, your honour."

"No," said Targas, "It'll be for us all. Alethea is very special to these people, so it'll be mainly for her."

"Oh." Cathar thought for a moment. "Anyway you should come and see the kitchens. They are big and there's always food there. I find that I'm so hungry after that horrible time we had."

"Yes'" Sadir gripped Targas's hand. "Let's go and see what's on offer." She pulled him after her and followed Cathar.

A light tap on the door, followed by a drift of Boidea's scent, woke Targas from a deep sleep. He blinked his eyes in the faint light of a dimmed lantern, wondering where he was. Sadir lay draped over him in the larger bed, exhaustion obvious in her odour, while a loud snore from his daughter reminded him they were in their room in Mlana Hold.

"A moment," he called softly, easing himself out from under Sadir's arm to stand on the rush-covered floor. He slipped on a robe to cover his nakedness and padded to the door.

"Sorry to wake you, Targas," whispered Boidea when he opened the door, "but the banquet is on soon and you'll need to get ready."

"Have we slept that long?" he groaned.

"It is late in the night, but most are sufficiently rested and Mlana is happy it proceeds. Is the voral behaving itself?" She lifted her lantern and peered over his shoulder.

"Yes, although I haven't heard a word from it. Is there somewhere it can forage?"

"Mmm," Boidea thought for a moment. "I suppose we can let him go up where the river comes through from the mountains. There's fish and lizards and the odd hive up there, enough to keep him occupied."

"Good. In that case we'll bring him to you when we come out. Thanks, Boidea." He closed the door quietly and turned up the wall lamps.

A long bank of glowing coals attracted them as they left their room. Anyar's intake of breath at the wall of scent and heat reflected their feeling of awe. The glow of the fire lit the whole area of the cavern in front of the rooms, painting the grey rock a flickering orange. Misshapen shadows, alternately orange or dark, filled the space as people moved on various errands amongst the long tables and benches. A light updraft drew the smoke and fumes through the entrance and into the night sky.

"This will be some banquet," whispered Sadir.

"Targas, I believe you have a companion for me?" Boidea's deep voice rose above the crackling of the flames and the background noise. "Anyar." The tall Rolanite leant down towards the young girl and the voral. "Would you like to help me take Vor, so he can go foraging?"

Anyar looked at her for a moment and then nodded.

"While I sort this out, you might care to be seated." She pointed to a double table, roughly central, with a view through the entrance to the dark sky.

Cathar met them halfway and escorted them to their table. Alethea, holding a small glass, began to rise as they approached, before being held back by Drathner and Undrea.

Alethea smiled and patted the seat next to her. "You will sit with me? I assure you we will have a warmer time than in the past few days. I trust you are comfortable."

"Yes," said Sadir, noticing a familiar figure down the table. "Thanks to you and Xerrita."

"Please be seated," Alethea continued. "Cordial for you, Sadir? And for you, Targas? Beer or wine?"

"Beer, please." He sat and looked along the table. Most were their companions from the trek, but there were several unknown older women and men.

"We'll wait for Boidea and Anyar to return, and I'll introduce you to those you don't know. In the meantime, enjoy the warmth and the drink. There are some speciality treats on the table to start with, and I think the kitchens have put on a fair feast so you won't go hungry."

"Thank you, Alethea," said Targas, as he picked up a mug of beer. "It is good to be rested and treated so well, but I do have a few burning questions—"

"I understand, Targas," she interjected. "Also, I'm well aware you have had a reoccurrence of your affliction this very day, but for the moment please relax. Next day will be the time for answers."

"Ah, here comes my favourite girl." Alethea smiled as she saw Boidea and Anyar approach.

Chapter Thirty-Six

The euphoria of magnesa had gone, leaving a sour taste in his mouth, a split-ting headache and an intense feeling of horror. Kyel had participated in the overwhelming of Faltis's forces in Hestrian Pass and enjoyed the power from his first controlled experience of the crystal, but the callous way Jakus had disposed of the prisoners was gut-wrenching.

They set up camp on the ridgeline while Jakus interrogated each person who had agreed to his terms. The man seemed like some sort of misshapen k'dorian lizard as he probed their scent memories while Kast held each captive immobile. It took him mere moments before he had ascertained their loyalty. Then he said "yes" or "no".

Kyel had to turn away whenever "no" was uttered, for Kast just flung the captive over the cliff.

The screaming got to him. If he had any reason to like the man before, it was gone. Poegna showed some sympathy as he walked past, but the glitter in her eyes revealed she condoned Jakus's actions. Kyel found his animal and began to rub it down. He couldn't see what was happening, but he could still hear the screams.

"Kyel?" Nefaria's scent wafted over him.

He pushed his face into the perac's flanks, trying to still the flashes of pain in his head. "What?"

"I'm sorry, but he has to show leadership. Anyone who doesn't support him can't be left behind. Surely you understand?" she pleaded.

"I don't want to talk about it," he groaned, then sighed and looked at her. "Isn't your head pounding after all that?"

"My head?" Her forehead wrinkled. "Oh, you mean the crystals, the magnesa. You must control it. See my Lord. He does. He has to. Push it to the background, you're skilled enough."

"Don't know if I can."

"Really Kyel, I sometimes wonder whether you're a scent master." She smiled and patted him on the shoulder.

"Lizards' teeth," he muttered as he delved into his scent centre, pulling to the fore the most powerful memories he had, the scent that had helped him to cope with headaches as a child in Ean—the bark of a particular tree, infused into water and drunk. Immediately the pounding faded, and he leant against the side of his perac in relief.

Early the next day they left Hestrian Pass, Kyel keeping his gaze fixed firmly on the path the perac followed, not wishing to see the miasma of foul odours that reminded him of what had happened. He saw everyone around him in a new light; that they could condone what Jakus had done seemed to tarnish them. There were none he could trust, even Nefaria, or Poegna, or Festern. And Bilternus seemed to be in the mould of the callous Sutanite. He appeared to accept Jakus's decision to either kill or spare his father, Faltis. What Faltis felt, now riding as a prisoner with the baggage animals, was another matter.

No, he didn't like Sutan.

Though, he thought, *the old woman, Xerina, is a friend, and there is…* Kyel moment-arily lost her name but the memory of her face and body caused him to blush. *Ah, yes, Sencia. I'd like to meet her again.*

The country was more of the same, covered with scrub but interspersed with trees poking through like sails on a grey-green sea. The hills, bisected by dark clefts, were higher and extended into the distance, lit by the rising sun.

A flurry of activity occurred in the trees. Lizards of a number of types were active, flying or thumping through the foliage. He recognised a similar scent trace to the Conduvian lizards back in Ean but the other animal scents had a distinctive Sutan feel. Kyel shivered and looked on down the track, noticing it was wider with signs of regular repair.

"We're nearly there," Nefaria said, pointing ahead. "You can see smoke from the cooking fires. I could really do with a time of quiet after what we've gone through." She saw Kyel's face. "Just go with it, Kyel, it'll be the best way to get through things." Nefaria shook her head. "And you'll like my home, you really will."

Kyel took a deep breath. "Just because I've thrown in my lot with Jakus doesn't mean I have to like how he does things. But thanks, Nefaria, I'll try." He resolved to show a calm outer face, at least until they reached Ean again. Jakus wasn't a man you'd cross.

A group of men in non-descript clothing more suited to the colder conditions than fashion met the head of their column as it rounded a wide bend. Jakus pulled up and spoke with them. Festern seemed particularly effusive in his greetings.

"Festern's men from the Steppes are here," Nefaria commented. "I think that means his force has already made it to Hestria. My Lord will be pleased."

"Yes, I imagine he will," said Kyel drily.

They continued following the road through a wide pass and into a valley. The green of the pastures almost hurt his eyes after the previous dull colours of the country. A broad silver river bisected land dominated by a long red cliff facing eastwards. Earth-coloured buildings ran in lines along its length, spilling down onto the flats of the valley where many dwellings clustered together.

Kyel's neck grew stiff from looking at the construction, marvelling how they were so much part of the rock. He barely noticed the crowds assembled along the way, men, women and children watching Jakus as he returned to the place he had lived during his recovery—there was little noise or feeling of anxiety from them. When they stopped by a large low building, the people gathered clad in loose tunics and trousers, most wearing straw hats, interspersed with cloaked officials and scent masters. Jakus slipped a hand into his mouth before standing in his stirrups.

He saw a drift of scent push out from Jakus and inexorably cover those around him. Kyel instinctively resisted the push of Jakus's will and the tingle of magnesa as he noticed the effect on the people. Some stood open-mouthed, others had blank faces while those with obvious scent mastery were accepting of the man's scent influence.

"My people," Jakus's voice rang, "I have returned as promised. Despite some slight…problems with those who saw fit to destabilise our progress, we are on schedule to create a united Sutan, with Hestria becoming the centre of excellence and prosperity." He looked slowly around the crowd of several hundred people and smiled. A cascade of rose-tinted scents drifted from him as he continued.

"No more will you have our young people conscripted to fight in useless battles in faraway places at the behest of one faction or the other. For I will lead. And I will not tolerate my people being subjected to the whims of Brastus or Vitaris, or even…Faltis." Jakus pointedly looked down the length of the column to his captive brother.

"We will soon be leaving on the next stage of this quest and will return more powerful than ever. I have with me representatives from all parts of our country who will help ensure that Sutan and Ean are reunited."

"This is an auspicious time, my people. And you are part of it." Jakus lifted an arm in salute. "So let us make our allies welcome and celebrate our prosperous future."

A roar began as if the crowd had broken free from invisible restraints. Hats flew into the air, people hugged each other, then ran into the columns of riders and helped them dismount. Kyel found himself being hauled off his perac by a large woman who hugged him soundly before a dirt-stained man shook his hand. He couldn't help getting caught up in the euphoria of the moment, even though he knew Jakus had orchestrated it.

"Come, Cer," said a man, "this way with your animal. The Shad will want you well served."

Kyel nodded into the lined, leathery face before him. The man smiled and took hold of the lead, pulling the perac out of the line and towards the side of the large building. Kyel followed, noticing a number of other animals being led in the same direction as his.

"There's stables here, Cer. I'll make sure your bags are brought to where you're staying, if you want to go on."

"Thank you, but I think I'll look after my perac first."

"You don't hafta, Cer," the man pleaded.

Kyel shook his head and walked into the long, gloomy series of stables filled with the strong scents of perac and dung. His feet crunched through fresh straw, bringing the smell of pastures baking in the sun and the memories of sitting on sun-drenched boulders back home. He hardened his longings and followed where his guide led.

"I'll stay for a while, uh…"

"Drothitis, Cer. And you'd be the Eanite they's all talking about, I take it?" His eyes glistened in the dimness.

"That I am, I suspect. Now would you give me a moment? I'd like to groom my animal."

"Oh? Right you are, then." Drothitis shuffled away.

Pulling a bristled brush through the short curls of the perac's woollen coat was curiously soothing. Kyel shut his eyes and let the comforting smells and the movement carry him away. He was here, in the middle of an unwanted adventure, having to rely on his own skills and intuition. His mind was still muddled but his thoughts were clearer. He wanted to get home, but more than anything stop this madman from carrying out his plan of regaining Ean. What could he, a youthful scent master do against Jakus and all his ardent followers? His mind was still vulnerable to Jakus's probing and if his thoughts were exposed he would almost certainly become a casualty of the coming conflict.

"There you are, Eanite." The voice was familiar.

"Damn." Kyel turned to see Bilternus.

"You're staying at our Shad's villa. I volunteered to fetch you since I'm staying there too."

Kyel nodded, a smile pasted on his face. "Lead on, then."

They came out of the stables into a bright sun angled a distance from the cliffline that dominated the city. As they trudged towards the main street, avoiding a generous scattering of dung, Kyel could see that the expanse in the distance was lined with wooden fencing up to the river. Workers dotted some of the fields while herds of a smaller, mainly white perac-like creatures, were in others. In spite of himself, Kyel was intrigued.

"Never seen so much fencing before. Different animals, too."

"Never been to Hestria before either, Eanite?" Bilternus grunted as they crunched along the main gravelled road. "Hestria's a rich place. Good cropping and fine pasture for peracs and chevracs. The fences are especially important where it reaches the Westforth river—stops the scartha from getting at them, the chevracs I mean—stupid animals. Good eating but easy prey for scartha."

"Is that why the city's so far away?"

"You're asking a lot of questions," Bilternus growled. "Don't you know anything? Hestria is here because of the floods. Every few years a heap of water comes down the river and floods everything. Reason why Sutaria is the capital instead despite the richness of this land, though the red cliffs contain iron as well as being above the flood line.

"Now this is where we're staying." He turned up a short, steep stone path that led between two columns of the red rock before moving along a long-fronted, single-storied building whose numerous small, dark windows looked across the valley. Backing the building was a sheer wall of the cliff, bulging as it curved backwards until the edge disappeared. Bilternus marched past two scent masters, through a narrow doorway and into the building.

Kyel took a lingering look at the panorama of the fields, river and distant hills before following.

"My dear Sharna," said Jakus with warmth. "It is most pleasant to see you in my home."

"My pleasure entirely, Jakus," said the red-haired, flamboyantly dressed woman. "There was no way I would wait in Southern Port when I knew you were to be in Hestria."

"Southern Port is in readiness?" Jakus asked of the small woman.

"You gave me a charge and I have carried it out," Sharna carried on blithely. "Any issues we had were resolved once your brother's influence fled the city, and our stores and ships are in readiness for when we're there." She smiled and stepped closer. "I assume I acted appropriately?"

"Sharna, it is appreciated. You shall sit with me at our banquet, and Poegna too," he laughed. "Two beautiful women. It has been some time since I've had the chance to relax."

"Kast." He turned to his second-in-command, who was standing with his back to the white-washed inner wall of the large, open room. "See that everyone is settled in and report back to me. We all need time to relax and freshen up before this night's banquet. Then next day I have something special in mind.

"Nefaria, make sure Bilternus and our young Eanite are settled—in the inner rooms, I think." Jakus walked with Sharna and Poegna into the courtyard off the room.

"Come on, you two," said Nefaria when she saw them in the entry hall. "You heard what the Shad said."

"Still doesn't trust me," mumbled Bilternus.

"He doesn't trust anyone, Bilternus," she said, "nor cares for them. I should think that is obvious."

"A nother early morning," said Kyel, as he followed Bilternus down the path they had used the day before. Jakus had required all his scent masters to be in the fields by dawn after a relatively late night enjoying a well-stocked table. Kyel's head was still heavy from an over-indulgence in the local beer and the effects of the battle in the pass. Somehow, Jakus was showing remarkable energy and moved quickly along the main street of Hestria with a long entourage in tow.

Kyel noticed a few others exhibiting the effects of a heavy night, especially Bilternus. But there he was sympathetic. The young man had to come to grips with a dramatic change in his life, with his father still a prisoner at Jakus's whim. The more the beer had flowed, the more he enjoyed talking to him. He had learnt Bilternus was upset at Poegna's indifference now that Jakus was taking her attention, and uncertain he had done the right thing in siding against his father's forces.

They turned down a narrow lane leading into a large field. At the far corner stood a shed built of interspaced wooden planks with a brush roof. Several chevracs huddled in an opposite corner against the post-and-rail fence.

Jakus moved to the centre of the grassed area and turned, a gleeful smile on his face. "Welcome all. I trust you enjoyed my hospitality last night?"

The assembled host watched, some with a puzzled scent aura. Kyel recognised most from his time in Southern Port, but there were a few more, all scent masters. Noticeably absent were Faltis and those of his scent masters who had accepted Jakus's term of surrender. He noticed many city folk lined up along the roadway paying close attention to Jakus, the early sun lighting their faces.

The stillness of the day, with the chill air, made an unusual backdrop to the man. He slowly raised his arms, grey tunic and trousers covered by his black cloak falling limply to mid-calf.

"I might apologise for bringing you out so early, but I won't. I have something to demonstrate for those of you who might have some misgivings about our direction, and concern about the opposition we may find.

"It will have the double effect of demonstrating our combined power and showing we have a weapon none can stand against. For this I can thank a mortal enemy from whom I drew valuable scent memories, one Targas, an Eanite sympathiser and a leader of the temporary revolution."

Kyel kept his face impassive as Jakus's eyes sought him out. "It is opportune to try this, with you all participating—even you, Kyel." He nodded towards them. "I think you, Bilternus, have also earned the right to taste the crystal."

Kast and several of the guard passed amongst the group, Jakus watching carefully as they accepted and swallowed the magnesa.

"Now let me explain. I will be leading this demonstration. You will follow my control and add to the effect. Come with me, closer to the shed." He raised his voice to the crowd gathered along the roadway. "Watch and spread word of my power."

Kyel walked down the field with the group, already feeling the heightened rush from the crystals entering his bloodstream. He noticed Bilternus slowly moving his head as if seeing scents in a new light.

They stopped near the building and Jakus turned side on. "I will begin to build a scent cloud. You will join with me."

Kyel was fascinated by what was happening. The normal pull occurred as it had when they participated in the blanket of soporific scent that overwhelmed Faltis's forces, but it soon changed. A distinct corrosive tang of scents filled the cloud, causing Kyel's eyes to water. He pushed it away far enough to help control the scents without it affecting him.

A familiarity with the form came to him, about the odour bonds. Targas had shown him how odours were made of minute parts, or motes, and if one was skilled enough, one could use these motes to combine, strengthen and extend the scent. It was the one thing that made a scent barrier almost impenetrable. But Jakus was doing something different. Kyel was only a participant as the master manipulated the scent cloud.

Soon the cloud was almost solid, and still expanding. The smell was overpowering but Jakus's control was firm. Slowly the cloud was forced towards the shed, drifting like a fog over the structure. It pushed through and past.

Jakus dropped his control and the cloud quickly dissipated. The scent masters composed themselves as their participation ceased.

"Done!" Jakus pointed.

Nothing appeared to have happened. All eyes were on the shed, searching for anything different. Then Kyel noticed that the rising sun was brighter around and through the building. It became easier to see as the wood let more light through, becoming transparent and crumbling away. Within seconds the building collapsed to the ground in a soft rain of dust.

The crowd along the road behind them gasped loudly.

Jakus faced his scent masters and the citizens of Hestria, scent aura pluming in the purples and dark reds of triumph, arms outstretched.

Kyel's eyes opened wide. *Wine's rot,* he thought, *he's found a way to break apart the odour bonds within the wood. They need to know. Ean needs to know.* He looked around; it had been such a strong thought that he wondered if he'd mumbled it to himself unintentionally, but even if he had, the people around him were all too focussed on what they'd just participated in.

Chapter Thirty-Seven

He woke with a sore head. The company had been friendly with the atmosphere, food and large quantities of beer combining to make him forget. The night had merged into sleep and he was in his room with Sadir and Anyar, unable to even guess how soon dawn would come. He strained to hear any noise from beyond the walls.

A wet nose pushed insistently into his neck. He groaned and reached out his hand. "I thought you were out somewhere. What do you want?"

Vor continued to push. Targas swung his legs out of the bed and stepped onto the rush-strewn floor.

"Par? Vor needs to go out," a small voice came from the single bed.

"Well," Targas said, rubbing at his eyes, "I suppose if Vor needs to go outside you might as well come too. We'll leave your mother trying to sleep, shall we? Come on, young one." He strode over and lifted her out of bed.

They dressed quickly and, hand in hand, walked from the room and along the narrow corridor. The light filtering through the cave mouth revealed a grey, oppressive day, light rain falling from a dull sky. Several people were cleaning up from the previous night while a delicious smell wafted from the kitchens. Vor's head lifted as Anyar drew in a deep breath.

"Par, I'm hungry."

"What about Vor? Doesn't he need to go out?" asked Targas as he breathed in the aromas of frying onions and meat.

The small girl shook her head and pushed the voral towards the cave entrance. The animal gambolled off and slipped over the edge into the misty rain. Targas tried to see if she'd used a scent command before a voice hailed him.

"Cer, you'll be wanting food?" A slim figure in a brown shift, thin face red from the hot ovens, came towards them holding a bread wrap in each hand.

"You're up early," he said as he took the food from her.

"Of course, Cer," she said, her eyes smiling from beneath a thatch of black hair, "someone has to clean up after yer fun."

"This is good," said Targas, as he took a bite. "I'm sorry, I've forgotten your name."

"Wouldn't have thought yer'd remember it after last night. I'm Cernea, an' it's my time helping in the kitchens. Happy to take care of yer young one later, as we've got classes she could join."

Targas saw Anyar's face light up at Cernea's words and nodded. "Thanks for the offer, but I better discuss it with her mother first." He smiled and walked with Anyar towards the opening.

The fires had died to black ash and the chill of the day infiltrated the mouth of the cavern. They stopped where the drizzle couldn't reach and chewed their food, looking out onto a new world. It was easy to see the strategic advantage of Mlana Hold perched on the head of the misty valley, enclosed by the shoulders of the mountains. Constant rain coming from the highlands to their right swept in sheets across the stone dwellings and fields until it disappeared into the tumbles of rock piling on the left. The river barely showed before it disappeared into the grey haze of the landscape.

"I hope it's an inside day today, Anyar," said Targas, his arm around his daughter's shoulders.

"Vor's coming," she said.

A bedraggled creature with a toothy grin burst over the rim of the cave and rushed over to them, before stopping and shaking.

"Vor," she laughed as water flew all over them, "stop."

The animal stilled and began to take an interest in Anyar's bread wrap.

"Thought I might find you here," Boidea's voice boomed out. "Still got that disreputable creature with you, Anyar?"

"Vor's not disr...disrbtal," the girl replied, letting the animal grab the remainder of her food.

"No," laughed Boidea, "of course not. Now let me get you some hot milk or tea and we can discuss Mlana's plans for this day. I don't think"—she looked out into the rain—"that we will be going far.

"And you,"—she bent down to Anyar—"will be spending some time with children of your own age. We have lessons going on in the Hold and you would most certainly benefit. Though what to do about the voral..."

"Vor's staying!" Anyar looked at Boidea with determination.

"Of course, but he will have to do something while you are in lessons. However, enough of that. Let's get those drinks, and perhaps more food?"

They followed the tall woman to the noise and warmth of the kitchens.

Sadir had joined Targas standing in the entrance to the cave, enjoying the warmth of the newly banked fires on their backs. The smoke rose straight to the ceiling before edging out to dissipate in the rain.

Anyar had disappeared with other children and for the moment they were alone, eating flatbread filled with onion and meat while watching the rain pound the rocky land beneath them.

"Comfortable, Sadir?"

"Mmm, I am." She leant into him. "A rather wonderful place to view the world. I wonder whether we can just stay here and relax." She looked up at him. "I suppose your problem hasn't gone away?"

"Just hidden for now," he said bleakly, "waiting for his chance, I guess. Whenever that will be."

"I think you have the best position in the Hold," Alethea's warm voice came from behind them. She hooked her arm through Targas's. "A wet day, I think. Perhaps a good time to look further into what ails you?"

"How to spoil a wonderful moment, Alethea," he said with a rueful smile.

"But necessary. We have a place, here in the Hold, a special place which will aid this."

"If you say so," he sighed, looking down the valley at the few people braving the rain along the paved road leading between the dwellings and larger buildings.

"If you'll come with me, we'll get a hot drink and then continue to the place of crystals." Alethea pulled on his arm and took them away into the darkness of the huge cave.

Cernea smiled wearily as she passed over cups of hot tea. "I'm soon to finish here, once the last few are fed. Then it's to lessons, which perhaps Anyar can join?"

"That is a good idea, Cernea, and my thanks for looking after our guests so well," said Alethea.

"Oh, definitely my pleasure, Mlana," she said with a bob of her head.

Alethea led them past the range of cooking fires and ovens to where the brickwork outlining the rooms merged into the soft rock forming the walls of the cave. The stone glowed a warm orange from lamps fitted into niches in the smooth, man-high walls. Occasionally Targas had to duck his head to avoid a projection from the roof as they followed along the passage to a small circular room decorated with lengths of cloth hanging from the ceiling.

Boidea rose from one of several stone seats when they entered.

"Welcome to our inner sanctum," she said.

Targas and Sadir looked around the sparse room, then at each other.

"Looks can be deceiving," said Alethea, "Try using your other senses."

Targas tasted the air, recognising the ever-present odour of the Rolan cordial had deepened, becoming thicker and syrupy. He could see floating scents even in the orange of the light, swirling and effectively blocking off lesser scents. He kept delving into the motes of odour trying to find what they were blocking and why they were swirling, until he heard Sadir exclaiming: "The shadow scent! It's the shadow scent. How clever."

"What?" he heard himself snap, irritation flooding from deep within his mind.

He saw Alethea look at him in alarm, then hurry over to Boidea. He pushed down on the threatening *presence* and waited, foot tapping. Sadir held onto his arm.

"I think," said Alethea, "we need to get changed to lessen any influence of our normal clothing on the process before we proceed." She held her hand out towards the curtains. "If you both dress in the shifts you will find there…"

"Come on," said Sadir, pushing aside the curtain to a small room.

They changed quickly and came back out to Alethea, now wearing a similar item of clothing.

"Targas," she said, touching his hand, "I fear you must trust us at this juncture. I am loathe to warn the *presence* in your mind."

"I'd prefer not to but I've little choice, I guess." He stood back watching while Alethea whispered into Sadir's ear. A feeling burbled and bubbled in his head, but he couldn't be sure whether it was Septus or merely his apprehension.

The three women appeared to drink something before Alethea walked back to him. "Please trust me, dear Targas, and allow me to cover your eyes." She lifted a strip of cloth and tied it around his head. "Now take my hand and come with me."

He moved forward, fearing that he would bang into the wall, but instead felt the brush of a wall hanging and then heard the crunch of gravel under his feet. As they walked the odour changed, becoming thicker, more minerally. Soon their feet echoed in a larger space. Moments later they stopped, and Alethea removed her hand.

"You may remove your blindfold, Targas."

He almost dreaded the moment as he untied the large knot. It fell away and he saw three sets of eyes watching him, almost luminescent in the darkness. Boidea placed the lamp she was carrying into a recess in the cave wall, allowing the light to direct its beams outward. Targas heard Sadir gasp as he struggled to come to terms with what he was seeing.

The ceiling was dark and low over his head, with the walls of the softer, paler rock extending around them in a vast oval. Occasional forms, seats or benches were scattered across the gravel-strewn surface. But that was not what drew his attention.

Light was caught and flung around the walls of the cave in an infinite number of points of red, flashing and moving as the lamp's flame flickered, everything having a reddish hue. Targas lifted his hand to watch the play of light across his skin before he looked at Alethea.

"It still takes me by surprise," she said. "To think this material can amplify light in such an amazing way."

"What is it?" whispered Sadir.

"It is one of the rarest elements in our world, a material able to enhance our senses, in particular our sensory abilities."

"Not magnesa," said Targas, "the crystal Jakus uses?"

"This is the base material, magnesite, from which the crystal is extracted, so you are correct, Targas," Alethea confirmed. "And this is the focus of his intent even now, if the Knowing is accurate.

"However, we are wise in its use, unlike the Sutanites. All peoples can use scent senses, some individuals more than others; such abilities are enhanced by our natural environment. Magnesite has its influence too, more in the background, but the crystals themselves must be used sparingly as they demand much of the user. We have developed rituals and meditations for this very reason and control the release of the substance. If I had my way it would not leave Rolan, but we are a poor country and need the income it brings, that and the cordial of course."

"Well why…"—he spun around, looking at the extent of the cave and the magnesite that filled it—"why tell me about this? You…you said you couldn't let me know because of the…thing in my head, yet you have. Why?"

"Targas," Alethea said gently, "it will make little difference, for this is the area where you must be if we have a chance of healing you. The location is well hidden—you will recall your blindfold?"

"Yes, but…" He walked over and sat on a flat rock, shaking his head. Alethea followed.

"This cave is unique, Targas. Normally the crystals are scarce and hard to find—this whole cavern complex is a result of many years of mining the soft rock that exists as a filler between harder layers."

"So you've been digging out crystals for a very long time. Must be a lot of waste material, then?" Targas looked at the flashing points of light with renewed interest.

"Our crystals are securely stockpiled further down the valley; however, you mentioned the waste. Here is the interesting thing: we use it in the making of the pottery tumblers that hold the cordial."

"I see," Targas said, nodding slowly.

"Does that mean," said Sadir, "it's the tumblers giving the cordial its special character?"

"My dear Sadir, you have uncovered the truth." Alethea face brightened in the red light. "For this is the essence of the matter. The powdered rock imbues the cordial with a vital quality that enhances the scent abilities, although it appears to have a bias towards women. None of our men seem to be the better for it, and we do not know why."

The crunching of feet on the gravel interrupted them. "We've brought cordial and warm drinks, Mlana."

Xerrita's smiling face appeared in the light, accompanied by Cathar. They each wore a shift and carried several steaming cups.

"Well done," said Alethea. "We will drink first and then prepare to undertake our attempt with Targas."

"We will?" Targas looked apprehensively at the women around him. "Where's Drathner or Telpher?"

"I am sorry, Targas. I seem to have brought this on you rather quickly. As I explained, the essence of the material surrounding us has the greatest effect for women; even your Sadir has felt it." Alethea placed a hand on her shoulder. "This place is normally used by women, protected through the use of the *shadow scent* as you, Sadir, referred to it. We rarely bring men in here.

"Now Boidea, Xerrita and I are probably the most experienced *other*, or *shadow* scent users in Rolan; Sadir has some knowledge and Cathar's is developing. We are here, in the crystal cave, isolated from most influences, the best environment to try to expunge the thing from your mind. This is why I was so keen to get you to Rolan, to this very place. We didn't have success in Sanctus so we may succeed here.

"You are willing to give this a try?" She looked intently into Targas's face.

There was movement in his mind, apprehensiveness at the thought of another invasion of his essence. He didn't know whether Septus was aware of what was about to be done. Or if it was that he didn't want to go through the process again. *After all, maybe the creature's influence has faded? Maybe I'm finally overcoming what part of Septus is in me?* he thought.

"Wine's rot!" he spat through gritted teeth. "I must!"

Alethea smiled, gently cupping his face. "It will be for the best, my dear. I know this is a necessary trial for you."

"Don't worry, my love," said Sadir quietly, "I'll be with you."

"Ah, damn!" He slumped on his seat and looked at the gravel darkly arrayed in the red light.

It swirled like blood, thick strands looping around his head, thickening, making the air too viscous to breath. He wanted to close his eyes, cut out the vile red but he was afraid to. For if he closed his eyes, then that within him would be trapped, writhing within his brain, digging and cutting into his stored memories, taking the very part which made him, leaving him empty and alone.

He kept his eyes open.

He could see the shadowy forms enclosing him, hearing their vibration as they weaved their magic. A rational part of his mind wondered what the shadow scent was, what it did that was so different to what had gone before, in Sanctus. Then he had been lost in memories drawn from Septus's mind and imagination. But here he was awake, imbued by the red scent around him and feeling nothing.

He squinted at the swirling coils of scent, noticing a change, a darkening of the material. It thickened even further, slowing, becoming solid, closing in until he felt it on his face. Targas took a quick gasp, surprised at the ease of breath as the scents entered his lungs and infiltrated his sinuses.

Then it began—a skittering within his head like the legs of so many spiders slipping and sliding on smooth surfaces. Something was backing away, refusing to confront the inflow of scent, seeking purchase, creating pain as if claws were digging into raw flesh. A skull-like head, bulging red eyes, blood-stained teeth showed Septus ripping with hooked fingers at the softness of Targas's brain.

He grabbed at his head, trying to scream. The push continued forcing the *presence* further into the recesses of his mind. The pain drilled into the centre of his brain like a spike being thrust into an eye. His throat ached with the intensity of the scream. A rush of blood burst from his nose, spraying across his body as he pushed his hands on each side of his head to try and crush the pain.

He took a huge gasp, his lungs filled with blood and then his head *exploded*. The red turned to black.

A wet cloth wiping across his forehead brought him to his senses. He tentatively explored his head, seeking the pain, seeking damage. There was nothing, apart from an overall ache.

He opened an eye. It was dark. The surface he was on was soft and comfortable. He smelt the familiar essence of his room, the odours of his family, Anyar and Sadir, even Vor.

"Did it work?" he croaked.

"We don't know, my love." Sadir's arms came around him and her head rested on his chest. "I...I was so worried. I thought you were dead. All that blood."

"I can't feel him," said Targas. "I think he's gone."

They rested silently in the darkened room, each in their own thoughts.

"I don't want to go through that again," Targas murmured.

"Neither do I, love," Sadir's voice was muffled. "Neither do I."

Chapter Thirty-Eight

The trek from Hestria with Jakus's sizeable force had been uneventful. Once the uproar from the demonstration of corrosive scent power had died down, preparations for the next stage of the journey began. It was a long day's travel through low hills and eroded plains to Southern Port, where the five ships Sharna had readied were waiting to take the army on to Rolan.

"What do you think, Kyel? We've several days in Port. Time enough to find a woman or two. Never know when we'll get another chance, not with our leader taking the best."

"I don't know, Bilternus," said Kyel. "I've got something else I need to do."

"Your loss," he said, shrugging his shoulders. "I'm headed to the Way House first thing next day. You know, near the tavern you were in when you first came to Port. Where Jakus held his gathering."

Kyel's thoughts of Sencia disappeared. "How do you know where we met?"

"Wasn't a secret," Bilternus smiled. "If you remember, it was my father who attacked you. I did have some knowledge of what was happening. Wouldn't be much of a spy if I didn't."

Kyel's attention was taken by the long, grey-stone building of thick walls and narrow windows; the darkening sky as night neared made it even more oppressive.

"Back again," he muttered. "At least this time we're not being attacked."

"Never been in Jakus's compound," said Bilternus. "Impressive but ugly. What's the layout?"

"Well, I know where we sleep and where we eat. Both big rooms, with little privacy. Out the back's a huge training ground, and the stables. I don't know how he's going to fit so many people in."

"Won't be a problem. My father's buildings are not far and will be empty, so some will go there." Bilternus scratched his head. "Besides Jakus pretty much owns this place now. Brastus may have a few spies but he's far away and won't have an influence."

"Do you think Faltis—I mean your father—will be on Jakus's side now he's had time to think?"

"Him? Never know what he thinks now, but I'm sure he won't even dream of crossing my uncle. Bilternus's face dropped. "Always was a coward, unless he was bigger than you."

"Come with me," said Kyel. "We'll take the animals around back, then I'll show you where to put our gear."

The darkness had fallen over Southern Port by the time Kyel took Bilternus to the main dining room in the compound, which was already filled with hungry people. Kyel saw familiar faces, but he was only looking for one. He thought he saw Sencia running into the kitchens before Bilternus nudged him in the ribs. "What's that they're serving? Not scartha by any chance?"

Hot platters of pale meat, along with tureens of gravy, flat bread and huge jugs of beer were being placed on each long table. Wooden bowls with a metal spoon and clay mug marked each seating place.

"Don't know, Bilternus, and don't care," said Kyel, filling his mug with beer. His table had with many people he didn't know, several scent masters he recognised but none of the women. He noticed they were with Jakus at the head table where wine and a finer bread were being served.

"Pass the beer," said a broad, bald man next to him. "It's good to have a tasty meal after a long day's travel."

Kyel nodded and passed the jug.

"Tretial's the name, from Hestria." His voice was gruff. "Was some show, wasn't it?"

"Yes."

"You'll be on the lead ship, with me and the Shad."

"Oh, I wasn't aware." Kyel searched the room.

"Just thought I'd let you know. You and your friend seem a bit out of it, the preparations and planning I mean."

"Thanks, Tretial." Kyel took a chunk of meat and washed it down with a swallow of beer. He ate in a cocoon of silence. Bilternus was talking to someone along the table and Tretial was trying someone more talkative.

A soft breath huffed in his ear. "Late this night, young Eanite. You know where."

He swung around to catch the slim back of Sencia as she returned to the kitchens. He turned back to his food and saw Bilternus watching him. Kyel went red as Bilternus raised an eyebrow.

The place settled quickly once the meal was over. The men had the large room, lying on thin mats stretched out on a hard clay floor, most soon asleep after the hard day's travelling. Kyel lay back, hands behind his head, waiting as the last few noises in the building died away.

He slowly pushed himself to his feet and manoeuvred his way amongst the sleeping forms to the door. He turned down a long corridor, feeling his way with a hand on the wall. The scent traces of Sencia became stronger the further he went, until he came to a dead end where several doors were set into the walls.

Kyel knocked quietly. It opened without sound and a slim hand reached around his neck and pulled him through.

Her scent overwhelmed him; a pleasing odour of sweat and musk. Her body pressed into his and he was startled to find she was naked. "You took your time, Eanite," she murmured, "I was getting cold."

Sencia pushed him towards the bed, slipping off his sleeping tunic with a practiced ease. He fell backwards holding her firm young body to him.

"Now let's see if you've learnt anything while you've been away." She bit his ear before nibbling her way down his body. His fingers slipped along her smooth back as she moved down, half attempting to stop her, half urging her on.

"This I'm going to enjoy," she giggled.

Any thought of what lay ahead, or regrets about what he hadn't done, were irrelevant, he just enjoyed the moment. The anticipation of meeting Sencia added spice to the experience and he had to bite his lip to stop his groaning as she wriggled over his body.

He was covered in a sheen of sweat when they stopped, squashed in the small bed, his arm around her shoulders, fingers playing with a small breast.

"So, Kyel, was that worth waiting for?" Her voice was soft and musical.

"More than I thought, Sencia. I missed you."

"No, you didn't," she chuckled. "I am enough of a realist to know what you missed. You are a man, after all, even if an energetic one."

"No, I mean it." Kyel rubbed his other hand across his forehead. "You've given me some direction, an understanding that Sutan isn't a place full of unpleasant people who want to rule the world and damn the consequences. And in knowing this country is like any other if we can only stop those who want to take it away."

"My, you are getting serious," she said. "Let me see if I can distract you." Her hand moved down as she spoke.

K yel noticed Bilternus's eyes on him as he slipped back onto his sleeping mat. "Does she have a sister?" his friend whispered.

"Shut up and go back to sleep," Kyel hissed.

T he next day preparations were in full swing, everyone roped in to help load the ships with their gear and perishables.

"We're sailing next day," said Nefaria when she sought them out at their morning meal. "That means we all have to help. Bilternus, did you have other plans?" she asked noticing his face drop.

"Uh…no," he said. "But what of my father? What's happening with him?"

"He'll be on the expedition. Not on your ship, though. He'll be kept confined."

"Does that mean we're all going on Jakus's ship?" asked Kyel. "I met Tretial last night and he said something about it."

"As far as I know, Kyel," said Nefaria. "Despite being out of his eye for the last while, he requires you to be with us."

"Come on then, Kyel," said Bilternus, "let's get busy."

S oon they were amongst a convoy of laden perac heading towards the docks and wide streets that paralleled the waterways.

"You were lucky, last night," said Bilternus. "The way it's going I'm going to have to make love on my lonesome if I don't get to a way house. Maybe we can slip away later?"

"Mmm," Kyel murmured. "She's very nice. I might even get a chance to see her this night. So, no, I don't reckon I'll go to a Way House."

"All very well for you, friend."

Kyel, lost in his own thoughts, hardly noticed Bilternus's mood as they walked onto the docks.

"Hold. Which ship?" A guardsman blocked their access to the ships berthed along the stone and wood jetties behind him.

Kyel could see the vessel he'd sailed on to Sutan, and pointed.

"That's Shauna's operation. Just head down to her and she'll tell you what to do." He looked past them to the next group leading peracs.

They followed a narrow path to where three similar ships were moored, threading through the bustle of loading and unloading, animals, carts and people spread along the network of piers. He could see the diminutive redhead in a lime-green cape covering dark tunic top and trousers and headed towards her.

"Kyel. Bilternus," she said. "You've brought cargo. Let me see where this goes. Better give it to the men loading as it'll get too confusing. I see you're both on this, Jakus's ship," she added, looking down at a parchment. "Good, good. I will be too. Off you go. I have a lot to do to sail next day."

"Shauna, when are the animals going on board?" asked Kyel as he offloaded the baggage from his perac.

"What?" Her forehead creased. "No. No animals are coming. We're picking them up in Port Saltus. No point in feeding perac on the longest part of the voyage." She turned away.

No animals, Kyel puzzled. *There's no way they can get them in Ean, I'd reckon. It's Eanite controlled. They can't do it, unless there's help; someone local. But anyone helping them would be a traitor.*

They led their animals through the oncoming crowd, each in their own thoughts until they had walked a few streets up from the wharves.

"Let's get some proper food," said Bilternus, looking down a side road. "I really have to get the taste of scartha out of my mouth."

"Sure," agreed Kyel, still puzzling over what Shauna had told him.

His nose was recognising the smell of the tavern as Bilternus stopped outside. "Best food in Port. You would recognise it, I guess?"

"Of course," said Kyel. "I was here before, and wasn't it near the Way House you mentioned?"

"Was it?" Bilternus asked, tying his perac to the rail outside the building. "What a coincidence."

"I suppose I could look the other way, if you're quick," Kyel laughed.

Bilternus disappeared into a narrow-fronted building next door. Kyel began to enter the tavern, then paused and looked back down the street. His eyes narrowed as he saw a dark figure step back into an alleyway. Even at that distance he could recognise one of Jakus's scent masters. So, still not trusted, he thought. Wonder whether it's me or Bilternus they're following. Well, they can wait while I eat. He fingered the few coins in his pocket. Might try some of that chevrac— make a change from scartha at any rate.

"My dear brother," Jakus said, walking into the small room, "I trust you are well?"

Faltis looked up from the narrow, barred window overlooking the gravelled training ground.

"I imagine you are somewhat bored with all this sitting around. Not quite what you thought you'd be doing when you attacked me, eh?" He walked closer, his black cloak rippling. "I'd prefer you looking at me when I'm speaking, Faltis, for I am about to offer you a chance to salvage something of your reputation."

Jakus sat on the narrow bed and leant towards Faltis, who had now twisted in his seat to face him, his lean face showing a yellowing bruise on one cheek.

"I had a request from our father that I wouldn't kill you if the situation arose," he said flatly. "I have honoured that, despite your provocation. It seems I am somewhat sentimental, to my cost. I hope I don't regret what I'm about to offer."

Faltis's dark eyes glittered, and he shuffled in his seat.

"I will allow you to come on my expedition to Rolan, even to have you co-captain one of my ships, if I have your absolute guarantee you will obey my direction and work with me to establish my rightful role as leader of Ean, and… Sutan."

"What?" Faltis jumped up.

Jakus's scent shield shivered slightly.

"You…you mean me help establish you as ruler of Ean. And Sutan?"

Jakus nodded.

"But that would mean deposing father. Working against him?"

"No, brother, it wouldn't. I told you, Vitaris and I spoke. He would not stand in our way." Jakus stood, placing a pinch of crystals into his mouth as he walked to the window, while Faltis paced the room.

"Brastus! There's Brastus. He believes he should be the future ruler of Sutan and beyond."

"Yes, there's Brastus and his ambitions. A problem, certainly, but not at this time. The results from my expedition to Rolan will make Brastus's return from his overseas campaigns merely an annoying issue to deal with in due course. It will not be a problem."

"So"—Faltis turned his head on one side and looked at his brother. "Where do I fit in, now I know so much?"

"You will be my right hand, serving in my stead whenever needed."

"What? After all we've been through, you'd trust me that much? No"—Faltis shook his head, "I can't believe you."

"You've heard what I've said," Jakus spoke quietly. "And I'm a man of my word."

"You surprise me, brother." Faltis sat and ran a hand through the greying stubble that covered his head. "And I'd be mad to turn it down."

"Yes, you would," Jakus smiled, sitting back on the bed, their knees almost touching. "You would. And there's no time like now to seal our agreement."

A wall of scent enveloped Faltis, pushing down his instinctive reaction. His eyes almost crossed as a tendril of odour emerged from Jakus's mouth and twisted up his nose.

"No, you can't…" he gasped as the probe entered his scent centre.

Jakus grimaced as he sifted through the scent memories to locate the loyalty area, searching for some tractability. He weakened the darkness he found, pushing hard with positive scents, *endeavouring to link his own odours with his brother's better emotions. Sweat poured down his face while he worked.*

Faltis groaned, stretching back, fighting the invasion.

Chapter Thirty-Nine

The room was dark when Alethea entered.

Targas picked her up immediately. She had a pleasant scent, floral but with the ever-present cordial smell. Her age and wisdom showed through as a steely grey push, just visible through his half-closed eyes. His immediate reaction was to snap at her for all the pain she had caused, but he knew her intent was pure.

"I'm awake, Alethea," he murmured, "though my head's on fire."

"I know, my dear. Sadir suggested you might see me, even after what we did to you."

"Never, never again!" he continued hoarsely.

"Can I help?"

"Mmm."

The flow of soothing scents was immediate. It tickled, flowing past the blockage of congealed blood, infiltrating his sinuses and pushing back the throbbing pain filling his head. Targas tasted astringent plant odours above the smoothness of Alethea's concerns and felt her practised expertise relieving the wreckage left by his trial.

"Does that help?" she asked.

"Uh huh," he sighed.

"We were concerned at what you went through. I have never experienced anything like this possession of your mind. It seemed that the scent memories of Septus had infiltrated your own memories. I can only hope that we have driven him away, expunged his essence."

"What?" Targas croaked.

"I think, with the power we had at our disposal in the crystal cave he should be gone. The shadow scent is different and our use of it in this way should have been too much for him." Her hand brushed his forehead. "Are you able to feel whether he has departed?"

Targas explored his mind. The pounding had faded to a background irritation, so he was able to navigate his memories without difficulty. The tracks felt clear.

Before, he had experienced a thickness, as if a fog had been at the back of his mind, but now it was gone. He pushed as far as he was able, with no impediment.

"You may be right. I can't feel him. There's no trace." The relief was obvious in his voice.

"That is well, Targas. Now you may care to come out, have some food and enjoy the air, for it is a fine day."

"You mean it's not raining?"

"That was last day, Targas. This day is fine and sunny," said Alethea. "I will leave you to get dressed. Well done, my dear." She turned and left the room.

A whole day lost, he thought as he swung his legs over the side of his bed. A whole day? He shook his head, standing as he did so. The faint pounding increased in response, and he cried out as a sharp pain pierced his brain. It quickly disappeared, puzzling him as to its origin. *Surely not,* he thought in mounting disbelief. *Surely not.*

"Par! Par!" The girl ran into Targas's side, followed by the thump of a too heavy voral.

"Careful," he laughed, "you might cause me more damage than I've had already." He picked Anyar up and held her in the crook of his arm.

"I missed you, Par," she said, resting her arm on his head. "Why did you go away?"

"She did miss you, Targas," said Sadir, holding a hand against Anyar's side. "It was all I could do to stop her climbing on you when you were sleeping."

"C'mon, little one," said Targas, sitting down at a table with a view into the distant valley. "Par needs something to eat. I'm hungry. And I'm alright now. Much better after my sleep."

"Oh," Anyar said gravely, then noticed the slabs of buttered toast being placed on the table by Cernea, who smiled at the girl. "Can Vor have some too?"

"I think Vor will eat anything," observed Sadir, as she sat beside them. "Let's wait till we've eaten, sweetling."

The food came in prodigious quantities: large bowls of steaming oatmeal, plates piled with fried onions and crispy meat, eggs and fried bread and a platter of round fruits. Anyar's attention was drawn to the jar of honey sitting in the centre of the table. She dipped in a wooden spoon, dribbled some on her toast and then slowly dropped the arm holding the spoon below the table level.

Sadir was about to comment on table manners and food etiquette, but Targas shrugged and asked: "Would you like some hot oatmeal to go with the milk and honey, Anyar?"

The child, missing the sarcasm, replied: "Yes, please." Her hand, with the now licked-clean spoon, reappeared. It was obvious what was under the table.

"I'd suggest we visit the village at the foot of Mlana Hold, Targas," said Boidea, intercepting him as he left the table. "There's some people you should meet, and it'd be wise to see what extends beyond the Hold."

"I would," he answered. "I think I've been here long enough and want to see more. Besides, Alethea feels there's some urgency for us all."

"We'll leave Anyar to her lessons, then, and I'll take you, Sadir and Cathar down into the valley. The Mlana and several of our leaders are there already."

They left via a well-travelled pathway below the cavern's mouth, winding their way through large boulders and several tall granite walls amongst a tumbled mess of small rocks, narrow crevasses and broken scree.

"This path's the only easy way to the cavern, and could be easily defended, if necessary," said Boidea. "There's a bridge ahead that could be destroyed to hinder any enemy trying to get to the Hold."

Targas nodded, looking over the valley and recognising features making it hard for an invader to approach without undergoing heavy losses. All the buildings spreading across the slopes were of heavy stone and had slate or wooden roofs, arranged to give cover against any force coming up the valley. Periodic walls of packed stone angled from the valley walls towards the centre ensured that the invading forces would be funnelled into the middle and be more vulnerable.

They came into a sunlit square formed by a number of buildings, the largest with two solid doors swung back against its dark stone walls.

"The small, solidly built building between the pottery and the meeting hall is where we secure the items of trade, processed magnesite and tumblers," said Boidea. "We'll go on to the hall." She pointed to the largest building, where many people were gathered.

"I'll leave you with Drathner, though," said Boidea as she headed towards the large building. "Cathar, you might come with me."

The younger woman nodded and followed her.

Drathner finished a conversation he was having and smiled at them. "Welcome Targas, Sadir. Welcome to our humble hall, our planning area. How are you feeling?"

"Well enough," Targas replied. "Not an experience I'd wish to repeat." He and Sadir reached Drathner and exchanged scents.

"It is good to see you up and about. Now I have a person I'd like you both to meet." He half-turned and took the solid arm of the man near him. "My friend, Xaner, the commander of the Port of Requist."

Targas took in the square-faced man with peppery hair, noticing with a start that he had the same light eyes as himself. His dark coat was open revealing a wool tunic and dark trousers covering scuffed boots.

"Ah, Targas, I am pleased to meet you, having heard much about the hero of

Ean." His smile was genuine, and his grey-shot scent aura echoed his words as they exchanged scents.

"My partner, Sadir," Targas responded.

Xaner's eyes lit. "I see you're a woman of some scent talent too."

"It's a slow leaning process, but rewarding," Sadir nodded at him.

"Come into the hall," said Drathner, turning towards the large building. "Let me show you our relief map. The Mlana is inside."

"You're not of Rolan?" Targas asked Xaner as they walked through the large doorway.

"You noticed my eyes were like yours? Well. I am a Rolanite, but my mother came on a trading ship and stayed. Tenstrian, she was."

"As am I," Targas replied.

"Welcome, my dear friends," said Alethea. The diminutive woman was sitting at a low table with several others. Xerrita looked up and smiled, while Boidea kept her eyes on the table, several lanterns suspended from wooden roof beams providing ample light to view the relief map constructed on its surface.

Drathner ushered them in to gather around the table. Targas nodded to Telpher before he looked down.

The relief map, moulded from clay, was coloured to reflect different portions—higher grounds grey, valleys and plains greenish, rivers dark and red lines appeared to indicate roads or tracks. The map began from the mountain range that backed the cavern. From there a depression showed the course of the river and its tributaries as it deepened and widened, heading for the southern coast. The arable area appeared very limited as the map clearly showed Rolan was a land of mountains; extremely rugged and imposing.

"Would you like me to explain the country to our friends from Ean, Mlana?" asked Drathner.

"If you would," she said, with a note of exhaustion in her voice.

"Mmm." He raised an eyebrow at Alethea before he ran a hand over the mass of clay mountains. "This is the backbone of Rolan. As far as you can see there are mountains—our benefit and our curse. This gives us little usable land and variable weather conditions, long winters and shorter growing periods except on the coast at the city of Request. In fact, apart from the small, exposed port of Sea Holm in the far west, Request is the only real harbour due to a very rugged coastline. It is here,"—and he traced a rough finger along the river to where it entered the sea—"that the Rolander river slows and gives us fertile plains.

"Conversely, the river is our main avenue of entry into the interior and the towns of Nosta and Mlana Hold—you can see where the roads go. Thus it is the route that any invader would follow." Drathner nodded to Xaner.

The solid man stepped closer and rubbed a hand across his face. "My thanks, Drathner. It is as you have suspected, Mlana," he said, glancing at Alethea. "Several trading vessels have reported rumours of a Sutanite force being prepared with the possible intention of coming to Rolan. While it may be another move on Ean, particularly in light of several events in that country, I rather think it's aimed at us. All this behoves us to prepare. Firstly at Requist, and secondly along the way to Mlana Hold."

A burst of conversation began at this announcement and Xaner waited until it died away. "For the benefit of our guests"—he glanced at Targas, Sadir and Cathar—"you may realise our country has defensive options for such an event. Our ancestors had the defence of Rolan in mind when they designed our city and towns. Any attack has to go along the river valley. The mountains and hills are too rugged, so Nosta and Mlana Hold are made to thwart any attack. Requist is a problem, being a maze of streets and low-lying buildings—the penalty of its trading nature, so it is an expected loss if that is the case, but the remainder of the country is our bastion. Our people will retreat there and never be defeated."

Targas nodded, wincing slightly as a burst of pain shot through his head.

Sadir squeezed his arm. "Thank you, Xaner and Drathner for explaining things. But I think we had better return to the Hold now. Can we see you again next day?"

"I agree," said Alethea, rising slowly from her seat. "There's much to think about and I'm looking forward to the warmth of the fires. Thank you all."

Boidea took Alethea's arm and led her from the meeting room.

"I'm feeling much better, Sadir, really," said Targas.

"Another day's rest won't hurt though, my love," she said firmly as they moved out into the greying day.

S adir worried about Targas. Despite his protestations, his face was white, and he hadn't fully recovered from their efforts to clear Septus from his mind. She kept hold of his arm as they followed the steep path up to the cavern.

The experience had been like no other. In the eerie red light of the crystal cave, being drawn in by the talented Alethea, Boidea and Xerrita, she had gone on a whirlwind of a ride.

In the Sanctus moon ceremony she had let her senses go, becoming one with everyone else, being guided and directed by the will of the people and the circumstance. Even when Lan and Alethea had tried to help Targas in the Sanctus cave's pool room she had been unable to resist, pulled into a dream-like state where Targas had fought Septus, screaming in reaction before she awoke. *No*, she thought, *this was different*. Whether it was the power surrounding them or their strong use of the shadow scent, she didn't know.

The red darkness had initially obscured the shadow scent, but the three women forced it to become greater, overriding the normal scents, pushing it towards her partner. She and Cathar had been mere passengers at that stage, but she could see it, feel it more acutely than ever before.

She had used the scent power when confronted by the hymetta in Nebleth's caves, but this experience was even greater.

The shadow scent became an extra force pushed into Targas's scent centres with the Rolanites' extreme skill, like a wary hunter travelling through the intricacies of nerves and memories seeking out areas of damage or ill. She and Cathar had added their abilities, to be used by the Mlana in this delicate operation. And the power was immense.

Sadir had never felt the thrill of such purposefully directed scent use before, even while knowing it was Targas who was bearing the brunt of their efforts. Then there was the chase, the feel of something fighting them, pushing back, blocking them. But this time it was only fleeting before the resistance collapsed and they sensed something, a frightened predator taking flight from what had seemed an easy kill. They followed, tracking it through the web of memories until it gradually faded away to nothing.

But the fight had caused damage as the evil resident resisted. Targas had bled heavily from nose, ears and eyes. They had been forced to stop to preserve his life, not sure they had truly succeeded.

"Mar!"

Anyar waved from a semicircle of children sitting around several women drawing on large boards with chalk.

Sadir waved back as they walked into the cavern.

"I think I'll rest for a moment," said Targas, and he headed through to their rooms.

"Fine, love. I'll see what Anyar's learning."

She watched the women engage with the children, recognising Cernea from earlier. Anyar, sitting next to a dark-haired boy and a brown-haired girl, was watching raptly as Cernea tapped the board's surface with a piece of chalk.

"How is Anyar fitting in?" Sadir asked Cernea when she had dusted off the board.

"Very well," she replied. They both looked at Anyar, in earnest conversation with her companions. "She is a bright young thing thirsty for learning. Come, let us get some tea while they're busy."

They noticed Alethea sitting on a soft seat near the fire nursing a mug, so they took their tea over.

"Well met," she said softly, her scent aura showing strain as they sat next to her.

The fire crackled and a spurt of sparks lifted to the roof before edging out into the open air. Sadir felt her eyes starting to close as they sat in silence enjoying the warmth. Alethea's voice penetrated her awareness.

"Sorry, I was dozing. What were you saying?"

"I was commenting on Anyar. Cernea was saying what a bright girl she is, as you and I both know. But you are aware she is even more than that, aren't you?"

"Yes, both Targas and I know she's showing some unusual attributes. Her scent power seems to be developing really early, and the way she controls that voral…"

"But she is more than that. Much, much more," said Alethea quietly. "With attributes from both yourself and Targas, she has no choice but to be special."

Sadir looked over at her daughter playing with her new friends.

"I think it is good that you, Cernea, are here at the moment, for Anyar will need all the help and protection she can over the next while, as on her shoulders rests the future."

"What do you mean?" asked Sadir, incredulously. "She's a child! What do you mean the future rests on her shoulders?"

"I have had Knowings reinforcing that belief for some time now. Should she…I'm sorry…survive the coming conflict, then she will develop quickly, and will become the Mlana, likely the greatest Mlana that has even been. And she will need to be."

Sadir's mouth dropped open at Alethea's words.

"However, should she fall, then darkness will descend on our lands." Alethea's voice trailed off and she gazed into the fire for a time before looking back. "It will not be my role—my time is nearly complete. You, Sadir, Cathar and those around you must nurture her until she reaches her full powers."

"But…Targas?"

"Sadir," Alethea said, holding up a weary hand, "I am uncertain, unable to see. His future is shrouded. Now, if you please, while I'm still able I would like to speak to you and Targas both. Could you bring him here?"

Sadir stood slowly, bemused by what Alethea was saying.

"Another tea, Cernea, please?"

She vaguely heard Alethea as she left. What was it all about? Did Alethea always have to speak in riddles?

A short while later, she had a sleepy Targas with her and was back to where Alethea waited. Cernea was with the children in the distance.

"Thank you, Sadir," Alethea said. "Please sit, Targas."

She waited until they were settled and took a deep breath.

"Next day, once you have rested, you must go with Boidea and Drathner, scout through the country, see Requist and the preparations for what is to come."

"Both of us, Alethea?" asked Targas.

"No, not Sadir, she has the responsibility of your daughter," she murmured. "It is important that you do so, Targas, for only then will you understand the land you are fighting in. Only then will you learn what you must for what is to come."

"Alright," Sadir said slowly. "Then you will be staying too?" She watched the old woman for a moment and then drew in her breath. "It's to do with your Knowing, isn't it?"

"Yes." Alethea looked towards the roof of the cave, her scent aura a dull green of concern and friendship. "Yes, it is. Ever since our near disaster in the mountains, I've known that I'm on limited time. I must remain and prepare. A war is coming, led by a cruel and single-minded man. If we are to survive him and be prepared for the hardships of the future, things must go this way. For if we do not stop him and force him to leave this land believing he has what he came for, then not only will our lands never be free, but the world will eventually fall under his domination.

"I must prepare for this, as must we all. Each has their tasks and their destiny. Please go with my blessing, Targas, and I will see you on your return."

Chapter Forty

Kyel was up early and hurrying to the dock with the noise and smell getting to him even though the ship was against the wharf. Chaos was everywhere, yet with a semblance of order, as the last of the carters bringing perishables was leaving and with all the scent masters and guardsmen on board. *Soon,* he thought, *soon.*

His eyes scanned the packed road leading into the city, hoping he would see a slim figure waving to him, but knowing she wouldn't be there. Sencia had left him feeling satisfied, but with an ache in his heart. She had seemed sad to let him go and was extremely inventive in the final moments they had together. He had tried to find her one last time in the bustle of the leaving but couldn't.

I'll miss her. I really will, he thought, running his hand along the oiled rail as if he could feel her skin.

"Hah!" Bilternus stepped next to him. "I know what you're thinking. I was lucky at the Way Inn. Not as lovely as your girl, but enough to give me something to remember."

"What do you want?" Kyel snapped.

"Not yourself? Don't let it worry you. There's girls like her in every city."

"What?" Kyel felt his scent aura change as he turned to face Bilternus.

"Sorry," Bilternus said, holding out a placating hand, "I didn't know she meant so much to you."

Kyel held his breath for a moment before looking down at the water lapping the hull of their ship.

"Just wanted to tell you our bags are jammed in the hold with everyone else's. Seems we'll be sleeping in bunks with a lot of the others, not in a cabin like you said you had before."

"Oh, I didn't think about it. I mean where else could we be?"

"Shows what his lordship thinks of us, doesn't it? The women, including Poegna, have the cabins."

"Look Bilternus, can't you find something else to do? I don't want to talk now."

"Can see that, my friend." He clapped Kyel on the back. "I'll be back when you're in a better mood."

Kyel heard him walk away.

The activity slowed as the ropes were cast off from the bollards. He could hear the bang of the rowing boats on the other side taking up the strain and easing the ship away from the wharf. It would be some time before they reached deeper water at the end of the long pier and were able to release the tow. He looked once more along the road, then turned away, heading down the stairs to find where his bags had been stowed. If his stomach didn't settle soon, he would be needing his bunk and the head.

They hit the first of the waves from the open sea around midday. Southern Port was well protected by man-made structures and the natural lie of the land, but now they were heading into a stiff sea breeze.

The crack of the sails caused him to appreciate the sight of the square topsails belling out. He watched as a sailor unfurled the jib, the spritsail already tight.

"Move out of the way, young Kyel," called the captain. "We're taking a tight port tack. You can come aft if you'd like to join me."

Kyel was pleased that Tibitis asked him. The earlier trip from Ean with him had only been several days long and he had spent most of it feeling ill, even sharing the captain's cabin, so was uncertain of his reception.

"Thanks." He took a breath of the air. The smells of land had already disappeared, leaving a slight tang of salt, seaweed and a freshness he had missed.

"Good to get on the way, eh? And you're getting your sea legs too," he said, glancing across at Kyel. "Don't like being in port much. Quieter here."

Kyel listened to the snap of the sails, the creak of the rigging, the burble and bang of the water hitting the vessel, the murmur of the people on deck, and shook his head. "Don't know about that, but it's good to be away from Sutan."

He watched Tibitis leaning on the tiller as the ship heeled into the wind on a southerly heading. "Isn't Ean more to the west, Tibitis? Why are we heading south?"

"You noticed, I see," the captain grunted. "Most wouldn't ask, not being sailors, but you've come this way before.

"Take up the slack, damn you!" he yelled at a sailor near the bow.

"Humph. As I was saying, you came from Ean with the wind. A quick journey, you might say, and easy for sailing, too. Now we go back. Against the wind, a longer, harder trip. Takes almost twice as long since we have to tack most of the way."

"I can see that," said Kyel, his body automatically moving with the ship, "but why south?"

"Best winds as it clears the coast. Sutan has this large bump which gets in the way of our tacking. Best to go south aways before zig-zagging back westwards. Be tired out by the time we get there. Might even get you to help, if you'd like? Not much else to do on board."

"Thanks, Tibitis, I'd like that." Kyel watched the play of the sails for a while before looking astern. The other four ships of Jakus's fleet lay close by, sails set, each beating on the same tack. Even further astern was the smudge of Southern Port.

If it wasn't for Sencia, I'd never want to come back here.

"Kyel," Nefaria said, from near the aft railing, "Jakus wants you in the cabin."

"Wants *me?*" Kyel asked. "Why?"

"Just go. I must get Bilternus, too." Nefaria spun around and edged towards the bow, holding onto the rail as she went.

"Better go, lad," said Tibitis. "We both know what he's like."

"We meet again, young Kyel," said the large scent master by the door to the cabin. "Looks like you've sailed before. Some of us are already a bit green."

"Hi, Tretial," said Kyel as he squeezed past and into the cabin. He endeavoured to keep his scents neutral as he saw Jakus studying a parchment on a small table; Shauna, Poegna and Festern were with him.

He waited just inside the door feeling the pitch of the ship, sampling the scents of the sizeable room. Jakus's scent aura showed he was intent on what he was doing and in a neutral frame of mind.

"Here he is," said Nefaria, as she pushed a decidedly ill-looking Bilternus inside.

Jakus looked up and frowned.

"Haven't had much time for you two, but you have your uses. Bilternus, you've had time on your hands since Hestria, and have proven your loyalty."

Bilternus gulped and put his hands to his mouth.

"Nefaria. Don't let him spew!" he snapped. Jakus's eyes fixed on Kyel while Nefaria drifted healing scents over Bilternus.

"You'll both be rowing the longboat when we reach Port Saltus. We need muscle power to bring several ships in, so be available. We won't be staying longer than necessary." His eyes narrowed as he watched Kyel's face. "I see I have been neglecting my prize Eanite. We must have some moments together before we arrive.

"Now, Bilternus." He turned his attention to the pale-looking man.

Kyel's mind froze. He kept his scent aura tight, preventing his alarm from showing. He assessed the people in the room. All, even Bilternus, seemed to be strangers, each with their own preoccupations. No one he could rely on. He'd never felt more alone. He had managed to travel through a hostile land, survive attacks and the invasion of his very being, until he had finally come out the other side, a stronger, more resolute and mature person. If anything, the time had helped him decide he needed to look after those who cared for him: his family, his people and his country. And Jakus would see that in an instant, if he decided to check.

Kyel wondered how Jakus would react to anyone who might to try stop him. Given what he'd seen before, he knew it wouldn't be pleasant. He moved past Tretial and out of the door. *Back with the captain, that's the safest place to be.*

O ver the next few days Kyel involved himself in the voyage, pushing his concerns into the background. He helped the sailors wherever he could, learning the ropes and even climbing the rigging; the experience of swaying at the top of a pitching ship was exhilarating. But at night, alone in his cramped bunk, he spent his time thinking things through, remembering his time with Xerina, recalling her lessons and her conviction he needed to know about the strange scent she referred to as the *other* scent.

He smiled when he remembered her, then the young acolyte who served them and then Sencia. He became aroused when he thought of Sencia, what they'd done, and went to sleep remembering her firm, exciting body.

A line of black scudded towards them early one morning, four days out from Sutan. Kyel was in his usual position next to Tibitus, resting from rope work, his hands already callusing, and pointed it out.

The captain nodded. "I know. Be in for a rough blow. Just need to keep on course. As well we don't have animals on board. Probably about time to tell your friends about it. Need to feed quickly, then batten everything down that could shift. Get wet-weather gear too."

Kyel sought out Bilternus. He had turned out to be a fair sailor after his initial sea sickness and was someone he could talk to and do things with. Together they told most of the scent masters to prepare—the sailors had already secured the ship for tight sailing, then returned to the aft deck.

"If you're going to stay, prepare to help at the helm. Tie yourselves to the mast. We won't be stopping for anyone overboard." Tibitis watched the ship as it plunged into the waves, the jib and spritsail the only sheets not furled, occasionally yelling an order against the rising wind.

The blackness now filled the horizon and the first drops of rain splattered into their faces. The deck was cleared of all but a few tethered sailors when a wall of water hit in a howling rush, smashing into the ship. Kyel and Bilternus bent into it, their waterproofed perac-wool coats giving little protection.

"Give me a hand!" screamed Tibitis. "Hold the helm."

Kyel hooked his arms over the long tiller which juddered and shook like a live thing. The ship heeled, almost flattening on its side as the wind hit. Kyel could feel his feet slipping and held on as tight as he could.

A high-pitched scream broke through the howling wind. A sailor was flung across the deck, crunching into the rail before flipping over the side. Kyel briefly noticed the man's tethering line snapping with a twang.

He drew a breath to call the captain's attention to the lost sailor, but his feet were swept away, and his grip snatched from his hold on the tiller. He slithered to the rail with the rush of water, his mind readying for the fatal plunge into the boiling sea. The line tightened painfully around his middle and held.

"Get back, fool, or we'll founder!" the captain yelled.

The ship rocked between gusts, giving Kyel a chance to scramble back to the relative safety of the helm.

"Help your friend. It needs the three of us."

Kyel glanced at the white face of Bilternus, who was clinging to the wooden tiller, relieved at his own narrow escape.

The nightmare didn't end there. His vision narrowed to the wood his fingers tried to dig through. Juddering and heaving his body like it had no weight, the tiller's attempts to flick him off like so much jetsam terrified him. His white clawed fingers were matched by Bilternus's, while Tibitus held tightly to the end, adjusting the helm in increments to allow for the weather's effect on the vessel.

As a huge wave washed over them and the wind tore at their bodies Kyel's gaze moved up to his companion's frozen face and saw a silent recognition of the ordeal they were sharing.

The howling wind began to subside after a while, enabling them to move frozen fingers and shift locked limbs.

"What about the sailor?" Kyel asked Tibitus.

"What about him? The sea's taken him. There's no going back."

"But..." He quietened at the captain's stern face.

Slowly the wind blew out, allowing the ship to right itself and the helm to respond more easily. The rain ceased abruptly, and a ray of sun broke through the grey sky.

"Let go, lads," growled Tibitis. "We're right for the moment."

"Set the sails!" he bellowed to his sailors, "we've got distance to recover."

"I wouldn't want to go through that again," said Kyel.

"If you're a sailor, then you'll go through it again," said Tibitis, his wet face glistening. "But that was just a gust, a short blow. It can go for days, sometimes. Better go and help clean up. Thanks for your strong arms, lads."

They sailed on with the wind blowing steadily across their bow, necessitating continual beating to windward. The five ships carrying Jakus's small army had regrouped, looking trim and preparing for their arrival at Port Saltus.

A day out, two vessels of different design appeared close to them from the west, before returning the way they'd come.

"Do we follow them, my Lord?" Tibitis asked Jakus, standing next to him at the helm.

"The Eanites must not get away, captain!" snapped Jakus, his scent aura blackening.

"All hands on deck. Make sail!" yelled Tibitis.

The wind had risen, driving in off their port bow, its strength causing the white caps of the waves to break loose and fill the air with punishing spray. It screamed through the rigging and tugged at the sails, stretching them to breaking. The ship heeled over, its topmast spar trying to kiss the waves.

"My Lord!" yelled Tibitus at the tall dark, figure braced next to him against the railing on the helm platform, cloak whipping and snapping with a life of its own. "We have to ease off!"

Jakus shook his head without moving his eyes from the two vessels several boat-lengths ahead and away to port. "No, you will not. Keep a close reach. I need to get nearer, ahead of them!"

The captain hesitated, mouth open, spray causing his face to glisten in the wan light of the sun lowering in the west. He eyed Jakus's rigid back then, signalled for a sailor to adjust the boom.

The ship heeled, its spritsail smashing through the tips of the huge waves, inexorably moving abeam of the Eanite vessels.

Jakus took a glance at the following ships, which carried the bulk of his Sutanese force. His eyes tightened as they slackened off, unwilling to follow his tight line towards the enemy in the heavy seas.

"Pah!" he blew a gust of air from his cheeks, then gripped the rail when the ship plunged into a trough, wincing as the pitching of the ship wrenched his body.

"Tretial!" he screamed at the scent master clinging to the rail amidships. The man gave no response, his bald head showing a circling miasma of sickness before the scent was stripped away by the strong wind.

"Damn!" Jakus yelled into the wind's wall of sound. He reached into his pouch, took a large pinch of magnesa crystals and pushed them into his mouth. He watched a large wave cascade over the line of scent masters clinging to rails, capstan and masts, even as the crystals reached his brain. The power relegated the pitching ship and angry waves to the background, and he perceived the flowing scents as a rushing blur, saw into the motes of odour and knew how to tame them. A burst of sea spray slapped his grinning face, but he continued concentrating.

He began to link the disparate scent bonds, pushing out with his mind, forcing the interlocking to spread, like ice forming over water, creating a floating pocket of calm amidst the turmoil around him. The pitching of the ship lessened as the waves were supressed by the blanket of odour, their very rhythm diminished. Curiously, the wind had little effect, such was the strength Jakus exerted.

Tretial lifted his head and looked over his shoulder at his leader as he felt a tug on his senses. Jakus glared at him, his face a rictus of concentration. "Take the crystals," he projected his voice. "Now!"

The black-cloaked scent master nodded hurriedly and turned to his companions, who were feeling the benefit of ship's easier motion.

Jakus smiled as he thought back to Targas years ago, when he had dredged the scent master's mind and taken his secrets. He could never have predicted how events turned out, but now he would be able to test his new techniques on a large target, the fleeing enemy ships.

A sudden crash, accompanied by a shower of splinters, threatened his concentration, causing him to move behind the limited protection of the helm. *Ah*, he thought as he surveyed the damage caused by the Eanite scent bolt, *impressive, but not effective enough.*

The ship heaved, mast lifting, sails losing wind as the captain reacted to the enemy attack.

"Keep it on course, you blood-cursed scartha!" Jakus yelled as his attention wavered.

Suddenly the links with his people expanded like a starburst in his brain as they took their magnesa. He grabbed their power into his scent web, pulling, building it into his own expanding blanket of odour. "Now!" he screamed. A powerful twist of his mind forced the blanket to spread at right angles to the wind, like a vast billowing sail, directly in front of the two Eanite ships.

He felt relief as he twisted the linkages to cause corrosive bonds to form on the fringes of the *sail* hovering in the enemy's path. Jakus knew this was an untried method of attack over a large area, but his understanding of the structures within the motes of odour meant success was moments away. And he was targeting wood, the material of the vessel, by breaking and *ungluing* the minute particles. He didn't understand how this worked, just that his bonds took something from the wood, causing it to crumble like iron turning to rust, but much, much faster.

A poignant beam of light from the failing sun struck the blanket of odour, causing it to glow against the scudding grey clouds and wild water. Then it happened. The leading Eanite ship was enveloped as it crashed through the cloud of scent. It sailed on as the second ship entered, to momentarily disappear in the gloom.

Jakus hissed an expelled burst of air. "It is done. Now it will work. It must!"

"There, my Lord," yelped Tibitus in Jakus's ear, releasing a hand from the tiller to point, "they're in trouble!"

Briefly obscured by the breaking white crests of the towering waves, the Eanite vessels appeared to blur, becoming indistinct as if being erased. The sails, drawn tight by the conditions, frayed as they watched, dissipating like frost in the sun. The masts stood out like skeletal trees while the momentum of the ships' bulk pushed them forward, before collapsing into the maelstrom around them; portions of iron, darker than their surroundings appeared briefly until swallowed by the water.

The Eanite vessels became part of the wild sea, vanishing as if they'd never existed.

"You may slacken off, Captain," gasped Jakus, his tight face relaxing as he released his hold on the links to his people and the odour blanket. "I think our passengers would appreciate a smoother ride."

"But my Lord, there are men in the water. They'll never survive. We need to pick them up."

"What?" Jakus turned to Tibitus.

The captain pointed at the scattered sailors in the sea behind them, being pulled high into the air by a monstrous wave. "They're drowning!"

"Set course for Port Saltus, Captain!"

Jakus looked back as the ship rose on the crest of a wave. He caught sight of the four sister vessels a distance off to starboard coming to a parallel course as he gripped the wooden rail. His stomach cramped and he bent over in reaction to the extensive magnesa use. He fought his rampant headache and glanced up through tears of pain before nodding to himself.

"That went well," he gasped as the cries of the drowning men came faintly to his ears against the howling wind. "Very well indeed."

Chapter Forty-One

"**B**ye, Par!" Anyar's voice rang above the noise of the moving animals and people.

Targas raised an arm in reply, pushing a burst of bright scent into the air. He waved to Sadir where she stood with their daughter at the mouth of the cavern, remembering the desperation of their goodbye the previous night, some of Alethea's prophetic words providing an impetus to their parting.

"Don't worry, Targas," said Boidea from the perac next to him, "they're in good hands. It's far better they stay where they and Cathar can learn from the Mlana. We, on the other hand, have a lot of ground to cover in harsh conditions, although not as bad as travelling through the mountains, I would surmise."

Targas grunted and looked around the group of people in thick woollen jackets and grey trousers surrounding him, calming their animals, some tying on the last of equipment and provisions. *Probably an equal number of men and women, though it's hard to tell,* he thought.

The sun fought through a bleak day, light frost on exposed areas of ground, as they moved through the village and on to the stone-paved road leading down the valley. Almost immediately they pushed through a set of walls, angling from the steep valley walls like a truncated V, numerous thick timbers piled on one side for defensive blocking of the gap.

Once through the road, they came alongside the fast-flowing stream that became the Rolander River. The noise was deafening and the pall of spray hanging in the air added a cold wetness to the ride. At several paces sheer cliffs bulged out, making the road treacherous and narrower, forcing them to go single file until the land flattened.

Soon the river widened and slowed, allowing for a more pleasant journey. Targas's head was clear, and he was able to appreciate the scenery. Clumps of fine-leafed trees pushed up into the hollows and folds of the foothills, giving a darker hue to the grassy slopes. Small animals with the look of peracs dashed away at their approach, leaving puffs of alarm scent. They reminded him of the softpaws he'd once hunted in his native Tenstria.

Rocks still dominated, with sheaths of mosses and ferns softening their effect, the road making a clear line through the rocks and grasses until disappearing through a lower pass in the distance. It was warmer now the sun had broken through the light clouds, and most of the party had thrown back their hoods or removed their jackets. He could make out Drathner and Telpher, together with the shorter, grey-haired Xerrita in the dozen or so people ahead. Twisting in his saddle he noticed a few larger peracs carrying big boxes slung across their withers, behind the last few people in the group.

He glanced at the woman riding comfortably alongside him, a thoughtful expression on her mature features.

"Boidea, those boxes the pack animals are carrying, I don't remember seeing them before. What are they?"

"Those?" She looked over her shoulder. "Just containers for the fermenters at Nosta—tumblers ready to be filled with cordial; it's made at the city, since they have the fruit and the equipment. Loads regularly go between the pottery at the Hold and the Nosta fermenters."

"So, if I remember from the map, we should reach it by the end of the day?"

"Yes, and the next day is an easier run to Requist, even if somewhat longer. How are you feeling?" she asked. "It is probably too soon for you to be travelling such a distance, but the Mlana was sure of the need."

"I feel well," he said. "Nothing really damaged, I think." He pushed up into his head as he spoke, seeking for the resistance he had become used to when Septus was riding in his mind. "And I think we may have fixed me. I feel, ah, content, even though I'm leaving Sadir and Anyar behind. I may even be ready to keep experimenting with scent again. It was hard with the feel of him, sitting behind my eyes, watching, waiting. Yes, I think he must be gone."

"That is well," Boidea said gravely, "for we have never encountered such resistance, and the way you reacted made us fear the worst. Still, if it worked, we can't ask for more."

They settled into a rhythmic pace, allowing Targas to immerse himself in his thoughts.

He was startled out of his reverie by a nudge from Boidea.

"Targas, we are coming to an area of particular beauty, but you will need to watch the road as we descend once we leave the pass, then you'll see. It's one of the things that make me homesick when I'm away."

The roar of the water hit his ears, accompanied by a strong honey scent. A myriad of water droplets hung in the air before them, grabbing and reflecting the sunlight. Through it all wove yellow-hued scent motes, assailing the senses. They moved through a wall of spray as they came over the lip of the pass, and headed down into a wide valley spreading almost as far as he could see. But he wasn't looking ahead, he was seeing walls of white-flowering trees extending along the escarpment in an east-west line, marking the division between the village of Mlana Hold and the plains leading to the city of Nosta.

Another stream joined the one they followed, both falling in an arc into the valley, emitting a tremendous roar and misting the air.

He noticed movement in the foliage of the trees, recognising lizards, including those with flexible skin flaps to help them glide, before he saw the distinctive shape of a large bee, a pria. It was half as big as Vor with black and white bandings on its abdomen. When one flew overhead towards the mountains, its buzzing overcame the sound of the water.

Boidea tapped him on the arm. "They make a good honey when we can get it. Unfortunately, their hives are a good distance into the mountains. These late-flowering trees attract all nectar feeders.

"What do you think of this?" She spread her arms wide to encompass the falls behind them and the plains extending into the distance. "The Cascade Falls behind us and the Nosta plains ahead."

The river had broadened and meandered in a silver band cutting through forests and grassland. Targas could see occasional herds of large animals that looked to be perac, and several different types of vegetation, again dotted with outcrops of grey rock.

"It is all remarkable, I don't think I've seen anything like it." Then he pointed at a far-off series of lines on the slopes extending each side of the river. "That puzzles me, though. What is happening over there?"

"You have good eyes, Targas," she said as their animals reached relatively level ground. "What you can see are the vines that produce the fruit for the cordial. It is not far from the outskirts of the city, which we should be near later this day.

"I think we'll be stopping soon to rest the animals, so you might like to question Xerrita; she comes from this region."

The fire made a welcome crackle amongst rocks, dispelling the faint chill that hung about despite the sun being directly overhead. While the animals watered at the river, tea, and bread filled with cold meat and cheese, were handed around.

"Enjoying yourself?" Xerrita approached him with her own mug and food.

Targas nodded as he chewed.

"Boidea tells me you're better—enough to be asking questions about Nosta, at any rate." Her weathered face creased into a smile. "Where to start, though?" she asked herself.

"Ah, the question you posed to Boidea: the vines." Xerrita chewed thoughtfully. "The cordial combines the fruit from the vines, even now being harvested, with honey and several herbs. They are fermented in large pottery vessels for at least a year, then poured into the tumblers to mature, much like that malas Tenstria is famous for."

Targas smiled. "A former profession of mine," he said softly.

"Of course," Xerrita nodded, "you would know the process well. Only the combination of the tumblers made from the clay of Mlana Hold and the cordial gives it that special quality—we believe it's the influence of the magnesite in the clay, but who can truly know?

"Back to Nosta. The city is in a star-shape pattern, with buildings following natural depressions leading out from a central point. At the centre are the administration and main storage facilities. Services and accommodation come next, then the houses of the residents—it is they who tend the flocks, grow the crops and operate the transport.

"The city sort of melds into the landscape. It is very rugged, set in a well-weathered section of the ranges where the rock acts as a moderator of the climate and also as a natural defence—you'll see what I mean later this day. But I like living there and find it better than the Hold. It is fortunate I'm not the next in line to be Mlana or that is where I'd be spending the rest of my days," she laughed.

"Oh?" Targas raised an eyebrow.

"Yes, Boidea has greater talent than I. Knowings come to her, and it is she who will be Mlana when…"

"How do you find out who is the next Mlana?"

"It becomes apparent. The existing Mlana usually knows first and trains her successor. So, barring accidents, Boidea will be the next Mlana."

"Has Alethea been the Mlana long?" asked Targas.

"Longer than I remember," said Xerrita, "but there's talk that she came into it late, after her sister, who was to be the next Mlana, disappeared. Only Alethea really knows that story." She paused, took a final sip from her cup before throwing out the dregs of her tea, and said: "Well, about time to mount up. It will be a comfortable ride to the city from here."

Shadows were lengthening across the valley when they entered the streets of Nosta. Many people were about, busy in the narrow streets. They were friendly enough, waving or sending scent welcomes as they passed, but they all seemed to be on a mission.

"It appears word of the Mlana's Knowing has reached here. I gather they will be preparing in case of an invasion. Still, it is better to be ready than not," Xerrita said matter-of-factly. She glanced at Targas in the dimming light. "You'll need to rest, as I'm not certain you are fully recovered."

They moved in single file along the narrow street, Xerrita ahead of him and Boidea behind.

It was fully dark when they entered a large hall in the centre of the city, lanterns on the walls and a roaring fire at each end of the room providing light and atmosphere. Servers in the familiar brown shifts moved amongst them offering food and drink. Targas had just taken a bite of meat pie and a large, satisfying gulp of his beer when Xaner clapped him on the shoulder.

"Haven't had much of a chance to talk with you, Targas," he said, his ruddy face splitting into a grin. "You're a hero of Ean's revolution and, I take it, not here by chance. The Mlana was particularly keen that I look after you, show you our country and our defences. What do you think of Nosta, so far?"

As Targas took another drink, already feeling the warmth of the alcohol, a wave of tiredness swept over him. He blinked and drew a breath. "A well-structured city I would say, hard for an enemy to overcome, although I haven't seen much."

"You can see more after we've eaten and then next day…"

"Xaner, leave the poor man alone," said Xerrita. "Can't you see he's all in?"

Targas watched the commander's eyes tighten and expected him to show anger, but instead he let out a huge guffaw. "Right you are, Xerrita. You can have him. I can annoy him later."

"Come, Targas, time for you to sleep," she said, taking him by the hand. She led him out of the hall, down a narrow corridor and into a large dormitory.

Targas slept well in the large sleeping room, a distance away from the centre, even the snoring of his companions not disturbing his sleep. He had an early rise for a meal of eggs, cured meats, honeyed cereal and juice before a quick tour of the city, Xaner keeping his promise from the night before.

They were leading their animals out of the city after taking a detour via the fermenting works, Xaner keeping up a running commentary of the virtues and weaknesses of the city. "So you'll have to tell me about your own brand of scent control, Targas. From what I gather it was your ability to bond scents that helped the Eanites rid the country of the Sutanite scourge." The big man clapped Targas on the shoulder in a friendly manner.

"I don't know," said Targas with a shrug, "it was just something I found I could do, particularly after my apprenticeship to become main tester and analyser of malas at the House of Versent in Tenstria. I could see the individual motes of an odour, recognise the differences between those from different sources and bind them to the greatest effect. In Tenstria it was for the taste and aroma, in Ean it was for the greatest strength and effectiveness of the bonding."

"So how does it relate to the skills our women possess?" He looked over to a set of granite columns marking the end of the city and waved at several people who appeared to be on guard. His light eyes watched Targas.

"Me? All I know is that they have an ability to strengthen a scent in a way I can't fathom. They used it effectively on me at Mlana Hold. Why, Xaner, don't you know?"

"I do know, but in general terms only. They are a crafty lot, always talking in mysterious ways and when you get near the secret, they'll say only women can use it. One thing I've learnt is if they don't want you to know then it won't do any good to try and find out." He gave a great laugh and mounted his perac. "Come, we've a way to go and I have much to show you."

Targas swung onto his animal and followed the group of riders along a wide road towards the south.

The valley made by the Rolander River wound through rugged hills covered with substantial vegetation, tall trees jammed in with thickets of shrub and large ferns. The climate was mild, with the early chill quickly disappearing to a pleasant day. The well-paved road followed the river, the gentle gradient making the journey easy on man and beast.

The smell of the sea was the first indication they were nearing the coast, and by the time the sun had set behind the rugged hills the undulating, grass-covered plains of Requist lay before them.

"Now this is my city," said Xaner proudly. "By the sea and the trading hub of Rolan; busy place, and people from all over the known world come here to trade."

Targas noticed a vague smoke on the horizon covering a substantial area.

"Fires already lit. Even though Requist is at the sea, Rolan is a colder country than what you're used to," Xaner commented. "Off to our left you'll see the cropping lands—where the grain comes from—for without it we wouldn't have the famous Rolan beers, and my preference is a well-malted beer with some body. You can have your malas, or even your cordials. Give me a good beer after a hard day's ride."

"Yes, I like a good beer," Targas grunted.

"Suppose I should outline what you'll see, for when we get there it'll be too dark," Xaner continued. "Not as well laid out as Nosta—built more for trade than defence. Just sorta developed around the waterfront over the generations, and the wharf area is a craze of streets and alleys. Locals know their way through it, but a stranger…"

"So, do we go there, or do you have somewhere else, a central point?"

"Of course!" Xaner nodded. "Wouldn't want to go to the waterfront at night unless it's to a tavern. No, we'll be going to Lookout Hill, a higher section behind the general trading area. Have my family there and it's where we do most of the administration and business."

"You've a family?"

"Don't sound so surprised. Of course I do. My partner's name is Sharia and I have three little ones, though not so little now. Just at the stage to cause trouble and answer me back. Have thought to move them to Nosta in view of the Mlana's Knowing, though." He turned and looked at the trail of people spread out behind him. "If we could get this lot moving we might be in time for a hot meal. What do you think, Targas?"

"Be good to stop," Targas agreed. "Been on the go for a while now," he said, thinking of the long trek from Ean to Rolan and here.

"Right!" Xaner stood in his stirrups and with a burst of scent, waved his arm. He sat back down and urged his animal on. Targas followed suit.

Chapter Forty-Two

The Salted Arms was a well-frequented tavern in Ean's Port Saltus showing clean lines of well-preserved planks of dark wood resting on a foundation of dressed grey stone. Double doors led into a spacious, well-lit room redolent of beer, spirits and vinegar cleanser. The light provided by long opaque windows revealed padded stools and benches with small well-used tables. The bar was the length of one wall, above which hung used wool wharf-matting.

The group comprising Lan, Lethnal, Brin and Jelm followed Ginrel, the administrator of the port, along a wall of people lining the bar and threaded their way past the well-occupied seats and tables.

"Busy," commented Brin.

"Always, 'specially at mealtimes. But don't worry, I hev me own table. One of th' few benefits of me job." Ginrel ushered them to a table at the back of the tavern with the bar extending off to the left.

"Sit 'ere an' I'll git Mar t' serve us. Yer'll want cordial, Lethnal? Beer or sumthin' stronger fer th' rest of yer?"

"It is late and I have a mind to try Targas's favourite, malas, if I might," said Lan.

"Rite." Ginrel waved an arm and in a moment a small, thin woman hurried over. Her bright eyes assessed them before she spoke to Ginrel. "Drinks first before yer try the fish?"

"These friends of mine hev travelled a way, so drinks first wud be gud," he smiled at her. "Meet Mar. She runs Th' Salted Arms. Looks after us well, she does. So, cordial fer me friend, Lethnal, malas fer Lan 'nd beer fer Brin, Jelm 'nd meself."

"Fish with spiced tuber 'nd flat bread is th' best this night," she said quickly. "Suggest yer would all do that?"

Ginrel looked around the table, eyebrows raised in his weathered face. "Gud. We'd like thet, thanks Mar. Help us talk, it will."

Mar nodded and disappeared through the throng of people around the bar.

"Ah," sighed Ginrel as he leant back, arms behind his head. "I tek it yer not 'ere fer th' scenery?"

"Sorry, my friend," began Lan, "our visit is much to do with the unrest in Ean, and the prime importance of Port Saltus in future conflict. Your role, as main administrator of the city, is to bear some of that burden."

Lan quickly briefed Ginrel on their journey from Sanctus, via Regulus and Nebleth, following up the unexplained death of the scent master, Brennyl, the subsequent disappearance of the hymetta from under the capital city and the defensive preparedness of country.

"Ah, 'ere be th' drinks." Ginrel's face brightened. "Thanks Mar"

The small woman grunted as she left.

"So yer reckon th' hymetta were barged down t' Port, 'nd that Heritis may hev 'ad something t' do with it?" he asked, swigging his beer.

"Certainly there were disguised traces leading to the river and a barge is the most obvious means of transporting the vile creatures."

"But Heritis?"

"Still uncertain," added Jelm. "But he had the opportunity and skill. The keeper of the hymetta is also involved, and may be easier to trace here, in the city."

"Yes," agreed Lan, "and there is a third, more disturbing element, one which hastened our journey. Jakus!"

"Jakus? No. 'E's not back? Last I 'eard 'e was dead or dyin' 'nd fled Ean."

"Jakus," nodded Lan. "Though I do wonder what he wanted so badly to risk coming here."

"There 'ave bin strange goings on 'ere"—Ginrel leant back in his chair—"whether it be associated with th' hymetta or Jakus, or merely irregularities in th' shipping… So it's vital t' expand our information gathering, trying t' track down where these creatures 'nd their handlers hev gone, 'nd increase th' Port's readiness for when th' enemy tries something," mused Ginrel.

"It would seem so. Jelm and I already have people working on it, so we will co-ordinate our efforts," said Lan, looking at his now empty cup.

"Cud yer tek another round of drinks?" asked Ginrel, signalling towards the bar. "I know I cud after what yer've told me."

With the meal come and gone, the tavern noisier and strong with the odours of food and sweaty bodies, Lan assessed what they had learnt from Ginrel.

Rumours had been circulating, adding to the concerns they had: a scent master in charge of ship boarding having severe memory loss, a missing barge being sighted then disappearing with no record of cargo, finding the keeper had indeed made it to the port only to drop out of sight, and the movements of numbers of people at odd times.

A further puzzle was the disappearance of Heritis. He had been obvious when seeking traces of the hymetta and the possible murderer of scent master Brennyl in Nebleth, but now he wasn't to be found.

Lan accepted another cup of malas and sipped it thoughtfully before speaking. "I think we need to stay in Port Saltus for a time. We must get to the bottom of all these mysteries and, above all, locate Heritis."

"Agreed," said Jelm.

"Yes," said Brin, "we most certainly do. Thet missing barge has me intrigued. It can't hev jest disappeared."

"Don't forget the hymetta," added Lethnal. "They must be somewhere."

"My friends," said Lan, finishing his drink, "I only hope we are capable for what is ahead of us, for I believe a storm is coming and we must be prepared."

"Come," said Ginrel, standing, "I hev quarters in th' administrator's house fer yer all. Next day we must be fresh t' search in earnest."

They pulled on oars in muffled rowlocks, towing three ships of the fleet into Port Saltus under the cover of thick fog. The smells of the land guided them this early in the day, for the port had its own unique odour, with export salt being dominant.

Kyel was in the long boat with a few guardsmen, several scent masters and Bilternus. He was rowing hard, trying to keep in rhythm with the others. His back strained from the pull of the oar, but his hands were callused enough to keep from being abraded from the repetitive action as they towed the great ship.

He didn't think why Jakus had him rowing, grateful to get off the ship and away from the leader's constant threats to investigate his *loyalty*. Kyel had strengthened his scent control while in Sutan, always knowing he had to conceal his true feelings and his determination to stop the Sutanite ruler's plans. He had to avoid Jakus testing him for he'd surely be found out.

The smell of the Great Southern River emptying into the bay brought memories. He had known the river all his life, it being the major artery of the country, and all he wanted was to head up it to his family and his people. But that wouldn't happen. They were here for another purpose, which meant ill for Ean.

"This is the life," groaned Bilternus, "rowing, in a stinking fog."

"Shush!" Tibitis hissed from the stern. "Noise carries."

Kyel could see his shadowy figure standing in the stern, steering with an oar. Behind him, the thick rope off the transom disappeared into the fog, the attached ship invisible but weighty.

The first of the posts marking the channel appeared and disappeared as they rowed past, their speed increasing as the incoming tide took effect.

"Not long now," whispered Tibitis. "Keep a sharp lookout."

Kyel's memory stretched to recall where they were. The layout of the docks included a few small wooden piers jutting out from one lengthy wharf running parallel to the shore, designed for ships to berth alongside and take on salt and wool from nearby warehouses. Normally they'd be packed with ships, leaving little room for the three Sutanite vessels now approaching to take on men, animals and provisions.

Two fewer local ships to berth there though, thought Kyel, recalling the sea battle with horror. *All those people left to drown. He must be stopped.*

The rhythm of dipping oars, pulling on them, then raising them to their original position was cathartic, allowing him to ponder what lay ahead. How could they possibly get away with it? Who was Jakus's traitor in Port Saltus who could arrange all this? *No point in worrying,* he thought, *I'll find out soon enough.*

Several spars and rigging of a stationary vessel emerged.

"Pull!" exhorted Tibitis, his voice low but strong. The top of the ship disappeared as the long boat veered to port.

Must be close. That ship must be berthed against one of the piers, thought Kyel. *Where will we find room for our three ships?*

A strong odour pulsed out from ahead with a distinctive smell of Sutan. It grew as they continued.

"That's the signal. We're near," said a scent master.

"Oars up," ordered Tibitis, as the long wooden side of the wharf came into view. Mats of weathered, stained wool hung there as buffers.

Kyel lifted his oar with relief, laid it into the boat along with the others and watched the wharf grow closer. They nudged into a corner where a pier pushed out from the wharf.

"Bring the boat along the pier until the rope is taut. Leave room for the ship. Use your hands to pull it."

All rowers on the starboard side pushed and pulled the long boat along. Kyel, on the port side, watched the indistinct lines of their towed ship as it nudged into place.

"Wait!"

They sat listening to the sounds of the other ships berthing. Kyel's back ached. He was keen to stand and stretch, get off the boat and disappear into the port. But he was given no chance. Time seemed to stretch as he hunched over in the boat, listening for the sounds of sailors quietly securing the ships and setting gangways in readiness.

The noise of the loading began as the fog slowly thinned. The nervous bleat of perac, the clink of weapons and stamp of feet began to get louder.

The watery sun showed figures on the dock. He recognised Jakus, lean and authoritarian, standing away from the loading. A taller figure stood next to him, having an animated discussion. Kyel strained his eyes, trying to make him out as he felt he should know who it was.

Gotta be the traitor, he thought, *I must find out who it is.*

"Still," hissed a scent master. "We're to stay here. Shad's orders."

Kyel drew in the scents, seeking even a mote of odour to give an indication but the man was obviously adept at control.

Then a slight breeze began pushing odours towards him from the shore. He started, controlling a gasp as an odour he would never forget infiltrated his scent memories. "No!"

"Quiet!"

Now he could see them, cages of nervous peracs moving towards the gangplank and onto the ship. The smell was the large killing wasp, hymetta, one that Jakus had used before, and one Kyel hoped he would never see again.

Chapter Forty-Three

"**A**t th' docks! Now! There's trouble." A hand shook him out of his light sleep.

"Ginrel?" Lan identified the shadowy figure.

"I'm t' th' barracks. Wake th' others 'nd I'll meet yer by Th' Salted Arms." He disappeared out of the door.

Lan threw his robe on over his undergarments, slipped into sandals and hurried to get the others.

A thick sea fog swirled around the administrator's house as they ran out. A detachment of guardsmen with several scent masters joined them, hurrying through the shadowy buildings towards the docks.

Lan inhaled deeply to pick up any unfamiliar odours, realising the breeze was flowing out to sea. It took a few moments sorting through the scents before he recognised something out of place. *Hymetta,* he thought. *They are out there, nearby.*

Noises, muffled by the fog, came through: clattering feet, the bleat of animals, clash of metal and the occasional boom of a scent bolt.

"Hurry," urged Jelm.

People came and went in the gloom, scent auras hard to see, recognition difficult. They neared the tavern amongst a swirl of activity.

"There yer are," snapped Ginrel as he broke from a huddle of guardsmen and scent masters. "Brin, I need yer t' tek charge of th' barge people 'nd yer scent masters. Go t' th' docks with Jahnl 'ere, but be careful. We reckon there's Sutanites, causin' trouble."

Jahnl grabbed Brin's arm and led him and the group of fighters away.

"Lan! Lethnal!" Ginrel focussed on them. "Cud yer cum with me? I think I know where th' worst of it is, 'nd if this Jakus is involved we'll need yer skill."

"Certainly," said Lan, "and I believe there are hymetta around. Their scent is becoming obvious."

"Hag's breath!" swore Ginrel as he beckoned the guardsmen and scent masters on, "thet's all we need."

"**G**o now, Heritis!" urged Jakus, distracted by fighting near the stern of his third ship berthed against the wharf. "Loading's almost done and you're more useful to me here, in Ean."

"They're not stupid, Jakus," hissed Heritis. "They'll know I've been involved with the men and supplies, and hymetta—the failure with Targas's woman makes that all too certain."

"Your initiative, my friend; pity you failed. But give them half-truths and only reveal I demanded supplies and men for my expedition to Rolan. Tell them I needed to obtain magnesite from Rolan to sort out problems in Sutan, then you may still be of use in the future."

"And the future is?" asked Heritis, a grim smile on his face.

"No more than I've said," replied Jakus with a similar expression, "no more than I've said, as far as you and the Eanites who interrogate you are concerned. Now go! Take no further part. I must gain time so we can get away to sea."

Kyel watched the hurried conversation between Jakus and the person he was now almost certain was Heritis. As the man hurried away down a narrow alley he saw Jakus gathering scent power about him.

The attention of those in the boat was on Jakus and as a particularly loud bang of a scent bolt reverberated, Kyel took out a cloth from his pocket he had earlier imbued with some of his scent experiences and flicked it onto the wharf. It landed, limp and innocuous, without anyone noticing.

It's all I can do, he thought, hoping it would be found.

The fog was thinning as Ginrel, Lan and Lethnal reached the docks, the sun beginning to make its presence felt. Already the noise level was high, the clash of arms and scent bolt explosions contributing.

"Where is Jakus?" asked Lan. "He will be at the centre of this, I have no doubt."

"I would think… *There!*" Lethnal pointed to the wharf and the indistinct outlines of three ships loading frantically amidst a flurry of action.

"You are right. And there are hymetta aboard, I can detect a strong scent. This is our chance to take Jakus. For he is there. Exposed." Lan gestured. "Come. We need to make a stand. But do not underestimate him, for whatever else, he is not a fool."

"We'll cum frum th' right side, frum th' bow of th' first ship," said Ginrel. "They're wedged in 'nd not likely t' git away easily. Brin 'nd th' others are cummin' frum th' back of th' last ship. We'll catch them from both sides."

"Wait," warned Lethnal, putting a hand on Lan's arm as they moved onto the exposed dock. "What's Jakus doing?"

An exchange of scent bolts between the defenders and invaders kept the groups from using more conventional weapons of spears and knives. Numerous figures, dark through the thinning mists, were facing Brin and his force. Lan could see a faint thickening of the air as they worked at something.

"Ginrel!" he snapped, "Have your scent masters concentrate with me. We must be ready to counter whatever the Sutanites are conjuring. We will form a scent blanket."

They gathered, harmonising as their minds co-ordinated and joined. Lan used their power as he pulled in odour from his surrounds, forming and strengthening bonds, extending them out and upward like a huge translucent bubble to cover his group and push out towards the ships. He was under no illusions about Jakus, who wouldn't have returned to Ean without considerable backing.

A cry echoed from the end of the docks, near the furthest ship. Many people had fallen and hand-to-hand fighting had begun. Lan could only guess at what Jakus had done to them even as he pushed the scent blanket further, with the intent of forcing the invaders into the sea.

An invisible barrier retarded their progress, countering effort from Lan and Ginrel's force. Behind the Sutanites the sailors were busy untying the ropes holding the big ships to the wharf, and the towing lines were tightening.

"Harder!" urged Lan. "We cannot let them get away."

A new pressure imposed itself on the structure of the scent-bonded barrier. It began to shiver where it met the countering pressure, as if the very odour motes were disassembling. *Cannot be*, thought Lan as the force came through him. *It is as if something is eating away at what we created.*

His hold on the structure began to crumble and it slowly folded into itself, moving back on them. Jakus's scent barrier forced closer, threatening to overwhelm them. With it came a corrosive odour, a scent Lan knew meant them ill.

"Hold! For Ean's sake, hold!" he shouted, his voice sounding suddenly foreign to him.

The pressure was intense as the attack ate into their scent shield, inexorably breaking it down. Lan dragged in his deepest scent memories, using odours of rock and metals to add strength to the shield. It slowed and finally shivered to a stop. A stalemate had been reached.

"Fire!" A panicked voice came from behind them. "Fire! The warehouses are on fire."

The pressure of the Sutanite scent attack fell away, dissipating in an instant. Lan staggered to the ground while the others around him buckled over, taking deep breaths.

"The ships," gasped Lethnal. "They're escaping."

"Leave them," said Ginrel, "we've got more t' worry about. There's fire right across th' warehouses. We've gotta stop thet. All th' stock'll go." He bent down and put a hand on Lan's shoulder. "Yer alright?"

"Go," croaked Lan, "I will be fine. Not as young as I used to be."

Lethnal sat beside him on the wet ground, still breathing heavily. "W…what was that? I've never felt such vileness before."

"I don't know, Lethnal. There is a *feel* there I have not experienced. Something has been added, giving Jakus more power than when last we met his forces. This is not good at all."

"Hey, yer two, yer alright?" called Brin, hurrying along the wharf. "We've bin thru a nasty fight back there. They caught us with sum kind of acid. It ate into us. Cudn't even make scent bolts. Then spears came. We've dead 'nd injured… Jahnl's gone too—blasted haggars." He looked over at leaping flames above the nearby buildings, sighed and sat down. "Left it t' th' healers, but too late fer Jahnl. Now they's gittin' away. Gotta stop 'em, but how?"

"We will leave the firefighting to the locals," said Lan, following Brin's gaze. "I fear there is very little we can do, but if you both assist me, we may gather some useful intelligence. Come." He stood with a wince and walked over to the wharf.

The sun had broken through the fog and although billows of black smoke were threatening the light, it was easy to see the scattered detritus left over the wooden wharf area by the departure of the ships. Lan, Lethnal and Brin methodically worked through the discarded material, picking up scent traces that confirmed the movement of troops, supplies and hymetta onto the ships. Lan meticulously filed away every useful scent he came across: unknown scent masters from different regions of Sutan, familiar traces of Jakus, and a smattering of the scent he knew related to magnesa use.

A mystery here, to be solved, he thought as he moved along a pier jutting from the wharf. Then he detected a very familiar scent, Kyel–powerful and flagging itself. He picked up a small rag snagged between two planks and drew in the scents.

Ignoring the youth's odour, despite it appearing more mature and powerful than he had known, he sought other scents that had been left. Hymetta, he picked. Jakus, Nefaria and another man's scent, like Jakus but not him—a brother, perhaps? But what really intrigued him was the scent of another, an old woman. He had to reach deeply within himself to work it out, for the scent was of Rolan, so reminiscent of his close companion, Alethea that it made his eyes mist over. A relative of Alethea's, a woman of power, a woman of strength. But where did Kyel pick up such a scent? Why did he put it so powerfully into the cloth?

"Brin! Lethnal!" He waved them over, showing them what he had found.

"A clever young man is Kyel," he said. "And we now are certain where the ships are heading—Rolan. They are going to attack Rolan. I feel Alethea's Knowing is right, and I can only hope they will be prepared for what is coming."

The ships took advantage of a light breeze as they tacked from Port Saltus to the rest of the fleet in Nebleth Bay. The breeze was cold, but it fitted Kyel's mood. He had seen little of the fighting around the wharf, having to stay in the boat to tow it out into open water once the loading had finished. He knew people—his countrymen—had been hurt, and that Jakus had achieved what he wanted, but leaving the port in flames showed more of the man's cruelty.

Kyel stood next to Tibitus letting the wind fill his lungs, taking away any vestige of smoke, giving him a last taste of Ean before they hit the open sea. The sails cracked as the ship heeled over in a slight gust.

"Good to get away, eh lad?" said the captain, his weathered face peering up at a sailor setting topsail. "Don't like being in a port, unable to move. Far rather be coping with the elements out here, eh?"

Kyel nodded as he scanned the waters, ignoring the rim of land they were to round later in the day. *New country, new terrors by Jakus,* he thought. He watched a flight of fish, disturbed by the ship, leaping out of the water and flitting a distance before sliding back in.

"Rain coming," Tibitus's voice broke into his thoughts, "off to the south-west. We're heading right into it."

Kyel could see the haze of grey marking the rain a distance off.

"Damn!" he muttered.

"What's the matter, lad?"

"Rain means I'll have to go below, down with those things, those hymetta."

"Know what you mean about them wasps. Don't like them on my ship neither, but the Shad requires them."

"I require what, Tibitus?" an authoritative voice came from behind him.

"Uh, Jakus," said Tibitus quickly, "I was just explaining to the lad here about the need to carry the wasps."

Kyel turned and saw Jakus coming up to him, and swallowed, thinking fast.

"Why have we got hymetta?" he asked. "I mean you've got all that power from magnesa, surely you don't need them."

"Hymetta?" mused Jakus, apparently in a good mood. "Yes, having them does seem somewhat out of proportion to their abilities. But your strategic brain is not working, young Kyel. Their chief value is shock, the unexpected. If the enemy expects your attack, be it scent or force of arms, the impact of hymetta tracking in from a distance and hitting them in such a horrific way is immeasurable.

"A good leader uses all weapons at his command. Magnesa is effective, but should be used sparingly." His eyes narrowed. "Besides, hymetta have good scent knowledge; they remember who they have been with. Your sister, for instance. If she or those related to her are with the enemy, then they'll be in for a surprise."

Kyel's mouth dropped open.

Jakus laughed. "Now leave. You will have work to do."

Kyel left the aft deck as fast as he could, with his head down. *That blasted haggar. How had Sadir been with the hymetta? What had Jakus done to her?* More than ever he resolved to avoid Jakus, for he would easily determine where his loyalty now lay. He hoped the voyage to Rolan would be short for he would have to be on his guard, as a traitor would have only one end.

Chapter Forty-Four

The Sailors Rest opened onto a wide busy street; pack animals and carts piled with goods and household effects moving past, on their way to and from the waterfront. Targas had taken the opportunity to slip away to the tavern, have an early beer and reflect on the last few days in Requist.

Rumours of the Mlana's Knowing had spread like wildfire and those with places to go or with secure storage for their goods were taking precautions. Invaders had never attacked the trading city and generations of complacency had affected many, but belief in their Mlana, the figurative and spiritual head of Rolan, made them take heed.

Targas had been billeted in Xaner's household, welcomed and accepted as one of the family by his partner, Sharia, a vivacious and engaging woman. Her three children reminded him how his Anyar would have loved a sister or brother. Sovira, a red-haired girl of his daughter's age could even be a friend, given the opportunity, he mused.

During the day he had met many of the local officials and toured the city to get an understanding of its layout. Requist was a maze of laneways and streets built up around the wharf and its hinterland. Goods came and went in the busy port with the highly valued tumblers of cordial, woollen products, minerals and processed timber being Rolan's major exports. There was little of the city or the country to attract the eye of an aggressor.

He had found he was somewhat of a celebrity, being one of those who had taken part in the routing of the Sutanites from Ean years before, and his opinions and explanations of his scent talent were eagerly sought.

Scent talent, he thought bitterly. If anything, his scent talent seemed to have diminished after the long trial with the *presence* in his head. When he had been fighting its influence back in Lesslas he felt he was improving the skills he had, working on the bonding of scent motes, stabilising the power until the blanket of scent was strong and almost self-sustaining. Since then he had been trying to come to grips with Septus's presence, tackling it with the help of well-meaning people, culminating in the horrific expulsion of the thing at Mlana Hold. He should have felt happy at his release but he experienced a loss, an emptiness and the occasional ache in his head.

"Another beer!" he called to the landlord, digging out a silver coin from the pouch of currency he'd been given at the Hold. Drink helped fill the void, but there were too few opportunities to cater for that need.

He had taken a first mouthful, inhaling the rich aroma and appreciating the twists of bronze-coloured scent lifting into the air, when he heard a familiar voice.

"Thought I might find you here," Boidea slipped onto the wooden seat beside him and signalled to the landlord. "Don't blame you slipping away. Been a busy time, especially with the influence of the Knowing on everyone."

"Needed to. Got a lot of thinking to do." Targas took another mouthful. "And I'm missing my family."

"Mmm," Boidea nodded as she accepted a small cup of cordial and passed across a coin. "A time of trial is coming upon us, Targas. I would like to be back with the Mlana for she is in need, I feel, but the Knowing is stronger than ever upon me."

"So," Targas said, looking up from his mug of beer, "you are next in line to be Mlana?"

"I don't know about 'next in line'," Boidea shrugged, "but it appears the fates are selecting me. I feel there are others, older and wiser, more suited for the role, but what will be must be." She watched Targas finish his beer before she drank the last of her cordial. "I have come to collect you, I'm afraid. We have to attend a council meeting; there's been a development which we're to hear."

"*Development*," Targas laughed harshly. "There have been nothing *but* developments since I first left home." He shook his head as he stood. "I'm sorry, Boidea, but times are not good."

"Understood, my friend," she hooked an arm in his, "but we best continue this long sorry dance while we may. Maybe it's good news for a change?" She laughed.

The administration building standing on top of the hill included brick columns supporting the roof, allowing unimpeded views through the windows, across the wharves and out to sea. The wooden shutters had been fastened back with the mild temperatures of the day, allowing light into the long, wide room.

Another table and another meeting, thought Targas, eyeing off the large wooden table surrounded by many people. *And I'm the last to arrive*. He fixed a smile on his face and followed Boidea over to Xaner and the small group around him.

The commander looked up.

"Good day to you, Targas. It is fortunate you're here as we have received tidings confirming Mlana's Knowing. Port Saltus has been fired and it is likely the perpetrators are coming here."

Xaner waited for quiet, a grim expression on his face.

"The report came from one of our intelligence gatherers who travels between the Port Saltus and Requist, for this is the best way to receive such news. He left in a fast pinnace as the Port was burning, having witnessed fighting between Sutanite ships and Eanite authorities. While it is uncertain we are the next target, what is certain is the ships picked up men and supplies from allies in that city. As we share a common border with Ean, it is logical we must prepare for an act of aggression." He scanned the grim faces around him.

"We'll follow the plans for defending against what will mainly be a scent attack, but in essence we will have Nosta as our fallback if this vulnerable city is taken.

"Dranthner, will you liaise with the city defence supervisor, Siliaster?" Xaner indicated a square-shaped man with greying whiskers and thinning hair. "Ensure too that the last of our civilians are out of Requist so their safety is no longer our concern."

"Telpher will be in charge of the scent master forces, at least those who are experienced in that art." Telpher nodded.

"Boidea?"

"Yes, I know my role, if it comes to that, Xaner."

"You're too important to us, Boidea. As discussed, your charge includes the women, and their additional known powers, but you must act with caution. If this attack lives up to expectations, then your part will be vital.

"And Targas…"

"And me? What do I do?" he asked with a lump in his throat.

"Your role?" Xaner asked rhetorically. "You will be with me as much as possible. I'm loathe to risk you. What would the Mlana say?" he said with a smile.

"I think we all should be on our way, then. Any last concerns for our people should be dealt with expediently so we can concentrate on the matter at hand."

Targas felt superfluous as people left the room. Soon only he and Xaner remained standing beside one of the brick columns and looking across the city. The sea beyond was dark highlighting the remnants of a storm tailing off across the distant horizon. An ominous, more threatening storm was brewing in the west.

"It's as grey as I feel, Targas," said Xaner. "We've planned for an attack as much as we can, but we're not a warlike people, have an insignificant navy, and so our contingency plans had better hold up. You can see by the layout of the city any determined invader will walk right through Requist, so our desire is to cede land to him with little impact on our people and property.

"Our defence is to restrict the invader's position and stretch his resources as much as possible, so that by the time he reaches towards Mlana Hold he will be happy to retreat. Our Mlana is canny and her Knowings would point to this man, this Jakus, leaving if he thinks he has what he wants. A dangerous game, but with some likelihood of success. Still, we will see, eh?"

Targas was lost in his own thoughts, watching the movement of people through the streets, then looking for the first sails that might indicate Jakus was nearing. He had no doubt the man, his enemy, was approaching and felt resigned that something was coming to a head. First Septus and now Jakus, both of whom hated him and had fought him. It seemed never-ending, but now he had something to fight for.

The squall, accompanied by driving rain, hit the ships hard, heeling them dangerously and forcing them to turn into the wind for relief. Men scrambled spiderlike through the rigging, tightening sheets where possible, leaving only enough sail to maintain headway.

Tibitus held grimly to the helm, eyes fixed into the mists ahead of the ship, rain mixed with sweat pouring off his face and running under his thick wool coat. The man standing next to him smirked at his discomfort.

Jakus was dry, unaffected by the wind and rain, and loving it. His scent control was complete, the blanket of bonded scents deflecting the elements around him while others suffered the full force of the weather. He looked back to the other four ships of his fleet heeling over in the wind, smashing through the rolling waves but essentially coping with the changed conditions.

Everything's going to plan, he thought, holding onto the aft rail as Tibitus changed tack. *Even these conditions will only serve to make my people tougher and ready them for our attack. The Rolanites won't see us coming in this.*

His euphoria was such that the delay caused by the rough weather didn't concern him. His ships were brimming with trained scent masters and guardsmen, animals and supplies. Jakus didn't anticipate a long campaign. He knew his target was at Mlana Hold, deep in the rugged terrain of Rolan, and he would do everything to swiftly capture supplies of magnesite.

The prize, he thought, his body twitching, *is worth it.* Unlimited scent power driven by the red crystal, magnesa. *No-one will be able to oppose me when I have that.*

Kyel was on his bunk in the hold, along with his friend Bilternus, and many sweating bodies of guardsmen. Someone had been sick, and the smell combined with the odour of nervous animals and acrid smell of upset hymetta. He found he could keep it out with judicious use of scent bonding, but every time the ship hit a rough patch he lost concentration and the smell returned.

He wondered whether the scent masters in the cabins on deck level were any better off. He could appreciate the women, including Nefaria, Poegna and Shauna were separate, but why he and Bilternus were relegated to the holds was harder to understand. *Still, I'm happy away from his notice,* he thought.

"I don't feel good, Kyel," said Bilternus from his cramped bunk. "It'd be better to be out in the weather, even helping the sailors, rather than being in this stink."

"I agree," he said. "If it slackens off I'm going up on deck." *Even if Jakus sees me.*

"Me too," said Bilternus, then gulped as the ship rolled. The perac, deeper in the hold, added their bleats to the slap of sails, the crackle of thunder, the creaking of boards and the crash of waters against the hull.

They lay in silence as the ship plunged through the waves, heeling every so often as it changed tack or the wind strengthened.

K yel became aware the ship's motion had reduced, the noises quieter. "I'm going on deck," he whispered to the white-faced Bilternus looking at the ship's beams above his head.

"So am I," Bilternus started, his face tightening. He swung out of the bunk and followed Kyel, manoeuvring through bodies and gear to the stairs.

G usts of rain-filled wind hit them when they poked their heads through the hatchway and clambered across the wet and slippery deck towards the open door leading to the rooms occupied by the female scent masters. Nefaria was in the doorway, Poegna beside her.

"Kyel," she said with a quick smile. "Out from the depths of the hold now the weather has lessened? You too, Bilternus?"

"Hah!" Bilternus huffed. "You ought to try it: smell of animals, puke and piss. Far better up here."

"No, Bilternus, it hasn't been," said Poegna. "I admit we had no animal smells, but it was even rougher up here. We were swinging about like a top. I'm sure we have the bruises to prove it."

"Is Jakus about?" Kyel quietly asked Nefaria.

"At the helm with the captain. Been there right through the rough weather. Do you want to see him?"

"No," said Kyel quickly. "I just wanted to get on deck, and he might not want me to do that."

"I shouldn't worry," said Nefaria. "He's in a good mood. We've all come through the storm well and Requist is only half a day's sail away."

"Requist? We're that close?"

"Yes," added a new voice. Shauna in her brightly coloured cloak and trousers, pushed past Poegna and Nefaria. "We have to ready ourselves for the landing and coming conflict. Do you two want to help or are you happy to stand there blocking our way?"

As if in answer to her words, the rain ceased and the mists began to lift, a pale sun breaking through the clouds. Sailors were aloft putting on more sail. The invasion of Rolan was imminent.

They stood on the nearly deserted wharf watching the last of the larger ships being pulled into canals and berths well away from the central part of the city. Groups of guardsmen and scent masters were strategically placed, and the populace had departed. For a city mainly reacting to the Knowings of their spiritual leader, the Mlana, the place felt prepared.

A shiver ran down Targas's spine at the eerie quietness, then his head pulsed painfully in empathy.

He had been placed with a group of scent masters in a street cluttered with irregular buildings and stalls forming a significant impediment to movement of invaders. Their view covered the obvious landing place for any ships where deep water led to two piers of different length which projected into the bay.

Targas observed the determined people around him. He had the security of Xaner and Telpher nearby; Drathner was liaising between the commander and Boidea several streets away. He knew most alleyways and streets had contingents of defenders, the strategy being to slowly withdraw while inflicting as much damage as possible.

While they understood Jakus was coming in a powerful invasion force, they were skilled in scent power, including the mysterious feminine-based scent, and they knew what he was after.

The only negative he could see was what they knew of Jakus's abilities—reports were that he had a different and reportedly more powerful scent ability.

So they were following Alethea's Knowings. The blind faith they had in her and what was happening was a concern to any strategist, but who was he to query that? As usual, he was being dragged into the unknown by a strong current. *As long as my family is safe*, he thought.

A clatter of feet alerted him and he heard a thin youth speaking animatedly to Xaner. Within a moment he was gone. Xaner looked across at Drathner and nodded.

"They come!" he said.

The fleet tacked into the bay. Requist lay ahead, a brown line in the blue haze of distance. Sailors worked hard, despite a cluster of scent masters and guardsmen holding onto ropes and rails as their ship heeled in a moderate breeze. The sun was just past midday, meaning they would arrive well before nightfall.

Jakus stood in his favoured position by the helm, his face set.

"What do you reckon you'll do?" asked Bilternus from where he leant on the rail.

"Haven't much choice. He doesn't trust me, so I'm in the group near him," said Kyel as he looked over his shoulder towards the Sutanite leader, relieved Jakus hadn't carried out his threat to interrogate him. He still had hopes the coming conflict would give him the opportunity to escape and find his way back to Ean. But being in the forward attack group would also be risky and lessen his chances of surviving.

The ship heeled and spray spotted his face. The rest of the fleet followed majestically, sails light against the dark grey of the far horizon. They look peaceful, gentle things instead of what they really were. Kyel's eyes misted over as he thought of what Jakus was about to do to these people, killing and destroying merely to achieve his own ends. *At least my family should be well away from this, if I ever get to see them again.* His fingernails dug into the salt-covered rail, face tightening.

A large puff of dark scent rose from Jakus. He pointed towards the shore and Tibitus ordered the crew to ready the ship for a final tack.

The wharf, with its two piers drew closer, revealing the lack of vessels along their length. The place was quiet, deserted, the slap of their sails the only sound.

"News of our arrival has preceded us. The cowards have fled!" crowed Jakus from the aft deck. He scanned the people crowding the deck, a scent aura rising from him. "You have your orders. We will take and hold the waterfront as soon as we land. Spread out in your assigned groups, link up with the rest of my forces and then we'll push through the city. We need to capture it in the shortest time possible as we must head to our goal without delay. The success of the mission depends on it."

He rested his hands on the rail, his dark scent aura flashing with red, until he saw Kyel and Bilternus in the crowd. Then a smile flicked across his face.

"A select group will stay with me," he commanded, his eyes boring into them, "to provide a distraction for those Rolanites deciding to oppose us. Yes," he said with cruel pride, "for we have some burning to do."

Chapter Forty-Five

The ships berthed unopposed, gliding into the pier with the light wind, decks bristling with Sutanites ready for any reaction from the inhabitants. The waves had become ripples, the day clear, the scents from the shore revealing little.

Jakus's ship berthed first. He alighted in a flurry of robes and stalked down the pier towards the wharf, shields held high. The scent masters followed enthusiastically, joining with Jakus's scents to support his scent barriers as a solid force against any attack. Kyel followed with Bilternus by his side.

The invasion force rapidly disembarked and formed up. Jakus stopped at the end of the pier in a cloud of dark scent and held up an arm as he looked along the wharf.

"The opposition is hiding and the city is ripe for the taking." His sharp-featured head swivelled slowly like a k'dorian lizard seeking prey, scanning the buildings along the waterfront, sifting the drifting scents.

Five large groups formed while equipment and animals were unloaded from the ships.

Kyel, noticing that Jakus's brother Faltis led one of the groups nudged Bilternus. "Looks like your father's been given charge of some of the army. Do you reckon he'll be trying to get you?"

"Him? Nah," said Bilternus, following Kyel's gaze. "Jakus has him under control. He wouldn't dare try, the coward. Besides, I'm a fair scent master myself."

"Uh huh," Kyel replied, losing interest as he sought familiar faces in the crowd behind them.

Despite the large army, the only real noise came from the animals, grunting and bleating with the relief of reaching solid ground. Kyel could see scent masters aligning with each section. Sharna, Poegna and Festern joined Faltis as leaders, while Jakus and his second-in-command, Kast, were at the head of their section.

Jakus's scent aura darkened as he viewed his army. "You have your orders!" His voice was tightly directed. "We have little time. As soon as you're able, move out and target your assigned areas. I want the waterfront and the city secured.

Our forces must be ready to move on at first light.

"Now take your crystals. Sparingly!" he warned. The scent masters throughout the army quickly reached into their pouches.

Kyel slipped a pinch of magnesa into his mouth, enjoying the instant rush as it hit his nerves and sharpened his scent sense; he stopped his hand slipping back towards his pouch with a start. He sensed Nefaria and turned as she approached.

"Come Kyel, Bilternus, the Shad wants you with him." She led the way to where Jakus and Kast were talking.

Jakus eyed them and several others, including the scent master Tretial, who Kyel remembered from Southern Port. "Kast will take my section up the streets as planned, with full shields. You will come with me to search the warehouses."

"Go!" he ordered. As the scent masters and guardsmen moved off into the buildings ahead of them, the first reactions of the defenders began. Scent bolts boomed and yells, then screams, sounded.

The army flooded into the city under Jakus's watchful eyes, his scent aura reflecting excitement. Far back on the pier the last of the supplies were being offloaded, while minders corralled the animals into a large herd. Kyel noticed the familiar cages of hymetta stacked alongside.

"Attention!" Jakus snapped at his small group. "You are here to locate any supplies of magnesite. The natives will have some ready for shipment unless they are hidden. Your task is to find them while the fighting keeps them occupied. The warehouses are not far, and we must be quick. Now move, shields high."

The Sutanite forces had already entered the maze of streets and buildings surrounding the waterfront. Little damage had occurred, largely due to swift movement of the troops and the guerrilla tactics of the defenders. Scent bolts coming from cover impacted on shields, having little effect except where several hit the same target at once or non-shielded guardsmen were exposed.

The magnesa-enhanced shields of the attackers were powerful, and they moved through the hinterland of the waterfront without much difficulty, forcing the defenders to retreat. Jakus followed at the back of Kast's force and then slipped off to a section of dark wooden buildings a street back from the wharves. His small force of Kyel, Bilternus, Nefaria, Tretial and several others moved quickly.

Kyel maintained strong, scent-bonded shields easily with the magnesa coursing through his veins. It made him feel invincible and not overly concerned about the situation. He eagerly readied his powers as they ran through a narrow street, one- and two-storey buildings on each side.

The clash took him by surprise. A group of people in green thrust dark bolts of scent and long, metal-headed spears at them, hitting their shields hard, slamming Jakus's force against a wooden wall as they reached a large warehouse. A spear snuck through a break in the scent bonds and took one of their number in the thigh; the man screamed, falling through his protection.

Jakus reacted, exploding his shields outward, taking and using his group's scent strength to roll an impermeable wall at the attackers. Kyel felt a sudden weakness from Jakus's action, making him realise how powerful the leader was, but he wasn't prepared for what came next.

The scent blanket pushed down on the defenders, overwhelming and flattening their own scent shields, leaving them lying battered and semi-conscious on the street's cobblestones.

Kyel prepared to run on, but Jakus hadn't finished. He kept drawing down on everyone's power, holding the scent blanket hard over the people on the ground. Kyel tried to ease back, reduce Jakus's pull on him even as he saw the contortions of the victims struggling to breathe. Finally the scent master relaxed the pressure and the scent blanket retracted, leaving the bodies where they fell.

"I felt some resistance from you, Eanite," Jakus growled at him.

"But they're all dead. You didn't need to kill them!" Kyel shouted, unconcerned at Jakus's threatening presence.

"The only good enemy is a dead enemy." Jakus stared for a long moment. "It appears I have been neglecting you." He glanced at the rest of his group. "Come! The way is clear to search for the prize. Leave our injured for the healers," he said, passing a wounded man lying against the wall. He strode off towards the door of the nearest building.

Kyel felt Nefaria's hand briefly rest on his shoulder as his eyes moved over the bodies and back to the wounded man. Kyel took a deep breath and followed them, feeling flat, the hit of magnesa having left him. His aching head was filled with the deaths, the cruelty and power of Jakus and that he had revealed himself to the man. What am I going to do? he pondered as he entered the gloomy wooden building.

Jakus acted as if the attack had never happened while he searched through the scatter of rubbish strewn across the wooden floor of the warehouse. They spread out, delving with their senses for the slightest trace of the red crystal, but it appeared the building had only stored lumber and wooden products.

"Useless," he growled. "Next building. There must be a trace." He hobbled through the gloom, pushing out of the door and into the building alongside.

"Ah!" he came to a stop, angular nose held high. "Slight, but there. The blooded scartha have tried to remove any evidence, but it's there. Follow its trace," he ordered.

The poorly lit warehouse was empty, but the scent of magnesite was apparent in a welter of odours. Kyel could vaguely see a reddish scent mixing in with an odoriferous background, with indications that its source had been recently removed.

"We need to keep on the trail, find where it leads," Jakus snapped.

They followed him to the door. Then Jakus grabbed both Kyel and Bilternus by the shoulders. "Keep going," he said to the others. "See where they took it but wait for us. There's a small job to do first.

"Since you have sympathy for the Rolanites, I thought I'd let you punish them," he smiled at Kyel, eyes cold. "Bilternus will help."

Kyel and Bilternus looked at each other as Jakus reached under his black cloak and into the pouch hanging off the belt on his tunic. He took out a thin-bladed steel knife and a slate-coloured rock before kneeling on one knee in the rubbish-strewn floor at the entrance.

He struck the knife blade with the rock, causing a shower of sparks to hit the ground. Jakus blew on the sparks with a scent-laden breath and immediately a flame sprung up. It rapidly spread across the straw and wooden rubbish on the floor.

"Use this fire to destroy these warehouses." He winced as he stood and stretched his back. "Do it now! Prove your loyalty."

Kyel's mind went blank, with the flame filling his vision as Bilternus added a volatile scent-stream to the fire. His first thought was to smother it, not allow the buildings to burn, but the knowledge that any hope he had of stopping the tyrant and getting back to Ean and his family would disappear stopped him. He had to play the willing traitor and pass Jakus's test. There was no choice.

He sought the scent memory of the most flammable substance he knew, remembering Targas's favourite drink of malas. He forced the scents into the mix and the fire roared in response, flames licking across the building and pushing against the far walls. He grabbed the soaring flames, and bent and twisted them to his will, dragging them across the gaps between buildings to ignite the wooden structures. Kyel felt the influence and strength of Bilternus as he worked, but a cold chuckle behind him reminded him of who was in charge.

The flames leaping into the air in coils of scents and soot attracted Targas's attention where he waited with a group of scent masters further back towards the centre of the city. He could see figures driving the flames in huge thrusts towards the wooden walls and roofs, causing a destructive conflagration.

"Too far away to stop them. Let's get closer," he said to Drathner.

"No!" Drathner took Targas's arm. "Don't even try. It's hard, but it fits our plans. While Jakus and his invaders are busy we can move out, with fewer casualties. Leave them to their mindless destruction as it'll only be short lived."

"Huh!" Targas grunted, loathe to leave the opportunity but realising the sense of the man's words. He stopped for a moment looking back at one figure in particular, puzzling at its familiarity.

"Hurry, Targas. We haven't long," urged the Rolanite.

"Coming." He shifted his pack across his shoulders and began to follow, then realised who he had been looking at. *Kyel! It's Kyel, fighting for the enemy. Can't be,* he thought, *can't be. Blood's teeth.*

They ran in double file through the darkening streets, a long green worm of defenders with Targas in the middle, still puzzling over what he had seen. They soon arrived at an agreed meeting place in the elevated northern outskirts where they could look back over the city.

A number of defenders had already arrived and were reporting to Xaner and Siliaster.

They learnt the defence had not been going to plan. The power of the Sutanite troops with their magnesa-enhanced shields had made it difficult to stop their progress, and casualties were higher than expected. They clustered around a parchment map, working out the deployment of their defenders. Each section had been fighting a rear-guard action, slowly moving back, filling the streets and alleys with debris and rubble; some buildings had even been collapsed to hinder the enemy. Fire in the warehouse district made the situation worse, although an onshore breeze hindered the attack by driving thick smoke through the streets.

Targas was frustrated at being kept from the fighting. The success of his scent bonding during the war in Ean encouraged him and made him want to confront the enemy using some of his knowledge he had worked on back in Lesslas, but Xaner and Drathner wouldn't hear of it. His head pounding in frustration, Targas listened to the reports which revealed the Sutanites had already taken a third of the city.

"Hold up," came Boidea's deep voice as she, Xerrita and a number of women arrived. "I...I take it," she puffed, "the enemy is hard to stop? Their shields are difficult to penetrate?"

"You are correct, Boidea," answered Xaner. "What news?"

"Our experience is the same as yours, only we have managed to infiltrate their shields with our feminine scent control. A small detachment entered our area and after considerable effort we defeated them, pushed them back, made them worry."

"And," added Xerrita, breaking in as Boidea took breath, "achieved a modicum of success in the total plan. This will make them more cautious, we believe."

"Good news," smiled Xaner grimly. "A setback for Jakus and something for him to think about—we'll be able to work with that. Well done."

With rations and hot drinks handed out, the leaders continued their discussions over the map of the city, tracing known concentrations of the enemy.

Thick, roiling coils of black smoke from the burning warehouse district darkened the sky and brought on a premature night, causing the group to break up. They'd decided to move most of their army to the hills outside Requist and then make a withdrawal northward before dawn, following the river. In the meantime, small guerilla units were to continue harassing Sutanite invaders, damaging their ships and supplies, ensuring Jakus would leave part of his forces behind while he followed the magnesite trail.

"You coming Targas?" asked Drathner as the army moved out in small units into the dimness now cloaking the last of the buildings.

"Not right now," he said, "I need to talk with Boidea. You go ahead."

The large man hesitated for a moment. "You sure?"

"Yes, I'm well able to look after myself," he said irritably.

Drathner nodded and hurried after the people moving out.

Targas slipped back and out of the way, pushing up a scent shield, thickening it to gradually obscure his body; for some reason he recalled that one of his first instinctive uses of scent power after his arrival in Ean had been to conceal himself. He pushed the memory to the back of his consciousness: it could not help him here.

After ensuring he hadn't been noticed, he slipped down a street leading back towards the burning warehouses.

The way was quiet, dark streets, empty buildings, no people, a feeling of sadness. He sampled the odours as he moved, senses open, alert for the first sign of the enemy. Targas sought the scent of Sutanites, knowing he should detect even the slightest odour if they were near. He briefly wondered if Kyel was masking his spoor to conceal himself, if he was that much of an enemy sympathiser.

His head began to throb in time with his heartbeat, picking at his concentration, eroding his scent control, forcing him to reconsider his quest. He drew a deep breath, squashed his doubts and continued on to the scene of the fires. *I must find Kyel,* he thought. *I must know what he is, what he's done.* Because of his attitude in Lesslas he had driven Kyel away and now he had to bring him back to the family, and if he had to go through the Sutanite invaders to do it, he would. But a nagging doubt remained. Am I doing this to prove myself? he thought, or is it really for Kyel and Sadir?

"Wine's rot," he hissed, and forced himself to concentrate as he neared the fires.

Movement rather than scent alerted him to the presence of the enemy. A thin line of shielded figures, black and grey blending in against the twilight and lit by flickers of flame, crept along a rubble-strewn street.

Targas dropped to his haunches and strengthened his concealing shield to a maximum, cutting off any betraying scent.

He couldn't recognise anyone; no familiar shapes and no known odour. He was caught in a quandary as he realised the foolishness of his situation. At the best he would find Kyel and then escape without the enemy realising he had been there. He had to get back and avoid the risk of a confrontation with Jakus and his scent masters.

The end of the line was disappearing around a corner when he acted instinctively. He dropped his shield and flung out a line of strengthened scent at the last figure, squashing the person's own scent shield with tremendous force and dragging him down. He pulled powerfully and reeled in the black-cloaked figure across the street, to swiftly wrap him within his concealing shield.

The reaction was quick. Like a flurry of ants the enemy came back, searching along the street, trying to find their companion's scent. Targas kept pressure on his captive while tightening his concealment, firmly locking the bonds of the scent motes around him. His practise over the years served him well and he watched passively as the search continued around him.

"We have to move on," hissed their leader. "Jakus will not tolerate lateness."

When the street quietened Targas relaxed his grip. At once his captive, a slightly built man with the arrogant look of a Sutanite scent master, pushed outwards with a thrust of scent power. With it came a familiar smell, that of magnesa, reminiscent of Rolan cordial. Targas pushed back, hard, his strength soon overwhelming his opponent.

The man's eyes widened as Targas's action cut off his air and he strained hard against the pressure, kicking out, trying to break free.

"Still!" Targas growled, pushing harder.

The Sutanite slumped at once, panting, eyes locked on Targas's, strong scents of fear and body odour rising. "You're him, aren't you?" he gasped.

"Enough!" Targas spat, looking around to make sure they were alone. "Tell me about Kyel. Is he here? Who with?"

"What?" The man's face slackened. "What? The Eanite? The Shad's boot licker?"

"So he's here!" A pain started deep in Targas's head as he realised what he'd seen at the burning warehouses was true.

"Hah!" an explosive gasp came from the scent master. "So that's what you're after. The so-called hero of the Eanite revolt is after an escapee? Well, it's too late. He's on our side, whatever use he is. Seems you've been betrayed!"

A rush of blood thundered through Targas's brain, making him feel as though he was an observer in his own head. Scent snakes speared out of his mouth and into the nose of his captive, driving into the olfactory centre, seeking his memories. While a part of him was denying what was happening, another part was eagerly delving through what he found.

What the Sutanite scent master had said was confirmed, the man convinced it was true. Other odours came to the fore: loyalty to Jakus, a love of magnesa, ship and sea smells, his homeland, but above all fear. Targas didn't want to know more but for some reason he continued to delve deeper, driving in, enjoying his captive's pain.

When the smell of blood broke through his senses he snapped upright, withdrawing his scent probe. A bloodied wreck lay under his hands, the man dead from his interrogation.

"What happened?" he muttered in horror, his head pounding. "How?"

A sharp pain shot through his brain, like nails dragging. Targas bit his tongue to prevent a rising scream.

It can't be, he thought. *He's gone!*

His mind, overwhelmed, closed down to blackness.

Chapter Forty-Six

Light pushed through his eyelids, a foul smell assaulting his nostrils as he woke to a headache, his body cold and sore from sleeping on hard ground. His companion was unresponsive, emanating thick and virulent odours with beetles investigating the smell.

Targas scrabbled away from the body of the Sutanite scent master, horrified at what he had done the night before. *Could it have been caused by the* presence *they had tried to get rid of in Mlana Hold?*

"No time to worry about that. The question is: why didn't the Sutanites find me?" Then he remembered the concealing scent shield he'd instinctively used to escape years ago in Ean. "Must've been that," he muttered, pushing at his hair with a filthy hand.

He stretched against the rough wall of the building, shifting the straps of the pack on his back as he assessed his surroundings. It was early in the day, with no scents indicating anyone had been nearby. He moved back from the corpse and dragged motes of stray odour in and wove them into a concealing blanket of scent, using the techniques for long-term stabilisation he had been developing in Lesslas. He laid it across the scent master's body, trapping the odours of death beneath.

He heard people coming his way so he rapidly tested the area, dissipating any of his own scents as best he could before slipping along the street, shields raised.

Targas came to a larger street leading out of the city, cobblestones covered by the detritus and animal dung of the recent passage of people. The air, still overhung with the odour of burning, revealed a Sutanite army had recently come through there. He tried to recognise individual scents amongst the odours before him, but nothing showed other than unwashed bodies, animals, equipment and supplies—too many to differentiate.

Targas's stomach reminded him he hadn't eaten, so he slipped down a laneway between two wooden dwellings set on brick foundations. He found a wooden bucket tied to a hook driven into a low brick wall, indicating a communal well.

He lowered it down a narrow hole into water a short distance down. Drawing up a clean bucket-full, he rinsed his dry mouth, washed away the crust of dirt on his face and the dried blood covering his hands.

Although his wool cloak and woollen tunic kept him warm, he still shivered in the shaded nook as he ate honeyed berry biscuit and dried jerky. He was alone, away from his family and friends, surrounded by the enemy and unsure of the powers which had risen in him last night.

He chewed mechanically, refusing to consider anything more as the stillness settled around him in the lightening day. A shaft of sunlight edged over the roof behind him, forming a pool of warmth at his feet. A small tuft of white flowers fought for life where the brick of the wall met the dirt. Targas looked along the horizontal line of bricks and saw more flowers lining the wall, small and compact. A drift of scent, thin but pure, rose into the still air. An early foraging bee followed it and landed on the flower head, reminding him of years ago when he had first met Sadir in Lesslas. He smiled and took a drink from his water bottle.

A wooden toy lay abandoned, half-covered by the flowers. *Anyar's had little time to play with toys*, he thought, *and now war is coming her way. It's not right. Why can't people be satisfied with what they have instead of taking from others?*

His mood darkened as he stood and returned the water bottle and food to his backpack knowing he had to get back to his family, which meant going through the Sutanites blocking his way. Targas had a last look around this tranquil haven before heaving the pack onto his shoulders.

After testing the slight breeze coming through the laneway for any signs of life he started to move off, until the merest mote of odour caught his attention, causing him to stop and shake his head in disbelief. *Hymetta?* he thought. *The Sutanites have hymetta. Why in Ean's name do they have those?*

Still shaking his head, he slipped out into the street and headed for the meeting ground of the day before, where the vantage point might show the disposition of the enemy forces.

K yel, covered with gritty soot, was engulfed in the dust billowing from the movement of the army. He held a scent shield around himself to keep out the dust and associated insects but knew it would be hopeless to hold it for long.

They had moved out before dawn, tracking the Rolanites ahead of them. A wide column of scent masters riding on perac preceded guardsmen on foot along a well-maintained road. Jakus had left a fifth of his forces behind to maintain control on Request and protect his ships, confident his army could handle any resistance ahead.

While the natives had left no supplies of the magnesite in the city the tangible scent trail pointed inland, to where all intelligence indicated the substance was mined, so that was where Jakus led them. The lure of quantities of magnesite in the depths of the country meant the army would continue to move at a fast pace and crush any opposition.

The army had merged, Jakus at its head with Kast and the remaining leaders. Faltis had contrived to be at the Shad's right shoulder and kept trying to engage his brother's attention. Bilternus had moved ahead to be with Poegna, leaving Kyel alone to his thoughts in the large, moving column.

While Jakus was fixated on his goal and less concerned with him than before, the burning of the warehouses appearing to ease his suspicions, Kyel was free to think things through.

They were climbing a slope covered by substantial thickets of trees and scrub, having left the plains and cropping lands behind when a nagging thought hit him: it was just too easy.

The fighting in Request had been brief and bloody, but they had managed to get through in a fairly short time and head into the country with no effective guerrilla tactics from the defenders. When Kyel had been involved in the fight for Ean over years ago it had been deadly, with many people killed and much destruction. Nothing had been easy for the Resistance in their push to rid the country of the Sutanites.

Here, Jakus and his army had simply marched up an undefended road and into the foothills of the mountainous country with relative ease. So what were the defenders doing? From what he knew of Rolan the people were strong and proud, ruled by a spiritual figurehead, the Mlana, and no one had ever invaded the country. Yet the Sutanite army was travelling through it with impunity.

Kyel shook his head, troubled by what he saw and wondering how he would be able to affect what Jakus was doing. There appeared to be no opportunity to cause a problem for Jakus's ambitions, and when confronted he had bent to the man's will like a coward.

"Blast!" he hissed under his breath. As he cast about in exasperation, a wizened face floated through his memory, shrewd but kind eyes peering into his. *Xerina, the soothsayer in Sutan,* he thought with a start. *She came from Rolan, and she taught me something about an other scent. What was it now? And how is it relevant?*

He cast his mind back. *Other* scent was important and lay behind the scents he, as a scent master, could see. But it was unable to be used by men, so why did he need to know about it?

A shiver ran down his back and the hairs on his arms rose. The time was coming and although he couldn't use it, he needed to be aware of it. That was the message from Xerina's Knowing. Something was coming and he would play a part in it.

Kyel's body melded with the rhythm of the perac and he idly watched the drift of scents around him, feeling calmer for the moment.

Targas bent and sifted the scents in the area where the Rolanite forces had been the night before. He closely examined the disturbed meeting site looking for any indication of when they had gone, and if they'd left a message. Not that he expected it since he had deliberately misled the Rolan leaders to slip away on his own.

The place was deserted, situated on a slight ridge between a series of stables and yards to the north, and streets of small cottages and other dwellings that led to the promontory of Lookout Hill and the sea in the south. Targas sought a vantage point to locate the road leading out to the hills, all the while keeping alert for any presence of the enemy. As he'd expected, light scents mixed with those of his friends revealed Sutanites had inspected the ground and no doubt assessed the strength of the forces against them.

He climbed onto a wooden railing and looked over the country that framed Requist. The black stain of the army stood out against the lightness of the road and the green of pastures. The leaders of the large force would shortly disappear into the first of the forested land on the slopes of nearby hills, while the baggage train bringing up the rear still had a distance to go. Targas scanned the vicinity and caught sight of several Sutanites a few streets away, and the scent plumes of many more.

So Jakus has a holding force in the city, he thought as he climbed down from the railing, *meaning I'll have to be on my guard when I try to follow the army.* Targas had no intention of remaining behind. His knowledge of Kyel being with the Sutanites, and the danger now approaching his family, meant he had to get back to his friends at Mlana Hold.

He grunted, stretching his neck in a vain attempt to relieve his burgeoning headache before quietly following a laneway to a street leading northward.

A few times he had to wait as a patrol moved past. The streets eventually converged onto the main road at a temporary blockade of several overturned carts and bales of hay between the man-high wooden walls enclosing the city. The way was held by alert guardsmen and a competent scent master.

Targas was not in the mood to be stopped by the flimsy barrier, but aware he couldn't reveal himself. Waves of pain coursed through his head before a calmness came over him. *A distraction won't hurt,* he thought, *and if there are casualties, so be it.*

The only opponent of worth was the scent master, and although momentarily surprised that it was a woman, he didn't let it worry him.

Targas carefully balanced a series of bricks and half-rotted timbers at the back of the street and then, holding a strong, obscuring shield, moved out into the roadway. He slipped across to a patch of shadow against the wall of a building that guarded the approach, then fired a scent bolt at the pile of material he'd left behind.

The crash brought a response. As several guardsmen ran past him towards the noise, Targas slid along the wall, pushing carefully between the shafts of an upturned cart and several hay bales. He kept his shield tight, being as quiet as he could. eyes fixed on the scent master.

She was sniffing the air while slowly scanning the area, body tensed with awareness.

"Blast!" Targas hissed between his teeth. She hadn't fallen for his ploy and was on double alert.

Her eyes narrowed and she focussed on where he was slowly pushing through the barricade.

"Halt!" she yelled, her voice breaking with alarm. A scent bolt smashed into the hay bale and knocked Targas to the ground. As he hit he lost his shield, and an explosion of odours lifted into the air.

Another scent bolt, dark and fast from her mouth, hit his hastily strengthened shield, before she leapt over the barricade, several guardsmen following.

"No!" A red haze filled Targas's mind, the implications of being caught scaring him. He automatically lashed out with a strengthened scent coil which knocked her off her feet. A spear dug into the ground and his scent bolt response blew the guardsman's head off his shoulders. In quick succession he hit the remaining unprotected guardsmen with scent bolts of such fury their broken bodies soon covered the ground.

He was in another place as he looked down at the white-faced woman, her eyes wide in shock. He dropped onto her chest with his knees, causing her to grimace in pain, and then slashed with a strengthened scent band linked to his hand. Her neck ruptured, blood spraying into the air.

Targas rested back on his haunches as she thrashed, feeling the blood splatter onto his uplifted face. He revelled in the moment with no regrets and no thoughts about what he had done. His blank eyes took in the dead around him as he fancied he heard a mocking laugh deep in his mind.

They marched through the heat of the day, snatching quick drinks and hard rations, alert for retaliation from the natives. Several times an attack came from a deep gully or thick stand of trees but with little impact, the magnesa-reinforced shields proving a match for any scent attack.

The road leading to Nosta was more hazardous; heavily treed slopes and deep passes meaning a nerve-racking time as an early twilight descended. The dark was amplified by thickening clouds hanging over the peaks of the mountains to the west and stretching towards Jakus's army.

They were on the outskirts of Nosta, dividing their forces to cover each of the arms of the star-shaped city. Poegna, Sharna, Festern and Faltis led the sections while Jakus held the main road that led into the city.

Kyel made sure he was near those he knew. Tretial, Bilternus and Nefaria were in the group led by Jakus and Kast. They camped in the near gloom, shields covering each other, Jakus using highly enhanced senses to test for the enemy.

Kyel didn't waste the opportunity, having reflected on what Xerina had meant. He avidly sought the *other* scent, assessing all the odours he could see, especially those coming from the city they surrounded. Anything that might reveal itself, be detectable, had the potential to help him in his attempts to stop Jakus's cruelty and oppose what he was doing. He had to find something, even if the darkness made it near impossible.

Targas took in the odours of the Sutanites and their animals before him, and waited in the dark to assess his options. He had come to his senses a short time after destroying the protectors of the barricade. His head was clear, headache gone, but the horror of what he had done remained like a pall over him. He hurriedly sluiced off the blood with several stolen water bottles before striking out on the army's trail, leaving the destruction behind. Now night had fallen, and he was blocked from either entering Nosta or continuing to Mlana Hold.

I can't be stopped, not now, he thought. *I must get through.*

He moved into the scrub lining the road and headed at an angle to bypass the army. The vegetation on the rocky ground made it hard to push through with so little light to see. A flow of scent reached his nostrils, mainly from leaves and soil, with a trickle of insect and occasional lizard smell. The intricacies of the scent flow allowed him to navigate in the darkness and avoid making too much noise.

The long day began to catch up with him, causing him to stumble and become more erratic. When he bumped into a large tree he slid to the ground, pulled off the backpack and tiredly retrieved his water bottle and meat jerky.

He reflected on what was happening to him, how he'd found himself on his own, avoiding the enemy and trying to come to terms with his own wellbeing. He knew he wasn't cured and his actions in a dangerous situation were frightening. What would he do if he was in an argument with friends, or worse still, Sadir? He needed to get to Alethea, to see what could be done, if anything.

He fell asleep to the gentle chirping of crickets in the undergrowth.

A tickling on his legs pushed into his subconscious. Targas relaxed at the feeling and he smiled at a memory. The tickling became more insistent, moving up his legs under his trousers, forcing his eyes open.

He stood in alarm, cracking his head on an overhanging branch, shaking himself at the same time. A cascade of small beetles fell from his trousers, tumbling to the ground in a black mass before crawling determinedly back towards him. At once, several small lizards with pointed heads ran from the undergrowth to snap them up.

Carrion beetles, Targas thought, *attracted by the blood on my clothes.*

Then he remembered where he was. Light from a rising sun lit a rugged landscape, thickly carpeted with grasses, bushes and trees around substantial rock outcrops.

Noise filtered through—animals bleating, metal clinking—revealing Jakus's army on the move nearby. He unwrapped a piece of honeyed biscuit and chewed while he thought. The choice was simple: either attempt to get into Nosta or head towards Mlana Hold.

The pull of his family and his knowledge that Kyel was with the Sutanite army made his decision easy. He rested his hand on the solid tree he had slept beneath and heaved himself up into the upper branches.

Targas took care not to shake the tree as he gradually climbed above the canopy, found a comfortable position and scanned the surroundings.

A mass of odours not far to his right showed the position of the army and the road. He didn't attempt to decipher individual scents but looked further ahead, towards the mountains in the north. Thick patches of animal odour revealed where portions of Jakus's forces were blockading the city, and how far along the road they extended.

Clouds were still gathered about the mountains, thickest in the northwest, but the day was generally clear. He caught a glimpse of the road where it led northward, free of the invaders, and determined to make for it as swiftly as possible. He slithered down the tree, dropped to the ground, retrieved his backpack and began to walk parallel to the road until he could be sure to be past the blockades.

Targas set off, desperate to reach Mlana Hold.

Chapter Forty-Seven

Targas tried a half-jog to increase his pace, but his body, protesting after the trials of the previous day, soon slowed him to a brisk walk.

The road wound through the rocky, well-vegetated terrain, allowing only glimpses of the way ahead. All too often he was walking in a cocoon of his own, out of contact with anyone but always testing the surrounds for enemy presence.

Stretching his senses he noticed a curious lack of scent, areas where existing odours were disrupted, indicating someone or something had interfered with them. The older traffic, including the group he had ridden with a few days previously, were still discernible despite recent light rains, but someone had come through within hours and attempted to conceal the fact.

Targas smiled despite himself, recognising familiar scents. A small group had ridden through towards Mlana Hold, and several of his friends were with them. Somehow they had escaped the notice of the Sutanites in their blockade of Nosta. He was relieved not to have enemies ahead, yet concerned they might be close behind him.

All the while he pushed himself. The enemy rode perac and could travel faster, and soon the land would flatten, making him stand out if he followed the road, yet he had to at least reach the pass of the Cascade Falls before any pursuit.

Targas paused where the river met the road to splash cold water over his head and fill his bottle. He climbed a large boulder and looked back for any sign. Grey cloud now covered most of the sky, making any odour evidence hard to see. A large group of riders would make a considerable impact on the rising flow of scents, but he could see nothing. Eventually he dropped down, still uneasy.

He made for the road and began a light jog while he was able, keeping his eyes fixed on the horizon, hoping to see the first signs of the escarpment and the pass.

K yel was in a group of over two hundred riders moving along the road north of the city. They had taken all available animals to mount the total force now heading deeper into Rolan, leaving Nosta blockaded.

Jakus, driven by the need to secure the anticipated stockpile of magnesite at Mlana Hold, had left a significant portion of his army behind to prevent the Rolanites from breaking the blockade and attacking from the rear. Nosta was well able to withstand an assault, being fortified and set in difficult terrain, so a blockade was the best option. They had tracked the native force from Request into the city and trapped them there, strong scent powers meaning a virtual stalemate in the fighting, each side suffering few injuries.

The opportunity to move a relatively large force to the source of the red crystal without enemy attack had been too much for Jakus to resist.

They had set out several hours from midday under a grey sky with rain threatening. While Jakus and Kast led, Faltis was tucked in behind his brother, for some reason having gained favour since his failed attack back in Sutan. Kyel made sure he was near the head of the column, just down from Nefaria and Poegna, and well away from the cages of hymetta Jakus had insisted on bringing. He watched the land for signs of anything familiar, a feeling nagging him that he had missed something. The teachings of Xerina kept floating into his mind, and he searched for the *other* scent without success.

His perac pulled sharply, bumping into the animals ahead of it. He stood in his stirrups and saw Jakus, Kast and Faltis crouched down, searching the scents of the roadway ahead.

"What's up?" called Bilternus from behind him.

"I don't know," said Kyel.

"Some unusual traces," answered Nefaria, turning around. "Not sure what, though."

The leaders had a hurried talk before climbing back on their animals and urging them to a faster pace.

As the column moved off, Kyel scanned the side of the road that came close to the river. *Something,* he thought, then shook his head. *Just imagining things.*

T he roaring sound told him he was nearing the Cascade Falls, even if stands of trees hid them. The stitch in his side kept him to a hobble, his feet were sore and a gnawing hunger bit his belly.

Targas needed to pass the falls to feel safe, but the ground was relatively exposed in the rise to the pass and the long climb almost beyond him.

He stood in the shelter of the last of the trees and watched the cascades of water looping out in a long arc before crashing into the rock-filled base of the cliffs and continuing into the Rolander River. The mist filling the area before him melded with the cloud that had thickened as the day progressed, creating a grey scene, one which should help him ascend the pass without being noticed.

Targas ate the last of his honeyed biscuits and took a swig of water before stepping back onto the road. He had no time to see who was following as the last of his effort had to be to gain the summit of the escarpment.

He shifted his light backpack and continued his scent concealment as he went, recognising his ability to do so was rapidly diminishing.

The brief halt had helped but it wasn't long before the stitch was back and his progress slowed. When he finally reached the start of the incline, he chanced a look back.

"Wine's rot!" he cursed and urged himself on. An obvious dark roil of odour revealed the existence of large numbers of peracs and people coming rapidly along the road.

Targas concentrated on putting one foot in front of the other on the long climb and maintaining an obscuring scent shield. He wanted to look back but resisted the urge with the effort of climbing the pass.

Water spray drifted across him, at times bringing some relief while his legs and body cried out in agony. The roar of the Cascade Falls was constant, pounding through his head, blocking his ears from noises of pursuit. The pain began, sliding in quick bursts through his head, bringing the feel of a *presence* in his mind.

"Not now!" he groaned, coping with the slope and the increasing wetness of the road. The way ahead closed in as the mists of the falls increased and his vision tunnelled.

Targas slipped, banging his knee on the rocky surface and skinning his hands. He slowly turned his head to look back, aware his scent control has been momentarily broken.

A mass of people and animals, black to his sight, were at the start of the climb, only a short distance away.

His gamble had failed.

"Targas!" screamed Jakus. "You Tenstrian scartha. Now I have you!" He urged his perac into an extra effort up the steep path.

There was a scrabble for position behind him as the column thinned to climb the road. Kyel automatically followed, about twenty people back, numb with the shock of unexpectedly seeing Targas.

Part of his mind was beginning to recognise what those twinges of familiarity were and another wondering where his sister and niece were if Targas was here. *Why didn't Xerina warn of this in her Knowings? How can I stop Jakus from killing him?*

The flow of the people followed Jakus into the climb.

Targas's panic was overcome by a controlling *presence* in his head. He fancied he could hear a cackling laugh as he faced his pursuers, his tiredness ignored. All his skills combined when he reached out with his senses, thickening and joining scents into a long band, angling it into the falls pouring past him. The water's impact jolted him, seeking to smash the scent band into pieces. But the bonds held, deflecting a flood of water from its natural course, angling it onto the roadway below him.

It washed down the road, driving a lethal mix of water, rock and gravel at the pursuers before it. The riders and animals in the lead lost their footing, rolling back onto the others behind. Screams rose thinly above the sounds of the Cascade Falls.

Targas directed the water on the road for as long as he could before he released his control and sat exhausted at the head of the eroded slope. Some impetus finally pushed through his awareness, overriding the gleeful *presence* in his mind, forcing his body to continue the long climb to the top of the pass and safety.

The animal rearing in front of him was Kyel's first indication of something untoward. Then a wall of water, animals and people hit him. Reaction was instinctive. He created a scent shield around himself, holding it as tight as he could while being battered and tumbled down the slope. The impacts pushed hard at his control and the rolling seemed endless.

A final bang broke his hold and the barrier collapsed. A flood of muddy water washed over him as he struggled to sit, trying to make sense of what had happened.

Cries and moans around him came from a sodden mass of humanity and injured animals. The remainder of the column that hadn't begun the climb was active behind him. He waved away an offer of help and slowly stood, testing his limbs for damage. His own perac lay near him, neck broken, gear spilling out of saddlebags. Other animals struggled to stand, some with broken legs and others merely shaken.

"A blasted mess, Kyel," croaked Bilternus from nearby. "Just as well we weren't near the front."

"Poegna!" he exclaimed, and limped by to begin searching amongst the people sitting or lying ahead.

"Nefaria," gasped Kyel, remembering she had been ahead of him in the climb. He followed Bilternus looking for the slighter forms of the women in the group.

He found her, body half-covered by a dead perac, her black curls flattened by water and mud. He slumped next to her, lifting her head gently from the wet ground.

Her dark eyes opened, and she smiled as she saw Kyel's concerned face. "I...I knew it was you, Kyel," she breathed shallowly.

"Let me get you out of here," he said urgently, "somewhere dryer."

"No. Kyel. No." Nefaria's eyelids fluttered as she took a shallow breath. "Is... is my Lord...hurt?"

Kyel looked up, hoping to see Jakus dead, but couldn't find him in the crush of bodies. He shook himself and smiled down at the pale face. "Sorry, I don't know."

"It doesn't matter," she whispered. "But you...you need to...get away. Get home...find a love...live. Don't worry...about me."

"No, Nefaria. I...I love you. I can't go." Tears began to trickle down his face.

"I know you do. For that reason...you...must survive. I was never for you; my heart...already taken. Now leave me...help someone who needs it." She lifted a hand to touch his face. Her eyes closed and her arm dropped to the soggy ground.

Kyel sat on his haunches, tears running down his face, oblivious to the noise around him.

A hand touched his shoulder and he jerked.

"Is she...?"

His tear-filled face looked into Bilternus's and he nodded. "A...and Poegna?" he remembered.

"No, she's fine. It seems the scent masters were able to protect themselves. It was those with lesser talent who suffered the most."

"So Jakus...?"

"Nothing'll kill him. He's ordering everyone around as usual."

"So he won't know about Nefaria yet?" asked Kyel.

"No," answered Bilternus.

"Well, let him find out for himself. I'm not telling him," said Kyel as he stood. "He didn't deserve her."

Targas never knew how he made it to the top of the pass and out of the mists of water vapour covering it. He found himself shivering on a ridge of rock looking back across the valley below, mind curiously empty. He couldn't see the result of the water flow he had sent down the road, but any pursuit had ceased.

The roar of the falls was muted and he was distracted. A scent tendril brushed his neck and he swung around in alarm.

A small group of people on animals were before him, dark and alarming. He began preparing a shield before he recognised the scents and slumped down.

"Well met, Targas. We were most worried about you!" cried Boidea as she slid off her perac and ran forward.

Targas managed to stand before he met her and exchanged scents. "I...I'm pleased to see you. You don't know how much."

She stood at arm's distance and eyed him critically. "You have been in the wars and…your eyes, they're red, really bloodshot."

Before he could respond the others came up to welcome him, including Dranther, Xaner and Xerrita.

"We must move on but firstly should provide you with warm clothes, for you appear to have had an accident with the Falls," said Boidea with a lopsided smile.

Xaner replaced his wet clothing with a woollen jacket and dry trousers before leading him to the waiting animals. "We saw what happened below from a ridge over there," he said, nodding to a projection of rocky ledge that curled around the edge of the escarpment a distance away. "A clever feat, which will put the Sutanites back a bit. It will take them time to negotiate the road after what you've done."

"You can ride with me," said Boidea. "My animal is strong and able to take double."

Targas grunted, his mind still dazed as he climbed up behind her. He could feel the animal's spine on his tailbone, so he slumped forward with his arms on Boidea's thighs. Waves of weariness rolled over him and his head began to droop as they moved off. When Boidea spoke he had to strain to listen.

"I suppose you're wondering why we're not in Nosta, why we're here instead?" She half-turned to glance back at him.

"Uh huh," he replied.

"It's all part of the plan, the Knowing, Targas. We haven't told you too much because of the chance you might have been captured, but you're safe enough now.

"Mlana has seen what is coming for some time, not in detail but enough to prepare and plan. So what is happening now is anticipated."

"Oh?" Targas began to pay more attention.

"Abandoning Requist and being blockaded in Nosta is all part of the plan to divest Jakus of a large portion of his army. You will notice we are a small group of leaders within Rolan and not locked away in Nosta. We slipped away with little trace to ensure the Sutanites thought we were trapped."

"So," Targas's voice croaked, "the fact that a large army is on our trail is part of your plan too?"

"Y…yes," she said thoughtfully, "although a significant percentage has stayed behind, and your actions have helped even more. What were you doing, by the way?"

"Ah, so your Knowing doesn't say?"

"Not everything is spelt out, Targas," Boidea said matter-of-factly.

"Well it's all to do with my family," he said. "Kyel is with the Sutanites, and I stayed back to see if it was him and whether the enemy had turned him.

"And I'll need to talk to Sadir and Alethea about this as soon as I can."

They continued at a brisk pace through the rolling foothills of the mountains ahead. Boidea said little from then on, concentrating on pushing the perac as fast as it could with its double burden.

At one stage they stopped and looked back. While the clouds seemed ready to release the rain they had threatened all day, the road above the pass was still clear.

"That was a deadly stroke at the Cascade Falls, Targas," she said as she urged her animal onwards.

"It wasn't my idea."

"Oh? Whose, then?"

"Septus's," said Targas flatly. "He's back."

The aftermath of the flood on the road hardened Kyel's heart even further. The wreckage was sorted, with bodies of people and animals separated. The animals were piled in a rough heap while the people were laid off to one side. Eight guardsmen, two lesser scent masters and Nefaria were left lying under the dull skies while the rest of them worked on the road attempting to make the huge scar left by the water's power passable.

Kyel stood above Nefaria for a time, watching her pale face, vainly waiting for her eyes to open and for her chest to rise.

A shadow loomed up next to him with a familiar scent aura. "Had enough time with her?" the hated voice asked.

He didn't respond.

"Help with the hymetta. Make sure they weren't affected as they're still needed, particularly now. And just remember"—Jakus's sharp face came into focus—"she won't be around to look out for you. So keep out of my way!" He walked off.

Kyel watched him go with unblinking eyes before he pulled at some recently cut branches. "He doesn't even care. You never, never should've wasted your life for him!" Tears flowed as he laid the branches across Nefaria's body.

The path into Mlana Hold was treacherous in the failing light; getting past the cliffs that bordered the river was hazardous, yet they made it without mishap. The stone walls at the village angling towards the road loomed out of the twilight and the guards at the entrance moved the timber barricade to allow them through.

"Straight to the Hold while the animals have strength," urged Boidea, pushing back at Targas's head resting against her shoulder.

He attempted to respond while floating in and out of exhaustion, but the effort was too much.

The animals finally pulled up. He was eased out of the saddle and held upright as his legs failed.

"Come, Targas," said Drathner, "let Xaner and me get you up to the fires. There's people there who are keen to see you."

He staggered as they negotiated the narrow path and up into the cavern. He barely felt the extra arms around him, just registering Sadir's scent before a blaze of warmth from the fires struck him.

"Take him straight to the baths. Get him warm, then food and sleep."

The authoritarian voice registered through his consciousness, making him aware he needed to tell the Mlana his news, that the Sutanites were not far behind, and Kyel was with them, but his protests were unheard.

Targas was dragged away, stripped and eased into a warm, slightly odorous bath. As he relaxed in the heat-giving waters he felt a body slide in and hold him.

"I missed you," Sadir murmured as she began to soap him down.

"As I missed you," he answered, wondering how to tell her about her brother, and repeated: "As I missed you."

Chapter Forty-Eight

"I can't rest," said Targas. "They're too close. We need to see Alethea."

"Quiet, love, let's take a moment," said Sadir, lying against Targas's chest on their bed. Anyar lay across her father's legs, hanging over the side playing with the voral, her movements against him familiar and comforting.

He had told Sadir about seeing Kyel and they had thought it through. She was convinced her brother was a captive and being forced to co-operate and Targas, despite what he had discovered, didn't dissuade her.

A shadow appeared at the door, a querying scent from Cathar drifted in.

"You ready?"

Targas pushed to his feet with a groan as Anyar laughed, falling over the side of the bed onto Vor.

Sadir helped Targas to his feet before bending down to her daughter. "Keep him quiet because we have to go and speak with Alethea and the others."

"Yes, Mother." She scrambled to her feet, large eyes glistening in the dim light. "Stay, Vor," she said, placing a hand on his neck.

Targas briefly wondered at his young daughter's sudden maturity as he made his way to the door.

The fires, banked into heaps of glowing coals, provided ample heat for those seated around it and he saw Alethea amongst the nearest group of people. She got slowly to her feet before he could stop her.

"Welcome, Targas," she said, leaning forward to exchange scents. "You have been having a difficult time of it?"

He moved to the seat next to her noticing how frail she had become, even over a few days. A bowl of fragrant soup and a chunk of buttered bread were given to him as he sat.

"Eat first," she murmured. "We have time afterwards. Sadir, Anyar, sit on these; they're nearer the fire." Alethea indicated several cushions at the base of the chairs.

Anyar sat where she could lean against her father's leg while she ate a slice of honeyed bread. Sadir was cross-legged on the other side, holding a mug of tea.

"Boidea tells me our cure hasn't worked," she said quietly.

Targas grunted, his mouth full.

"I anticipated as much."

He gulped down the mouthful. "What? You knew?"

"Don't get upset. We had to try, even against the Knowing. Unfortunately, you've had to bear the awful consequences of the *presence* in your head. There is a reason behind all this."

"Do you know what has been happening? Do you know what I've done?" He glared at the woman, whose tired wrinkled face and sympathetic eyes immediately made him regret his anger.

"I do, my friend," she said. "I most certainly do."

The fire cracked and sparked, throwing light across the ceiling of the huge cavern. The murmur of the large number of people scattered across the space formed a backdrop to their isolated group.

"Make use of this night," she said, her voice growing in volume. "For this is the last night of calm, the last night before it all comes to pass. We hope to survive for the future, but for those of us whose path finishes, it is meant to be. The Knowing ends and begins here. Your role, my friends will end and begin next day. Do not be afraid. Play your part. Know it is meant to be."

Alethea paused, looked at her wrinkled hands lying in her lap, then her dark eyes pointedly caught Targas's, and she nodded sadly.

The fire flared, casting a surreal light on their faces. Alethea took a deep breath. "Please bear with an old woman's ramblings. We are prepared for what comes, following a plan that we have known for some time, and understand the outcome.

"Look after the young one, Sadir. She is most important." She leant down and placed a hand on Anyar's head. "Now I must leave you in the hands of others, for I am weary."

Boidea appeared at their side out of the darkness of the cavern and helped Alethea to her feet. Together they disappeared to her rooms.

"Lizards' teeth!" hissed Kyel, breaking out of his melancholy as a rattle of hail hit his face. The hooded figures in front of him were hunched over against the freezing weather blowing in from the west. He twisted to see the covered cages of hymetta a few animals back and wished they had been destroyed in the flooding of the pass.

Though he had been relegated to the back of the column of around one hundred and seventy riders to assist with the baggage and hymetta, he didn't mind—anything to be out of Jakus's sight.

They had made the top of the pass before dawn and were pressing on in the rain and hail that had been threatening. The dead and wounded were left behind to await the army's return from Mlana Hold. Kyel wondered whether Nefaria would be given a decent burial, but wasn't able to say anything.

Even if it hadn't been a grey and depressing day, he would still have seen the dark, determined scent aura at the front of the column. Whether Jakus was angry at the obstacles in his path and the loss of his most faithful servant and companion, or just focussed on his goal, Kyel didn't know. Faltis, Kast, Poegna, Festern and even Bilternus were with him, keeping up a steady pace to get them to the village by midday.

One way or the other he knew this day would resolve things and, if he had the remotest chance to help put Jakus down and protect his family, he would do it.

"My family," he mouthed to himself. The words always put a slight glow of hope in his chest when all was going wrong. *I wonder if Anyar is with them. If she's grown much. Whether she'll remember me.*

Another rattle of hail stopped that thought.

They met at the entrance to the cavern, standing in groups along its long lip, eating bread filled with fried meat and onion, watching the rain and hail sweeping in from the western mountains to a cold and bleak village below.

From his vantage point Targas could see numbers of people in hooded green jackets and dark grey trousers manning the V-shaped walls that angled to the blockades on the road. The corners of the granite and slate buildings were also manned and built up with more barricades while far off, people were positioned where the road ran alongside the river and past a towering cliff.

He had woken clear-headed, had some time with Anyar before he left her in rooms at the back behind the kitchens, being the safest place for children and their carers. He was relieved Sadir and Cathar would be with them when the fighting came.

Xerrita tapped him on the shoulder. "It's time to discuss our tactics."

A large group of leaders gathered around a seated Alethea with Xaner and Boidea by her side, so Targas and Sadir slipped into a space near her.

"Go through relevant parts of our deployment if you will, Xaner," said Alethea, looking small in her large woollen cloak.

Xaner nodded and moved into the centre of the group. "You will have seen from here where our defenders are. All areas of approach are covered, and we will have scent masters with them when the enemy attacks. The magnesite storage in the village is well guarded but if it is captured then the fall-back position is here—the Hold.

"Whatever happens they must not take it. We are outnumbered but our women, along with the Mlana, will be based here. We don't anticipate them being able to break through with the *shadow* scent against them."

"Drathner, why don't you use the magnesa against them?" Targas asked. "It's obvious that the enemy is using it to aid their scent power, so why don't we?"

"I'm sure you would know our strength is in our women, and this comes through the cordial. The use of magnesa, as you say, is not our way. Directly taken, it is only for the mystics of our world, not for such use as you suggest. It would lead to madness.

"However, Targas"—Drathner caught his eye—"I will initially need you with me in the village as you have the most familiarity with the enemy. We have easy fallback lines to the Hold. So, whatever happens, you must return here. Your family is very important and despite the vagaries of the Knowing, the Mlana believes this is where you need to be."

"Fine," he agreed, "I think I'm up for it." Targas felt Sadir squeeze his hand and wondered if she was thinking about her brother out in the enemy's force. As Xaner continued to outline other details, he wondered how he could help Kyel in the middle of the fighting, or if he might have to do the unthinkable.

When the group broke up, Targas walked with Sadir to check on Anyar. She was playing happily with other children, leading them in a complex-seeming game. Vor was a messy flop of fur settled in a corner, eyes fixed on his mistress.

"Can't do better than that, love," said Sadir. "I'll make sure I'm with her if things get too dangerous. Please be careful." They hugged desperately, melding scents, before he left to wait with several others.

"They've been sighted," Xaner said from nearby. "Be on us soon. We best be down in the village."

They descended the narrow track winding its way through the rocks and areas of scree. Targas had an anticipatory feeling in his head as if the *presence* was looking forward to the coming conflict. He hardly noticed the small bridge they crossed or the two axes strategically placed to cut through its wooden struts. They entered the square formed by the large meeting hall, the magnesite storage building and several other huts. It was a hive of activity, men and women carrying spears and knives joining with scent masters to move to strategic locations.

Close up, the rock walls of the buildings and the angled rock barriers across the small valley, meeting at the road, looked formidable. Targas wondered how anyone could even think to attack and succeed with such natural defences, let alone the scent power at the Rolanites' disposal. Then he remembered the magnesa-enhanced power of the enemy.

"You can see well from here," Xaner's earnest face gazed into his. "Our first point of defence is where the road narrows, under the cliff. We've weakened the rock, and with concentrated scent strikes we should have some effect on the enemy's numbers.

"As you'll know we're outnumbered, but our efforts to tie up the enemy's forces in Requist and Nosta mean we have some hope, so, at the very least, the Hold will not be taken, not with the Mlana and her talents."

The wind worked in favour of the defenders, blowing scents apart and leaving little for Jakus to pick up and analyse.

The road narrowed and dived through an extension of the mountains to the east, leaving a cliff on one side and the fast-flowing river on the other. The road, though well-formed, was too wet and treacherous for any attack.

They halted in a mass of steaming animals and people to consider their options, the hail becoming a light, icy rain. A bivouac of perac and supplies was established in a grove of stunted trees, since the final push would be on foot.

Jakus understood the layout of the land and how the village was set in a small valley with the Hold at its head and knew where the defenders would likely distribute their forces. He was numerically superior, even with the large part of his forces tied up at Requist and Nosta, but as he looked into the windswept skies to the craggy outline of the rocky ridge blocking their path, he had some misgivings.

The fact Rolan had never been conquered was not just due to the lack of attractive resources in that mountainous country, but because of the resilience of the people. Rolan had a reputation for being a wild land peopled by mystics with unusual powers and was considered not worth the bother. Jakus believed a lot of that reputation was fuelled by the resources of magnesite and the influence of the magnesa crystals.

He shook himself against such negative feelings and considered the barrier before his army. Poegna thrust a hot cup into his hand as he stood there, and she noticed his momentary surprise at receiving if from her and not from Nefaria, before he disguised the thought. His force was clustered around him, taking the opportunity to eat and drink. He noticed the hymetta moving in their cages and pondered the value of these predators in the coming conflict. His gut told him that it was worth bringing them to cause disruption in the enemy's ranks, for if Targas was there his woman, Sadir, would be too, and they had her scent from the time in the caverns.

"We've only several hours of daylight, Shad," growled Kast at his shoulder. "We must make best use of it."

Jakus grunted as he considered his strategy. Due to the terrain he had little option but to take the road into the village, where he expected his use of the red crystal would give him an advantage. His leaders were fully committed, even his brother Faltis; the only one he was unsure of was the Eanite. He had been less forthcoming of late and since Nefaria's death had even shown hostility.

"Kast," he said, "make sure the Eanite is with the hymetta. He will have the role to release them on my command; that will prove his loyalty. Don't give him any magnesa. Any resistance, kill him!" Jakus scanned the people around him. "We'll attack as soon as we're ready, with maximum shields."

He raised his arms, dark scents gathering in his scent aura. "My people," he addressed them, his voice growing, "we are to undertake our assault on the village in the next valley. Our primary objective is the stores of magnesite kept there—this must be achieved.

"Our secondary objective will be to dig the so-called Mlana from her den.

"Do not cease in these objectives until you hear my order. For our success here will signal the rise of Sutan to its pre-eminent position in the known world, with ourselves as rulers.

"Take your crystals. We begin our attack."

K yel took a deep breath, attempting not to breathe in the unpleasant hymetta odour as he waited at the end of the column. He knew his links with the ruler were tenuous, and his chances of survival when he made his move slight. He pushed a hand into his pouch and felt several crystals of magnesa left from when he was trusted.

Everything to play for, he thought as he urged his animal, with its load of wicker cages, to move, *for my family must be near.* He glanced at the dour hymetta keeper next to him holding a similarly-laden beast, then looked away—he wanted nothing to do with any of them.

T he comfortless granite walls of the village square did little for Targas's mood as he looked down the wet road to where it disappeared around a cliff. River spray and rain obscured the defenders clustered behind a low wall. His rational mind was almost overwhelmed by the anticipatory hunger of the spider-like *presence* in his head as he waited for the coming of the enemy.

He tried not to think of Alethea's lack of concern for his condition or her enigmatic look at him when talking of the future conflict. *Am I to survive this?* he wondered. *It can't be my time, not after all this. Cursed woman. Cursed Knowing. And cursed Septus. What will that creature do?*

He gritted his teeth. No time to reflect, for the moment was now and he'd have to do his best.

Drathner touched his shoulder and pointed to the front line of defenders. "They've been seen. Won't be long." His mouth hung open in anticipation, while Targas clenched his teeth.

He looked at the small group of defenders so far away and felt a moment's pity. Their role of first contact with the enemy was not an enviable one.

The Sutanite army surged towards them.

The defenders reacted, causing sections of the cliff in front of them to crumble and fall. The action wavered, fluctuating, shards of rock bigger than a man's head flying up and out, some hitting the defenders, others causing splashes of water to rise from the river. A wedge of attackers emerged along the road, several figures spilling into the river; powerful scent shields clashed darkly against the lighter shields of the defenders.

A sudden break occurred and a staggered line of Rolanites ran for the barricades at the apex of the V-shaped rock walls. Some made the temporary sanctuary of the barrier but others were left lying along the rocky ground.

"It begins!" Drathner said harshly. "Much as expected, although they're powerful. We will wait until they break through—not go down to them. With any luck the river and our barrier will prove to be a significant stumbling block.

The perac pulled at its lead, reluctant to follow the narrow road with its smell of blood and entrails; a black-cloaked body washing down the river added to its alarm. Kyel jerked back, needing to get to where he could see what was happening, while the keeper behind growled at the delay.

Jammed on the road with a frightened perac, looking into the black compound eyes of an agitated hymetta, all the while trying to keep his feet on the slippery surface, was not a good introduction to a battle. The sky, darkened by the huge scent shield held by the scent masters made his way difficult. Once past the cliff face, he tripped over a body, seeing a pale feminine face and sightless eyes.

"Who?" he gasped as he fell.

"Keep moving," growled the keeper from behind.

Kyel pulled himself up by the reins and staggered along the rock- and body-strewn road. Here the army had spread out, the shields thinner and in places non-existent. He only had time to wonder why when a rock hit him sharply on the thigh. He yelped before strengthening his own shield.

Killed while I'm gawking. Some scent master, me.

The yells of the fighting around him, combining with a push towards a rock wall, kept him occupied. He and the keeper remained in the centre of the group, ensuring the animals were as well-protected as possible, leaving the fighting to Jakus and his scent masters with their magnesa-enhancement.

He caught sight of buildings ahead through a brief gap in the shield, and thought he saw a scent belonging to Targas. *Can't be him, fighting, can it?* The thought made him concentrate even harder and watch for an opportunity, any opportunity, to take part in stopping Jakus.

"Kyel?" gasped Targas, in the group holding a scent shield against a push of determined Sutanites. His immediate relief at seeing him was tempered by realising Kyel was jammed in a wedge of black-cloaked enemy. He released a scent plume, revealing himself in the hope of Kyel seeing it, continuing in Sadir's belief that he was not a conspirator but an unwilling participant. Then his view was lost as another push came from the determined enemy.

"Targas!" said Drathner, beside him against the stone wall of the meeting hall. "We'll have to fall back, leave this place, and get to the Hold. We've fought well, reducing their numbers without revealing too much of ourselves. Now it is time."

"But they'll take the village, and the magnesite." The pressure of the *presence* in Targas's head caused him to shout as he watched the enemy swarming the last of the barricades, leaving a trail of bodies behind. "And they're not having it their own way. Their shields can be broken; your scent masters are holding the line! We should stay!"

"This has been planned for, Targas," grunted Drathner as the enemy came closer, driving a long scent cloud above the wedge-shaped barrier Targas's group had created in the square.

"What's that?" Xaner moved over to them. "That scent cloud."

"Quick!" Targas yelled as he rapidly pulled in scent motes from the vicinity and bonded them tightly, feeling others add their strength as he did so. "We need to cover against it."

A slight tang came with the cloud as it moved against the wind and hovered over them. A trailing edge drifted past a wooden cart barricading the approach to the square. Out of the corner of his eye he saw the cart collapse and realised what the tang and the effect meant. *Acid. That blasted haggar's using acid.*

The *presence* in his head chortled as a redness came over his vision.

Chapter Forty-Nine

He lashed out at those carrying him. They only held tighter, running, jostling his body in their haste.

Targas's eyes flicked open, and the grey stone moving past made him realise he was on the steep path leading to the Hold, the *presence* in his head quiescent.

"Let me down. I'm fine!" he yelled.

His feet dropped to the ground and a red-faced Dranther looked into his eyes. "Thank the Lady you're alright. Now come, we must hurry."

Targas steadied himself, grimaced apologetically at the solid scent master who had helped Drathner carry him, and began to climb the path. He risked a glance over his shoulder in the dimming light to see a trail of Rolanites following him up the path to the cavern. The bridge was just wreckage on each side of the deep gully bisecting the approach to the Hold. The square in the village was changed, with some buildings leaning, others crumbled to the ground. The black of the enemy filled it, leaving exposed ground to the gully as a significant gap between the forces. He noticed many bodies heaped where the fighting had been thickest and hoped his failure to keep control hadn't led to more casualties.

"What happened?" he yelled at Drathner's back.

"We're away, out from that," the other man flung back over his shoulder. "Your warning was in time, but we couldn't hold it off once the buildings started going. Thought you were dead when you dropped."

"Targas!" cried Sadir, flinging herself into his arms as he reached the lip into the cavern. "You're not hurt?"

"No!" he snapped, still worried how his mind had failed him in the crisis. "Kyle. I saw Kyel," he added to distract her.

"He's here then? Where? Where is he?" she gasped as they moved back from the crush of people.

He pulled her to a vantage point where they could see the Sutanites beginning to move to the destroyed bridge. "He's there, where the two animals are. Can you see?"

Sadir excitedly released a plume of her unique scent to show her brother where she was. "Oh, I hope he notices that."

"Best leave it for the moment," said Targas, moving her back. He noticed Boidea beckoning and took Sadir over to where Alethea, Xaner and Drathner were in close consultation.

They waited for a moment until Alethea looked up and briefly smiled at him.

"Not a good time, my friend?" Her light eyebrows rose over her lined face. "Still, not unexpected."

"But they've got what they came for," said Targas, pointing down to the village.

"That they have," agreed Alethea, "but it is tainted and no longer of concern at this time. It is what comes next that is of most import and will require each of us to play our part."

Targas shook his head at Alethea's cryptic remarks.

"Yes, Targas. And for your role, let what happens happen. Do not be overly concerned at your perceived failure. I trust the end will prove the means."

Targas nodded vaguely as he stilled a sigh.

"This man, this usurper, will now attempt to beat us here," Alethea said, looking around, voice rising as she opened her arms to address all in the cavern. "And we will stop him. We will make him leave, take his perceived prize, and run from our country. He will use it for a time to establish his rule in Sutan, ultimately doing him no good. It will eventually weaken him, while we have time to strengthen ourselves and our allies for the final conflict.

"Now we will confront him with a force he has little knowledge of, and being the coward he is, he will flee. But my friends, we must be on our guard and those of us who have a protective role must carry it out to the best of our ability. And above all, don't be distracted by what you see. Don't be distracted by who is hurt. Who may fall. We will prevail. It is in the Knowing.

"Trust in the Knowing."

She began to hum, a resonance building. Everyone in the cavern joined in, and a scent aura of wellness and strength filled the area. Targas could see scents moving in swirls, the thickness dragging, leaving lines in the air. Behind it was a darker scent giving solidarity to the odours and bringing belief for those who were beginning to doubt. The humming stopped and a faint fragrance, reminiscent of cordial, remained.

"They're coming!" yelled someone.

As they rushed to see the Sutanites crossing the gully on makeshift bridges, Targas noticed something that wasn't right, something missing.

The hum was still echoing in his ears. Then a flicker of yellow and black caught his attention. The distinctive odour of hymetta made him swing around, searching for sight of the creatures. But the dark of the cavern and the lingering wellness scents made it hard to see.

He must be targeting me, he thought, remembering how these predators needed a scent spoor to hunt. *Jakus knows my scent.*

He spent precious seconds trying to spot them until he heard a sharp scream. He recognised Sadir's voice and looked to find her, but she was gone. *Where?* he thought frantically, before his mind blanked in horror, his feet already running. Sadir was to look after their daughter when the attack was on. *She's the target! That blasted Jakus knows her scent. Anyar's there too.*

Targas barged through those in his way, past the kitchens and into the room where the children were being kept.

The odour of hymetta blood rising into the air greeted him as he entered. A flurry of stick legs and yellow bodies were fighting a furred creature that snarled as it slashed with teeth and claws, spinning away from the snap of the large insects' jaws and the sting from bulbous abdomens. Several hymetta were writhing in pieces on the floor and the rest were in a corner, penned there by the ferocious voral.

Sadir was against a wall holding her daughter behind a scent shield, watching the scene with horrified eyes. Anyar was intent on what Vor was doing. She was calm and using a strong scent power, unbelievably through Sadir's shield, to keep the creatures in the corner, away from the other terrified children and their carers, while the voral showed its prowess.

Targas's mouth dropped open as he watched the last hymetta die. Then the voral, still emitting a low growl, raised a hind leg and squirted a stream of urine at the six misshapen bodies and their scattered parts, before trotting back to his mistress's praising hands.

Targas started to speak, then realised there was nothing to say in the sudden silence. The noise of fighting came loudly from the front of the cavern, and he realised that the hymetta attack was a distraction. He swung around and ran.

That was all the time the *presence* in Targas's head gave him. As he ran towards the fighting, a red mist built up in his vision and a rising anticipation filled him. This was the moment Septus had been waiting for as Targas joined the defenders in the Hold, trying to keep control of his body while protecting his people from Jakus's army.

The time for scent bolts had passed and the use of scent shields was the main form of defence against the attack. Jakus, leading a wedge of Sutanites, gained the lip of the cavern in a swirl of thick scent. Targas could see the familiar skeletal head of the leader surrounded in an odour haze, his scent aura scarlet and purple. Behind him was a similar figure with a lesser scent aura, and many others of comparable strength supporting the push.

But Septus, in a magnesa-red fog within his head, forced Targas closer to the enemy.

The strength of Jakus's assault had initially overwhelmed portions of the defence, leaving bodies on the floor, the defenders being driven back to the centre of the wide cavern, blocking off the attackers' strong scent blanket filled with the tang of acid.

Jakus's confidence was growing, his scent aura flickering with brilliant yellow flashes in the purple and scarlet of his passion. "I will have you, you old crone!" he shouted towards the Mlana.

The strength of the fighting pushed the opponents into small groups until a space opened revealing a group of women, Alethea, small and insignificant at their head.

"You have no place here, usurper!" Alethea's voice came strongly over the noise of battle. "Take yourself from our lands while you still can!"

Jakus laughed, his voice echoing around the cavern. "Why, when I am winning? When I can destroy you all!"

His laugh suddenly died away and his face whitened.

Targas, even while under Septus's control, could see a dark scent emerging from the small knot of women as he quietly edged behind the fighters. The shields in front of the attackers began to collapse in on themselves even as they reacted to this unanticipated assault. A strong scent of cordial filled the space as the odour streamed through the fighters' defences and pressed down on their bodies.

"Hold!" screamed Jakus. "Hold. We have them." He snatched a spear from a nearby guardsman and flung it at Alethea, enhancing its flight with a strong band of scent. It pierced the shields protecting the Mlana's group, hitting a woman in the shoulder. The injured woman screamed and fell. The dark scent shivered at the disruption and the attackers' shields strengthened.

Jakus surged forward.

Alethea, her body weakening with the effort, slumped. Quickly Boidea grabbed and held her, a grimace on her face.

Alethea straightened, and her voice came to Targas's ears: "You will go, usurper, or you will die!"

He could see Jakus's push slowing and the women's defending scent growing, building into roiling clouds streaming through from the rear of the cavern, impacting against the enemy.

But then he saw no more.

He lost the last of his control. Septus filled his vision, his evil *presence* taking over, forming the tightest of scent shields as his body ran through the wedge of enemy. Jakus was his target, his mantra. Such was Septus's control that Targas's mouth chanted "Jakus. Jakus," as foul scents were pulled from his memories and readied for the strike at the enemy leader.

Jakus noticed the disruption, even in his fight against the *shadow* scent, and half turned to face the oncoming Targas.

Ah, the *presence* in his mind chortled, then forced Targas to drop his shield, channelling all effort into flinging bolts of scent at Jakus.

Something hit Targas in the side, knocking him to the ground even in the moment of Septus's expected triumph. A strained visage, looking like a thin-faced Jakus, pushed into him, black and yellow odour snakes oozing out of his mouth, seeking to drive into Targas's scent centres. Targas was a passenger as Septus screamed inside his head and counterattacked.

The red mist filling his head deepened and pushed at the very edges of his consciousness. The pressure increased painfully until he felt his eyes bulging from their sockets. Then it released. One moment the red mists filled his vision, the next it was gone. Black replaced red and his consciousness faded.

S adir came running from the children's area just in time to see Targas fall, with a dark Sutanite on top of him.

"No!" she screamed and ran forward.

Jakus caught sight of her running figure and fired a black scent bolt even while backing away from the *shadow* scent attack. "Targas's woman! You should be dead!"

A figure dashed in front of her, taking the impact of the attack as he did so. Both fell to the ground and rolled into the bodies already littering the ground.

Chapter Fifty

The wave of fighters, both Sutanite and Rolanite, had broken into small knots of intertwined battles, the dark green of the defenders inter-mixed with the black and grey of the attackers. The Rolanites' scent had successfully countered the scent clouds of the enemy until fighting was reduced to hand-to-hand combat. The desperation of the defenders slowly began to tell, and all forward motion into the depths of the cavern ceased. Jakus was still an obvious presence in a group of scent masters, but his strength was being used for defence and his eyes flicked towards the outside.

Faltis started the retreat, rising to his feet from Targas's body. A vicious smile twisted his face, and he felt a *presence* building in his head before calling to Jakus and pointing out of the cavern. Others noticed and urged Jakus away.

"We have what we came for, Shad!" yelled Kast. "We should go!" The advice from the large figure of Kast at Jakus's shoulder finally tipped the balance and the Sutanites began to edge towards the opening.

"Keep at them!" yelled Drathner. "Make them pay! Every step." His fellow defenders pushed against the retreating foe, using scent bolts, spears and anything that came to hand.

The enemy reached the path leading from the Hold, leaving many bodies behind them as they retreated down it. The narrow way, rather than being a viable escape route, coralled the triumphant invaders, making the victors more vulnerable to the attacks of the defeated Rolanites. The Sutanites, in their hurry to leave, stumbled and fell while defending themselves, every scent barrier thwarted by the unexpected *shadow* scent. Rocks and boulders added to the carnage of the retreat. Jakus's rage was palpable, but he was forced to protect himself, unable to counter the defenders.

"Get to the village!" he yelled as they staggered away, oblivious to the slowing of the defenders' attack. "Take the magnesite to the camp, at the cost of your lives!"

They wove their way in small groups through the village in the descending night until all that was left was mounds of dead and wounded.

The defenders followed cautiously, making sure no one was left behind, checking the wounded and dead. Drathner quickly organised a pursuit party with orders to follow, harry but not directly engage the broken army, the imperative being to drive them back to the coast and from the land.

S adir lay stunned on the ground, slowly recovering in the cavern as people began moving through the carnage. She felt the familiarity of the body lying entwined with hers and she felt across his form, breathing in his scents, feeling the thud of her brother's heart.

A wave of thankfulness filled her as she realised Kyel had returned to save her and was not an enemy. Her family was whole again, finally. Another thought came to her.

"Targas!" she gasped, remembering how she had last seen him, and attempted to get from under her brother.

"Sadir?" Kyel whispered in her ear. "Are you safe, not hurt?"

She relaxed, briefly melding scents with him, showing her concern and her happiness for him. "I am fine, Kyel," she murmured, "fine."

"Ky?" a high voice sounded nearby. A black nose pushed into her face with a gust of hymetta smell, causing her to gasp.

"Vor!" Anyar commanded, and the nose withdrew. A comforting scent closed around them, and Sadir recognised the strong presence of her daughter. "Oh, Ky. I've missed you."

"Huh?" Kyel's voice sounded muffled against Sadir's body. "Anyar? It can't be."

The weight lifted from Sadir, and she saw Kyel sit up and hug his niece. "You've grown, tremendously."

The voral sitting nearby, long red tongue hanging and eyes glistening, caught his attention. "What's that?"

"Vor," stated Anyar, proudly. "My Vor." She raised an arm and the voral moved under it to accept a pat.

"Sadir?" Kyel turned questioning eyes to her.

"Long story, Kyel," she said, struggling to her feet. "But we must find Targas! He was over there. Hurt! We must find him!" She pointed to where people were already moving amongst the dead and wounded lying across the cavern floor. "Stay!" she ordered. "I'm going to look."

"No, mother, I'll go too," Anyar said, gripping Vor's grimy fur in one hand.

"My responsibility as well." Kyel stood, flung off the hated black robe and took Anyar's hand before following his sister to the bright opening of the cavern, frightened at what they would find.

Fires already being built provided light and warmth to the huge space while everyone looked to the needs of the wounded. The groans and cries of the injured drew attention, but Sadir had eyes for the place she had last seen Targas.

His scent came strongly from amongst a pile of black-dressed bodies. She hurried forward. "I…I don't think Anyar should see this," she gasped as she came closer.

"No! Mother!" Her daughter's voice was strong.

Sadir dragged a black-robed corpse away to reveal Targas's slumped body lying in a small space. She knelt in a pool of blood, its scent rising around her in a cloud barely noticeable in the dark, odour-filled surrounds.

She held Targas, cradling him to her chest, pressing her head close to his. His stubble-covered face was calm, eyes closed, body slack. She put her lips to his bloody ones and attempted to push invigorating scents into him, trying desperately for a response, wanting his eyes to open, for him to give his familiar half-smile. But he lay limply in her arms. The anticipated smile never came.

Sadir screamed, shaking his body, trying to pull him to his feet. People, strangers, came around her, placing hands on her shoulders and releasing comforting scents. Anyar pushed under Sadir's arms and against her father's body, with tears rolling down her face, the voral quiet by her side. Kyel crouched down with her, adding his presence, releasing his grief.

The light of burning torches helped the Sutanites find their small camp where the animals were waiting. Jakus, adrenalin keeping him going, turned to find the men carrying sacks of the precious magnesite.

"Get it on the animals!" he ordered. "Tied securely. Then we ride. We must get to the rest of our army and out of this land. We have what we came for."

"What about the wounded?" asked Bilternus, his mind still a daze after the horrific turn of events, and the loss of his friend, Kyel.

"Pah!" exploded Jakus. "Anyone who can't ride is useless. Leave them behind. We need to get out of this cursed country."

Bilternus turned to see his father standing nearby, gaze fixed on Jakus.

"Do what my brother says," Faltis said, looking disinterestedly at Bilternus. He gave a high-pitched triumphant laugh before swinging onto his perac. Bilternus was stunned. As much as he didn't like his father, he knew him. What he had seen wasn't Faltis at all. A stranger had been looking at him, out of his father's blood-shot eyes.

"Move yourselves!" came Jakus's order as he spurred his animal along the road and into the darkness.

His diminished force followed.

The night passed in a blur as they came to terms with their losses, caring for the injured and clearing up the cavern from the battlefield it had become. Most eventually fell into an exhausted sleep on the floor around the fires, in the company of friends and loved ones.

Sadir woke with Kyel on one side and Anyar on the other. The fires were crackling, and the delicious smell of frying drifted from the kitchens. Her grief was a dull ache in her heart, her mind rationalising what she had already subconsciously known once they had failed to rid Targas of the *presence* in his head. *At least*, she thought, tears streaming down her face, *he died a hero, fighting for those he loved.*

A gentle scent attracted her attention and she saw the sympathetic face of Cathar smiling down at her. She crouched next to her. "Your brother?" she whispered, looking at Kyel.

"Yes." Sadir placed a protective hand over his shoulder. "He's been through much."

"A brave man," she nodded before glancing over towards the tables. "I've come to bring you to Boidea. There's more bad news, I'm afraid."

"What?" Sadir mouthed as she stood quietly in the nest of blankets, careful not to disturb her family. *Another failure in the Knowing*, she thought, her rage rising. *My love! My Targas! It can't get any worse.*

Boidea and Xerrita greeted her where they sat near the fire, mugs of tea and bowls of oaten porridge in front of them.

"Sadir, please sit," said Boidea, indicating a seat opposite her. "We can see your anger, your concern, but, for the moment, eat with us."

Sadir looked back to where her brother and daughter lay before sitting. "Cathar says there's more bad news. But how can it get any worse than what's happened. How?"

"It can," said Boidea, eyes glistening with tears. "Your loss is profound, one we would not wish on anyone. But there is another. One expected, which will bring significant changes to us all. For it is the Mlana's time. She is dying."

"What?" asked Sadir, slumping on her seat. "No," she said, and shook her head, "it can't be. How can she go when there's such a mess? She hasn't answered for Targas. She can't get out of it that easily."

"Were it so, Sadir," said Xerrita. "If she were able, she would be all too happy to answer you, to lessen your grief. But the battle has taken too much from her. Her body simply cannot sustain life."

Sadir sat glumly, still shaking her head. She started as a small hand covered hers.

"Mother." Anyar climbed onto the seat, Vor pushing his head into her legs.

Sadir clasped her to her side, put her chin on her daughter's head and began to cry.

"Sadir," said Boidea gently, rising to her feet, "we must attend the Mlana. Time is short."

She nodded mutely as she stood. "I suppose I'm ready. Nothing better to do. Could you go, Anyar? Stay with Kyel for a while."

Anyar looked at her mother, not moving.

"Anyar must come with us, Sadir. The Mlana is waiting for her."

"No! She can't have my daughter too! Not after Targas. She can't!"

Anyar took her mother's hand and pulled her into a walk, following Boidea across the cavern floor and down a corridor to an open door where Cathar was waiting.

"She knows you're coming, but be quick, there's not much time," Cathar whispered.

They walked to a narrow bed seemingly swallowed up in a large dimly-lit room. A small figure lay unmoving, propped up on pillows.

Sadir, holding Anyar's hand, looked down on the shrunken figure with an uncaring heart. This was the woman who promised so much yet didn't save her love, her mate.

A voice startled her. The Mlana was still alive. "I'm glad you are here... Please forgive me for all that has happened. It has taken much from you, Sadir." The eyes peeped blackly from the wizened face.

"Take my hand, Anyar," Alethea whispered.

The young girl slid her other hand across the coverlet to Alethea. "You have the Knowing. You are ready?" Alethea softly asked.

Anya nodded.

"Ah, it begins."

They waited for a long moment before she spoke again. "Boidea, my friend... you know your role."

"Yes, Mlana," she replied gravely, "I will rule until Anyar is of age."

"What?" gasped Sadir, gripping her daughter's hand.

"Please, Sadir." sighed Alethea, "They have gone and will leave Rolan without further conflict. Our countries are safe for now. But you've known your daughter...is special. She has a momentous destiny... That is what this has been about. Who knows what...will be...without her. You all...must look after her... protect her...that is your charge."

"No, not now. Please," begged Sadir.

Alethea's chest ceased moving. Sadir was wondering if she had died when her head moved.

"Anyar," she wheezed, her voice a hoarse whisper. "Come closer."

Anyar let go her mother's hand and climbed onto the bed.

As soon as she settled, Alethea's face relaxed and a ball of shadow scent built up, covering her head, moving over her body, thicker and darker in the dim light than Sadir had seen.

Anyar leant forward, touched the ball with her finger, tracing a line from it to her face. The scent flowed along that line and into her nose. The girl's eyes closed, her smile serene, her breathing slowing.

Then her eyes, light like those of her father, opened, and she looked at the four women surrounding her.

"The Mlana has gone," she said calmly. "She lives in me still." Anyar slipped off the bed, and took her mother's hand.

"Come, Mother," she said, "we need to tell the people of our hope for the future."

Sadir followed in a daze as Anyar led her into the sunlight streaming into the cavern of Mlana Hold.